SEIZURE

LASZLO VARSZEGI

Copyright © 2023 Laszlo Varszegi.

All rights reserved. No part of this book may be reproduced, stored, or transmitted by any means—whether auditory, graphic, mechanical, or electronic—without written permission of both publisher and author, except in the case of brief excerpts used in critical articles and reviews. Unauthorized reproduction of any part of this work is illegal and is punishable by law.

ISBN: 979-8-89031-520-5 (sc)
ISBN: 979-8-89031-521-2 (hc)
ISBN: 979-8-89031-522-9 (e)

Because of the dynamic nature of the Internet, any web addresses or links contained in this book may have changed since publication and may no longer be valid. The views expressed in this work are solely those of the author and do not necessarily reflect the views of the publisher, and the publisher hereby disclaims any responsibility for them.

One Galleria Blvd., Suite 1900, Metairie, LA 70001
(504) 702-6708
1-888-421-2397

Jeffrey Clark's presentation at the international symposium held in 2012

The Past, Present and Future of the Human Race
An analysis of human interactions

Intended course of presentation:

-Greeting
-Personal introduction
-Plainly speaking (Here and everywhere)
-Follow the highlights on your pamphlet
-Raising consciousness

Topics:

-Evolution
    The appearance of humans
-Basic human relations, past Basic human behavior
    Did we learn anything from the past? ...why are we still making the same mistakes?
-Human relations, present
    Summary of the past 100 years in contrast to previous centuries (As they are the consequence of each other)
    The Establishment
    Development and control of human behavior, role of parents and schools (teachers)
    Work related manipulation-motivation (socialism<>capitalism)
-Medical care
-Globalization
    Nationalism/Heritage, accelerated mixing of races (few exceptions)
    Economic consequences
-The Economy
    Banks, money, supply and demand, cheap labor, cheap products, (consumer products- not expected to last?)
-Where are we going? (The future)
    Closing

Good evening, Ladies and Gentlemen!

Please accept my warmest welcome this fine evening! It makes me extremely happy to see so many brave people gathered to hear my lecture, especially in light of the seemingly boring topic.

You may soon find that it is anything, but boring!

Before I would begin my presentation, I must clarify a couple of things that, I feel, are rather important.

Firstly:

I would like to introduce myself more thoroughly, as your invitation pamphlet only provides limited information about me.

My name is Jeffrey Clark. I was born on December 25, 1964, right around sunrise in Los Angeles, California.

My parents were Roman Catholics for most of their lives. Therefore, people may assume that my siblings and I are also Catholics. During our childhood, we learned the basis, and practiced the traditions of this faith, but our parents left us to decide what we will ultimately believe in.

Believe me; I have been working on that all my life.

The best I can say about my current belief at this time is that I believe in a higher power, a higher intelligence, most people would refer to as The Creator, or simply God. I also believe, in fact I know, that there are those WHO constantly try to make the rest of us believe that THEY personify that higher power and intelligence. More on that later.

Currently, I am a tenured professor of history at a prominent university in my home state and I have been working there since 1989. I choose not to name the institution because the views I'll be presenting today are my own, distilled from my comprehensive studies over three decades, as well as my life experiences. My private studies included anthropology, archaeology, geology, and human psychology to gain a better understanding of the way we relate to each other. I devoted considerable amount of time to researching economic development and finance and their combined affect on the life of the masses. Consequently, I studied numerous business forms as they emerged with the advancement of technology. Finally, I briefly studied the word "business" to clarify its various meanings, if only for my own amusement. Then I realized, the way Italians tend to pronounce it as "busy-ness", might just be its secret.

Secondly:
Since you may anticipate that I will use language, typical of the sciences mentioned above, which usually goes right over the heads of the audience, I want to assure you that my goal is to speak as clearly as possible. Here is why.

From time to time, in the course of our lives, we must read and understand legal documents, business contracts or simple advertisements. The purpose of the difficult language in those documents is to discourage us from deciphering its true meaning on our own. Feeling intimidated and short on time, we usually accept the enticing terms obediently. To have an attorney review the document would cost money most of us are unwilling to spend. Therefore, we take on risks that may or may not come back to haunt us. Even after signing such documents most people rarely take the time to read the fine print. The presence of "fine print" on legally binding documents is a cunning way to hide undesirable consequences, in plain sight, that may result from the deal. Upon signing such document, essentially we accept all liabilities and relinquish all our rights.

Consequently, "fine print" is proof-positive of malicious intent. For this reason, I embrace the style of speaking plainly.

That is the only way I can expect you to trust what I am about to share with you.

The pamphlet you received shows the main points and time line in which I intend to proceed. To accentuate similarities between ancient and modern events or behaviors, it will be necessary to jump back and forth in time.

To address each point, according to their significance, will take, an estimated, three hours. That maybe too much for some of you to digest in one sitting, so we'll take a twenty-minute break at about half way.

Many of you maybe wondering about the real purpose of this event, and why do I put so much effort into a benign subject, I offer this to clarify: I wish to raise individual and collective consciousness about what we are doing to each other on this amazing planet. Having said all that, let the "show" begin.

How would you summarize human achievements? What historical events would you highlight? Would you exemplify our greatness or our flaws? Would you list our inventions? Would you say that discovering the laws of nature is our greatest feat? Do you admire architectural wonders, like ancient pyramids or modern skyscrapers? Do you approve the way we structured our societies and belief systems? How do you feel about the ways we treat one another? How do we relate to our environment and all the wonderful things our magnificent planet has to offer? Is this really the best we can do with our accumulated intelligence?

Finally, where are we going with all of this?

Let us examine our progress from the beginning.

Primitive life may have started forming on our planet as early as 3 to 4 billion years ago, and that my friends, is a scientist's way of saying "We have no clue". The beginning of life remains shrouded in mystery, to this day. Despite of all the sophisticated equipment available to scientists today the answer to how it really began still eludes us. From all the data collected throughout the centuries by conscious research, a "theory" is all they can propose.

If our true beginnings were discovered, it must have cost an arm and a leg to keep it a secret this long. Maybe quite literally, meaning the loss of limbs.

Looking at history often brings up the question of understanding time.

When we think about time in lengths far greater than the lifespan of human beings, we tend to lose track quickly. Just think, for a moment, about your childhood and those school years when you first started to learn about history. Most of you, just like me, simply accepted that this or that event took place at such and such time, but we never stopped to think it through. Ancient times always seemed so far out of reach that, perhaps out of laziness, we trusted our teachers to tell the truth.

To get a better idea, during your teenage years you may have stopped for a moment wondering about your future. How far ahead in time, did you dare to imagine the way your life may unfold? It was not easy then, and it did not get any easier, but one thing seems certain. Your best reference, the one you can easily relate to, is your current age.

Therefore, when scientists talk about time in terms of centuries, millennia or even longer periods, try to compare that to the length of your own existence. It will become clear in an instant just how insignificant we really are. Then go a step further, and think of great distances. Lean back in your seat and go beyond the limits of our planet. Go into space, where time takes on a new perspective. This is where most of us lose our grip instantly, but few of us would ever admit it.

Measuring distance with elapsed time can easily exceed the average person's power of imagination. I am sure all of you have a good idea about the length of a minute. Perhaps at times that minute may seem like an "eternity", while other times it maybe gone undetected.

Based on the associated experience, we perceive the length of time differently.

When we speak of happy moments, they may have lasted for several hours or even days. However, a single unpleasant incident, lasting no longer than a minute or two, can turn an entire day or week into a memorably bad one.

The negative feelings generated by an event, and how long we hold on to them, can greatly skew the perception of time.

Someone illustrated this phenomenon by saying:
"The length of a minute greatly depends on your physical location in relation to the bathroom."

The saying may seem juvenile, but if you ever waited for a restroom, with any urgency, you must know its wisdom.

Lighthearted remarks aside, the scientific community has agreed that the speed of light, being nearly constant in space, should be the benchmark of measuring interplanetary and interstellar distances. Yet, they still resort to estimating when they inform us about the distance of certain objects in space. Imagine now looking at the night-sky and you may see a star that is said to be a thousand light years away. Let's assume now that star exploded, or imploded, five hundred years ago and no longer emits any light. Yet, we will be able to observe it for another five hundred years before it disappears from our sight. Consequently, when you look at the night-sky you always see the past and the future at once, but never the present. You see a forecast of the future, because whatever you observe happening to galaxies, stars and planets will, with all certainty, be the faith of our Solar system and our Galaxy as well, so we are told.

Since now we all feel comfortable with time expressed in billions of years, we will begin with the creation of our planet. Scientists say that planet Earth formed about 4.6 billion years ago. How it really happened, I leave it up to your imagination. Violent things kept happening for a very long time; that much is certain.

Let us skip most of that by jumping forward to about 1 to 1.2 billion years ago.

Trust me! We did not miss much by so doing!

Most of what follows, is available online for all to research, and believe, if so inclined.

We skipped some prokaryotic life forms, which kept cloning themselves, leading nowhere. Now, we arrived at a time when sexual reproduction began in earnest.

But not quite the way you may imagine it.

Back then, all sexual activities took place chemically, at the cellular level. Cells identified and communicated with other cells by chemical signals. If all went well, they reproduced, meaning they combined some of their content to form a new cell.

Interesting parallel to humans is that our word for initial attraction is chemistry. Women may argue that they mean something else by it, but believe me, they too are responding to that ancient chemical signal. Physical attraction is a complex process that begins at the chemical level in our brains. When chemistry seems mutual, we contemplate many things before we proceed. Women especially do. The social status and monetary worth of the contender became a deciding factor, quite some time ago. This altered selective process presents an unnatural twist on things, to which the evolutionary code has not yet found a response.

Suffice it to say, that many influences are at work, negatively affecting individuals, and the future of humanity.

Continuing our time-line, Mother Nature ran a myriad "trial and error" tests for viable species and the time of the first mammals was steadily approaching. Around 250 million years ago, the first animals appeared that are thought to be direct ancestors of "modern" mammals. You see, with the advancement of technological instrumentation, old archaeological, geological and other collected samples can now yield new information, because humans have accumulated intelligence to formulate new theories.

Therefore, history changes, as new theories now serve as "evidence" of what might have been!

That means, what you now know, maybe rendered obsolete by someone with credentials, putting forth a new idea. Ultimately, that new idea would still be someone's speculation, nothing more.

We should skip another 190 to 200 million years. Do you remember how many things happened just last year?

Now imagine thousands, or millions of years!

I could literally sit around for hours wondering about what has been going on during those ages!

If we could go back in time, we would then see small, furry, warm-blooded animals living in the jungle.

They mated in a relatively modern fashion and produced milk to feed their offspring.

Relatively soon after this period, about 40 million years ago, the first species of primates developed that can still be recognized today in their descendants.

I think it is safe to jump forth yet another 35 million years.

Evidence exists to prove that some apes were able to walk on their hind legs as early as 4 to 4.5 million years ago. About a mere two million years later, we see Homo-erectus appear in Africa.

While I intend to keep my presentation enjoyable, making any pun about Homo-erectus would be inappropriate. One fascinating fact is worth mentioning about the Homo subgroups.

Homos persistently reappeared throughout the ages, making their presence known for a while, only to exemplify the concept of an evolutionary dead-end. Having said that, let me set the record straight: Humans have been placed on this planet. Anything less than Homo-Sapiens is NOT human, in my humble opinion.

Therefore, Homo-Sapiens is the beginning of modern humans, and humans have changed very little, overall. Creation, folks! Creation.

There it is. I've said it out loudly.

The next brief segment will cover the time during which they came and went.

You will see that time estimations are becoming more accurate as we approach modern times.

Once again, I'd like to stress that this is what you'll find, if you take time to research this topic online.

If you're lucky, you might find some opposing view points. Researching in libraries is highly recommended! Roughly three hundred thousand years after Homo-erectus appeared and migrated north-northeast, the species named Homo Georgicus came forth and colonized Eurasia.

We have fossilized evidence from this age suggesting that he, and of course, her of the species were both able to start and extinguish fire independently, as they needed it.

(Question: How long ago did Greek Mythology assert that Prometheus has stolen fire from Mount Olympus to help humans? Or was it the Romans'?)

If you find that I do not conform to the idea of "Political Correctness", it is because, it is a form of censorship. Political Correctness serves to confuse the meaning of similar sounding expressions, thus leaving the true meaning of the conveyed information open for discussion. PC is also a way to silence opposing views to the standing powers.

That is crucial when we are given information by people we should be trusting, specifically our leaders!

Whenever I use the common the noun "he" or "man" referring to humans, in my mind, it includes both sexes equally as it has for many centuries earlier.

(On a side note: He and She are both Human, and both nouns have "he" in them. Some believe that the original spelling of woman, or women, began with woe followed by man, or men. I do not wish to create more division between women and men, for we have been divided far too long. We must come together, as often as possible.)

Around 500 thousand years ago, the species Homo-Heidelbergensis dominated the landscape. Although physically similar to Homo-Erectus, they had larger brains, about 93% of that of modern humans. After shedding much of their body hair their skin color lightened as an adaptation to their new environment. Males, on average, stood about 5'5" tall and the females were about 5' tall.

Even though they were much stronger than we are, accidents did occur during hunting. Aside from environmental factors, the injuries so suffered, most likely contributed to their relatively short lifespan.

It was a long journey, but 300 thousand years later Homo-Sapiens finally arrived. Earliest fossil evidence points to around 195 thousand years ago, creating a bit of an overlap in time. This only means, as pointed out earlier, that members of several evolutionary levels coexisted simultaneously. Some 25 thousand years had past until Homo sapiens began to show most of the characteristics of modern humans. Fully erect posture and the shape and size of their skull became very much like ours. As we see, they had to put up and contend with lesser-developed human species for more than 40 thousand years. I give them a lot of credit for patiently waiting for them to catch up.

Worth mentioning of this period is the alleged discovery of "Mitochondrial Eve", the mother of all modern humans who live today, as we all carry some of her mtDNA. (mitochondrial).

What ever happened to the Giants that roamed the Earth and allegedly mated with the daughters of men, I wonder.

For the most part, we accept this information at face value, because we receive it from fellow humans, whom we respect based on their knowledge and we have no reason to doubt their intention. Do we?

Interestingly, Homo-Sapiens still did not have a way of verbal communication at that time, but we can be certain that they were able to understand each other's body language, facial, hand and even vocal expressions. Just like whales, dolphins and other land mammals of sufficient intelligence, they must have had a range of sounds by which to communicate important information.

By the way, would you accept whales and dolphins, alligators and crocodiles, eagles and other raptors, bears, and last, but not least, all large cats as powerful, intelligent creatures, who have also reached the top of the food chain in their own branches, as equal?

If not, would you say that humans are on the top of all food chains?

Then I'd ask, have you ever watched "survival" shows to get an idea of what it takes to survive in the wild?

If you have, would you volunteer to try your current skill-set, say, in the middle of a very "civilized" European forest? Before you start laughing, consider that you would not have any modern gear available to you at all. For a week, you would not be allowed to leave the forest to find civilization. You could pick the season and your clothes and then left to rely on your wits and physical abilities to survive.

Now let's go back to about 150 thousand years ago, with over a million years of human evolution behind us!

Imagine that! We have risen to the top, and we did not even know it! What if all predecessors of modern humans have gone extinct, one after another, for not having been properly suited to survive in the wild?

It would still take 70 thousand years before humans could express their thoughts or feelings intelligibly, but who cared? It was enough to know, without much discussion, that when it started to rain or the temperature dropped below a comfortable level, they would seek shelter in some form. Preferably a cave, but for some a boulder and a few fallen branches and leaves may have seemed like a good start.

Clothing was most likely seasonal, and consisted mainly of animal skins, as evidence suggests. However, during summer months, they were probably going around shamelessly naked. We can see that most of their actions were dictated by instincts imprinted during their million plus years of evolution. These instincts are so essential that, to this day, they could help most of us survive a brief calamity. "Brief" is the key word.

As we evolved out of the animal kingdom, or, rather have been removed and reinserted, with established new species, we were made to retain certain primitive characteristics to this day.

In those days, one had to be a good observer, alert, strong and fast, as a human can be, to ensure the survival of the self and their offspring. There were no questions about any deed being right or wrong. There was no shame in hiding or running away to save one's hide. There was no guilt attached to killing an opponent, animal or human, that posed to be a threat, only elation. The goal was and is to survive. This is true evolution, nature at work to select the most viable specimen to pass on their genes and acquired knowledge. The young had to learn all the skills of survival quickly before their mother and father would die. Self-reliance is a prerequisite of survival for both, the individual and its species.

Smaller groups began to merge for increase protection. It is self-evident that at some point they realized the advantage in numbers, possibly while hunting large animals. This behavior later became valuable against other humans as well. Due to their limited population it is unlikely that they would have run out of natural resources in any given location, therefore, following the behavior of animals they hunted, they would only need to migrate as the seasons changed.

Naturally, some of those who first made that expedition became our ancestor's ancestors. It was another crucial evolutionary step, without which we may not be here today. Let us simply call it the Learning Curve. We must also give credit to those who, having honed their skills of survival for their geographic location, decided to pull through the winter.

They had to have accumulated additional knowledge of all the local animals and plants and figured out ways of gathering and preserving enough supplies to last until next spring. Throughout winter, they still had to make brief excursions for various reasons, during which they learned even more about their environment.

Neither group could claim a hundred percent success rate, but obviously, they survived in sufficient numbers to carry on. We are living proof of that fact.

As we see, evolution, was and is a painfully slow process. There were great advances as well as major setbacks all along. About 10-12 thousand years ago, Homo-Sapiens had finally triumphed over all lesser developed humans. The power of thought is undeniable! Proper education is evolutionary, as it gives descendants an edge to live a better and longer life.

Basic human relations in the past were, as the word suggests, basic. As we had seen, most interactions stemmed from the need for survival. The cooperation of individuals served the advancement of the group and serious competition moved to the group level, for the most part.

Early on, the smallest human unit consisted of a mother and her child or children. She had to protect and provide for the little ones, as any other mammals do. For quite some time males did everything on their own, so the role of a father, even as a mere protector, took a long time to realize. Once that happened a new unit had formed and it offered a greater chance of survival. We call this unit a family. Beside the family, another unit began to take shape in which small groups of families, bound by the same basic needs, they banded together in a tribe.

One aspect of human existence did not change at all since the beginning of time. Just like every other living creature, we need food and shelter constantly to prosper. For the most part their early shelters were made of larger branches tied together by twines made of tree-bark or animal sinew and covered with large leaves or animal skins.

We refer to a group of these huts as a village and people who live in them are the villagers, who are of the same tribe.

Regardless of the added security of living together, things did not always go smoothly. They had to be constantly on guard against impending dangers, like predatory animals that would consider them prey or accidental encounters with other creatures like snakes, spiders and such. Accidents did happen on their hunting trips and it was just a matter of luck if one would only suffer a minor cut or break a limb or possibly die. They did not dwell on misfortune very long, they were just happy to be alive.

It is important to understand that at this stage of human development people were not emotionally equipped to express much of sorrow, happiness, hatred, love, guilt, or pride. To express those emotions would take hundreds of years more to perfect. They had two basic states of existence. They were either peaceful (happy), or frightened (unhappy).

Therefore, when I say, "they were happy to be alive", I only mean that they returned to their calm state after having been frightened.

Around this time, our planet was also experiencing one of its cyclic climate changes. Mind you, these changes have been ongoing since the planet formed, and we are fortunate to live in a pleasant phase, called the "interglacial" period. Some twelve thousand years ago, the last glacial period slowly ended.

Until then, human habitat was confined to an area, scientists refer to, as the "fertile crescent".

(We must wonder, however, how many other places on the planet were different human groups surviving, as twelve thousand years was not long enough for all the various races, or, if you will, ethnic groups to separate out from a single line of humans. I am convinced that the people of Far-East Asia do not consider Adam and Eve their ancestors. I'm also certain that the black people of Africa would also beg to differ.)

The diversity of life in the region was well suited for human development. Due to its moderate climate at the time, it had most of the flora and fauna that later became the foundation of agriculture.

While glacial ice gripped the northern and possibly the southern hemisphere as well, a region greatly neglected throughout history, early humans took great strides in developing verbal skills, domesticating animals and growing crops. As the ice retreated, the northern hemisphere became habitable once again. The ecosystem of the region was quite different now. Most large mammals became extinct and most plants, not being hardy enough, also vanished. Over thousands of years, the land recovered and humans slowly spread northward. They may have over populated the "fertile crescent" and had to find new living space, as the area began to lose its fertility and was not able to support them all.

According to credible sources, earliest bows and arrows found are nearly 40 thousand years old. Their compact size offered a definite advantage over spears in tight quarters. Until about 4 thousand years ago, people mostly used tools made of stones and bones, sharpened to cut meat, carve wood or to point their arrows. Approximately 3500 years ago, people had enough knowledge to seek out and smelt copper ores. Thus the Bronze Age began. (God keeps nudging us forward...)

Time seem to have accelerated slowly for a few thousand years now. At least to our perception, it will continue accelerating as our accumulated knowledge grows and we develop new technologies. Nevertheless, a day has always been and will remain twenty-four hours long, regardless of how many activities we intend to cram into it.

(Here, I'd like to address time once again, because we have been thought that it's based on an ancient system developed, you guessed it, in the Fertile Crescent, or Babylon as it was called back then. We know it today mostly as Iraq. Time as we know it consists of seconds, minutes, hours, days, moths and years, to only concern ourselves with its most basic units. But I must ask a serious question here, for I am not aware of single human who dared to question the validity of them.

How can we know for sure how long each unit of time really is? That is a question for another Dei.)

Let us step back for a minute to examine life in a Stone Age village. It may have contained a dozen huts. For quite some time, in moderate climates, people dressed lightly in the summer, wearing only a loose cover around the groin area and not much else. The hotter and colder climates forced them to cover their body more thoroughly. Life in the village proved safer from animal-attacks, as the scent of people and the smells and noises generated by their activities deterred most animals. They might have had hunting dogs too to alarm them. Their safety did not last long, as an unexpected foe emerged from the woods.

This new threat turned out to be other humans.

We can only speculate as to why humans have turned on one another. Basic instincts of survival surely played a role in it. Another possible explanation could be that not all humans are willing to work equally hard, not even to support themselves. The villagers worked together, more or less, to provide for all members of the village. Ideally, they shared the fruits of such work relatively fairly. However, even in small communities there are a few, who would not willingly contribute. Those who work hard to provide food, shelter and other comforts would not tolerate selfish behavior for long. Naturally, they would care for an injured or sick member, but an able-bodied person who refused to participate in the daily chores, would not be welcome for long. When the villagers came under attack and had to flee to save themselves, they abandoned even the injured or sick. Have no doubt about that.

(To overcome that instinct it would take a great deal of sophistication.)

Then why would anyone tolerate unacceptable, anti-social, behavior for any length of peacetime?

This is the motive why the lazy rejects have turned on their fellow men. They would not risk their lives to hunt dangerous animals, or spend hours trying to catch fish, nor would they bother learning to plant crops and wait for an uncertain result, to support themselves.

Instead, they joined in arms and raided unsuspecting villages to take what they needed. Even the most peaceful people will arm themselves against their vicious attacks, eventually.

Living creatures only need a strong will to live and the presence of immediate danger for self-defense. Humans are no exception. It is part of the genetic code of all creatures, to prevent override.

Ridiculously, and contrary to nature, our acquired intellect may actually suppress that instinct!

Very few people can realize the lurking dangers in time. When someone would try to warn us, we respond with ridicule. Thus, we have become the most dangerous predator of our own kind.

Humans could not survive or hunt successfully without effective tools. Therefore, perfecting weaponry was a necessity from the very beginning of our existence. One very important tool was/is cunning to lure an animal into a trap by using its own habits against it. Once the animal was cornered, they used everything from throwing heavy rocks to spears and bow and arrow to bring it down.

Then, the need for protection against other humans prompted early men to devise and produce more-effective killing instruments as well as armor. Some specialized in making weapons only, and they traded their merchandise for everything else they needed.

For those engaged in farming and animal breeding, producing excess was inevitable. They offered some of the excess crops and animals in exchange for other goods or services. For a while, the barter system was a natural way to go. This system actually worked well for, say, a few hundred years, but some shortcomings began to emerge. The biggest fault being that greed always finds its way into the simplest of human endeavors.

Deceiving innocent, honest, peaceful people is easy.

It has always been easy, and it will be easy for a long time to come! Our basic traits make us gullible prey.

From the very first time humans deceived one another, to this day, the goal remains unchanged!

History shows us, the goal is personal gain, at the expense of others.

Without exception, those who benefit from the labor and/or stupidity of others, think of themselves as superior.

In their eyes, there are only two types of people in the world, the illuminated and others.

You and I are nothing to them, but udders.

The phrase, "cash-cow" takes on a new meaning, does it not.

However, let us not wander too far from the time when barter was still a decent idea. In those days, people got up around four or five in the morning, as we have learned of time, tended to their animals, organized, cleaned and repaired some equipment. Loaded a wagon with tools, and depending on the season, perhaps with seeds; harnessed an ox, donkey or horse and drove it out to the field.

(Allow me to digress here for minute. Have any of you ever pondered why we use Horse-Power in reference to the power of man-made engines of all types, and even electric motors, until the mid-twentieth century? Why not Ox-power, or Donkey-Power? Well, Horses produce more uniform and more reliable power, per animal, as compared to the others. Also, the reference alludes to the era of horse-and-buggy, powered by one, two, four and even six horses. Not to mention "Driver" which was and still is reference to anyone using a whip to drive those horses. "Driver's License" anyone?)

Back to our early farmers: When they arrived, without much fanfare, got right down to tilling the earth. Then they took a break, ate a simple meal and rested a bit. The animal that pulled the wagon and the plow, also had to eat and he may have had a guard-dog that was hungry too. He had to feed them too. In the afternoon, he would spread all the seed properly and make a final round to cover it all with soil. If the soil was moist enough, he was done for a day or two. If the soil were dryer than needed, he would have to water the land somehow. He could do this early next day, before the sun got too hot, or he could wait for rain, risking the loss of his crop. Experience helped him decide. The seeds needed moisture for several days to start germination.

A heavy rain would be devastating, for at least a couple of weeks, as it could wash away seeds, sprouts and soil. After seven days or so, roots take hold in the soil and seedlings begin to grow vigorously. Anyone who ever spent at least one day on a farm knows that his work was far from over; in fact it had just begun. He would have to check progress of growth, remove weeds that threatened the tender young plants every few days. On other days, he would not be idling either. On a farm, there is always plenty to do. He may still have to take excess crops to market, or store it for feed, mulch and compost plant stalks to use later as fertilizer. He had to repair frequently used tools or make new ones, tend to livestock from dawn until dusk.

He then would have to find the strength to be a father and a husband, just as his woman would still have to be a mother and a wife, after a full day's work of her own. They had to play with their children a while, then feed and bathe them before putting them in bed. The remaining time was theirs, alone.

Thousands of years later, we still live more or less the same way. Wouldn't you say? Our tasks of the day are somewhat different now, but we are just as busy. Our time and labor is devoted to the need to earn money, the common medium of exchange, and we find ourselves living in servitude. We no longer receive any goods for our services and we can no longer sell the products we produce. Instead, our employers paid us with paper money and coins, made of metal that is no longer precious. In this age, we are no longer receiving either paper or coin currency, and very few still receive checks. Most of us receive electronically transferred digits in our bank-accounts. How did this happen?

To find some explanation we have to go back in time to examine the invention of money. Before we do that, I'd like to tell you more about the development of agriculture and industry.

Earlier I mentioned an area where human civilization flourished even while the northern and southern hemisphere suffered the ice age. The "fertile crescent", or Mesopotamia, as its name is in the history books, was the "cradle of civilization", say scientists. This area is located in southern Iraq.

Even if we do not spend time on them, note that other civilizations were also making great strides during this time.

The surplus that is a natural result of farming and ranching allowed people to settle in suitable areas. By this time, they had enough information about the most important edible plants and animals to schedule their activities. Until now, they kept most of this information in memory and verbally conveyed it from one generation to the next. The amount of information, gathered about their environment, was now so overwhelming that it led to the development of writing and reading. Each family member handled a portion of the workload, but some families had more land and animals that they could take care of by themselves. They had to hire help. Some of you might say, to avoid this necessity, they could have opted for a smaller parcel of land and perhaps fewer animals. But, based on events of the past, they learned to prepare for circumstances beyond their control. A drought for a year or two, or an occasional pillaging party sweeping through the area, would leave them with short supplies. Aside from arming themselves, producing surplus when possible seemed like the logical solution. Excess also represented wealth.

Over time, the number of workers settling in the area increased the population density dramatically.

The worker's living conditions were less than desirable and their pay was barely enough to live on. Discontent closely followed that realization.

Having all time in the world, the wealthy and therefore influential members of society were contemplating many ideas behind closed doors. To maintain order, the need for laws became pressing. Reading and writing were the skills necessary to create them and they were in possession of those skills. They appointed themselves to guide the ignorant masses. Maybe it was not a conscious decision, but class separation deepened, as most common people were illiterate during those times.

The wealthiest thought, it was just as well, as it gave them more power to keep the ignorant busy working. People keep toiling on the lands of land-Lords and the only education they get is the crack of the whip.

Education should be available to everyone equally. It would boost human evolution like never before.

Anything we learn is eventually registered and chemically stored in the genetic code of our cells. The volume of that information is staggering, even in simple organisms. To create a human body it takes an astronomical number of cells, each of which comes with its own code. The miracle of life is that each new cell knows exactly what to do! In a blade of grass, within the cocoon of a butterfly, as well as in a human baby, cells grow and go where they belong and do what they must. They act, with complete disregard for themselves, for the benefit of the entire organism. Blades of grass, butterflies and humans live individual lives, but, for the most part, remain in sync with their own kind.

Only humans managed to deviate from the grand plan. We have forced individuals into compliance for centuries.

Have you ever wondered how can children learn to use electronic gadgets so effortlessly these days?

Children always start their lives with a slight advantage over their ancestors. Possibly because the accumulated knowledge of thousands of years gets compressed into DNA and passed on in minute amounts. Obviously, for lack of education, not all children are equally fortunate. The good news is that we can positively affect future generations by exposing ourselves to all the accumulated knowledge. Deliberately withholding knowledge from the people for any reason or by any means is a crime against humanity. Surely, equal education would promote humanity's growth, while the current state of affairs breeds retardation.

The wealthy created laws that secured their rights over the people. Soon after that they wrote more laws to regulate the lives of all others. They needed someone to enforce these laws, so they hired deputies. The deputies would catch whoever committed a crime, even if the person had no idea about the law he had broken. They would have to make him pay a fine or lock him up, if he could not pay.

What is considered a crime, anyway? The wealthy sat down to think again.

It became quite clear to the smug that all this protection is going to cost money. As they are more willing to spend other people's money than their own, they found the idea of taxation irresistible.

Their logic went something like this: "There is a multitude of ordinary people out there. They are but an astonishing human resource of energy and wealth. We should not let it go to waste. Since, because of our wealth, we are in a position of power, we shall order them, by law, to pay a small individual tax. This tax should cover the cost of a court of law, were people appointed by us create new laws and punish the people for breaking them. Further more, taxes should also cover the expense of deputies needed to enforce the laws, the cost to build and maintain a place of incarceration and pay the guards. And, by the way, not knowing the Law should not absolve the person breaking it."

If any of this sounds vaguely familiar, it is a mere coincidence. Remember that I was talking about a society that existed nearly six thousand years ago.

In our current time, for at least the last few hundred years, crime was considered to be any act, deed, and their consequences that caused harm, injury or death to another human. That was not enough.

For, those who imagine to have inherent rights to everything our planet has to offer due to their accumulated wealth think the rest of us are useless eaters, and that we are plundering the resources of the planet. But, may I ask, who owns and runs all the for-profit industries? And who is in control of the production levels of their factories? Is it not their greed to blame for exploiting the resources for increasing profits? Economic growth is only important to those who own the industries, and aiming to own the whole food production chain, by purchasing large swats of lands.

It is indeed a bizarre aspect of human history that we have mastered the abuse of our fellow men, and we seem to glorify those who proved to be the most ruthless abusers. We readily commemorate their names in the history books much the same as we memorize the names of our most significant scientists, philosophers for their intellectual contributions. I know there are many outstanding people out there in many different fields in both, past and present. I have deliberately emphasized these two categories, because they represent the physical and intellectual sides of our being, respectively. Scientists are the cutting edge of human intellect when it comes to uncovering the physical secrets of our world. Philosophers on the other hand, literally dwell in the realm of untouchable and convey to us the essence of our spiritual being.

Let us now discuss the topic of tyrants.

Throughout history, tyrants were the most arrogant and ruthless individuals of their time. Their actions usually resulted in the loss of human life and resources of devastating proportions. It takes a lot of effort to build a peaceful and harmonious world in which people can prosper. A tyrannical ruler can easily destroy such a fragile world, if the people allow it.

Tyrants came in many different forms since the down of time. Here are three of the most common ones.

The first kind is a person with a strong urge to surpass the fame of another by any means necessary. Once in power, he may not accomplish much beyond the destruction it takes to get rid of him.

The second one truly believes he can change things for the better. He may build a large following by speaking about a future in terms that most people find desirable. To achieve his plans, it would take a radical deviation from the course envisioned and set in motion by a mysterious power-group. Therefore, he encounters tremendous resistance from a visible coalition. They systematically undermine, discredit and morally humiliate him, until he becomes politically irrelevant. News of his tragic suicide will shock his former supporters.

The third kind of tyrant is as difficult to understand, as it is to detect. It is no longer a single, easy to identify individual, but rather a mob, controlled by a "League of Extraordinary Gentlemen".

Usually, only members know of the existence of this clique. The mob works towards a common end.

This tyrannical organization is the most cunning and dangerous of all. Picture a multi-headed Dragon, or a Hydra.

As a fun fact, consider that your local government is taxing your property on behalf of the Fire-Department, which has established a network of fire-Hydrants all over town. You know...

Just in case they need them for crowd control, ahem..., I mean to extinguish fires.

That common end is, as we have identified it for our era based on Agenda 21 and Agenda 2030, the End of commoners. Their minion's role will be that of a movie extra's, who may watch the final product, but will not benefit from it.

Some times, these tyrants existed simultaneously. Some were local landlords; others ruled entire nations. They frequently battled one another and their subjects as well, to maintain or expand their power.

They derive their power from money and ignorance, or if you will, the ignorance of money. Now it is time to examine the invention and intention of money.

As you had seen, ancient societies, well before the Roman Empire, were becoming rather complex. Merchants, who's only goal is to create profits, realized that lacking a base value leads to disagreements in exchange, so they devised a standardized system. Their solution offered coins made of precious metals, such as gold and silver, as well as tin, zinc and copper and their alloys for every day use.

There were some variations, from people to people, but let us not hang up on that.

It was easy to see the logic behind this idea, as each coin represented a set value, for which everyone could get the same amount of goods every time, without much argument.

However, even then, this system was not perfect, and it is certainly not perfect today.

At the beginning, coins were scarce and general use of them spread relatively slowly, while other means of exchange were also in use. As minting of coins increased to produce enough to go around, it became apparent that precious metals maybe in short supply. This perhaps, lead to the first ever price-increase. We may speculate that certain people held onto coins of precious metal, thus increasing their wealth.

The treasury held a stockpile of coins, some of which they put into circulation to replenish the dwindling supply, as needed. This helped to restore balance to the system for a while. The supreme ruler of the time could never allow the complete depletion of the treasury, as his power depended on it. As always, the surest solution, to hold onto one's power, was to form a standing army. With this army, he could attack neighboring city-states, colonies or villages for monetary gain. He could dispatch it to conquer new frontiers and far-off civilizations as well. The mere taking of the enemy's possessions was, of course, never enough to replenish the treasury. Gaining control over the resources of the conquered land became the main objective. Besides looting the enemy's treasury, mines were prime targets as they provided a continued supply of precious metals, among other things. Other important resources acquired during these campaigns included the new territory's forests full of game animals for hunting, lakes and rivers for fishing, mines for stones and minerals, domesticated live-stocks, and even the people, to pay taxes. Tribute, as they called it back then.

Armed conflicts always have devastating affects on the geographic location and the people involved.

Aside from the destruction of resources and habitat, the conquered people suffered the loss of freedom. The most significant negative effect, however, is the loss of the most viable male population.

I believe we can all realize the implications of that fact.

Although forcing the losing party into slavery was common practice, it escalated to new levels. Keeping slaves had a new benefit. At first, slaves performed time consuming and unpleasant tasks. This practice allowed the master and his family to ponder new ways of expanding their territory. When a master had to decide between paid help or slaves, the choice was obvious.

At this point, I wish to remind you all that I am talking about slavery as it was practiced by the Roman Empire, by the Greeks, by the Egyptians, by Babylonians, Africans and Asians alike.

America will not be disc-overed, or re-disc-overed, for a few thousand years more.

Historically speaking, manual labor is expensive and hence undesirable for profit-making.

For this reason, slaves were and are profitable, regardless of how immoral we may find such a notion today.

The ugly truth is, people would use slaves for everything they are too lazy to do themselves and too cheap to pay for it. Make no mistake about it! Slaves pay for their own keep by their own labor, while producing profit.

Slavery still exists today for that reason, but almost no one is aware of it anymore. A new, invisible system exploits every imaginable human weakness to keep us in bondage.

The system is constantly refined to yield ever more power to those in control of it.

Money corrupts whole societies, to varying degrees, from top to bottom. Generally, the most corrupt people are at the very top and the very bottom of such societies.

-Is this some kind of conspiracy theory? —someone spontaneously shouted from the audience.

That depends on YOUR definition of "conspiracy theory"! - Jeffrey replied without skipping a beat.

As far as the government is concerned, whatever people might find to be the cause of losing their jobs, homes, automobiles and why their marriages may fall apart in large numbers during an economic downturn, is conspiracy theory. Never mind that the government and most employers suggest and believe that personal financial troubles are the direct result of one's laziness. They consider you lazy for not willing to work harder and more hours, while they pay you less to maximize their profits.

When our lives become shockingly similar to the punishment of Sisyphus, but our task is rolling a snowball of money uphill, toward retirement, in the middle of summer, that, my friends, is a fact of conspiracy.

You and your family, your relatives, and friends may talk about things that had happened to them, or others, during a party or family gathering. If, at any time, a pattern develops, you can rest assured, you have just stumbled upon conspiracy facts having an effect on your lives.

Instinctively, deep down, every one of you know this to be true.

The television, radio, and newspapers tell us a different story about the world. They tell us that the causes, we may find behind a series of events, are just a theory, they do not exist.

Yet, they produce palpable results. How is that possible? We must discern fact from fiction.

My intention is to show, how the few constantly outsmart the many.

We still have to cover about two thousand years of history. That may take another hour or two. I suggest we take a quick break now.

Fifteen minutes later... Welcome back!

Please take a moment to look around you. What do you see?

A large number of wonderful people are present, who are truly interested in our shared destiny. We should also note the empty seats left behind by those who are now hopelessly indifferent. They need our help, as they represent a segment of society that is near the point-of-no-return.

They clearly show signs of the propaganda at work that we all experience daily. They have become numb from over- stimulation and they now live in a fantasy world. They are giving in to the idea that the world is what it is, and there is no way to turn it around. We have to shake them up and out of their lethargic state, so they could actively participate in reshaping the world.

Let us continue following money and its effects.

It is clear that money corrupts and has been doing so from the moment of its inception.

Is that the true nature of money? No, money is an inert object; human weakness is at fault.

Blaming money for committing fraud would be exactly the same as blaming guns for killing people.

It is people, who misuse both! The second amendment and owning firearms is something I wish to address later. Circumstances influence and sometimes force people to act in desperation.

If a person feels safe, he will not resort to violence, nor will he feel the need for self-defense. Likewise, if he is financially secure, he will not commit fraud. However, he may find power irresistible and do awful things to grab it or to increase it.

Human evolution has been slow and painful. Slow is good. But inflicting pain on one another for money and power, as if it was the only way to happiness, is never good. This is why, when pushed too far, even the most tolerant people can become extremely ruthless, taking it all back. I say again, when the advancing interests of a few inhibit or prohibit general prosperity long enough, conflict is inevitable.

History is a testament to that fact. By the way, the word history sounds as if it is a collection, or recollection of events and their causes by someone else, perhaps the victorious one, and thus the record is His Story.

So far, we covered nearly eight thousand years of human progress. It is time to look at our modern interactions.

Conflicts of all sorts and magnitude mark every turn of our history. We could say that the most dynamic events happened during the last four hundred years. Having passed many social and economic stages of development, the underlying problem shockingly remains.

A tight and relatively narrow band of people, who feel supreme to the rest of us, still exists. They refer to themselves as high-society and expect you to do the same.

Dare not, and you will find yourself marginalized.

Life is simple and always revolves around two basic needs: food and shelter. If we can have that, most of us will be content with life for quite some time.

Yet, when we become aware that those needs are no longer accessible within reason, we begin to feel compelled to take matters into our own hands.

Historians cataloged all the rebellions that resulted from such neglect of the people's needs.

We abolished physical ownership of slaves a little more than 150 years ago. Little did we know that a new system was in the making. This system, as you may have guessed, is all about money. To the freed slaves and their former masters it opens a new chapter, better yet, a whole book of struggles, as they are tossed into the fray, as individuals.

Only those in control of this system reap its true benefits.

Money is nothing more than an accessory to separation, as to this day, literacy and illiteracy has been.

Having learned to read, we are obliged to make that basic knowledge available for others. Likewise, knowing how the financial world works obliges us to teach our fellow humans its cunning ways.

As long as we live in a world that requires the use of money, everyone should know how to use it safely.

The church condemned usury a sin and forbade its practice to Christians in Europe in the 15th century. Islam forbade usury from the day it became the religion of Muslim peoples, and they never allowed its practice in their nations.

The institution of slavery became obsolete, as a new realization took hold in financial circles.

The benefit of using slaves would be far outweighed by the profits that could be made of an ocean of "employable" people.

This concept needs further clarification. The truth is, the civil war in America could have been avoided, if the Masters of the north would have sat down with the Masters of the south to discuss the matter in detail. But once again, the profit that could be made from the war was too great to pass up.

The fact, that making profit out of war always costs dearly in human lives, never seems to bother the profiteers.

I wish to honor all the great men and woman of the general population who has willingly laid down the ultimate sacrifice for the good of the people throughout history. At the same time, I must question the motives of those who willingly join military service and risk their lives, knowing full well, it will only serve the interests of a few. The question is: Are they truly aware?

Morality is frequently cast aside in business circles in favor of cold calculations; thus, the aim of converting slaves to employees was only to increase profits.

The southern Masters had to be educated to see the logic behind the numbers. I'd like to show you some numbers now to demonstrate what I mean.

Let us say, the population of the states was around 20 million. It is a round number, easy to divide and it is realistic for the mid-eighteen hundreds. Some of the most brilliant human minds have discovered the arithmetic operation called division in ancient times.

Did they realize that it could be viewed as an alternative for multiplication?

Visualize this. You take something whole and start dividing it into more and more pieces. The pieces seem to multiply, but they become smaller and weaker as they are separated from the whole.

It takes a politician's mind to apply the principles of division to whole nations.

When preparing to conquer a people, the first order of action would be to divide them by any means necessary. That deserves a chapter of its own, and it is something we shall examine later on.

Now, we have twenty million people to divide. They could be divided many ways, but we want to know how many of then actually work and earn wages. Statistics show that in any population, the number of working people is around thirty-three percent. Mark that number! Given the basic structure of a healthy society, the remaining sixty-six percent would include the elderly and young children.

The census figures for 1850 puts the number of slaves around three million out of the whole population. Once again, I rounded that number off for easier figuring.

Now add them to the taxpaying population and we will see a staggering jump in profits favoring the usurers.

Let us assume that a person earned one dollar per day, or, working five days a week, around two hundred fifty dollars per year. A mere 1% tax on his earnings would make him send two dollars and fifty cents into the treasury.

Multiply that by three million and the treasury will be 7.5 million dollars richer, each year. That amount is dwarfed by the total estimated cost of the war, being nearly 6.2 billion in 1860's dollars. You can search that online, to see that I am not fabricating any of this information, as the media does.

The seven and a half million dollars from taxed earnings alone, is a handsome addition to the vaults. Revenues from other transactions such as, tariffs on purchasing goods, export-import, tolls, fees, property and sales taxes, legal stamps, agriculture and manufacturing all added up to several billion dollars every year, even in the mid-eighteen hundreds. Let me remind you, the total population then was just over twenty million. The Census Bureau reported federal debt for the 1850's, around 47 million. Question: If the government had control of the Treasury and had the power to issue the nation's money, by which I mean printing and minting it physically, at no interest at the time, how did they account for a debt of 47 million dollars?

If we compare that, to a few billion dollars of yearly revenue, what does the word debt really mean? I believe, to explore that topic in its full dept, deserves yet another, separate presentation.

As the leading nations of the world moved ever closer to full industrialization, certain aspects of the lives of individuals had to change, fundamentally. Forced by their circumstances, people in cities, have already made this change. Country folks would not be so easy to convert. What that means is that people in the cities could no longer have a vegetable garden or keep farm animals to provide healthy food for their families. They did not have the space or the time to do it.

They quickly became dependent on a new industry that manufactures foodstuffs, which could be stored for extended periods of time.

People seemingly accepted this idea, as they found themselves working in occupations that take every bit of ten hours each day, while some take even longer. After those hours, people just want to get home, have a quick meal, spend a little time with their children and spouses before crashing into bed, so they could repeat the process the next day.

Does this sound familiar to any of you? I think people have been here before; but back then they worked for themselves. As more and more people lost the ability to be self-sufficient, they ended up working in the businesses of others.

As a result, they were usually paid the lowest acceptable/negotiable amount, on the basis of "take it, or leave it". While the Masters of today continue their discussions to increase profits behind closed doors, the common people are too busy "earning a living", and so, have no time to pay attention.

They are too busy, figuring out how to make ends meet by the end of the month.

Hence the question: "Why do we have so many days of the month, after the paycheck runs out?" circulates as a cruel contemporary joke.

For quite some time, only men worked outside of the household. They were proud to be the sole provider. Soon, the emancipation movement sent women off to work as well. That alone nearly doubled the working class and the number of earnings for taxation. Also, sending women into the "work-force" took the private affair of raising their children out of their hands, and landed it in the hands of strangers, in the form of baby-sitters, day-care, kindergarten, preschool and finally the fully government controlled School System. Ponder that for a moment!

To increase the speed at which money circulates, the sales tax came into being. Every time a we buy something, we pay to enrich the Money Masters, who are not amused. From their point of view, money flows very slowly. In a capitalist economy, the numbers of Masters multiply rapidly, and they are impatient, when it comes to collecting returns on their investments. Gradually all goods had to be taxed to satisfy their hunger. But, wait!

Perhaps to maintain the appearance of decency, food products are still tax-free in thirty-five states. Why the rest of the states chose to differ, is any one's guess.

The food industry developed as a side effect of the industrial age. Large masses of people are working long shifts, who find no time to cook a healthy meal at the end of the day. Fast food attempted to fill the bill, but soon another side affect became apparent. People fell ill more often, and began to develop weird allergies. Worn-out, stressed-out, and suffering from malnutrition, people became dependent on medical care just so they could go back and work some more. Doctors and hospitals kicked into high gear when they realized the potential for higher profits. Profits are irresistible.

Legislators enacted new laws that allow cartels to operate with little or no accountability to anyone. Hence the corporation was born.

We are aware of the fact that the law considers a corporation a legal person. A corporation shields the living people who run it from the living people who receive its products or services. Think of it as a bulletproof vest. I am sure many of you enjoy that protection right now. If your business is successful, are your business practices decent enough to afford you a good night's sleep? If not, the remnants of your conscience may disturb your peace. If you sleep well, but you feel compelled to set the house alarm each night, your conscience may not be as clear as you think. You may worry about the existence of needy people and the off chance that they might break into your home in search of food or something other.

As an employer, how much did you contribute to their plight? Do you believe in karma? If you do, you may want to discard that belief in order to sleep better at night.

Whether you like it or not, as an employer, you are responsible for the well-being of your employees.

It does not matter what activity you engage in, be it education, marketing, any other business, religion, politics and even finance, as long as you employ people your business affects the lives of fellow humans.

So you see, the way money flows, matters a lot. You work very hard, neglecting your children and your spouses, just to make more money that may or may not be enough to afford your expectations of life. Then you pay taxes, day-in, day-out, every time you shop. On April 15th the government expects you to hand over a percentage of what you made, so you'd better saved up to pay them. They use much of your taxes to pay themselves, and if there is anything left, it was a good "fiscal" year! Next morning, you may find yourself stuck in traffic, surrounded by a jungle of barricades to keep you safe, and you notice that your tax-dollars are hard at work financing what appears to be an unnecessary project of "improvement".

The phrase "trickle-down-economy", of the Reagan era, describes almost all my examples so far. This phrase alone should have caused a public outcry, not to mention the implementation of measures for which it was the code word. With the help of "none-existent" inflation, earnings now seem to trickle down, while taxation has increased to great torrents. I must admit that until recently, most people lived good lives, at least in the western world. But even they begin to feel the trickle.

Their good life came at the price of exploiting people in lesser-developed countries, as well as people at home. We ignored their needs and rights with indifference. The same kind of indifference a corporation feels towards us, when they pollute our waterways, fields and forests that could support us all. Instead of demanding organic foods, we accept tightly packaged, processed foods that only met nature on the road to the store. When we read the nutritional label on a food product, we do not understand the meaning of "natural flavors". Naturally, we believe so much in the people who made that food to mean no harm to us, that we accept the unnatural. We ignore the fact that "natural flavor" is just a chemical compound used in place of something we remember as real. "Imitation Crab Meat", anyone?

We carelessly spend our hard-earned dollars on food "products" that are synthetically made, loaded with preservatives and are deceivingly labeled.

That is why it is called the Food Industry.

Now that we know why we are undernourished, yet over-weight and hence more prone to illness, I would like to tell you about the "Medical Industry".

Keep in mind that "medicine" is the art and science of healing. Healers can use a wide range of methods to maintain or restore health, by preventing or curing an illness.

The number one rule of Medicine is "Do no harm"!

When I was little more than two years old, I became very ill. I had high fever of 102-104 for many days. The pediatrician could not identify the disease correctly. The best advice he could give my parents was to keep my fever down. After a few days of trying to keep my fever below 100 degrees, by which time I looked like a rag-doll, they took me to the emergency room of a major hospital nearby.

The ER ran a couple of tests and within twenty minutes, they had the right diagnosis.

The ER doc's thoroughness and my parents' parental instincts saved me, not the pediatrician, sorry to say.

Many years later, in the mid seventies, I came across an article by accident, that spoke of a Japanese doctor who just discovered a "new" and mysterious disease. The description of this disease sounded very similar to a number of childhood diseases that produce some type of rash accompanied by fever, but some of its symptoms that help identify it may not show up for some time. According to my mother's account, I had red, swollen lips, strawberry tongue and the skin of my palms and bottom of my feet began shedding after several days.

It also resulted in a heart murmur that a cardiologist monitored for years before I was in the clear. The disease is Kawasaki's, named after the doctor who discovered it.

If the name sounds vaguely familiar, it maybe because I am not the only one who ever contracted it. Most notable in recent memory is Jett Travolta, who lived with the consequences of Kawasaki's disease, which may have contributed to his untimely and tragic death.

Dr. Kawasaki discovered the disease in the late sixties, but to date the exact cause of it remains a matter of speculation. I want all of you to know that I am a fierce advocate of timely dissemination of vital information about any new diseases! Doctors can accurately diagnose diseases and save people if they have that vital information. The public should also have that information so they would know how to prevent, recognize, or care for people with certain diseases.

Withholding vital medical information should be punishable as a crime against humanity! A professional doctor intends to heal people and he, and she may rightfully enjoy the financial benefits of so doing. People who recognize the compassionate care of such doctors would express their gratitude by an honorary fee in addition to the usual cost. On the other hand, a doctor, who is practicing exclusively for monetary gain, is no different from any capitalist. These doctors inconsiderately medicate their patients; therefore, the patients would never pay any extra for such a treatment. This doctor may sleep peacefully through the night, knowing the dog is alert and the alarm is set. He does not concern himself with the patient's well being or chances of healing much beyond the amount he can collect from the Insurance Company.

Do you ever wonder why your medical insurance keeps going up?

I believe every person is entitled to the same level of healthcare, the highest level. Patients should be able to choose a doctor or hospital based on their reputation and their specialties for the patient's needs.

Medical insurance should be affordable enough, so hospitals and doctors could treat even the less fortunate without the force of law. To make medical services even more affordable, since health care suppose to be a humanitarian service, the cost of medical schools should also be affordable.

I am not in favor of enacting new laws, as I believe we already have more laws than we need. However, reducing the cost of medical services in such a way is a cause worth writing into law. No, it should not result in socialized medicine.

It should result in fair pricing. The basic premise of medicine is to heal, equally. People who can afford to, could then spend all the money they please on additional treatments for enhancement.

Wealthy people have been doing it, for they can afford to have their doctors on payroll.

Just so you understand where I am coming from, I should tell you that my sister died of breast cancer a few years ago. She has had every imaginable and available treatment at the time, yet she had three recurrences within ten years. She lost her hair to chemotherapy and radiation every time. She ended up disfigured after a bilateral mastectomy and a series of reconstructive surgeries after her second recurrence. At the third occurrence, she volunteered to receive a new type of chemo, in a final attempt to beat this curse. Her kidneys, damaged by years of processing toxic chemotherapy, failed her.

I firmly believe there is a cure for all cancers, but the medical establishment simply prefers to maintain the health condition of people. HMO, anyone?

Most cancer survivors will tell you that the right mind set wins half the battle. For some, all it takes to beat cancer is to be in the right frame of mind.

As far as prevention is concerned, a naturally tranquil mood, not giving in to fear and the ability to keep stress out of one's life is the key! How could you get rid of stress? It all comes back to money.

The perpetual pursuit of an imaginary sum, we think we must have to be happy, causes all of our stress. Most of us are going about it in an honorable way. For the most part, we stay within the boundaries of decency and obey the law. Thus, we are doomed to failure. If we cannot let go of the urge to compete when we see the neighbor in a brand new Jaguar, or parked in his driveway a huge boat, we will never be happy. In addition, if we find out what that neighbor does for a living we might get quite upset. Naturally, we would never allow ourselves to sink to his level of corruption.

If you do not have neighbors like that, it is most likely because you live among decent people. Your neighborhood is open and is without deed restrictions. You and your neighbors enjoy making your own decisions, for instance, about what color to paint your house or garage. Where you park on your property is also at your discretion. Most likely, neither you, nor your neighbors have need of an alarm system. You personally know at least your immediate neighbors, and by sight, most vehicles that belong in your neighborhood. Out of respect for yourselves and your neighbors, you regularly mow your own lawns, not needing a community notice to prompt you.

The apparently well-off neighbor I described above would very likely prefer living in a gated community. Living there, he would not be able to keep his boat on his property, so he'd be a member of a Yacht Club. People in any gated community seem to enjoy self-imposed rules in ever-increasing numbers, decreed by an elected association.

To me, this concept is alien.

I do acknowledge that many hardworking people can earn above average salaries, which, unfortunately, may appear a bit suspicious when viewed casually by the less fortunate. Some of these hard workers may even prefer a closed community to an open one. I do applaud them for being so organized and having sufficient foresight to meticulously plan their course and consistently follow through with it! Their willingness to commit more energy and time to achieving their goals, than most of us would feel comfortable with, is also admirable. Their numbers have been steadily increasing over the last few decades, aided by the electronics-age; still, they only represent a small percentage of the populace. I want them to know that I would never suggest any solutions to bring up the rear, which might appear to be an attempt to deprive them of their successes. Their cooperation to do so, would be highly desirable. Their expertise are indispensable for making the world a hospitable place for all peoples.

I also realize that changing course mid-stream may seem frightening, but I must insist on getting started! Artificially induced economic conditions can have a profound affect on quality of life, for anyone. People may experience tremendous stress due to hardship, as they face loosing their jobs, their savings, their homes, even their families. They do not understand that it is beyond their control and thus they are not to blame. Sadly, this stress may damage even a seemingly stable marriage beyond repair, as spouses blame one another for their increasing hardship. Times like these can be highly profitable for those poised to take advantage of the downfall of others.

Profiteers would rather push people into the grave than help them in any way.

The ideas I have presented tonight, are mine and they are simply pro-people, humanistic in nature. If any organization interprets my pro-people views as anti-establishment, the opposite must also be true. The pro-establishment mindset of any organization must be anti-people!

In light of the ongoing worldwide economic crisis that occurred seemingly without reason, I urge every one of you to pay close attention to the world of finance.

I would like to quote a few famous people from history to illustrate my point. Benjamin Franklin said about the revolution of 1775 "The refusal of King George to allow the colonies to operate an honest money system which freed the ordinary man from the clutches of the money manipulators was probably the prime cause of the revolution".

Thomas Jefferson had this to say about banks, "I believe that banking institutions are more dangerous than standing armies. If the American people ever allow private bankers to control the issue of currency…the banks and corporations that will grow up around them will deprive the people of their property until their children wake up homeless on the continent their fathers conquered."

And finally, one of the most famous quotes of all time from Mayer Amschel Rothschild, the founder of the Rothschild banking dynasty, "Give me control of a nation's money supply and I care not who makes it's laws."

These quotes are rather old, yet they fully capture the essence of today's central banking based on fractional reserve. Remember that my lecture is about human relations. As such, does it make you wonder what kind of person would do such things to his own kind? You should look into that as a homework assignment!

While billions of souls toil daily to make ends meet, the self-proclaimed elite continues to perfect their agendas. In a simplified way, I have described how they acquired their wealth and power by keeping the rest of us overwhelmed by our daily chores. I have hinted at the subtle way they manipulate our lives without ever alerting us to the fact.

They will never flinch to use drastic measures to gain control of any situation, so neither should we.

Until now, the second amendment guaranteed our right to bear arms, but I am afraid the time will come when THEY will want to proceed faster in executing their plans. Soon, they may pass a law that will require all of us to hand over our firearms in a sheep-like manner, as they had done with gold, in the 1930's.

That would mean the end of America!

Let me bring up an example from the early twentieth century, so we may learn from it.

In 1917 a revolution took place in a far-off land. There was no television then, even radio was a fairly new invention and scarcely available. But, power-hungry people understood its potential and began using it to broadcast propaganda slogans to the public on the streets by way of loud-speakkers. The working class people of Russia were so over-worked and impoverished that it did not take much to ignite their fury.

Carl Marx and Friedrich Engels wrote "The Communist Manifesto" that was published in 1848. Soon after, people with special interests adopted the idea of "class struggle" and began to infuse the masses with it.

Vladimir Ilyich Lenin became the leader of the uprising of the Russian people, and proceeded to execute the Tsar and his whole family, followed by most of the intelligentsia and nobility of Russia.

The short version of their story is that the people of Russia took power into their own hands by 1922. Or, did they really?

Under a self-proclaimed, or should I say volunteer, leadership, they United many sovereign nation-states into what was called the Soviet Union for almost seventy years.

Instead of recruiting them by reasoning, they decided to force their ideology upon them. Where did they get the idea from, I wonder.

Meanwhile, most of Europe was ablaze in the first deadliest modern human conflict of our common history.

Excuse me, if my allusions are in anyway offensive to your nationalistic feelings, but as mach as I share your sentiment, it is time to regard a conflict between or within any nations as a human conflict.

History books would have you believe that WWI broke out as the result of the assassination of Archduke Franz Ferdinand, the heir to the throne of the Austro-Hungarian Empire. That was just a false-flag operation to kick-start that conflict.

In reality, it was nothing more than a series of failed financial negotiations by Germany and other countries to get out of debt.

Germany was forced into an economic and financial corner by Britain, and the Rothschild banking dynasty.

Do not look for this information in the history books. It had to be omitted to conceal its far-reaching implications. Years ago, I have traveled to many European countries and spoke with scores of people old enough to remember those times. The differences between their recollections and what children, all over the world, are being thought in schools are staggering. Industrialization and the financial arrangements that "helped" make it happen, resulted in economic hardships in many countries. As a major industrial nation, Germany became an arch-rival of British Empire, both commercially and financially, a fact that did not sit well among British industrialists and financiers. Something had to be done to change that.

Economic sanctions came to mind as a solution. What does one do when cornered? Fight or Flight? We all know what happened.

I have already pointed out the enormous loss of human lives and the unimaginable destruction of assets resulting from conflicts of such magnitude. You may have heard varying numbers about the actual losses. The death toll of WWI is estimated to be 16 million, including military personnel and civilians. The sinking of Titanic, two years prior, was the result of complex and multi-faceted dirty dealings, all around. I urge every one of you to investigate that on your own! Barely two decades later, WWII claimed the lives of nearly 60 million people, in Europe alone.

Sadly, almost half of that were civilians, which the media now calls "collateral damage".

Please excuse my expression when I say that banking dynasties also "made a killing" by financing both sides of both wars and have been doing so in every conflict since Napoleon lost the battle at Waterloo.

Talk about ethical dealings!

From the day money was invented, every human conflict revolved around it, one way or another.

With the help of technological advances, those conflicts have grown ever larger, ever bloodier and destructive, and ever more expensive! From the humanitarian perspective, large-scale massacres like these are no longer desirable, and much less acceptable.

At some point in the history of banking, bankers realized that a "sustainable warfare" is a virtual gold mine. Not only do they make astronomical fortunes by financing military operations, but also by creating national debt. The reduced loss of human life curtails public outcry, for the most part. Habitats are continually destroyed and rebuilt, and, according to bankers, that is beneficial for the economies of the countries involved.

Entire nations become debt-slaves in this fashion, as common people always pay the price.

While these wars raged in Europe, America had its own problems to solve.

Coincidentally, WWI began soon after the Federal Reserve Bank established itself in 1913. Was it really a coincidence?

G. Edward Griffin wrote a book called "The Creature from Jekyll Island" about the creation of that monopoly.

He clearly explains the concept of fractional reserve banking and how the Federal Reserve Bank "creates money out of thin air", in his book.

Money really is a fiction, as its value is what the FRB says it is. This type of currency is known as FIAT money. There is no gold, nor any other precious metal or commodity backing it; nor does a nation's Gross Domestic Product have anything to do with it anymore.

The natural resources of a particular geographic area and the population occupying that land, maybe considered acceptable as collateral for lending money to the government of that nation.. Their government can then lend it to its subjects, but only through a prescribed path. Originating from a fractional reserve system, no monies can ever reach the people without an accumulated interest attached to it. Just as in any other business, all parties that have anything to do with a product or service, money in this case, add their cut to its price-tag before passing it on. Those who understood the power that comes from lending money at interest were bound to make it their monopoly.

Debt is the primary instrument of slavery today.

If you do not think so, you should take some time figuring out just how much of your possessions do you truly own. Then, find out who really owns your belongings, as lean-holders.

How much do you owe for your most important properties and how many ways are those properties taxed? Does the phrase, human resources, bother anyone?

Then consider this. In some countries, which might fit the description of being "third-world", whole families can actually live on approximately 800 dollars for a whole month. The price of gasoline in some of those countries now exceeds $6/gallon.

How do you suppose they manage that?

For one thing, they may still own their homes free and clear, even after the collapse of the communist system. Up until recently, they had affordable medical care, referred to as "socialized medicine" in the west, which covered every citizen more or less equally. They did not have to rob a bank, as a figure of speech, before seeing a doctor.

Yes, you may point out that their facilities were of inferior quality. Yet every body was able to use them and they could count on caregivers who happened to care. It was not perfect, no, but people were able to live. If those former communist countries would have adopted the western model of medicine, their foolish system would have collapsed much sooner.

Public transportation in most European cities is also affordable and is set up so well that those who live within cities do not have to own a car at all. Of course, people who choose to own automobiles must be able to afford the gas as well as everything else related to its ownership. Large numbers of people are still relatively debt free in these third-world countries.

Under EU membership, however, they are now being forced to barrow money by enforced economic measures.

On the personal level, the only REAL value they have for collateral is their homes; on the national level, the country's natural resources maybe presented as collateral.

Now, imagine a life in which you would not need a mortgage to buy or build your home, you could save money for a car, you did not need a student loan to get a good education, and have no credit card debt, but you would be paid the same money you earn today!

What would happen to all the stress in your life?

Sadly, the US military is an accessory to forcing these peoples to accept credit, instead of a fair wage. Thus, little by little, they lose everything to creditors their families owned, in some cases for centuries!

As a nation, they are forced to give up the right to their own natural resources! If they do not, they will be taken from them by force.

Is it any wonder they do not like the United States of America Inc. very much?

American "leaders" send innocent children in uniform into those foreign countries, to steal their natural resources and kill their way of life, on behalf of Big Banks. (B B)

No, those people did not want to kill our way of life. They wanted to keep their own, and wanted to be left alone! We did not leave them alone. They are rightfully angry now.

This is also true at home, in America.

In a country, where people have a strong desire for freedom, the military should stand by the people when it matters. Soldiers should clearly understand their purpose, which is to defend their country and people against foreign interests. Officers are few, soldiers are many; someone will have to make the right decisions.

Ladies and Gentlemen, thank you for your patience and attention to the problems we face together. These problems concern us all equally.

The world is different now!

Millions of peace loving people are working together, communicating over the internet, to bring true freedom to regions where freedom only existed in the schoolbooks.

I wish to close my presentation with a quote from Johann Wolfgang von Goethe, who said:

"None are more hopelessly enslaved than those who falsely believe they are free."

CHAPTER 1

"Open your eyes!" Jeff heard a muffled voice calling. He could barely understand the words through the blaring of the siren.

"Open your eyes!" The voice sounded much closer and louder this time, and he felt the touch of a hand. It was warm and gentle as it opened his right eyelid. A bright light pierced into his brain instantly and he jerked his head hard to avoid it. His evasive action caused a sharp pain on the top-left side of his skull as it bounced back from the metal frame of the gurney.

"You're okay, calm down, you're okay!" The voice reassured him.

A female's voice; he now recognized the tone, but could not yet see her face.

His current reality began to register slowly, as his senses returned to normal. He felt his sweat soaked clothes stuck to his skin, making him shiver even under the blanket.

Soothing warmth began to flow through his veins, comforting his whole body. It emanated from his left arm, where a plastic tube was tugging on a needle, causing negligible pain. The ambulance was rocking in all directions as it raced through morning traffic. All his pains vanished, replaced by a fuzzy calm feeling as the low-dose morphine took effect. He could not see clearly, but his mind was still searching for answers; He reached out and grabbed the woman's hand. "What happened to me...?" he whispered faintly.

When he fully regained his consciousness, the world came rushing back in. Even with his eyelids closed, he could sense a bright light illuminating the room. Cautiously opened his eyes, expecting a brain-stabbing pain again, but it did not come. The room was too bright at first, but the intensity of the light quickly normalized. While staring at the ceiling tiles, the smell of the sterile environment made Jeff realize that he was in a Hospital. His lips and throat were very dry. He managed to press the call button with some difficulty. He heard voices from a distance, outside his room, but none sounded like the voice in the ambulance. That voice clearly burnt into his memory, but he could not remember her name.

While he waited for someone to respond, Jeffrey began to analyze his surroundings to make sense of the situation.

There were four beds in the room, but only two of them were occupied.

The other person was tightly wrapped in bandages.

The poor fellow wasn't as lucky as I was, Jeff discerned with sympathy.

The door flew open just then and a middle aged nurse, currently on duty, burst in with some medical supplies in her hands.

"Hello, Mr. Clark." she greeted him as she placed the tray on the cart next to his bed. "How are you feeling?" Her voice was of a well-trained professional accompanied by a smile that comes from many years of practice. It is meant to be reassuring and one can barely distinguish it from a genuine smile.

"Not bad, considering…" "May I have some water? My mouth feels like I just swallowed a handful of chalk." he pleaded to the nurse.

"That is quite normal at this point Mr. Clark." she said matter-of-factly, as if her words could quench his thirst.

"I will bring you some as soon as the Doctor gives the okay." she added, pushing a syringe into the port just below the IV bottle and emptied its contents directly into the line.

It's all just a big game.

A game, in which his needs are deliberately ignored to avoid any liability.

Jeff hated corporate policies as they curtailed any natural human behavior in the workplace, distorting them into PR maneuvering.

He opted for a request that maybe less of a threat to the medical establishment. "Can you tell me why am I here, nurse…"

"Freedman" she finished his sentence and removed the needle from the line.

"Let's see." with that she flipped up the chart hanging at the foot of his bed.

He watched her poker face as she decoded the information scribbled on it.

"Well, it says here that you were brought in during the nightshift. You have suffered a severe concussion, some minor bruising and fractured three ribs when you fell down the stairs during an episode of seizure. A condition which resulted from the Kawasaki's disease you had when you where about two years old."

Mrs. Freedman was, as her demeanor suggested, a seasoned nurse with twenty six years under her belt. In her mid fifties, she showed signs of sitting around for long hours each day, year after year. Being head nurse of this new facility, she was in charge of assigning tasks to her subordinates, whom she regarded and handled accordingly. She spoke in a tone of authority even to her patients and demanded respect when she did not get it readily.

Seizure?

I do not have a history of seizures. Not that I remember. Why am I uncertain now? I can't seem to think straight. My mind falters at the slightest effort, trying to conjure up a coherent line of thoughts. How do they know I had Kawasaki's…?

Jeffrey Clark wondered.

"Mrs. Freedman!" He intended to yell, but only managed a soft whimper and being exhausted, he slipped into unconsciousness again.

Several hours later he found himself in a different room. This one was equally bright, but here he was alone. Am I in isolation? He wondered in a state of despair.

Why am I here?

I am not contagious, and I am certainly not dying!

Jeff struggled to remember what happened…

It seemed awfully quiet out there; wherever "out there" actually was.

He looked around curiously, noting every little detail about the room. Undoubtedly, it seemed like a real hospital room with all the usual fixings. He saw an E.K.G., which displayed and recorded his heart rhythm. An I.V. pole, from which electrolytes dripped slowly, hydrating his body, or whatever it was supposed to do. Another instrument measured the oxygen saturation of his blood and there was a crash-cart by the door.

He kept looking around, feeling weird, for not realizing what made the room so odd. Then his eyes settled on an unusual feature of the room. He gazed at a large, heavy drape that covered the entire wall on his left, floor to ceiling.

Is there a window behind that curtain? He could not tell.

The clock on the wall, in front of him, read 9:11, then 9:12, but whether it was AM or PM it did not tell.

That's great, I don't even know what time of the day it is.

He completed the examination of his surroundings.

As he tried to recall the events of the last few hours, or days, he heard the voice of the female E.M.T. in his mind, once again.

"Open your eyes!"

Too bad, I did not get to see her face. I should have asked her name at least. Maybe I could find her, whenever I get out of here, and ask her how she found me.

This idea made him feel a little more upbeat about the way things were. Regardless of how beat up he actually felt.

He could see dark bruises on his arms and now he felt a throbbing sensation that connected the visual clue with his brain.

With every breath he took, his ribcage felt like it would fall apart at any second. His brain could only process so much pain before sending him into unconsciousness.

"Mister Clark?"

Jeffrey woke up hearing his name being called by a man he never saw before.

"My name is Henry" the man introduced himself pointing at his nametag, with a reassuring smile.

"You are safe for now, but we have to get you on your feet. They'll be looking for you soon!"

Henry lightly patted him on the shoulder. He turned around and began to replace the I.V. bag with one he had brought in.

"Wait a minute! Who are you again and who is looking for me?" Jeff sounded confused.

"I do not have a lot of time to explain, but they announced you dead on prime time news last night." Henry answered frankly. "I am glad to see you alive and I am here to help you get out of here ASAP. We need you."

"Where is Mrs. Freedman?" Jeff inquired with obvious concern in his voice. Henry seemed ready with an instant answer.

"She was the leader of the "other" team, here at ERIS."

"What do you mean she was?" Jeffrey's concern doubled instantly.

"Mister Clark." Henry turned to him now with a sobering tone. "I understand your confusion, but her whereabouts should not concern you. As I said, we want to keep you alive. She was responsible for your drowsiness since you arrived and she would have done even more unpleasant things to you if we had not stopped her. I have to go now." Henry was already heading for the door.

"Why..." Jeff started to ask, but could not finish it, as Henry disappeared behind the closing door. Jeff looked at the clock; the numbers showed 7:30. The sun illuminated his room now with bright golden rays that bounced off every chromed surface and glass. Its brilliance told him it had to be sunrise.

Henry hurried back to his friend Ed, who just got off the phone after speaking with someone at the Good Samaritan Hospital.

"Hey, Henry! I just spoke with the E.M.T. Supervisor at Good-Sam, her name is Katherine Kelly King. I told her I was you, and that I had a few questions for E.M.T. Janet C. about the patient they dropped off here. She said she'll let her know and she will call back soon." Ed informed him right away.

"Nice work, Ed! Now would you make sure nothing happens to our valued guest while I am writing the accident report on Freedman?"

"No problem, boss! By the way, it was a good call moving him downstairs." Ed saluted his friend and went to make sure that Jeffrey Clark was indeed safe and regaining his strength and senses.

"Ester Freedman suffered a tragic accident while transporting a deceased body to the morgue. She was pulling the gurney along when she tripped, losing control of her footing. She fell down a flight of stairs. I could not hold back the combined weight of the gurney, the dead body and Mrs. Freedman by myself. I sprained my ankle trying to hold it from going down, but it was unstoppable. I bruised my chest as I fell on top of the gurney when it landed on head-nurse Freedman, crushing her to death on the landing below."

Henry sat quietly for a moment, recalling the event, after writing his report.

"Henry! Come and help me take this DOA down to the morgue." Mrs. Freedman called to him.

"This poor thing did not have a chance surviving; those guys, you know, should take it easy sometimes." she continued without waiting for a reply. Pulling the gurney in the front, she went on. "We can only do so much to save them; yet, sometimes, they even bring in victims they could have pronounced at the scene."

Henry listened to her attentively, waiting for his chance to ask about the new patient. "Mrs. Freedman, what about the patient we admitted in the morning? He seemed to be in good shape, don't you think?" he ventured.

Ester Freedman glanced at him for a moment while slowing down to consider her reply.

"Well, he appeared to be in fair condition, but you never know. I've been told to care for him personally, because they have doubts about his condition."

"But, Mrs. Freedman, we do not know his name, we do not even have an address for the man. Does he have any relatives we could contact?"

They were heading toward a corridor that led to the elevators.

"Listen, Henry. How many times must I tell you to stick to your tasks and do not mind the details! We are well paid and our boss is very concerned about the privacy of these people." "Besides, what do you care if the government gets rid of a few unwanted elements? Think of your family's safety!"

She tried to divert his attention from the missing information.

"But, Mrs. Freedman, this patient..." at that moment they were passing an employee lounge where a television set was broadcasting the evening news. Henry looked to see the picture of the patient in room 305. He stopped, setting the brakes of the gurney, while he listened to the announcement of the man's tragic death, then his accomplishments, including his most recent and controversial lectures on human relations.

"...is still alive." he mumbled to himself.

"Mr. D'Guard! I've had enough of your buts for this evening! Now push this gurney along!" She commanded sternly. After releasing the wheel locks, Henry D'Guard leaned into the back end of the gurney while Mrs. Freedman pressed the wall plate to open the double doors. Just beyond the door, they had to make a tight turn to the left to reach the elevators. The gurney now required two people to control it. While moving forward Ester Freedman turned around to grab the gurney, but her shoe got caught on the threshold. Facing the gurney, she was forced by its momentum to step backwards to avoid it. The threshold peeled the shoe smoothly off her left foot. She felt the cold of the polished stone floor as she stepped back trying to swing the gurney to the right. Without her left shoe she started to slip as her pantyhose offered no traction on the floor. To regain her balance she stepped back with her right foot. Missing the floor of the hallway, her foot landed one step below on the stair behind her, while she was still clutching the gurney. With her weight added to the momentum, the gurney accelerated effortlessly. Over five hundred pounds pulled Henry across the floor, his shoes screeching as he struggled to keep it from falling.

The front wheels dropped onto the stairs violently. His instinct of self-preservation kicked in and Henry let go of the gurney to grab the railing. All this took only five seconds from the time the door opened until the gurney stopped thirteen steps below. Mrs. Freedman's head slumped forward lifelessly.

"Serves her right, the arrogant, two-faced bitch that she was." Henry concluded the event without remorse.

The phone rang loudly on his desk just then, as he pushed the finished report aside.

"Henry D'Guard speaking. How may I help you?"

he answered the call automatically.

"Hello Mr. D'Guard! Janet Carter here, you wanted to talk to me?" the EMT's voice came over the phone with some excitement.

"Oh yes, Ms. Carter, thank you for returning my call so quickly!" Henry replied with equal amount of excitement. "I am sure you've heard the news last night about our mystery patient's sudden death and maybe wondering what happened to him. I assure you he is fine and we are doing everything we can to keep him safe." he told her honestly. "I will also tell you, even though it may cost my job, that E.R.I.S. is a new government funded facility in town. (E.R.I.S. means emergency resuscitation for injured suspects). Our job is to keep alleged suspects from expiring and facilitate their easy debriefing by various agencies, as they see fit." Henry explained in a single breath.

"Yes I saw the news and I had spent most of the night reading about your patient. I can see why he might be a wanted man! So, tell me, what can I help you with, Mr. D'Guard?" Janet offered to help calmly.

"Ms. Carter, we have a second gate on the same street two blocks north from where you first came in. Get there from the Avenue to the north of us…"

Ed burst through the door interrupting the call.

"Henry, we have to get him out of here, now!" Ed blurted out. "Agents are approaching the main gate; we won't be able to stall them very long!"

He added frantically.

Henry hung up the phone without a word. They both ran out while Henry redialed Janet's number from his cell phone. Janet answered on the first ring, by this time, they where standing in front of the security monitors. There were only a few cameras installed around the place to keep speculations to a minimum.

They could clearly see two vehicles stopped at the main gate.

"Janet, we need your help taking Mr. Clark to a safe location."

Henry had to know how long they would have to stall the agents at the gate.

"How soon can you get here?"

"Ten minutes tops." Janet answered confidently.

"Make it sooner…" Henry shot back, flipping his cell-phone closed. They watched in amazement, as the agents were trying to open the gate manually. Their RADs must have failed by some miracle. The gate is designed to open on time, every time, even if you approached it at 60 miles/hour traveling in an unknown vehicle, as long as you had a Remote- Activating-Device on you.

Ed and Henry ran all possible scenarios they could pull off to further delay the entry of these agents. To their surprise, another vehicle approached the gate, this one from the inside.

On the side of the vehicle they saw "Carl's Security Gates. Installation and Servicing".

They looked at one another with satisfaction and took off in two directions.

Most everybody was still busy cleaning up the mess after the deadly accident that killed Mrs. Freedman and writing their reports. Being slightly under staffed, no one was watching Jeffrey Clark for the moment.

The opportunity was perfect.

Sophie Herd was a twenty-nine year old nurse, who started working at this facility nearly a year ago, fresh out of college. By now she proved to be a resourceful and reliable employee.

When the intercom started buzzing, she answered it promptly.

"Who is it?" she asked with obvious authority in her voice.

"This is ATF agent Brown. We need to ask a few questions of Jeffrey Clark. Could you open the gate, Ma'am?" the answer crackled over the speaker.

"I am sorry sir, but the gate is automatic, we can not control it. If you'd watched TV last night you'd know that Mr. Clark "tragically" expired around 8:40 PM. He is not available for questioning." She answered sarcastically. "Ma'am! I told you my name and rank, now open this gate! We have to see Mr. Clark!" agent Brown demanded in frustration.

"Sir!" Sophie snapped back at him in an instant. "I told you that patient is not available! You have NO business being here without proper clearance. This is an NSA facility!" with that she shut off the intercom.

Dr. Ruben, at the end of his night shift, witnessed the exchange.

"Way to go, Miss Herd!" he said, approvingly holding his thumbs up.

Smiling with authority, Sophie walked into the security room to look at the same monitors Henry and Edward were watching just a second ago. Her smile widened when she saw Carl's service men waving the agents away from the gate.

Jeffrey had no idea about any of this.

He began to feel more collected and alert within minutes after Henry D'Guard changed his I.V. fluids. He did not miss that fact! Naturally, he still felt confused and really wanted to get an idea of where he was. However, he did not feel quite strong enough to investigate.

For now, he took comfort in the fact that some one was looking after his safety.

He began to remember that he was at home reading his e-mails, when he heard a strange noise. The noise came from the hallway, as if the wind had blown thru it. It was gone as quickly as it came. He remembered that in an instant, day turned to night. Stillness took over his senses and while certain parts of his body where trying to tell his brain something was very wrong, his mind only registered faint noises and sensations. It seemed to him that he heard his son's voice calling. Later he felt like a mushy rag doll being scooped up by careful hands and then he heard that angelic voice!

He opened his eyes struggling to recall its tone, but all he could bring back was the name of the Hospital he read of the ambulance. "Good Samaritan" "That's it! I have to find her!" Jeffrey knew in his heart he could trust her.

He had no idea that he would meet the person to whom that sweet voice belonged, within the hour.

He had not seen Bobby in more than six months and now he began to worry about his son's well being. Was he really there? He wondered. Was it just a figment of his blurred mind? He could not tell.

He now recalled the stops he had made during his series of lectures. All arranged by his childhood friend and esteemed colleague Eugene Herald.

Six countries. He could still not believe Eugene actually managed to generate that much interest!

You did it my friend! The six most influential countries, on six continents! Unbelievable! He hailed Eugene in his thoughts.

I was pretty good too; Eugene said so himself!

Jeff finally accepted some glory of his own.

His injuries triumphed over his mind once again.

While asleep, in coma-like state, he could hear any noises and felt no motion as his mind no longer processed them.

"Ah, shit! He's out, again!" Edward shouted when he realized Jeffrey was not going to cooperate in his own escape! At least not right away.

He ran out to get someone to help dress Jeffrey up. They came back and immediately disconnected the I.V. that ran out almost completely, because Henry opened it fully. Hurriedly, they put his clothes on and sat him in a wheelchair.

Sophie Herd was the person Ed brought to help. She was not aware of this patient being here, or who he was, but she knew better not to ask. After Ed released her, she quietly returned to her usual duties.

Ed wheeled Jeffrey Clark out of the building and continued on foot toward the north-gate.

Henry, considering the situation, realized they needed more time. He drove straight to the old water tower located halfway between the two gates, accelerating to over 60miles per hour. Without delay, he rammed the base of the old frame that supported the reservoir for more than fifty years. A slow leak had rusted metal connecting parts of the wooden frame over the years. The steel-banded, wooden tank began to sway from the jolt imparted by the two-ton vehicle. Thirty-five thousand gallons of water sloshed back and forth, its dynamic forces flexing the frame to the point of failure. Dry-rot and decades of weathering weakened the supporting elements and the tank finally tipped toward the street, bending and breaking the supporting structure outward. With tremendous rumble, sheered off completely.

Truckloads of wood, steel and water hit the pavement with cataclysmic force.

Henry took off running in the direction of the north gate as soon as the Humvee he drove into the water tower stopped. He started to sweat profusely when he realized how incredibly lucky he was.

The water-tank could have fallen inward!

The tidal wave of water picked up the first Chevy suburban and crashed it into a building down the street. The second suburban made it through the water but crashed head on into the pile of rubble that used to be the water-tank. The agents, now bruised, wet and immobilized, were not so keen to gain entry into the compound anymore. Reluctantly, they called for help.

Henry could move much faster, since he did not have to carry anything. He thought he would beat Ed to the gate, but he found that it was already open. The gate had been knocked of its track, and laid in a twisted heap of tubular steel near a brick-wall, that had lost its stucco years earlier. He could see from the tracks that a vehicle came in rather fast, but it did not leave yet. He was relieved to notice a mid-nineties Ford Aerostar Van, turning around.

They picked him up seconds later thru the sliding door on the passenger side.

The right front fender was badly mangled; the right headlight was busted and the fiberglass hood's right corner broke off due to the impact of the gate.

-Hey, what happened? –Henry asked referring to the damage, looking at the unfamiliar faces. "We made it!" Janet answered with a smile that was out of this world.

"Meet Jon at the wheel…" She said still smiling and pointing at their driver. "…and I am Janet Carter!"

"Hello Mr. D'Guard!" saluted Jon, while maintaining full control of the speeding vehicle with his left hand. "I thought this place should be blown wide open, so I rammed the gate." Jon pointed at the wrecked gate on their left as they passed it.

They were heading north on the side streets for now, obeying the traffic rules as they went. "Where are we going?"

Edward was not aware of what the plan might be, or if one existed at all. "Excellent question! Since I'm driving, I'd need to know that soon!"

Jon exclaimed as he rocked the van by jiggling the wheel left and right.

He wanted to ease the tension and excitement of the escape somewhat, but no one was laughing.

Henry jumped in the passenger seat next to Jon, seeing that Janet was already taking care of Jeffrey Clark with Edward's help.

The rear seats of the van folded into a queen-size bed.

"Get on the 210 freeway west-northwest. Connect to the I-5 north…and don't do that -he imitated Jon rocking the vehicle- we do not want to get pulled over for reckless driving." Henry finished his instructions.

"Okay, boss!" Jon nodded.

None of them spoke a single word for quite a while. They were preoccupied by the awareness of a new chapter beginning in their lives.

All of them accepted it voluntarily. They reflected on the possible results of their actions, none of which looked very promising at the moment.

Jonathan turned on the radio; he wanted to break the silence with music.

The first thing they heard was breaking news: "…several fugitives are on the loose after a serious accident in (this) area.

The authorities ask the public's help in apprehending these dangerous criminals, who left behind four people hurt, and several vehicles and an old water tower in ruins. If you have any information that may lead to the arrest and prosecution of any of them, call your local police station and you could receive 5000 dollars for each person".

–Cheap bastards! –observed Jon.

Jeff explained why the police offered five grand to the public. –The economy is on their side! People are getting tight all over the country, so they figure "why pay more when you can get the same info for peanuts". They can always find spineless people, who'd be willing to turn in their relatives even for a little money. It is a sad fact of our human history.

-Jeff concluded his assessment. The others silently nodded their heads in agreement.

-Do you have "lo-jack" in this van? –Jeff asked Jonathan suddenly.

-No, I never believed in that stuff. –answered Jon smiling.

–You know, from now on it would be best if we did not use our credit cards or cell phones. –said Jeff clarifying their situation. –Would you, please, turn them off and remove the batteries?- he asked.

He did not have to repeat his request.

The mini-van was flowing with the speed of traffic in a long right hand turn. Jon suddenly swerved right to catch the exit they were about to pass.

-Where are you going? –Henry asked Jon in a bit of surprise.

-I live in Simi Valley; just want to swing by my house for a moment. –Jon answered. – I figure, we'll need some money and I have fifteen grand saved for a new car. I'd like to offer that for the cause. –he added soberly.

With a steady hand, he maintained seventy-five miles per hour following the left sweep of the transfer ramp as it crossed over from the 210 Freeway to the 118, west bound.

-Are you sure?–Jeff did not know what else to say to the generous offer.

-Oh yeah! The "rainy-day" has arrived! –replied Jon with a strange grin on his face.

Jon pulled into his driveway twenty minutes later. His modest home stood in an average, working class neighborhood. Neatly kept lawn and shrubs surrounded it with a colorful flowerbed separating the garage and the font door. Only fifteen hundred square feet, but it seemed larger on the inside. The floor plan created open spaces and no hallways. They took a quick break to freshen up, while Jon retrieved his money from the safe he had installed years ago in the master closet.

In fifteen minutes, they were back on the road.

-A friend of mine lives in Frazier Park. We should go see him next. –Ed offered to help next, before they got on the freeway.

-That seems like a bit of a detour, doesn't it? –asked Janet, but Jon had the answer to that problem.

-This is my back-country, I grew up around here hiking, biking, horse-back riding. I know the area like the back of my hand. You are right, it is a bit of detour, but it is much less likely to be found on a mountain road than be picked off I-5 by the highway patrol. It is also a very scenic rout. –Jon reassured them with another charming smile of his.

-You've got the wheel! –Ed declared -And I'll give you directions in Frazier Park. –he patted his new friend on the back.

Ed's friend did not want to be connected in anyway, so the best thing he could offer was a vehicle exchange at the local wrecking yard. He made the arrangement with the owner of the yard over a landline, who agreed to bring up the SUV personally. The Ford Aerostar was shredded within an hour of the exchange, according to their deal.

Two days earlier.

Jeffrey Clark was at home reading his e-mails in his second floor study. Suddenly he heard a floorboard creak behind him, but before he could rise from his seat two masked men subdued him by chloroform. They struggled, dragging his limp body thru the door and were preparing to carry him downstairs when the front door swung open. Jeffrey's son, Bobby arrived at home right then, announcing himself loudly.

–Hey Dad! I am home! – he shouted with a big smile on his face. His smile contorted in disbelief seeing his dad's seemingly lifeless body tumble down the stairs, landing in front of him.

The two masked men, using the noise of the falling body for cover, quickly hid, not having enough time to exit undetected.

Bobby jumped to his dad's body to check on him, noticing his shallow breathing immediately called an ambulance. Then he went upstairs cautiously to see what may have caused his father to fall. He'd found nothing other than his computer being on displaying e-mails, some from fans, some hate mail.

Hearing the siren of the approaching ambulance he went back downstairs to meet them.

The two men, now unmasked and their jackets turned inside out to blend, used the cover of the siren to get out the same way they came. They exited by way of the balcony of the room at the end of the hall that faces the backyard.

As they turned from the alley that runs behind the property onto the side street they nearly collided with the arriving ambulance. The two EMTs called them names and blasted them with the siren.

They noted the vehicle being a black Chevy Caprice, possibly a decommissioned "black-n-white".

The EMTs quickly took Jeffrey into their care and sped off toward the hospital. Jeff's son wanted to follow them in his Mustang, but a black Chevy Caprice cut him off while another ambulance pulled up behind him. The masked men circled the block to escape suspicion, but had to do something right, so they came around to detach the son from his father. They called for an ambulance thru their boss at the agency while hiding in the house, but the local emergency service beat them to it.

Few minutes later and only a couple of blocks from its destination, another, more government-like, vehicle intercepted the ambulance that was transporting Jeffrey. An agent jumped into the ambulance from the passenger side and ordered them to follow the car in front of them.

Some twenty-five minutes later, they turned onto an empty street. It looked like this neighborhood has been abandoned for many years; they could see plant life sprouting from every crack of the pavement.

They arrived at a gate that opened automatically as they approached it, then shut swiftly behind them. "Danger-Keep Out" signs were posted every 50 feet or so on perimeter buildings and sections of 12 feet high fences connecting them. Less then a minute later, they pulled in front of a building that seemed well maintained given its surroundings. Some people emerged from the building to help bring the "patient" in. The driver, Jonathan Doering, stayed in the vehicle, so did the two SAs in the car they followed here. The rocking of the cot brought Jeff back to semi-consciousness. He was able to make out the name of the hospital on the side of the ambulance. All people entering this building are required to hand over their RADs, if they have one, to a guard stationed by the entrance in a booth. He hangs them on a board behind his desk, neatly arranged. The RADs are about half the size of a standard garage-door opener. Janet noted this exchange and smiled sweetly at the guard who found it extremely alluring.

Within a few steps from the entrance, the head-nurse intercepted Janet, separating her from Jeffrey.

She questioned her briefly about the patient, but NOT thoroughly enough, Janet thought. The head-nurse told her the patient is in good care now and she can leave the way she came in. On her way out, Janet stopped by the guard booth. She greeted the guard, who came to the door of the booth. She charmed him by a few kind words then asked him directly about the device's purpose. He told her they were high-frequency "remote access devices" (RAD) that opens the gate.

-Well, its been nice talking to ya. I got to run now. –she said to the guard in goodbye, still smiling at him.

-Likewise! –responded the man, but the phone rang behind him. –Shit –he said to himself while turning to get the phone. –I won't be able to see that fine…-but he could not finish his thought.

Janet whacked him with the door at that instant; shoved him inside the booth and finished him with the chair. Quickly pocketing a RAD she hurried back to the ambulance. They left, escorted to the gate by the same car that lead them here. Jonathan and Janet agreed to memorize the way to get here, because this whole place is very suspicious.

They were riding in a dark blue GMC Yukon that is registered in the San Diego area, on the winding road towards I-5 freeway. Jeff was still confused about what happened in the last couple of days, so he asked Janet to tell him how they found him.

-We were dispatched in response to a 911 call, where the caller could not tell what happened to the victim. That was you. All we knew then "he fell and seems unconscious". –she said. –When we arrived, you were laying at the bottom of the stairs with your head towards the entrance. You were unconscious all right; bleeding lightly from a small cut on your forehead, -she poked him about two inches above the left eye, just below the hair line -right here –she said continuing - and your son, Bobby, was at your side. –Janet told him as she remembered. –Right Jon? –She asked him looking for some confirmation.

-Oh yeah! That's precisely how it happened. –Jon helped her out.

-So Bobby was really there? –asked Jeff with surprise and satisfaction at the same time.

-Yes, and he was going to follow us but he never did. We have no idea why. –Janet confessed uneasily.

-Wait a minute! –injected Jon. –Do you remember those lunatics who nearly hit us? –he asked Janet.

-Oh yeah, these two morons cut us off just before we got to your house. They came out of the alley that runs behind your property, rather fast, only missing us by a few inches. –Janet recalled.

-They drove, what seemed like an ex cop-car, a mid-nineties black Chevy Caprice. It sill had those searchlights, you know? –Jon continued.

-Bobby is a sweet kid; he was sooo worried about you! – Janet cut in taking back the story. –He told us that you fell in front of him tumbling down the stairs. He thought you had a heart attack or something! –Janet went on.

Jon hushed up when he realized what was happening. He could see a genuine interest bordering a full-blown crush in Janet's eyes. Her voice could barely hide it.

Edward also picked up on it and now was staring at Janet in amazement.

Excitedly glancing around, from the events of the day and her yet unrealized, but fast developing feelings for Jeffrey, Janet caught Ed's long gaze. -What?- she asked instinctively.

Edward reacted just as fast saying, –Nothing. –and looked away to hide his embarrassment of being caught. The fact that he discovered her secret even before she realized having one made him smile.

Henry was planning their next step and completely missed the exchange.

Jeffrey was so over taken by emotions for his son that he too was oblivious to what was transpiring.

-Let's get something to eat! I'm hungry! –Ed offered now to break the uneasy silence.

-What do you want from me and who are you people? –Bobby demanded to know after jumping out of his car.

An early nineties jet-black Chevy Caprice was in front of him and an ambulance was blocking his way from behind. He saw the words "E.R.I.S. - revival by G.O.D." written on all sides of the rear cab, bordered by a six-pointed sheriff's star. The letters were black with gold outline, the sheriff's star was gold with a thinner blood-red out line, all on white background.

Bobby, having been boxed in by them for several minutes now, has lost his patience. –I am going to sue you for… -he started to shout, but was silenced by a loud-speaker that was ungodly loud!

-Get back in your vehicle! NOW! –the words blasted him.

Obedient citizen that he is, Bobby got back in his late model Mustang in a blink of an eye.

The sound of police sirens approaching made him feel even more uneasy. Looking around to see where they were coming from he noticed the ambulance behind his car backing up and swiftly driving away.

The two men in the black Caprice took off their civilian-looking jackets and stepped out in full ATF uniforms. They had no idea anybody else was coming, as they were too busy communicating with their superiors.

None of them wanted to reveal their true identity to another agency, because this whole thing was supposed to be a covert operation. However, their secrets will be out in the next few minutes.

Racing to the scene were two FBI SUVs and two police cars, from the local precinct. They converged on their destinations at full speed. All of them arrived just after the NSA ambulance exited the area unseen by them, except the two AFT agents now standing in full view next to Bobby's car.

-Oh shit…-managed to say one of them as the four vehicles came to a screeching halt next to Bobby's car.

People from the neighborhood were watching the event unfold from a distance; they called the local police on what they perceived to be a domestic disturbance development.

Police officers and FBI agents jumped from their vehicles with guns drawn.

They all ordered the ATF agents and Bobby to surrender. When the AFT agents flashed their badges and shown their uniforms confusion set in, but only for a moment.

The police officers immediately insisted that this is their territory; therefore, they are in control, ordering the only civilian to move towards them. As Bobby opened the door of his Mustang, the ATF agents ordered him back inside, shutting door on him. The FBI agents just stood there for the moment with their guns trained on others.

The ATF agents argued that their orders came from higher up in the federal government, so they would take Bobby into custody for being first on scene.

At that point the FBI agents had to act. They moved forward and ordered the all the others away from Bobby's vehicle. One of them pulled a loudspeaker and declared the scene to belong to the Federal Bureau of Investigation.

-Based on whose authority? –the four police officers and two ATF agents demanded to know, now all turning to face the eight FBI people.

-Enough of this nonsense! –chief FBI agent Timothy Brooks shouted. Setting down the loudspeaker, he continued in normal human voice.

–One, you are out gunned; two you are out ranked as my orders come from the very top. I advise you to back down immediately! –he informed them.

-We need to talk, inside! –he added holstering his gun and walking towards the front door.

Bobby watched the whole event from his car in astonishment. He had never witnessed such a power struggle during his military service. But, then he was part of a single organization with a single mind. The Marines.

One police officer and one ATF agent followed FBI chief Brooks into the house. They reappeared in less than two minutes and in complete agreement on the situation.

All police officers and the AFT agents quietly returned to their vehicles, got in and drove off carefully observing the applicable traffic rules.

Two FBI agents escorted Bobby into the house.

–Robert Clark? –chief agent Brooks opened the dialogue by asking the elemental question.

-Sir! Yes, Sir! –Bobby responded military style as he came to attention.

The FBI agent's Intel about the Clark family is limited because they lead an old-fashioned life-style. In the short amount of time, since Jeffrey Clark became a "person of interest" to government officials less than a week ago, they could only pull up phone records for their residence, driver license information and the fact that at some point all members of the Clark family had Passports.

Even though it is rather important, Bobby's military record went unnoticed because he was not considered a suspect in anything.

The Clarks are open and friendly people. They do not approve of any means of controlling one's life. For generations, they raised their children to be independent and thought them to keep their lives simple.

Within the last few decades, however, certain signs emerged, in politics, in popular culture, in economics that indicate an imminent worldwide sweep to crown a more than century old series of covert operations. The rapid advancement of computer technology within the last twenty years has enabled power structures around the globe to operate more effectively.

Until about thirty years ago, the amount information that was feasible to collect and maintain about the identity of individual citizens was largely limited by physical volume and manual handling.

Properly kept and maintained paper records of the citizenry were transferred to microfilm during the cold-war era. These still serve as the backbone of data bases that are susceptible to unauthorized access by hackers. This vast amount of microfilm-data is being transferred, thus further reduced in size, to electronic storage devices since before the invention of Apple 64. Microsoft came along with a slightly different approach, writing programs that can now be deciphered, or hacked even by some children in eight grade. The inherent vulnerability lands this system perfectly to government surveillance. Ninety percent of the population does not have enough knowledge to operate it properly beyond a limited job related functionality. But most people use it for something or other regardless. All that usage can be and is monitored not only by governments to keep tabs on who's doing what and when, but also by major corporation for marketing purposes.

The Clarks know that all too well. They also know what the signs of the past few decades indicate.

The time is near when the powers behind the most violent events of the twentieth century will reveal themselves. One does not have to be a history professor to see that clearly. Being impartial, when analyzing these signs, can help to understand them sooner. A much bigger, uglier picture may emerge.

Agent Brooks had no idea that Bobby served in the military. Looking at him with a degree of surprise, he considered this bit of info for a few seconds. Then decided to find out more about the young man in front of him.

It might just lead somewhere.

-So, where did you serve, son?–he asked Bobby trying not to let on that until now he had no idea.

-I served in Iraq between 2004 and 2006. Sir! –Bobby replied.

-That is enough military talk, son. Speak to me as a civilian; after all, you are no longer in the service. –Brooks could tell that much by looking at his hair cut. Obviously, he hasn't had one in a few months.

-Have a seat. –Brooks pointed at the couch in the living room. He sat in an arm chair across the coffee table.

-I need to know where they took my father. –Bobby said in an even voice. –And, what is all this commotion around my father's house, anyway? –He could not hide his disapproval any longer.

-Well, we are surprised by that too. – Agent Brooks admitted being out of the loop somewhat.

-I came here to ask him a few questions, but obviously, I missed him. Maybe you could answer some of them. –Brooks tried to get Bobby to open up a bit.

-I don't think so. I have not seen him in three years. –Bobby declined to offer any help.

-He was not happy about my enlistment in the Marines; we have not spoken since my deployment. –he allowed that much.

-You mean to tell me you had no contact with your father in over three years? –agent Brooks wondered aloud if Bobby was telling the truth.

-Aside from a single letter at the end of the first month of my service? No. –Bobby reaffirmed his statement.

-Are you aware of your father's recent activities and his contacts of late? –Brooks continued to pry.

-Agent Brooks, you're wasting your time asking me about my father and his "activities". –answered Bobby using the that funny hand gesture for quotation marks.

-Now, if you have no reason to arrest me, I have to go. I must find him. – Bobby stood up abruptly.

-You are free to go, but if you remember any information that might help us out, give me a call. –said agent Brooks stepping in Bobby's way and handing him a business card.

Bobby accepted it with a wry smile. He examined the card briefly and put it in his pocket.

-Agent Brooks, your employer's effort to appear as some kind of legitimate business always makes me laugh. –with that, he turned and left his father's house.

Timothy Brooks looked after the young man for a few seconds and issued an order.

-I want all attainable Intel on young Mister Clark, ASAP! –and he left the house as well.

Still inside, other field agents were searching the house without much success for the rest of the morning. They've found Jeff's vault, in which he keeps his firearms and perhaps other valuables, but they did not want to break into it just yet.

Outside the house, agent Brooks summoned his subordinates.

–I want a tail on him. Now! –his voice left no room for questions.

One of his men walked off and commandeered a vehicle from traffic on the street.

Jeffrey Clark's house stands in a respectable neighborhood (not too far from Good Sam hospital) just about a block south of W. Sunset Blvd. on N. Palm Dr. (?).

The original structure was built around 1925 and had 2500sf living space. Jeffrey's parents expanded it to its current size of roughly 4500sf. The property itself decreased in size from fifteen acres to just under one acre. They sold off individual lots parceled from the property by way of financing. The current owners of the last two lots, the Clarks sold in the early eighties, are still paying their mortgages.

The Clark's home has a "glamorous" curb appeal, as any Real Estate agent would word it, built in Mediterranean Revival style by a prominent architect of the era.

The landscape of the property is also Mediterranean with trees and shrubs native to Italy.

The front yard is approximately sixty feet deep. A semi-circular driveway that runs around a large fountain provides access to the house for visitors. There are two temporary parking spaces, one on each side of the main entrance, attached to the circular drive. A narrow walk passes around the fountain allowing close viewing of the fish in its pond.

The driveway runs thru an arched gateway on the right side of the house. It meets a double garage about 55 feet from the gate. From the garage, a single door leads to the house between the laundry-room and walk-in pantry. Here a hallway runs between the kitchen and pantry to a door that leads to the back porch. There is a large arch on the kitchen side of the hallway thru which the doors of the garage, the pantry and the laundry room can be seen from the kitchen. Looking into the kitchen from this hallway one can see another arch that opens to the dinning room. The center of the dining room is occupied by a large, ten-person dinner table that is now rarely being used. Every room of the house bespeaks of a desire for space, hence they are sparingly furnished with luxurious simplicity.

CHAPTER 1

Robert Clark served two and a half years in the Marines. He had been all over Iraq during his eighteen months long tour of duty. Luckily, his instincts of self-preservation, combined with his combat training saved him in every firefight. Classroom theory and playing out war-game scenarios on a well-defined training course does not even come close to the nightmarish chaos of live combat. That kind of experience simply cannot be reproduced on a training base without casualties, and that would not be good for moral. Only on the real battlefield can the soldiers' training be completed and can they be forged into a solid fighting force. A successful first mission, with minimum losses, is highly desirable to achieve this cohesion beyond what basic training can provide. The presence of the enemy and the life-threatening danger they pose will reinforce this cohesion. Casualties are now acceptable because it further enrages the soldiers against their enemies. When all hell breaks loose, only two things can happen to a soldier. He will either live on, or die. Bobby's first combat experience was just such an event. He knows a guardian angle was with him that day.

He still breaks out in cold sweat just thinking about it; even now, sitting in the 140-degree heat of his car, generated by the relentless California sun.

-Private Clark! On your feet! –His squad commander's shout brought him back to reality in a blink of an eye. Bobby dozed off in the shade, enjoying a rare occasion when he did not have to carry out any orders. He jumped to his feet and replied.

–Yes Sir! Sergeant, Sir! –now standing in attention.

-As you were. –Sergeant Pete "Heartless" Harland softened his voice a bit.

He is a fifteen-year veteran who stayed on after serving in the first Iraqi war. His unit did not participate in any combat back then and now he is eager to see some action before his final tour is over.

-Hey, we got a scout mission. I need your skills. We received Intel on a village, about ten k-s from here. It looks like the goat-herders are amassing some serious firepower over there. Take a look. –he unfolded a recon picture of the village and a sketchy map.

-Now, to get there we need to cross some open desert and the road leads into a narrow gorge just before the village. The way I see it, we can attempt this either as kamikazes and head straight into the killing zone here, -he continued explaining his idea by pointing at the entrance of the gorge, -or we can do it like Marines and split three ways about here, -he pointed at the road about three k-s from the village.

-What can I do for you, Serg'? – Bobby asked calmly.

-I think right around here we'll be a kilometer or so from the village. We'd still be out of sight 'cause of the bend in the road and the small hills on either side. I'd like to put you up here so you could get rid of any sentinels before we rush in. – Sergeant P. "Heartless" Harland outlined the rest of his plan.

-Sounds like my kind of mission Sir. – Bobby said calmly.

The temperature was a hundred and ten degrees in the shade. The eighteen marines truly appreciated the luxurious accommodations offered by the military Humvee that had a canvas top to shield them from burning alive. Each of them had over fifty pounds of gear, truly an over-kill for most operations. Even though they were extremely fit due to their constant physical training and young age, logging around all that equipment could mean the difference between life and death.

In an ambush, it could mean certain death if one could not drop it fast enough and take cover.

A soldier only needs his firearm and ammunition to be effective in combat. Aside from that there are only a few more things a soldier needs to survive; a qualified commander, for instance, quick access to other resources by radio or by other means and accurate maps and Intel. In the desert, he will need a canteen full of water, salted peanuts to replace salt-loss and to hold him over, and some luck never hurt.

Properly managed, the excess gear does mean life. Under field conditions, before, after or between combat operations it supports the individual soldier for several days, as food and water is not always readily available. Logistics has been an important element of successful warfare for centuries.

For now, they were slowly approaching what they expected to be a small village. They have been on the road for over an hour, moving along cautiously at around twenty miles per hour. Keeping the dust cloud they stirred up light and low, and not giving away their position, and presence. The road was completely void of traffic due to constant flare-ups of hostility in this area for months. There were, however, ample amount of carnage and destruction strewn about that no one ventured out to clean up, fearing an ambush. The smell of decomposing corpses and burned out vehicles still lingering in the air, made the marines queasy. Soldiers eventually become desensitized by the sight of mutilated corpses, but there is something about the smell of rotting flesh that sets off an internal alarm and turns their guts inside out.

-Hey! What's going on man? Are we lost? –the only medic in the group shouted to be heard over the awful noise of the Humvee.

They were all sharp and on the edge. Looking in all directions, they could only see rolling sand hills alternating with jagged piles of rocks and very little in the way of vegetation. The marines sensed being watched, as the hills are sure to have eyes even in the most desolate locations.

The locals no longer traveled on known routes. Staying off them, they still managed to conduct essential business between villages and were able to observe enemy troop movement.

Visibility was pretty good, but they knew that could change rapidly if the wind picked up.

-According to the map I've got, we still have ways to go, Corporal Turner. –replied Sergeant Harland.

-Somebody fucked up scaling it, big time. -he admitted.

-I've been tracking landmarks and only counted 'bout half of them so far. It'll be another hour before we get there. –he added wearily.

The radio crackled to life just then. –Hey Serge! Are we there yet? –Corporal Monroe inquired from the second Humvee. Even though they were profusely sweating and felt miserable, the question forced a smile on their faces.

–We're wondering if we ain't lost here; or something…-Monroe conveyed the concern of his men. The marine in charge of the third Humvee cut in to let them know of the needs of his men.

–Sir, requesting permission for a piss-break, Sir! –Lance-Corporal Fuller came over the speaker.

-There's an idea! In a bind, we take a leak and consider our options. –Private Cooper mumbled to himself in the backseat, behind Bobby.

Sergeant Pete "Heartless" Harland wasn't cruel as his name might suggest. Actually, he had a sense of humor, which managed to surface occasionally.

-Well, since you ladies can't seem to control your bodily functions, I guess this time is as good as any. –he answered their request. –Stop at the next heap of rocks, Private Jackson. Let's see if they're hot enough to sizzle. –he added, pointing ahead about fifty yards.

-Yes Sir, Sergeant, Sir! –Private Jackson acknowledged looking at his CO with a big smile. The three Hummers stopped.

The rock pile was quite large and provided good cover for their pit-stop. Eighteen young men jumped out and stood in semi-circle between their vehicles and the boulders.

Rifle in one hand, their toy "gun" in the other; relief was right at hand in the middle of the desert.

-It's mighty generous of you, Sergeant! –Bobby said with a sigh of release.

-No need to thank me. I am just trying to keep you all alert and alive. I'm also trying to save you the embarrassment of pissing your pants when the lead starts flying. –Sergeant Harland replied, adding, - 'Cause something tells me it will...- Within a couple of minutes they were back on the road, which was nothing more than a pair of fading tire tracks mixed with human and camel footprints.

-What's that? Look! Over there! – Private Jackson asked pointing at columns of smoke up ahead and slowing down. Sergeant Harland was too busy reading the map that did not make any sense to him. He glanced up now and saw several columns of heavy smoke rising not too far ahead.

-Stop! –he ordered Private Jackson with a hand signal, who stepped on the break hard, but the Humvee did not react. They were already standing still.

Sergeant Harland pulled his binoculars out to have a better look. He stepped out of the vehicle and staying in its shade stabilized his hand holding the binocular by resting it on the hood of the Humvee.

He, Cpl Monroe in charge of H2 and LCpl Fuller of H3 were intently observing the smoke for about a minute. The smoke and the village now appeared to be less than kilometer away.

-It looks like a few structures and vehicles burning, but the light grey smoke is suspicious. It's almost like smoke cover. – Sergeant Harland assessed the situation.

-Suspicious indeed! –Lance Corporal Fuller concurred.

-Let's check it out! –Corporal Monroe suggested enthusiastically.

Sergeant Harland was still analyzing visual clues. He now stood up and faced the men.

-This is it boys! This is what we came here to investigate and investigate we shall! –he said to his squad of eighteen marines.

-The village is eight hundred and forty yards from here, according to my range finder, so I want you all to be extra sharp! Man the MGs and let's roll! –he ordered.

Like a well-oiled machine, the marines peeled the canvas off, raised the 50 caliber in the middle of his Hummer. The other two vehicles were equipped with M240 machine guns.

They approached at snail-pace to keep the trailing dust to a minimum.

About four hundred yards from the edge of the village, they had to stop. The road was out.

A zigzag obstacle course lead to a checkpoint, but smoldering wrecks blocked each and every turn. God bless the Hummer!

-H2, left; H3, right! –Sergeant Harland gave the order without hesitation, using both of his arms flinging over the windshield of his vehicle as he stood up to clarify his order.

-Go around the village; see if you can find another way in and report. We'll go straight. –he looked at Private Jackson, as he sat back down, while signaling him to take the ditch on the left side of the road.

Private Cooper was ready for action, gripping his 50-caliber M60 machine gun. He watched the two Hummers drive off in their assigned directions over some rough terrain.

When he looked back toward the village, he heard a loud metallic thump followed by the whining of a ricocheting bullet fading in the distance. The rumble of the shot came a split second later.

He felt a warm splatter on his face and something fleshy bounced of his forehead. The tumbling bullet tore off his left shoulder strap cleanly. Cooper began screaming when he noticed his left thumb was missing. The pain set in as he fell backwards. The second bullet hit him in the groin then exited just below his sternum; making him the first KIA of the mission.

Private Jackson's and Sergeant Harland's face was peppered with glass fragments. Several FMJ bullets punched through the windshield. One of them broke Private Jackson's right collar bone, who was sitting in the middle. It zipped by Pvt Reich's head, splattering his face with Jackson's blood, and tore an acorn-size hole in the canvas exiting the vehicle.

Another tumbling bullet core shredded Sergeant Harland's left ear. It blew off a small chunk from the edge of his helmet then lodged in the door a few inches above Bobby's right thigh.

Without delay, Bobby and the rest of the crew jumped out of the Hummer.

They only passed the first obstacle on the road when the hale of bullets hit them. The other two crews came under fire at the same time, except they did not have any cover around them.

Bobby and his mates ducked behind some wreckage on the road and their own Hummer. Private Jackson and Sergeant Harland also managed to clear the Hummer. Because of the extent of his wound, Private Jackson could only crawl with his left arm. On the ground by the Hummer, he was low enough not to get hit anymore while he dragged himself under the Hummer.

Sergeant Harland, on the right side of the Hummer, also found relative safety for now.

Bobby new they had to return fire as soon as they could or they would be slaughtered. He shouted to the other two marines to find a spot and fire on the enemy position. He too maneuvered carefully to find a spot to take a clear shot.

The other crews also had two KIA and two WIA in all, before they managed to hide. Luckily, the Hummers are well built and they can sustain a lot of damage from small arms before they would be immobilized.

Bobby was finally in firing position. Looking through the scope of his M40 sniper rifle, he saw enemy soldiers on both sides of the road in slightly elevated positions. He took aim at one shooting a long rifle. He clearly saw the enemy soldiers face even though he was at least 350 meters away.

Bobby's finger gently pressed the trigger. His rifle recoiled hard, but he kept his eye on the target. A pink mist hung in the air where the enemy's head was just a split second ago. The soldier's lifeless body slowly slid behind a boulder. A thunderous return fire erupted all around Bobby. He looked at the enemy soldier once more, but he could only see the muzzle of his rifle sticking up aimlessly.

-You! Keep them pinned! –Sergeant Harland shouted to the men of the other Humvees.

- We move on them! –he shouted to his men and took off running towards the next wreckage.

Cpl Turner took it upon himself to check Pvt Cooper's condition. He climbed back up into the Hummer.

Now covered in a thick dust cloud kicked up by firing many rounds close to ground level, Bobby and Reich had no choice, but to follow their Sergeant. Pvt Jackson was covering their move from under the

Humvee firing his M16 with his left hand, in the general direction of the towel-heads.

The marines' return fire intensified as both M240s joined in after the initial shock of the ambush had passed.

The sound of the M240s had a reassuring effect on the actively fighting marines and gave hope of survival to the wounded.

At the same time the Iraqis found it disheartening, as they came under a barrage of lead and steel every time they tried to make a move. They were effectively pinned.

The Iraqis only lost four of their men so far, but their advantage of surprise was now lost. The twenty three remaining Iraqi soldiers were far less trained in combat than the dozen marines.

Equipped mostly with old K98 Mauser rifles, equally dated 303 British rifles and a handful of Chinese-made SKS carbines they could only hold out so long. The marines would come charging their position soon and they did not want to be there when that happened.

Mean time Sergeant Harland, Bobby and Pvt Reich got to within two hundred meters of them.

Keeping low, they hopped from cover to cover. Bullets whizzed by from both directions, some impacted on rocks producing that ominous whine of a ricochet. Other bullets just hammered the wreckage they hid behind with little other effect.

The M240s kept enemy fire at a minimum by forcing them to take cover more often then firing. Suddenly Sergeant Harland heard the sound of an approaching vehicle behind him.

Cpl Turner quickly noted that Pvt Cooper was dead. There wasn't a whole lot he could do about that. He pulled Cooper's body into the back of the vehicle. He jumped out to see if he could do something about Pvt Jackson's shoulder. The bullet hit his right collarbone about four inches out from his neck on the top edge, instantly snapping it. Continuing its path, the bullet ripped a thumb-sized piece of flesh from Jackson's upper traps, and cleanly missed the top edge of his scapula.

Pvt Jackson felt as if a horse had kicked him in the shoulder. He would have passed out soon if Cpl Turner had not come to his aid.

–Hey! –Turner yelled at Jackson pulling him out from under the Humvee, grabbing his left arm and leg.

–Can you drive? –he asked as he pushed Jackson up into the driver seat.

–We must help the guys. –he added without waiting for Jackson's answer.

–Here. This will help! –he smiled as he popped a shot of morphine into Jackson's chest, a few inches below the broken right clavicle. He climbed in the middle of the Humvee and grabbed the M60. –Now go! –Turner shouted.

To much of his surprise, Sergeant Harland saw his own Hummer pull up just a few yards from him. He had no time to cover his ears before Cpl Turner let loose from the M60.

The 50caliber machine gun sounded almost like Navy artillery at a distance of a few yards where Sergeant Harland, Bobby and Pvt Reich were taking cover.

The sudden deafening noise made Bobby miss his next target. He could see the Iraqi's hat fly off from his shot and the stunned expression on his face. A second later, his head also disappeared in a red fog as one of Cpl Turner's fifty caliber rounds decapitated him.

The Iraqis threw out smoke grenades to cover their retreat. As soon as they turned to run, our marines went after them. Bobby moved quickly to the right to get out of the horrendous dust cloud kicked up by the M60 and to get a better view behind the smoke.

Sergeant Harland led the attack while Pvt Clark picked off five more enemy snipers.

The engagement ended a minute later when the first mortar shell landed. Pvt Clark suffered shrapnel wound on his left thigh as he jumped up in order to fall back. Fall face forward, was what he ended up doing.

He could hear the ripping sound of incoming mortars and their explosions, but he could no longer hear his teammates firing.

Only six Iraqis made it back to the village. If their brethren did not commence shelling when they did, those six would now be part of the landscape as well.

The mortar barrage lasted maybe a minute and a total of fifteen shells struck. Only seven shells came close enough to the marines to matter. It was the second shell that wounded Pvt Robert Clark, but not too seriously. The seventh shell wounded another marine from H2 team. Unfortunately, he lost his left leg below the knee, but he is alive. The other five mortars only had psychological effect.

Nevertheless, our marines disengaged from pursuing the remaining enemy.

They had nothing in their bag-of-tricks to match the firepower of a well-trained mortar team. Let alone three of them.

Sergeant Harland's assessment of the mortar fire was that they must have a minimum of three teams. He based his opinion on the frequency of fire and the pattern of shells that landed.

Three other Hummers arrived on the scene.

They could hear the gunfight from a mile away so they came quickly to help their fellow marines. But they waited out the shelling just beyond the point where Sergeant Harland's Hummer took the first hit.

Someone at base camp realized that something has gone terribly wrong with the scout mission. Sergeant Harland and his men should have been back long ago, but when they did not show up at camp they sent out the others to look for them. One of Harland's Hummers was a total loss. The seventh mortar shell hit it and it is now ablaze with a gaping hole where the driver seat used to be.

With the help of the fresh marines, they gathered their wounded and drove back to camp.

Bobby received a purple heart and a promotion for his actions during combat. They promoted him two more times before his honorable discharge. He advanced two levels each time and his final rank is Gunnery Sergeant. He had seen enough gore to last a lifetime. He is not proud of the things he had done.

Bobby started his Mustang, rolled down the windows and shook off the memory of that day in the desert. His first thought was to visit Good Samaritan Hospital.

At the ER he inquired about his father's whereabouts. Katherine K. King was in her office when the phone rang in front of her. The ER nurse informed her that a young man is looking for Jeffrey Clark.

Katherine walked over to meet him in the ER, located just a few yards from her office.

–Hello! I am Katherine King, the supervisor of EMS operations. –she introduced herself.

–My name is Robert Clark and I am looking for my father. Can you tell me where he is? –responded Bobby while curiously observing the woman in front of him.

Katherine wanted talk to him in private, away from the noise and curiosity of all the people working in the ER. –Let's talk in my office. Shall we? –and she lead the way.

–Please, have a seat. –she pointed at a comfortable chair as they entered the room.

–No, thanks, I don't have time to sit around. Just tell me where my father is, please. – Bobby added the word, not wanting to be completely rude.

–Well, I can tell you that my best EMTs are looking for him as we speak. They were supposed to bring your father in yesterday, but they got hijacked and forced to take him to some kind of compound. –Katherine conveyed the word as she heard it from Janet.

–What compound? Where? –Bobby became agitated by the word and his voice gave it away. It is the one thing he could still not control, not even after all those years in the Marine corps. Certain words, situations, behavior of people got on his nerves and he could not hide it.

–I do not know exactly. The last time I spoke to Janet Carter, whom I believe you've met at your father's home, was about fifteen minutes ago. She said they were going back there. –Katherine pointed at the chair again. –Let me see if I can reach her. –she said reaching for the phone.

Bobby pulled the chair back a bit and sat down. –Please do, Mrs. King! –he urged Katherine to make the call. The phone conversation between Katherine King and Janet Carter took only a minute and Bobby was on his way shortly after.

Katherine told him that his father is with Janet and they are going to Tahoe. Bobby did not ask for Janet's number because he knew this was the last time she used her cell phone.

In this traffic, it will take him over an hour just to get out of the city.

-Maybe even longer. –Bobby thought looking at the creeping line of cars ahead of him.

The infamous Los Angeles morning "rush hour" was under way. One could spend over two hours to travel thirty miles that should not take more than thirty minutes under normal conditions.

He remembered; when he was little, his parents took him to the park and let him play with the other children. But things have changed. Strange people from many different countries slowly flooded decent neighborhoods and turned them into "ghetto"-s. Gangs formed and soon started marking their territories. Some parts of the city became dangerous to visit after dark, some even in broad daylight. Nothing was sacred as graffiti spread far and wide. It ultimately spread way beyond gang territories, where no one understood this unsightly scribbling.

–If they had anything sensible to say, no one understood out side of their ghetto. –Bobby thought sadly. –Thank God it's better now. –he muttered as he looked at the sign mounted on the overpass.

They used to be covered with graffiti so badly traffic had to slow down to read them.

A couple of men from NSA escorted the ATF agents inside the ERIS compound. Their suburbans were towed to an ATF lot somewhere in the city.

-Wait here. –One of the NSA agents pointed to a small room provided for visitors. The four ATF agents stepped inside and the NSA agent closed the door behind them.

-"Novus Ordo Seclorum". –agent Karl Gunter Brown muttered the words as he sat down.

-What did you say? –an irate agent Silver turned to Brown.

–Three Latin words for "Now we are in seclusion". Get it? –Brown mocked Silver with the looniest smirk he could muster.

-Schmuck! –Silver turned away in disgust.

The tension between the two rival ATF agents did not subside before the door swung open again.

Another agent appeared in the doorway, as the door bounced back from a chair.

-Gentlemen! I believe we have a slight misunderstanding about the events of the last couple of days. –he addressed them while stopping the door's rebound with his hand. –My name is Larry Smith and I will bring you up to speed on what's been happening. –agent Smith tried to sound official and reassuring at once.

-About time! My name is Simon Silver from ATF and I have questions! –Silver could not help bursting out. Looking straight at agent Smith, Brown could hardly suppress a contemptuous chuckle.

-Good for you, Mister Silver! – Smith acknowledged him for the first time. –You can turn them in to your superiors as part of your damage report. –Smith stepped forward and condescendingly patted him on the shoulder.

Karl Brown nearly rolled off his chair, fighting to suppress the urge to laugh out loud.

-…and your name is…? –Smith stepped in front of agent Brown, his hand extended for a handshake.

-Agent Brown. –Karl stood up taking Smith's hand, his eyes still sparkling, but he managed to put on a poker face.

-I see. –Smith already heard his name from Sophie. –Come with me please. I'll brief you in my office. –he turned and left the room with Karl right behind him.

Smith did not have an office in this facility. He just wanted to talk to Karl in private and for that, he could use any of rooms here.

He already took possession of the small office Ester Freedman occupied until last night.

-Were you present at the time when Jeffrey Clark was admitted? –he asked Karl Brown as soon as the door closed behind him.

Karl looked back uneasily to note a closer mounted on the door.

–Fire code. –Smith answered the question just forming in agent Brown's head.

- No, I was not. In fact, none of our guys made it passed the gate, as far as I know. –Karl replied facing agent Smith again.

-Agent Brown. I trust I can count on your discretion when I say this whole thing is a big fuck-up. What ever else I'm about to tell you is for your ears only. –Smith began.

-I'm all ears! –Karl Brown said pulling out the chair from the desk to sit down.

-Only a few weeks ago did we become aware of the existence of the man in question … -Smith began to recount the information he had on Jeffrey Clark.

-…and that is why we need to find him. –Smith finished his briefing of full two minutes.

He told agent Brown about Jeffrey Clark's life-long studies, his recent lectures about a "conspiracy theory to top them all" and about his collection of firearms. He exaggerated the part about Jeff's firearms, since he was talking to an ATF agent.

Now, I have a vague idea who Jeffrey Clark is, but I still have no clue about what happened here today. –Brown summarized the briefing. -Why did I get nearly killed by a collapsing water tower and why is it that my Bureau does not have jurisdiction on these premises? –Agent Brown took the conversation back to its beginning.

-Like I said, this facility is maintained by NSA to deal with dangerous elements in our society. –Smith blurted out.

-Well, you did not. –Agent Brown caught him in a lie.

Did not, what? –Smith asked him back, attempting to stall Brown, while covering his own rear.

-You did not say anything about "dangerous elements" and all. –Agent Brown would not let him off the hook.

-Lets stop beating around the bush, agent Smith! –He changed his tone a bit.

-It seems to me, you lost the man and now trying hard to cover it up. I think you referred to that part as the "big fuck-up". But, the "why" eludes me. Maybe you did not have a valid reason to detain him in the first place, especially if we assume the "freedom of speech" part of the Constitution still applies.

In an open society, like ours, an individual's concerns about his government's actions should be heard. So tell me, agent Smith, exactly what crime did Mr. Clark commit against his country? –Agent Brown leaned forward attentively.

-I'm afraid I won't be able to share any more information with you, Agent Brown. –Smith attempted to shut down the conversation.

-Why in the hell not? –Karl Brown demanded an answer sharply raising his voice.

-Because, obviously we are not working for the same government! You should have more loyalty to your employers, agent Brown! Your superiors will surely question you about that! –Smith hinted at his connections and a resulting disciplinary action.

They looked at one another long and hard without a flinch.

Finally Smith got up and said, -I'll be seeing you again, agent Brown! – showing him out the door.

-Just make sure it will be in a public place! –Karl Brown jumped to his feet and stormed out of the room.

Simon Silver spent ten agonizing minutes with the other two AFT agents in the waiting room. They also enjoyed his humiliation at the hands of agent Smith and agent Brown.

They found it too irresistible not to drive it home.

-So, what was that all about? –the younger one dared to ask as soon as the door closed.

-Aren't you running this show? –pointed out the other agent.

Agent Silver stopped pacing the room back and forth. He gave the others a deadly look they will not soon forget.

-Your pay grade and years of service does not afford your fucking with me now! –said Silver in a chilling tone, clarifying the meaning of his facial expression.

Agent Fox, the younger of the two, has been with ATF for five years. Agent O'Bryan is going on seven now. Neither one of them knew Silver until a year ago when a major shift occurred in the ranks of their ATF branch. That is when Simon Silver suddenly appeared and out ranked their favorite lieutenant.

They got the message and retreated into silence.

ATF agent Karl G. Brown opened the door.
-Let's go. –he called to his colleagues. –I think we're done here. –he paused for a second noting the chill in the air, then turned toward the exit.

The men followed him closely.
-Agent Silver! –the sudden call of NSA agent Smith took them by surprise.
–May I have a word with you, please? –he asked in a tone of voice that surprised agent Brown even more.
-Certainly. –Silver replied with detectable satisfaction in his voice that could not be mistaken.
-Wait in the car. –he ordered his entourage pointing outside. After all, he was in charge.

It was late in the afternoon when Sophie Herd finally managed to finish the report, Larry Smith ordered her to write. She walked over to the office he now occupied and knocked on the door.
-Come in. –Smith answered barely audibly.
Sophie stepped into the office. – Sir! You asked for my report. –she handed it to Smith across the desk. Smith accepted it without looking up or saying a word. He placed the paper into a tray on his left.

A lot has happened since the departure of the ATF agents. "Carl's" crew removed the remains of the north gate, but did not have enough material to build a new one on site. They elected, and received permission from agent Smith, to weld it shut until a new gate could be made, delivered and installed.

Head Nurse Ester Freedman's body was taken away to the coroner's office for autopsy. A campus wide search has been conducted to locate Henry D'Guard and Edward Forsythe, but it turned up nothing. Agent Smith began seriously considering them as accomplices in the escape of Jeffrey Clark. He was now reading the last words of Henry's report about the accident that took the life of Ester Freedman.

Can I help you with anything else, Sir? –Sophie asked Smith before leaving his office. He looked at the young and pretty woman surprised.

–Ah, you're still here? I'll read your report as soon as I'm finished with these. –he said, being somewhat scattered.

-I can make some espresso if you feel the need! –Sophie offered with a warm smile.

Her white garb did not hide her astounding figure as she leaned forward slightly, waiting for an answer.

Agent Smith's eyes were scanning up and down her body at lightening speed, trying to take in all there was to see, before settling on her face.

-Well? –Sophie's lovely voice sent a shiver down his spine.

–Would you like some before your eyes pop out… –she paused just long enough to see Smith's face turn beet red.

–…from all that reading? –she finished her question pointing at the paperwork on the desk.

Ohh, suuure! –agent Smith answered awkwardly, feeling ashamed.

They both heard the buzzing of the Intercom, from the other room. Sophie had to get that quickly, so she asked –How'd you like it? –before stepping out of the room.

Black with lots of sugar. –Smith answered with some returning confidence in his voice.

Be here in a minute. –Sophie smiled again as she vanished from the doorway.

The intermittent buzzing continued until she pressed the "Answer" button. The speaker at the gate crackled as it became energized. When Sophie looked at the security monitor, she slipped her finger onto the "Open" button, before the men could say a word, and let them in. She could see the rear-end of a departing cab in the background.

The two men were still facing the speaker when the gate started to roll open suddenly.

In manual mode, it moved slower than normal and only opened three feet wide. Set to only five seconds of open time the gate reversed and closed rapidly behind them.

Sophie already left the "com-center", as they called it, to make coffee.

The espresso maker was a high quality machine normally seen in coffee shops. It had two dispensers for espresso and one for regular coffee. Sophie appreciated the machine's ability to make strong espresso, comparable with espresso being served all over Europe. Particularly in France, where she had come to love this heavenly treat while visiting relatives some ten years ago.

So, using both ports, she made enough coffee for six people.

The two men entered the ER and Sophie greeted them with her warmest smile and hot espresso.

They looked dead tired. –Hey you two, I bet you could use some of this! –she said handing them a cup each. Henry and Edward accepted them gratefully. –I am glad you're both okay! –she added picking up a single serving of espresso from the tray with lots of sugar on the side.

Sophie knocked on the door of agent Smith's temporary HQ of operations. Her knocking was too light and no reply came from within. She opened the door and was about to step in, but agent Smith halted her with his raised left hand. His gaze was fixed on a document in front of him and he was attentively listening to someone on the other end of the line.

Yes Sir! I understand. –he replied to instructions only he could hear.

-Of course, Mr. Secretary. We'll handle it as discreetly as possible! –Sophie now heard him say.

-No sir. Thank you for giving me the opportunity to make things right. –he expressed his gratitude for getting another chance.

-Good evening to you too Mr. Secretary. –Smith said goodbye to the person on the other end, placing the handset on the cradle.

Your coffee, Mister Smith! –Sophie reminded him.

Oh, yes. Thank you, Miss Herd! Just put it on that filing cabinet, lest I might spill it on these documents. –he said losing his composure fast.

-Damn it! –agent Smith finally allowed himself to burst out. He jumped to his feet, shoving the wheeled office chair backwards with his knees and angrily swept a stack of documents off the desk. The chair bounced off the wall with a loud bang.

His coffee already secure on top of the cabinet, Sophie stepped forward. –This office is such a mess. Let me clean it up while you enjoy your coffee. –she offered calmly, moving in to pick up the papers.

-Thanks. –she heard Smith say as he walked out of the room, with coffee in hand.

Agent Smith walked in on Henry and Edward, who were sitting in the break room by the ER.

-Where in the hell have you two been all day? –he demanded to know without greeting them.

-Hello there. Agent Smith. –Ed took another sip of his hearty coffee. –How was your day? –he looked Smith straight in the eye.

They never liked each other much because, Ed thought, Smith was a born-bureaucrat, incapable of normal social behavior. Edward, on the other hand, was a kind, social being with an independent mind.

-You both look like shit. –Smith attempted to act like a real person. The others were not buying it. He sat down next to Henry, since that was the only space he could take.

–Looks like you guys had a shitty day too. –he said in a voice of resignation, hanging his head low. That time he hit the mark.

Agent Smith had no idea how he would be able to save face, as it were. He was not ready to question the two men sitting next to him, but he sensed that they might hold the key to his salvation. Smith was banking on the smooth outcome of the Clark-case to help his promotion to Section-Chief of the LA area.

When he learned about Jeffrey Clark's controversial tour, speaking about a lot of "conspiracy-theory" stuff, not just here at home, but abroad, he took that as a sign to his advancement. For about a year prior, he was becoming a regular at E.R.I.S. He knew almost all the staff personally, although he did not know much details about them. He was so focused on the individual, yet insignificant, cases that he missed the intricate inner workings of the facility. Smith had a few trustworthy people here, he could count on, but he lost his most powerful player,

Ester Freeman. Without her, he was on shaky ground. Despite of all the scientifically designed "employment application" questionnaires, that attempted to weed out the disloyal, dishonest and discontent, and displace them in a timely fashion, they invariably got through. Not even the newly implemented AI system could weed them out.

HR personnel suspected that this was the case, but had no practical solution at hand.

They all knew about the hole in the wall that was supposed to be impregnable, but could not do anything about it without authorization from the very top.

Maybe it was intentional, -some thought, feeling their impotence in the matter, -and so be it. –they did not waste anymore time thinking about it.

No one dared to question authority anymore. –Pathetic. –Smith concluded without including himself.

- ...Larry! –he now heard his name. His eyes fluttered for a split second as he returned to reality.

Henry shook him out of his daydream, or is it a nightmare, he wasn't sure.

Edward noticed his spacing out and jabbed Henry in the ribs, but it was too late. Smith spilled his coffee on the right leg of his trouser and now started to feel its heat. It ran straight into his shoe.

Agent Smith kicked off his shoe, cursing to sky high. Then he ripped off his sock too.

He crashed back in his seat and meticulously, took off the other shoe and sock as well. He felt relieved.

-Have another! –Edward handed him a fresh cup of coffee from the tray Sophie left behind. They all cracked up instantly.

Jon is an excellent driver.

Janet and Jeff totally agreed on that by now.

Janet decided to entertain Jeff with the story of Jon becoming a "get-away" driver.

The "chauffeur"! Jon corrected her mercilessly every time. They laughed about that for a while.

But the burden of what their future holds sat heavily upon their soul. They were still few hours away from Henry's place. Lake Tahoe is a fancy yet remote hideaway for people seeking solitude. It is not completely void of human life as a sizable community lives there year round. But, those who own real estate around the lake, whether at the edge of the water or in the woods, can still find and enjoy privacy in abundance.

At the same time, every luxury in the world can also be found nearby, if one so chooses.

The place Jeffrey Clark is going to call home and share with his volunteer companions for sometime is located near the south end of the lake. Very close to the Nevada borderline. It can comfortably house a party of six people. It boasts four bedrooms and three baths, a kitchen, a dining room and a family room of ample size all included in the 2200 square feet of living space. The two-car garage is part of a separate structure. It also contains a storage space for all winter and summer equipment that can be very useful and a lot of fun in the mountains and on the lake.

-We still have over two hours of drive ahead of us. I don't know about you two, but I am hungry and I'd like to stretch my legs too. –Jon interrupted the low conversation behind him with his strong voice.

Janet and Jeff were speaking in a soft voice for the last half an hour or so and they completely disregarded him.

-So, what do you say if I stop in Stockton at a nice Restaurant? –he concluded his line of thoughts with another smile.

-Yeah, sure! I'm ready to have some real food; after all, they fed me through a plastic tube for the last couple of days, and who knows what! –Jeffrey agreed to stopping for dinner.

-Guess what, guys! The "Lady" could also use some plumbing! –they laughed at Janet's remark so hard Jon almost ran off the road. He turned around laughing at Janet for almost thirty seconds while maintaining eighty-five miles per hour and slowly drifting. Janet's changing facial expression and the intermittent rumble of the "shoulder" grooving so typical of California freeways saved the day.

He was back in the middle of his lane in no time.

Traffic was getting a little thicker at this time of the evening so Jon eased a bit off the gas pedal. Usually, he would fight the traffic for fun, but now it was more important to blend.

He pulled into the parking area of a place called J.C.'s Family Restaurant.

-Hey guys! Look what I've found for you! You'll feel right at home in here! –Jon just could not help smiling.

As soon as the vehicle stopped Janet flew out the side door, giggling. Jeffrey was close behind.

Jon locked the SUV calmly, feeling happy for the two of them. He paused for a moment before he entered the restaurant, trying to remember a time when he witnessed such connection. Maybe never.

Jeff was already sitting at the bar, ordering the first round of drinks. Jon settled on his right. If there was some sort of convention about the proper seating of one's lady, he did not know about. Very few people ever consider such things anymore.

-I really wanted to offer you a cold one, -Jeff turned to him now, - but I am not sure if it would be a good idea? –probing his character.

-I was really looking forward to having a cold one, though! –Jon admitted of being thirsty. He waved at the bartender, who quickly came over.

Being a workday, even during "Happy-hour", the bar of this restaurant was nearly deserted.

-What can I get ya? –the bartender had a hoarse voice, but seemed friendly enough to serve up anything they ordered.

-Been on the road for hours. I could use a refreshing, but stiff coffee, partner. –Jon said to the man.

-Do you mean stiff, as an Irish coffee, or stiff as an iceberg? –the bartender wanted to clarify the order.

-Good thing you asked. I'd like it stiff as an espresso, poured over some ice, and blended with cream. –Jon could not make it any clearer.

Janet hopped on the bar-stool on Jeffrey's left.

-One Irish coffee with a double shot, one white Russian with a double Kahlua and an iced double espresso blended with cream comin' up. –the bartender recalled the order.

-What shall we eat? –Janet asked the two men. She seemed neutral for a moment.

Jon did not feel any jealousy, even though he had more feelings for her than he would dare to admit. He and Janet had been working together for the past two years and he hinted at his feelings for her, from time to time, without acknowledgment that it did not matter anymore. They remain friends, that is all.

-You guys go ahead, I'll be back in a minute. – he said, but the other two were already busy looking at the menu, so he just got up and left.

The bartender set down their drinks and asked if they were ready to order, while Jon was still absent. Jeffrey asked him for a little more time, until their friend returned.

The restaurant smelled very enticing, as they even offered some home-style meals. It was more intended for the local folks, than for travelers. People, who lived around here, however, mostly came in to get drunk. Bar fights were part of the entertainment here, but mainly on weekends.

-Shouldn't there be a mirror, behind all those bottles? –Janet asked the bartender unsuspecting.

-Well, yes ma'm. There should be. Ricky, the owner of the glass-shop's promised to have it installed today, but they never showed. I spend a fortune on mirrors around here. –the bartender regretted the shortcoming solemnly.

-So, where are you folks headed? –Jon heard the bartender ask just as he walked by the U shaped bar counter.

-We spent an awesome week in Yosemite and now we are on the way home. We're hoping to do a little wine tasting in Carmel and Santa Ynez on the way. –Jon surprised them when he shouted his answer over the music playing from the overhead speakers. There were seven muted flat-screen TV's broadcasting sports games, but no one was watching them. His companions took a split second to catch up.

-And where might home be? –the guy inquired right on cue.

Jeff caught on and winked at Jon before he replied, -My parents are expecting us by Friday evening at their home in La Jolla. That's nearly six hundred miles from here! Dear God! That's gonna take two more days the way you drive, sweetie! – Janet looked at Jeff in shock when she heard him say that. She did not think he would put her on the spot like that, but now she had the ball.

-I know! –she smiled like a loony person to buy some time, - and if I did not have to GO every two hours, we might just make it in one! –she delivered the punch line smoothly.

The affect was instantaneous laughter. The three men then took turns telling tales about the female bladder's apparent inability to hold fluids. To appease Janet's dwindling mood, they concluded that it might just be the reason why women live longer than men.

-I lived here all my life, but never been to Carmel. I know they make fine wine there 'cause I have some for sale. Not many people ask for it, though. –Cliff, the bartender confessed in regret not having been outside of fifty miles in over forty years.

-Have you tasted their wine at least? –Jon asked him wondering.

-Not yet. –they heard the simple answer from Cliff. –So, what will y'all have for supper? –he changed the subject quickly. Their dinner was served shortly after. They ate rather quietly only speaking the most necessary words.

They never called each other by name, either. Not too far from their table, a group of youngsters sat down to have a few drinks, possibly something to eat. Cliff greeted them as one would greet a friend. Obviously, they were some of the most regular guests of this establishment. It was about time for the "after-work" crowd to file in, they had to be the first of them. Cliff spoke soft enough not to be overheard by Jeff and his new friends.

But they did not miss his gesture as he pointed in their direction with his head over his shoulder. The four young people acknowledged them by looking over briefly and saying "howdy" to be polite.

Jeff returned their greeting with a nod and that was that. The youngsters lowered their voices somewhat realizing they were not alone and out of respect for the business of their friend.

The rest of the dinner went by smoothly. Before asking for the check, Jon ordered a bottle of fifteen years old wine from Carmel, unopened.

They left the check with a cash payment, including ten percent tip, under the bottle. After they left Cliff came to collect their payment and found the wine addressed to him.

"Thanks for the great food and friendly service! Enjoy! Frank, Lee and Donna" he read their message.

-Nice folks. –he mumbled. Cliff did not mind the small tip since the wine made up for it, costing twenty-five bucks. He cleared the table quickly in anticipation of the evening traffic. He placed the bottle neatly back on the shelf where it came from. It stood out shining among the other dust-covered bottles.

The rest of the drive to Tahoe was uneventful, although rather scenic. Amazing mountains border the winding road on either side, creating canyons of immense proportions. Thorny evergreen shrubs mixed in a wild array with deciduous species cover the hillside among old oak threes at lower elevations. As the road climbs, the scenery slowly changes. Yuccas, a succulent plant belonging to the Agave family, begin to appear in the chaparral sporadically. It is one of many drought resistant evergreen plants native to California. Sometimes it's called "Our Lord's Candle" as it puts on a spectacular flower show at the end of its life cycle. In some years, like this one, the show is more breath taking than in others. It all depends on the total number plants flowering in each season. The plant has blade like leaves that grow about two feet long right from the ground. They are rigid and have serrated edges that end in a menacing sharp spur. Each plant may consist of a couple of hundred leaves that give the plant a spherical shape. The flower stem grows upward from the middle and can sometimes reach twelve feet in height. The upper four to six feet of the stem is covered with yellowish- white blossoms that look like the flame of a giant candle from a distance. When you find a hillside covered with dozens of these plants in bloom it is truly a magnificent sight.

Jeffrey, Janet and Jon silently admired the ever-changing view while the sunlight slowly diminished.

They stopped briefly at Carson pass to enjoy the last few minutes of daylight. Soon all the mountains and valleys vanished in the dark. Only the headlight of their SUV gave them a sense of direction. Forward.

There was no traffic up here at this hour. It was all wild life out there and Jon knew that. He eased off the gas allowing the road to dictate his speed. Especially in the turns, where the headlight swept over open space and dispersed into the dark without touching anything, Relying on the painted road markings they just passed by one of a thousand deadly ravines. In the next turn, a group of white tails jumped off the road as he approached.

Luckily they did not want to confirm the accuracy of the phrase "deer in the headlight".

His passengers fell asleep a while ago, another reason for Jon to drive smoothly. The rhythmic sway of the SUV, as he passed turn after turn, was wearing him down too. Nearly in a hypnotic state, he noticed some distant lights.

-Thank God! –he said aloud. He reached for his thermos to have the last of his coffee.

-What's up? –Janet asked, half asleep.

-We're almost there. –Jon wanted to say, but only managed to think it.

He stopped at the very first gas station in town to pick up a map. He found their destination in less than a minute. From there, Jon pulled up to the cabin within ten minutes.

At eleven thirty PM, they were home at last.

CHAPTER 2

Agents Silver, Brown, O'Bryan and Fox arrived back at their ATF headquarters around two PM.

Their boss, Arthur Coleman, was anxiously waiting for their return, because he had to report about the success or failure of their mission.

Upon entering the building, the concierge informed them that A.C. wants to have their reports on his desk within the hour. Urgently, they all rushed to their desks and began writing. Karl Brown received a brief message from Arthur Coleman by a colleague. Karl dialed Coleman's number right away.

-Boss! It's Karl. –he announced himself.

–Shit, Karl! Like I cannot tell who's calling? –Coleman rebuked him jokingly. –Now, get your ass up here! –the line clicked off.

Couple of minutes later Karl was sitting in Coleman's office.

Located on the sixth floor, the office had an exceptional view of the city to the south.

Even through that notorious L.A. smog hanging over it. Angelinos sometimes jokingly say :"We can't trust the air we cannot see". Well, in this great city, it is more visible than most would like, and it may very well be the reason for a large number of illnesses around the state that have not yet been linked to air pollution.

Viewed from the sixth floor, it is even more obvious; a thousand feet thick nasty, brown blanket separating people from fresh air.

It is no wonder than that airplanes approaching LAX for landing fly mostly by IFR, even in daylight.

-You still have the best office, Boss. Except for the smokescreen. –Karl commented on the hundred and twenty degree wide-angle view of the city engulfed in exhaust fumes.

-Yup, I do, but it seems to be seeping in here. –Coleman responded by referring to covert operations of late that are becoming commonplace.

-Coffee? –he asked Karl.

-No, thanks. It's way after lunch, I'll have something stronger, if you got 'em. –Karl smiled at his boss.

-Unofficially…-Coleman turned to treat Karl with a whiskey on the rocks, fully aware of how he likes it.

-…as always. –Karl finished his thought, accepting the drink.

-What do you think of the news? –Coleman got down to business.

-Nothing much. It has not changed any since Vietnam, maybe even before. –Karl hinted at the corruptness of the media.

–Obviously, objective presentation of the news has died a long time ago. –he added to express his sorrow.

-Okay, okay. I know that. –Coleman got a little impatient. Took a swig of his Scotch and sat down behind his desk, facing Karl.

-Don't you think it's going to blow? –he asked Karl straight. –I mean, I can only do so much to hide fuck-ups, for crying out loud! –he vented his exasperation.

Karl just sat back and let him unload. He knew his boss well enough not to get in his way of stress relief.

-As far as I am concerned you guys did a fine job in the last two days. Having to deal with a prick like Larry Smith is enough to warrant hazard-pay! –Coleman started to show a sign of change in his mood.

-Karl. Are you going to tell me how it all went down or should I take away your drink? –he demanded to hear the story now, smiling at his friend.

That was the cue Karl wanted to hear. Swiftly downed the rest of his drink and said –You can take it –handing the glass to Coleman, -but only for a refill, Art. 'Cause if you don't, I'll take that story to my grave. –Karl teased his friend in return, but in a serious manner.

–Get your own damned drink, moron! I am your Boss! –Arthur Coleman asserted from a position of power with a laugh. They both got up simultaneously to get their next drink. Art emptied his glass as he reached for the bottle. Being the "Boss" also meant that it was okay to pour a drink for his friend whenever he felt like.

This was such an occasion.

-You're the best boss I've ever worked for, without a doubt. –Karl accepted the next drink.

-Well, here it is…- he began to recount the story of his last two days, as he sat down again.

-Where are they? –was the question agent Brooks had to answer now to his boss, Donald Clamp.

Agent Smith was struggling to put together a story at E.R.I.S., in response to that same question, he knew someone would ask of him very soon. He had no immediate superior at NSA, to whom he had to answer regarding this case, so the next level up, in the hierarchy of government agencies, was DHS.

"This organization is not to be confused with a similarly named and rather harmless shipping company."

Smith thought with a smile. The person he had to worry about at DHS is David Price.

Timothy Brooks was standing in Donald Clamp's office ready to continue his verbal report.

-For now, I have put a tail on Robert Clark. We have very little info on him, so we are stepping up efforts to remedy that shortcoming. We are in the process of contacting ATF chief Coleman also to gather more information. I intend to find out how Jeffrey Clark disappeared so smoothly, ambulance and all. As for his exact whereabouts, we have no idea at the moment. Sir. –Brooks summarized the situation.

-What is it we know for sure? –Clamp needed something solid to work with.

-We received information, a little over two weeks ago, about Jeffrey Clark spreading a dangerous conspiracy theory world-wide. He spoke in six highly influential countries in front of several thousand people each time. His audiences consisted of a variety of people from all walks of life. Since he returned home, his website has seen an increase of hits up to thousands per day. Also, on the Net, the frequency on certain search words that could be related to his tour have jumped to alarming levels. –Brooks made an effort to present the vague information as professionally as he could.

-On a more personal level, we know where he lives, where he works and that he lost his wife in a nasty car-wreck a few years ago. We know he keeps guns in his house, but they are safely locked up. His car is, naturally, in the garage of his home. He has a large volume of books in a small library. Most of them are about the history and development of humanity, as I could see from the titles. He and his son both have cell phones, but they appear to be off, hence we cannot get a fix on them. Nor have they used a credit card in over six months. Jeffrey Clark's parents moved out of LA long time ago to an unknown location. –was all Brooks could tell for now.

-Splendid! –Clamp exhaled. He was highly annoyed by the fact that his number one man cannot locate this Clark person.

-Expand your search to include DMV records, phone and Cable TV bills, all other utilities, birth certificates, and marriage licenses, legal and criminal records. –Donald Clamp instructed Brooks to be more vigilant in his inquiries.

-Sir! We have already exhausted all those options. They turned up nothing incriminating. We also know that Mr. Clark is a member of the NRA since the passing of Charlton Heston, most likely to honor his legacy; but not even that makes him guilty of anything. –Brooks sighed heavily, not knowing what else to say.

-Have you checked medical and bank records yet? –Clamp inquired with a twinkle of hope in his eyes.

-That is an excellent point sir! I'll have my men on that in a few minutes. Sorry I did not get that far on my own. – Brooks took the advice and managed an apology.

-We do know that Mr. Clark has been teaching at UCLA in the Social Sciences department. He is a professor of human history who also teaches a number of related classes. –Brooks tried to regain some lost ground with that bit of info.

-Well, you've got the idea, Tim! –Clamp encouraged Brooks in a friendlier tone. –Check into that. See where it leads you. I want to know what kind of guns does Mr. Clark owns and why. Does he hunt? Does he shoot trap? How many guns does he keep in his vault with how much ammo? We have to make a case out of something. –Clamp's gotten carried away a bit in his excitement.

Timothy Brooks left his superior's office feeling rather uneasy. He knew his boss expected results, but he did not know how badly needed it, or how far would he go to manufacture evidence.

Clamp's position at the agency seems rock solid, so, the reason for his anxiousness must lay elsewhere.

Agent Brooks ordered the search for Jeffrey Clark's medical and bank records. He decided to take his investigation to UCLA personally. On his way there, he was still contemplating possible reasons for his boss's sudden interest in Clark's collection of firearms. He nearly ran a red light when his phone went off, very loud for the small space of his car.

-Damn! –he muttered as he came to a screeching halt. Picked up his phone to look who's calling.

-Yella? –he said, answering the call of the man he sent after Bobby, holding the phone to his right ear.

-Where are you now? What's your status? –He was also eager to get some positive info for a change.

-I lost him. –came a dishearteningly flat answer. The agent told him how he followed Bobby through rush hour traffic. First, he drove northbound on I-5 then onto SR 2 north.

-I got a little too close to him and he pulled into a gas station. I went past it and came back around to find him filling his tank. Then he pulled into a stall and parked. –the agent continued his explanation.

The light turned green and agent Brooks took off again. –And? –Brooks burst out in anticipation.

- I lost him. –he heard the agent say deeply ashamed.

The traffic flowed smoothly for the moment and Brooks accelerated a bit to pass a few vehicles. The phone still on his ear, he asked in disbelief. – How? –but he did not hear the answer.

A "black and white" was on his tail and another to his left as soon as he finished his pass. He could barely hear his own thoughts inside his head thru the blare of police sirens within a few feet of his car.

He nearly dropped the phone again, and it might have been better if he did, as he quickly assessed the situation. There was something familiar about the face of the cop on his left.

Holding up traffic in both lanes, the two police cars forced him to stop within seconds.

Brooks quickly stashed his phone in the center-console with a stealthy swing of his right hand and elbow as he stopped at the curb.

-Remain in your vehicle and put your hands on the wheel! –came the order over the loudspeaker from the police car behind him. Those speakers are usually installed replacing the standard horn of the vehicle. It filled the street with 100 decibels of sound, freezing even innocent bystanders in the process.

Brooks complied.

The time was around 18:00 hours, still daylight at the end of September. The traffic jamb reached epic proportions in less than a minute.

-What do we have here? –agent Brooks heard the muted voice of the officer now standing at the driver side door. The soft country music of the station he tuned in before leaving Coleman's office, and the closed window to keep him cool almost made the officer inaudible. Brooks continued to stare out the windshield, as he realized why the officer was so familiar to him.

-Agent Brooks! –he heard the police officer's voice much clearer now as he leaned forward to get a better view of the interior of the car. A loud rap followed as the officer knocked on the side window using his baton. Timothy Brooks could see from the corner of his eye that two other officers moved up on his right. One of them had a citation pad in his hand; he was writing something.

He heard another rap on the window; this time from the right.

-Sir! Open your window slowly! –another familiar face ordered him from the right.

He had no choice. He opened the passenger side window, slowly enough not to prompt the cops to draw on him. They had their hands on their weapons ready for action.

It is a tough job being a police officer in L.A. They have had the highest mortality rate of any department in the nation during the nineties. Things had gotten somewhat better since then.

-You were using a cell phone while operating a motor-vehicle. According to state law, that is a moving violation. Do you have a valid reason why your seat belt is not fastened at this time? Sir! –the officer asked Brooks courteously.

- This way I can easily get my license and registration out for inspection. –Brooks tried to remain as civilized as possible in tone of voice as well as in body language.

-May I have your Insurance and Registration for the vehicle, please? –the officer asked politely. Brooks slowly reached over to the glove compartment and opened it.

As he lowered the door, a bunch of maintenance documents slipped out along with the registration and insurance papers. He reached out to catch them when his holstered 9mm Beretta slid forth to Brooks' horror. It landed on the floor, next to the documents the police officer asked to see.

-Hands in the air! Now! Slowly, get out of the vehicle on the driver's side! –he heard the police officer shout! They all drew their weapons on him in a blink of an eye.

Before he could reach for the door handle the door opened and the officer on his side grabbed his left arm and roughly pulled him out. Two officers were now on his side and they shoved him against the side of the car. Hands behind his back, he was cuffed in less than thirty seconds.

-What were you thinking, agent Brooks? Going for your firearm like that while surrounded by police officers could spell disaster! You should know that. –the officer said disapprovingly.

-You have the right to remain silent. Anything you say can and will be used against you in a court of law… –Brooks heard the officer holding his arm begin to inform him of his Miranda right.

-You do realize that you are messing with a federal agent. Don't you? –he asked the officers calmly.

-You do realize that by now you have violated five laws of this state? Agent Brooks? –the officer asked him in return.

-What five laws? –Brooks cried out in disbelief and building tension in his voice. The officer laid it on him without mercy.

– Using a cell phone while driving, not wearing a seat belt, speeding, failing to use turn-signal while changing lanes are punishable moving violations. Threatening an officer with a firearm is a felony. –Brooks heard the officer's reasoning.

-"Is it really that easy to turn someone into a criminal?" –he reflected on the progress of the incident. He opted for one last comment even though he should have stayed quiet.

-You cannot take revenge on me because I out ranked you at a scene earlier… -but he already regretted opening his mouth.

-Where was that? –the officer inquired curiously. Brooks however, did not say another word.

-Oh yeah. I guess you mean the scene we've never been to, never heard of and will never speak of. It was such a covert operation that the suspect's face was allover the national news last night. He mysteriously disappeared a day after he was announced dead. –he made fun of Brooks. –Bravo! If I'm not mistaken that was an FBI case. –the officer added chuckling with his colleagues as they lead Brooks to the patrol car.

Needless to say, Timothy Brooks was furious about this incident, but for now there wasn't much he could do. Just before he got into the back seat of the patrol car, the ringing of his cell phone in his car stopped him.

-I have to answer that! –he objected against the unjust treatment. –I am investigating the mysterious disappearance of Jeffrey Clark, that is an FBI case, and my superiors will have your ass for interfering. –he dared the lead officer to hand him the phone.

The officer leading this patrol walked to agent Brooks' car and after putting on a latex glove, from his pocket, retrieved the phone. Holding it very carefully between his thumb and index finger, he slipped the phone into a plastic bag he pulled from his other pocket. –We now have the evidence for the "cell phone use" charge. –the officer handed the bag to one of his partners. His partner took it to the other patrol car.

They cleared the "roadblock" and waved on all the upset motorists whom they inconvenienced for almost ten minutes. They drove Brooks to the precinct for booking. His cell phone rang two more times in the "evidence" bag, where the officer put it along with Brooks' firearm.

The agent, who called Brooks, had no idea why his boss vanished so suddenly. He assumed that Brooks might be in a dead zone and it would be best if he waited some time before calling again.

With no target to follow, he was on his way back to his office where he would write a formal report.

Bobby pulled in to a gas station in La Canada Flintridge, just off I-210. He had been aware of being shadowed since he left Good Samaritan Hospital. The thought of getting innocent people into trouble that way bothered him a great deal. For sure, they will question the hospital staff about him. He blamed himself for slacking off. After a quick fill-up, Bobby parked his Mustang close to the exit, facing north at a Japanese red leave Maple tree. He admired its deep fall colors briefly and walked towards the station. At the age of 25 he was not ashamed to engage in such silly activities as bird watching, site seeing or occasionally watching the Sun set.

Bobby learned how abruptly a person's life could end so he makes every minute count. From the corner of his eye, he could see the vehicle that followed him all this way.

The man had parked at another gas station across the street, ready to pounce.

Bobby opened the door, but before stepping inside the convenient store, he gave that vehicle a fleeting glance.

-Now you see me, now you don't! –he said aloud playfully as the door closed behind him. First things first, he hurried to the rest room.

The agent began to feel uneasy for not being able to see inside the convenient store from where he was. Only a blurred reflection of the outside was visible in the tinted glass of the relatively small storefront. He had to wait.

Waiting for anything in life is a boring and unwanted task for most people, and he was no exception. To make time pass in a more efficient way he tallied all the people around the station.

Then he made a mental list of all vehicles and other objects he could see as well. Currently three vehicles were fueling; four vehicles are parked in stalls. Three of those were cars, including Bobby's Mustang and a single truck. He saw one vehicle inside the shop and a mechanic who was working on it. Smaller details, however, were hard to make out as he was nearly one hundred yards away. He could see the exit of the car wash located behind the station. As he completed the assessment, a Jeep, painted flat green, pulled out of the car wash. Only its windshield was glistening in the late afternoon sun. It had a hard top on and appeared to be dry. The driver was dressed in a mechanic's overall and cap. Two vehicles finished at the pump and started moving at the same time. He watched them closely as they exited the station. The first car turned left and headed south on Angeles Crest Highway passing in front of him. The Jeep and the other car turned north. The Jeep crossed over I-210 and continued up the hill while the other car took the on-ramp, heading east.

Bobby had an icebox full of food and drinks on the passenger seat courtesy of Fred Gilmore, his childhood friend. To keep it from falling down, he weaved the seatbelt through its handle and buckled it up. Now that he was several hundred yards from the station, he looked into the rearview mirror to make sure his tail was left behind. Relieved, he took off the cap and placed it on top of the cooler, wiser facing forward.

-There, you look handsome in it. –he smiled at the cooler.

Bobby never was much of a hat-person. Not even in the Marines where he had gotten in trouble many times for "being out of uniform".

He unbuttoned the top three buttons of the overall his friend, Fred, put on him at the station. He went a little overboard helping Bobby when he buttoned him up all the way to his neck.

It made him look like a "Chinese Dictator", as Bobby teased him.

Fred Gilmore was a simple, goodhearted soul all his life. He and Bobby became close friends in elementary school where they first met, in second grade. The Gilmore family moved into Bobby's neighborhood that summer reaching the pinnacle of their American dream. His parents, Adam and Kristine, made a series of successful stock market investments that paid off nicely. They also ran a family business quite successfully for many years they started with the rest of their fortune. But, around the end of the nineties, their business went belly up for reasons that remained unknown to Bobby and he did not want to pry. So the Gilmore family moved out of their mansion to save what they could and settled in La Crescenta. Their new home was less than half the size of the one they left behind in Beverly Hills.

At twenty-eight hundred square feet, it still offered plenty of living space for the family of five.

However, their streak of bad luck continued for several years, as Fred's parents tried desperately to adjust to a lesser lifestyle. Ultimately, his father became the co-owner of a small advertising firm. The new business took a long time to become successful, and even at its best he made less money than his wife did as a Real Estate agent. This unfortunate shift in earning ability led to continued and unresolved tension between them. They held the marriage together for their children's sake, until they all finished their college education. To their disappointment, Fred dropped out after his sophomore year to join the Marines. His two sisters, Suzy, who is older by two years, and Katie, younger by two, both completed college with high marks.

Bobby would only refer to them as the "Gilmore Girls" after the popular WB-TV show that first aired in two thousand. Their parents divorced about five years ago. Fred and the girls stayed with their mother in La Cresenta.

Adam Gilmore moved out and in with his partner, Sherry Klinsing, whose natural feminine charm accounted for about sixty percent of the success of their advertisement business.

-What a shame to see a nice family, like theirs, fall apart from economic stress. – Bobby thought. He pulled off at a lookout point a few miles up. Fred told him about the spot that overlooks 210 and from where he could see the station by using the 10x50 binocular from the glove box.

Looking south at this time of the day the sun was off to his far right. Holding the binocular steady, he could see the man still sitting in his car, but he was too far to realize he was there at his father's house.

Bobby could actually take him out at a distance of little over a mile, using his Marine sniper rifle. Bobby saw Fred come out, at the end of his shift, and get in his Mustang. The man in the car quickly checked the traffic and the Mustang seemingly getting ready to follow him. Fred backed up and smoothly merged into traffic, going north. In less than thirty seconds, he turned left onto I-210 westbound. Bobby watched the man angrily pound the dashboard of his car. He realized he was made, having sat here for over half an hour. He had no way of knowing when and how Bobby got away from him, but he did.

Bobby stashed the binocular away and headed back down toward the 210 freeway at leisurely pace. Hoping the man would be gone by the time he got there, since he had lost his objective. As he approached the intersection, he saw the black car crossing the bridge over the freeway, coming straight toward him. Bobby carefully slowed down to see what his pursuer would do. The black car merged left into the turning lane that will put him onto the freeway going westbound.

Bobby was now less than a hundred yards from him. As the light turned green, the black car began its turn following two other cars ahead of it. Bobby eased into right lane and made the turn westbound as well. He was only two vehicles behind his pursuer as they merged onto the freeway with increasing speed. Bobby could now see why the agent did not notice him. He was busy talking to someone on his cell phone. The agent remained in the outer lane and Bobby moved left a couple to stay on the 210.

Daringly, Bobby accelerated to pass him as the agent followed the ramp onto the Glendale freeway. They drifted apart gradually as the two roads separated. The agent never saw Bobby zoom by as he was too busy talking on his phone. He had to return the vehicle to its rightful owner, and negotiate the appropriate compensation for the inconvenience.

Sophie finished picking up the mess within minutes after Larry Smith swept a stack of documents off his desk in anger. He was upset over a phone-conversation with his superior. Sophie is very skilled in organizing office space and making order out of madness. To her surprise, she heard laughter from the break-room. In this instance, it was the last thing she expected to hear.

When she returned to the break-room, the three men were still shooting around silly remarks.

-What happened to you, Mr. Smith? Did these two attack you or something? –she asked puzzled seeing Smith sitting there in his underwear.

-No, Miss Herd. They just told me that spilling the coffee you gave me probably saved my life, as it was surely laced. – Smith smiled at her, showing a humorous side they never knew.

-Remember? You ordered it with "lots of sugar"! –Sophie responded to the accusation by throwing the ball back with a smile of her own.

Edward took that as a cue and said; -I don't need any sugar in my coffee, if you serve it, Sugar! –They all cracked up again, but Sophie stopped laughing and ended the jovial mood.

-Edward Doering! That remark of yours was sexist and some might even label it as harassment! –she said in an unmistakably cold voice. –Lucky for you, I am not like them! –she softened her voice to ease the blow.

Then she turned to Smith.

– We'd better wash your clothes before the sugar sets in those stains. –she said taking his wet pants and socks. Ed could not believe the way Sophie reacted to his harmless joke.

-What is the world coming to? Can I not joke with a woman without getting in trouble anymore? –he was furious, disgusted and intimidated at the same time.

-Well, my friend, -Henry began responding to his mumbling –if you have paid any attention to the world around you, you should have noticed a trend. –he pointed out his friend's narrowed vision.

-What trend is that? –he had triggered Ed's interest.

People have been systematically alienated from one another for a long time. –Henry wanted to say, but instead he decided to postpone the explanation.

-We don't have the time right now. Smith's waiting for our report. Come! –he said waving to Ed to follow him.

Agent Smith received a pair of blue-green pants, a piece of the garb medical personnel wear around here, and a pair of disposable slippers so he wouldn't have to go bare foot until his clothes came back from the in-house laundry.

Smith's interview with Henry and Edward turned informal the instant he spilled his coffee. They were sitting in his small office. Larry Smith slowly regained his old self; he was now sitting upright, in an official posture, but his tone remained friendly. He was in a bind and desperate for any information he could get. He was willing to settle for less than believable, if that was all he could get.

-Sooo. What happened today? –he asked the two men sitting across from him.

-Well, it is very confusing. –Henry volunteered to start. -As Ed will also tell you, they broke in at the north gate. As you know, we have cameras looking at all points of entry and we have cameras pointed at most intersections leading to the facility as well. Yet, and this boggles the mind, somehow we had a surveillance failure in the northern sector for almost an hour. –he went on explaining.

-I took Mr. Clark outside to get some fresh air. -Ed took over the story now, surprising his friend.

-Few minutes later I heard the sound of a crash as I turned a corner with Mr. Clark in the wheelchair, heading back to building 5. I looked in the direction of the north gate, but it was gone, and a fast moving vehicle approached us. –Ed laid it out fluidly.

-I heard the crash too, and I saw this van pull up next to Ed. –Henry continued Ed's line of the story. They were building on each other's ideas, combined with elements of what really happened. So far, it seemed to hold water, as Smith appeared to listen intently.

-I figured the fastest way to help him was by jumping into my own car. I drove as fast as I could, given the distance… - he slowed down a bit to allow his brain to compute a new idea, but Ed came to his rescue. -…the two masked men shoved Mr. Clark and me in the back and started moving rapidly. They realized Henry could block their escape so they gunned it to intercept him before he did! –Ed let it out excitedly. Smith was looking at them back and forth as they took the word from one another. A picture started to form in his head.

-So how did you end up crashing into the water tower a block south from the gate? –Smith injected a logical question to see if he could derail their story, or just make them stall momentarily that would indicate hesitation or improvisation.

But, the answer flowed smoothly, like the rest of the story.

-Flying down the road, I noticed they turned south, so I pursued them. They forced me off the road as soon as I got next to them. Their vehicle was heavier and they had four people onboard. That guy could really drive. Like he took a driving course from the police, or something. –Henry got excited too, as he continued building the story and saw that it was very effective.

It was indeed. Smith was now convinced that they were telling the truth. It was the best story he heard in years. He did not mind the possibility that they were rounding off the corners a bit, what mattered to him at the moment was the fact that he did not have to work very hard to make it news worthy.

-The morons did not have enough gas to get far away. –Ed signaled Henry by lightly kicking his right foot as he took the lead again. –They drove about half an hour east and pulled into a gas station. After filling up, Henry and I were shocked and relieved at once, as they ordered us out of the vehicle. As soon as our feet hit the ground, they were off. This was so unexpected; it took us a minute to gather ourselves. By the time we looked around, they were at the traffic light, two blocks east. –Ed solved their biggest problem and Henry leaned back in his seat, nodding his head acknowledging this clever move.

He did not want to add anything since Ed was on the roll and he took Ed's foot signal as "just listen".

However, Ed fell silent and that made him a little anxious. They were both considering Smith's reaction and were watching him closely. But, all they could see that he was deep in his thoughts. The tension grew as the silence dragged on.

-…and why do you think they did that? –Smith asked, taking a deep breath as he came up from the dept of his thoughts, after noticing the silence.

-They did not want additional hostages, or witnesses who, if left alive beyond that point, could rat on them. —answered Ed fluently from the tip of his tongue.

Henry had no idea his friend was such skilled "story teller". He looked at him in awe, approval and appreciation for a job well done.

-That makes sense. —Smith accepted their story.

They both let out a careful sign of relief and stood up, getting ready to leave. Smith remained seated and that stopped them from taking the next step.

-I have some questions about the events prior to Mr. Clark's abduction. Please sit down. —Smith pointed at their chairs. Somewhat reluctantly, they sat down again. Instead of asking questions right away, Smith just kept staring at them. It made both of them very nervous, but they sat their ground steadfastly, anticipating his questions.

Smith knew that prolonged silence while questioning witnesses or suspects could have different effects. It could make an average person nervous and confused so that he would make a mistake. Or, it could give time to a stronger person to make his story even more credible. To keep that from happening, an interrogator should ask such questions that could break up any logical or linear thinking. However, this was not Smith's intention, he was merely summarizing the information he received so far.

-I would like to know the circumstances of Mrs. Freedman's regrettable death and why Mr. Clark was moved from the room on the third floor. Also, I need to know if either of you had seen or had any contact with the people who brought him in yesterday. —Smith finally broke the silence.

Now it was Henry's turn to cover their tracks, although he could not deviate much from the truth.

-I have already written my report about the accident that occurred during the night shift. —Henry began by referring to Mrs. Freedman.

—But I will tell you how it happened in my own words and in full detail if you require it. —he was probing to see if Smith would cut him a little slack.

Friendly as he may have seemed, Smith was not about to pass up the opportunity to hear the event from the only person who witnessed it.

-I do require it. –he said flatly, and, with an expressionless face, he pulled out Henry's report from the stack on his desk. Henry just wrote that report yesterday, because it wasn't very long he could almost recite it word for word. But, he was not about to do that. Instead, he began right after Clark's admission.

-We were all taking care of our assigned tasks, around 10:30 in the morning. I noticed that a new suspect has arrived, as I was heading to room 108, just down the hall. I had to make sure the person in there was in a stable condition. He is no longer with us, however, as he was practically beat to death when they captured him. –Henry began to remember the events of the day before yesterday.

-I want you to refrain from using words like "suspect". –Smith cut into his words when he noticed an edge in Henry's voice.

-I did not know where Mrs. Freedman put this new person for treatment. I did not really care. Like every one else around here, I do not ask questions, I just do what I am told. –Henry retracted to an obedient employee's position.

-And what about you? What have you been doing all that time? –Smith turned to Ed, all of a sudden.

-I can't really say much about that morning. I was busy doin' my chores in the psych-unit. You know? Keepin' all the loonies in check. –Ed gave Smith the short version of his day.

Smith did not want to hear about the psych ward.

-That's alright! –he said, stopping Ed from continuing.

-So, –Smith shifted his gaze back to Henry, -what was your task after checking room 108? –

Henry took a couple of seconds to respond, as he made an adjustment in attitude. Then he told the entire story of yesterday, as Smith needed to hear it. Even without knowing for sure, he figured Smith had an obligation to his superiors to report promptly and he sensed its urgency.

Later that evening Smith made his report to David Price. The ripples of inter agency misalignment began to smooth out slowly, seemingly by themselves. Key power-players pulled some strings in their control and things fell into place.

Employees responded with varying degrees of eagerness and aptitude to produce the desired effects. But, thankfully, there are always those who feel a higher obligation to their fellow men, beyond the duty of a government employee. They began to see a pattern of deception that leads back through history.

Henry and his friend Ed talked about it over dinner. They brought their families together at Henry's to unwind. In the background the television was on, but none of them were watching it until now. Lisa, Henry's wife, turned it up and called them over to watch when she noted the headline.

"Dead man missing in action and maybe alive! – Where is Jeffrey Clark?"

They all sat in front of the flat screen HDTV Henry bought for Lisa's birthday less than six months ago.

-"And now, the local news! In the past couple of days, we have received contradicting information about the fate of, the now world famous historian, Jeffrey Clark. His fame began with a series of seminars he held in six countries around the world. In his lectures, Mr. Clark discussed human history and human interactions with a disturbing twist. He seems to suggest that certain groups of people (he did not attempt to identify) have perpetually played and continue to play with people's lives at will.

Two days ago, Mr. Clark suffered a tragic and deadly accident in his home in Bel Air. Authorities believe the accident occurred during an episode of seizure, the result of a rare childhood disease. He fell down the stairs of his home, an ambulance responded to a 911 call placed by his son Robert Clark taking him to the nearest hospital where he was announced DOA.

However, anonymous sources report that he is in fact alive and well at an undisclosed location."-they heard the announcer read the story.

-They're not going to admit any involvement, other than investigating the circumstances of the accident. –Ed injected with disgust. The others did not respond at this time.

The news cast continued...

"We have been told that Jeffrey Clark mysteriously disappeared shortly after he was declared dead. If he were alive, authorities would like to question him to rule out any foul play surrounding his accident. You may call the number on your screen if you have any information about him"

-Oh yeah. They're doing it again. They're calling for public help, making people spy on one another. For them it's just another handy occasion to deepen the lines of division among people, just like after 911. Remember? Your neighbors began to look at you strangely and became curious about the contents of your home and garage even though they knew you for years. –Henry could not stand it any more.

He was angry with the government for manipulating people into a precarious position of distrust, because he understood the reason behind it.

Divide and conquer; has been a tried and true concept for centuries, to rule any number of people.

This division is the reason why more and more outrageous laws pass around the world, because people can no longer unite. He now realized that his beloved country, America, is just like that. A country of over three hundred million individuals, proud to be individuals, which is why they formed a Union of fifty states instead of a true nation.

Shockingly, people still have faith in the government and anything it does, even while being told not to trust one another. Lisa turned down the volume so much it was barely audible after the Clark report has finished.

The anchor was now talking about a new opportunity to donate to a local non-profit organization.

-"'Kids at Play', a non-profit organization is planning to build and operate a spacious five acre recreational park for all ages." –they heard the faint voice of the commentator.

-Hey Henry, do you wanna write them a small check? –Ed teased his friend, not realizing that he accidentally poured oil on red-hot ember.

Henry's discontent, about how the world works, has flared up instantly.

-Fuck "Kids at Play"! Charitable people can never see the lies. –he jumped to his feet shouting and stormed out of the room.

-Hey! Calm down! Maybe we could help them to see! That is what this Clarke fellow is doing! –Ed shouted after his friend.

Lisa and Cindy just sat there in awe. They have never seen their hubbies behave like that. Never have they gotten so serious about politics either. Neither of them had any idea who this Jeffrey Clark was until yesterday, but he sure stirred up their cozy lives.

-I know, but look what happened to him! He nearly died and now he is a fugitive! –Henry returned, still being upset, but sounding more reasonable.

As the situation slowly diffused, Ed and Henry told the story of Jeffrey Clark to their wives.

The police had finally released Timothy Brooks after Donald Clamp clamped down on them in a "courtesy" call and vouched for his man not to cause any more headaches. At the same time he managed to get the point across that, the FBI's authority supersedes most local police division's authority in matters of national security.

The police chief felt it necessary to remind the FBI chief that even he had to answer to a higher authority now, namely the DHS. They both agreed that the current system was fast becoming intolerably cumbersome and they were happy to retire in just few years. Clamp had a nearly decade long working and personal relationship with the police chief, to whom he was informally introduced at a target range shortly after his own appointment as section chief in L.A. They hit it off so well that since then they regularly got together at the range every other week for a match. They both have been firearm enthusiasts most of their lives and do own a number of firearms, each.

They further agreed that the four police officers should be reprimanded for over-stepping their authority by harassing a federal agent and obstructing a federal investigation. The police chief has also decided, on his own, to promote them as soon as he could for executing the arrest in a textbook manner.

Timothy Brooks knew it was already too late to visit the Good Samaritan. His suspects, as he thought of them, were far away by now and there was nothing he could do about it. Having lost his best chance, the tail on Bobby, he wanted to search the Clark residence again. While on his way, he called two of his men to meet him there in twenty minutes.

The Clark residence was anything, but quiet when Brooks arrived. His men were already there waiting for him. They did not want to get involved without their boss. Agent Brooks was beyond upset after all he had to endure on this day. From the looks of things, it was going to continue that way. NSA agents were working with CSI personnel, gathering evidence of whatever perceived crime they had in mind. Outsourced and outnumbered, as their mission was supposed to be covert, the FBI team resorted to the most thorough visual inspection their expertise would allow. Brooks could only hope that the NSA agents would cooperate and share, at least visually, some of the evidence they already collected.

It did not take long before Larry Smith, now fully dressed in a suit, intercepted the FBI agents.

-Well, what do you think of this place agent Brooks? –he greeted his colleague with his left hand extended for handshake.

-Hello Larry! - being right handed, Brooks responded instinctively with his right. They both realized their mistake and followed up with their other hands.

This created even more of an entanglement as they found themselves in a four-handed, crisscrossed handshake.

-That was fun. –Brooks withdrew his hands with a chuckle.

-Yup. –Smith concurred and swiftly pulled back his own, lest someone might see him being silly again.

- At best, my information is sketchy about Jeffrey Clark, but looking at his home it is hard to imagine him being anti- establishment. –Brooks finally responded to Smith's question.

-It would seem that way, wouldn't it? But, we know from historical evidence that the educated ones are more dangerous.

–Smith countered with his official opinion.

–Add money to education, -he continued, –coupled with skewed ideology and it spells trouble! –Smith summed up what could lately account for a terrorist in the making, according to government guidelines.

-Where exactly did you receive your training? –Brooks inquired in a curious tone, wondering how a seemingly intelligent person can become so brainwashed.

-My last training was at FLETC. Why? –Smith responded unsuspecting any mockery.

-Your analysis is right on; sounds like something one could find in a manual for "law enforcement professional"-s. But what is your personal opinion? –Brooks wondered if he even had one.

-The man is obviously crazy to risk all this, -Smith swung his arm around pointing at the luxurious interior of the house, -for the enlightenment of the poor. –he stopped facing the FBI agent.

Smith actually expressed a human thought, but Brooks did not like the reference at the end. He never looked down on the less fortunate just because they had limited means.

"Poverty does not make them criminals automatically either. The great majority of people who live under less than desirable conditions do manage their lives within the law. However, some people, regardless of their social status or financial means, would always be on the lookout for injustice. They will stand up for their fellow men." He thought.

-Right. –Brooks agreed not wanting to start a moral debate.

–Do you have any information you can share with us, about how this man earned the scrutiny of the highest levels of our government? –he asked, referring to the "enlightenment of the poor" part of Smith's statement.

-We have seized his computer and all his written documentation regarding his "Human History and Relations" seminars. We are going through his contacts to sort out who is who, maybe he has deeper roots in some homegrown terrorist group than meets the eye. In addition, we have a locksmith working on his gun safe to see what kind of arsenal he keeps on hand. –Smith informed his colleague.

-"Arsenal"? –Brooks frowned at the word.

–How many guns do you have, Larry? –he asked Smith with rising suspicion. The NSA agent proudly answered him.

–Just the one I'm obligated to carry as a federal agent. It's government issued.–his response did not surprise Timothy Brooks.

-And you? How many guns do you own, Tim? –Smith addressed him by his first name for the first time after being his acquaintance for over five years.

Brooks smiled and held out both his hands, side by side, in front of Larry.

-Put me in irons, Larry! I must be a terrorist since I own a dozen different weapons. I also enjoy target shooting at anything man-made, you know, for special effect. –Brooks pleaded guilty of being a firearm enthusiast with a smile to match it.

-Don't tempt me, Tim! –Smith swept agent Brooks' hands aside smiling.

-We've got work to do. –he added leading the way upstairs into the study.

They inspected every square inch of the place in less than an hour. The locksmith finally opened the gun safe and they examined its contents.

-Here it is, Gentlemen! –the locksmith turned it over to them stepping out of their way.

-Gee, Larry! The guy only has six guns! –Brooks pointed out in a tone of sadness, yet teasing.

-Yeah, but look at all the ammo he's got in there! –Smith replied appalled by the site of about six hundred rounds of ammunition, one hundred rounds for each.

-I guess this may come as a surprise to you, but if he is a passionate shooter, the ammo in here is only enough for about fifteen minutes of leisurely practice, with any one of his guns. Taking all six guns out is a bit of hassle, but would make for a decent day at the range for an enthusiast. At an open range, this ammo, would quite possibly be gone in less than three hours, especially with the help of a friend. –agent Brooks informed Smith.

-Thanks for the insight, but I view it as grave danger to civilians! –Smith countered as a true bureaucrat.

-You cannot be serious! –Brooks burst out in disbelief. -The man is a scholar with a strange hobby for Christ's sake, nothing more! –he added to change his colleague's mind.

-Oh, but I am! –Larry Smith declared.

-Larry! –Brooks did not give up that easily, -Have you ever considered that blindly following orders can inadvertently aide something awful? As much as I am grateful for this steady and well paying job, in twenty years of service, I have seen a disturbing shift in politics! –he pressed his colleague.

Smith, however, was left untouched by his logic. The distance between them grew by the minute and they both felt it. There was no stopping it. A deep chill ran down Brooks' spine as he observed the change in Smith's body language. Brooks had gone too far trying to explain something human to a "block wall" and that wall threatened to come down on him with all its fury.

-Agent Brooks! I suggest you take the evidence I gave you and report it to your superior. I will request Chief Clamp's summary of your investigation later tonight. Good bye! –Smith dismissed him coldly.

Timothy Brooks rounded up his men and departed promptly. His partners suspected that something happened between their boss and the NSA agent, but thought it wise not to inquire.

After Henry's rare outburst of anger, he and his guests have settled back in the dining room. Having cleared the remnants of their dinner working together, Ed took the liberty to serve up everyone's favorite drinks. Sipping quietly, they allowed time for tension to dissipate.

More or less, they all agreed that things weren't the way they used to be.

They all experience small changes regularly, they never thought possible. During dinner, for instance, they talked about how just a few years ago one could travel around the world without having to endure the scrutiny of the government, that is now bordering harassment.

In the past, typically communist countries and other dictatorships were associated with that kind of mistreatment of people. The traveling public is manipulated into submission of the new laws by fear.

By fear of being arrested or denied the opportunity to travel for nothing more than carrying shampoo, perfume, drinking water, or just about anything else that is now banned from luggage. These limits may have been imposed on passengers only to reduce dead weight on the planes, thus improving their fuel efficiency. Then, by fear of an unsuspected hijacker, lurking among the passengers of one's flight. By fear of Muslims, fueled by the media, whom we have angered in the first place. Muslims, who have peacefully coexisted among the people of many nations, now find themselves singled out. Sadly, during the nineties, the former Yugoslavia burst into flames by politically spurred ethnic differences.

Edward Forsythe knew that, his friend, Henry D'Guard would not calm down for a while, because he was such an idealist. That is to say: he was hoping to achieve the impossible. Ed also believed that the world could be a much better place, if the common people would find a common ground. The way most humans are conditioned to view the world makes it very difficult to change direction.

They were not expecting any visitors for the rest of the night, so the doorbell startled them.

Henry stood up, jolted out of his thoughts by the noise, and went to the front door.

Sophie Herd was standing outside with a man Henry only saw briefly, when he viewed the security cameras, just before Jeffrey Clark's escape.

He froze halfway reaching for the doorknob.

-Hey! Henry? –he heard Sophie's voice resonate through the door. –It's me and my friend. –she said, but Henry was not convinced by the word "friend".

-Mr. D'Guard! I know this may shock you, but I have known Ms. Herd for over ten years, socially. We are here to help. –the man, standing next to Sophie, said putting his arm around her shoulder.

Henry did sense all along that, Sophie was somehow different from the other people working at E.R.I.S. Trusting that feeling now, he opened the door.

-Mister D'Guard! So nice to meet you! –the man greeted him as if he had been waiting for this moment for years.

-Henry! Thanks for letting us in. I was afraid you might blow us off. –Sophie hugged him so tightly, she had to explain herself to Lisa a few seconds later. Ed came to her rescue, almost getting himself in trouble with his own wife. It took a few minutes to introduce each other properly, but after that, the mood elevated rapidly. Sophie and Karl brought a case of beer to celebrate Oktoberfest! They were all game for a good party anytime, so the rest of the evening was a great success.

Karl took Henry aside for a moment, when he thought it was safe, to inform him that Bobby was about to rejoin his father. Henry did not ask for any more details. He would be visiting his new friends in less than a week. Curious to see how much this "friend" already knew, he asked him about the next move Larry Smith might take.

-He is hard to predict, but we know that earlier this evening he conducted a seizure at Mr. Clark's home.

One of my guys have been watching the place all day, unofficially of course. –Karl informed him without any apprehension. –Not too long ago the FBI showed up also, but they left after a while, empty-handed. Sophie told me that you guys spent some forty minutes in his office explaining yourselves after you returned to E.R.I.S. Smith is a real jerk of a bureaucrat, he does not have a human bone in his body. –Karl spoke very casually, not at all like a federal employee.

Henry slowly relaxed, and accepted Karl as Sophie's friend. He sensed him to be an honest and true private person.

Henry saw the sparkle in Sophie's eyes every time she looked at him. Just as Ed told him how he discovered Janet having a crush on Jeffrey, Henry found it quite heart-warming to witness the process first hand.

-Thank you, Karl. I think that's enough official business for tonight! Let's mingle! –Henry did not want to keep him from Sophie any longer.

Karl took off towards her shooting a quick "thank you" smile and a nod back at Henry.

He watched Karl gently slipping his arm under Sophie's and the way she received it, pulling him to her side.

They kept the conversation on the light side for the rest of the evening, about culture, friendships, families and sports.

CHAPTER 2

Bobby drove approximately four hundred and fifty miles in six hours flat. He had been very lucky, even though he exceeded the speed limit periodically, by twenty miles for five to ten minutes at times, CHP did not catch him. He knew keeping the hand of the speedometer pinned to the right was the only way he could achieve the 75m/h average he needed. He appreciated the Jeep's endurance because he had no mercy for it at all.

The vehicle is intended for off-road use at relatively low speeds, for the most part, but Chrysler, despite struggling to survive the economic crash of 2008, with help from foreign auto makers, managed to improve its highway speed with a new gearbox and two-wheel drive mode. The longer and wider wheelbase also helped negotiate the winding mountain roads.

Thus, Jeep remains relevant in the world-wide automobile market.

It was just after midnight when Bobby arrived in Tahoe. The first gas station he found was still open. He jumped out at the pump, filled up his vehicle, and went inside.

-Hello! –he greeted the operator of the station from the door, startling him even more than the sound of the chime did, hanging on the door.

The man's voice indicated mild annoyance and tiredness as he responded.

-How is it going? –and his eyes followed Bobby's movement in the store attentively.

–Would you mind if I use the rest room? –Bobby asked walking in the direction indicated by the sign.

–No, go ahead. –the clerk agreed waving him on.

Bobby reappeared in a couple of minutes, relieved and a bit refreshed. He washed his face with cold water; the only kind availble, to revive his senses. He grabbed a cold energy drink from the fridge and went straight to the cashier. There, he picked up the last local map from the rack.

The clerk noticed, but did not think much of it. –Are you visiting us for the first time? –he asked without any intention of snooping.

–I am here to visit a friend. He is expecting me, but I do not want to disturb him this late. I think I'll just crash in the closest Motel and surprise him in the morning by ringing his bell. –Bobby gave him something to chew over.

–The closest Motel is just up the road, 'bout a quarter of a mile on the left. –the clerk offered the info free of charge.

–You are the second person buying a local map in the last hour, you know. I haven't sold any maps in six months before that. So, you see, we can't help noticing strangers up here. –he warned Bobby, casually pointing at the surveillance camera behind him, up in the corner.

Bobby did not find his observation amusing and he did not want any trouble. He did manage not to look directly at the camera, and wished that he had Fred's cap on now, but it was too late.

–Well, ya ain't much different from the rest of us, then. We do the same, to keep honest people honest. –Bobby replied, showing his folksy side.

–Say, what did these strangers look like? The ones that bought the map? –he inquired, hoping to gain a bit more of the man's trust.

–Two men and a woman. They looked pretty tired, even more than you. They appeared to be in their forties. The two men were about the same height, 'round 5'-10" or 11". One of them had light brown, almost blond hair; the other's was dark brown. The woman's hair was shoulder length; she's also a brunette, maybe 5'6" tall. –the clerk gave the most accurate description he could, considering the late hour and the length of the encounter.

Bobby thanked the man for his help and after pocketing the change opened his drink as he waved good night to the clerk. He hopped back in the Jeep and drove into town.

Bobby realized that from now on they would all have to mind those damn surveillance cameras.

"What is the world becoming? Can people not have privacy anymore? What is the real reason for constantly watching people? Is it to gather data about how they behave in convenience or department stores to refine marketing techniques? Maybe. Is it really aimed to increase security as they say? Hardly. Small-time, desperate criminals do not care about cameras; they will break into places, rob people at will or even kill them if they can justify it by some morsel of logic. Normal humans would never kill for pleasure. It takes a disturbed mind to experience pleasure by taking the life of any creature."

Bobby knew that. He remembered all too well the horror of taking a human life, even when it was necessary. One must be in a completely altered state of mind for it to happen.

For the rest of the trip, he shifted his thoughts to contemplate the reasons why a nation would go to war. He realized that somehow the "war on terror" is just a cover-up for something much bigger. Something, he could not figure out on his own. But, he knew the person who could make some sense of it. In that moment, he began to see the reason why his idea to enlist in the marines was met with such furious opposition.

"We are not at war. We are not spreading democracy in the world, only the seeds of hatred, by gutting other nation's cultures and economies on behalf of an ambiguous entity. As in many conflicts before, the reason is purely monetary." Remembering his father's lectures on history and economy, it gradually became obvious.

"No human conflict ever begun without the pressures of greed! Only the means and the scale of the conflicts have changed."

"Wow!" Bobby exhaled sharply as the idea dawned on him now, many years after he heard the words from his father. Bobby was not sure what else could be involved, so he forcefully cleared his mind. These were way too heavy subjects to ponder at this late hour.

He eased the Jeep onto the driveway of the cabin, slowly approaching in first gear. The light on the front porch was still lit. He could see light inside the house.

Someone passed the window and the door opened.

Bobby stopped the Wrangler and engaged the parking brake. He shut the engine off. Suddenly the mountain's silent solitude engulfed him. He could only hear faint noises from the woods, as the nightlife of nature was in full swing already. All kinds of critters, large and small, were hunting and being hunted.

The lamp on the porch cast a ring of light about twenty-five feet out, barely reaching the Jeep. When Bobby finally shut the lights off, it nearly disappeared in the dark.

Jeffrey stepped out onto the deck as he recognized Fred's vehicle. Janet did not tell him that Bobby was coming. But, who else could it be?

-Bobby? –he called out into the darkness.

The faint squeak of the Wrangler's door echoed from the line of trees surrounding the cabin as Bobby eased it open.

-Dad! –He shouted back and ran up to the porch to meet him.

They hugged each other in a manly fashion, tightly and swiftly, lest the others might catch them being soft. They quickly moved to arms length, as if to get a better view of each other.

-Let me see you! You've turned into a grown-man since I last saw you! –Jeff said with pride.

-You ain't bad, yourself. –Bobby replied, earning a frown with that expression.

-You're looking great Dad! –he corrected himself.

They were still holding each other's hands and shoulders when the door opened behind Jeff.

-Hey you guys! Won't you come in? It's getting chilly out there! –Janet's voice caused them to release one another even quicker then they hugged.

Janet noticed their reaction but kept it to herself.

-Janet! I believe you have met my son, Robert! –Jeffrey's pride rang clearly in his voice.

-Hello Robert! –she stepped outside to greet him with a smile that could melt an iceberg.

-Hi! Nice to see you again! –Bobby smiled back at the familiar face. There was something about the way she stood at his father's side, but Bobby had no time to get a better feel for it.

-Hey! Would someone introduce me already to young Mr. Clark? –Jon would not let them ignore his presence.

-Oh, yes. I'm sorry Jon! This is my son, Robert. –Jeff said stepping aside.

-This is Jonathan Doering, our intrepid "chauffeur"! –Jeff pointed at his new friend with a grin.

Although they have met briefly at Jeff's house, Jon and Bobby shook hands as if they had known each other for years.

-How's it going? –Bobby's tone made it clear that he expected an answer while grasping Jon's hand.

-So far so good! –Jon looked him in the eye and said the best thing he could, under the circumstances.

-Inside! All of you! –Janet ordered the boys, in a motherly, but indisputable manner.

The temperature already sunk below fifty degrees and it was expected to drop to the lowest of forties by dawn. The fireplace was ablaze, loaded with logs sitting atop a bed of coke. It provided plenty heat for the living room, but the rest of the house had to be heated by other means. In this case, by ducting hot air into the rooms from a gas furnace, located in the laundry room by the water heater flanked by a stack unit of washer/dryer.

In the cozy warmth of the house, they all began to feel the effect of this hectic day. It felt great to have a soothing drink at first, especially to Jon, but soon it turned into a dull numbness that sent them all to sleep.

The next morning, Janet was up by eight o'clock and began to make breakfast. As the smell of toast, bacon, sunny-side- up and freshly brewed coffee spread throughout the house Jeffrey and Jon awakened around the same time.

Jon decided to delay his appearance for breakfast, out of consideration, so Jeff and Janet could have some time alone. So, he quietly occupied one of the bathrooms.

-Good morning! – Jeff's voice pleasantly surprised Janet.

-Morning! –she said already smiling as she turned toward him.

Jeffrey stood on the bottom step of the stairs, staring at her. She was dressed in the same clothes she wore yesterday. It just dawned on Jeff that none of them had a single change of clothes due to their hasty departure.

He found her very sexy in casual clothing, and wondered why. Very odd thing, how anticipation can skew a man's perception.

-Is something wrong? –Janet asked, bringing him back to reality.

-Oh, no! I was just thinking that we'll need some new clothes very soon. Maybe today …-he answered, giving away part of his thoughts.

Janet instantly guessed the rest, as any woman with a little finesse, would.

-Indeed! –she agreed. –We had better get some winter clothes, if we want to survive up here. –she said pointing out the window.

Jeff stepped down into the kitchen and went straight to window.

-Holy smoke! Is that rime? –he said excitedly.

-Sure is! –Janet handed him a warm cup of coffee with just enough cream to make it drinkable without burning his lips.

-Awesome! –Jeff's response was meant to adore both, the frost covered world outside and the coffee as he reached for it. The warmth of the cup felt welcome to his cool hands. When he took the first sip, he noticed the dark-blond color of the coffee, exactly as he would have made it. Its flavor was perfectly balanced yet accentuated by the cream.

-No sugar? How did you know? –the surprises kept on coming.

-It seemed a logical choice for you. Now, come to eat before it gets cold! –Janet sat on the opposite side of the small table.

It felt like they had known each other for decades, like neighbors do, mostly by sight, without much knowledge of the other's true origins. That had to change. While eating the hearty breakfast that was needed to cover their high energy needs, their hands met from time to time. First it happened by accident, as they reached out simultaneously to get the salt. Then, while looking at each other, intentionally, to see how it feels. Within the last twenty-four hours they held hands and had been in close body-contact, but this was different. This touch had meaning.

With every word they shared the shrouds of mystery slowly began to retreat from their past.

Using a slice of bread, Jeff wiped his plate to a shine, making Janet smile, then stood up, gathered their dishes and rinsed them off in the sink.

-You wouldn't happen to put down the toilet seat after yourself, would you? –Janet asked teasingly, but sincerely.

-As a matter of fact, I would and I do! –Jeff declared without hesitation.

-Even if my reason for doing so might be judged selfish. –he added mysteriously.

-How is that? –he managed to arouse her curiosity.

-Well, to save time in case of an emergency...-he explained bursting into laughter just as Janet did.

-The all-serious Jeffrey Clark actually has a funny side! Fresh! –she noted aloud with approval.

Jon heard their laughter as he exited the bathroom. He headed straight to the kitchen, not wanting to miss the fun. As Jeffrey and Janet came into his view, descending on the stairs, he saw Janet step back, away from Jeff. Jon did not see that she just landed a quick peck on Jeff's cheek.

-That's the spirit! –Jon greeted them by clapping his hands applauding their joyful mood, causing a slight blush on their cheeks for no apparent reason.

-I love the sound of laughter in the morning! Not to mention the smell of bacon, eggs and coffffeee!! –Jon exaggerated the word to emphasize his delight.

-Morning Jon! –they welcomed him and his good-natured humor, as the blush vanished from their faces.

-Have you seen Bobby yet? –Jeff inquired casually.

-I have not, but I heard noises from the other bathroom. I assume he is up already. –Jon said taking his place at the table. Promptly, he began devouring his share of the servings. He dabbed pieces of toast into the yolk, emptying the center of both eggs. Then he cut the bacon and remaining egg whites into bite-size chunks, scooping each load into his mouth with pleasure.

-More toast? –Janet asked him as he shoved the last piece into his mouth.

-Uhm, hmm! –he nodded, lifting his coffee to flush some food.

Do we have any orange juice? –he asked, fully aware of the answer.

-Remember what we've got from the store last night? –Janet asked hinting that he should know.

-Just checking! –Jon smiled and buttered the fresh toast.

-Care for some milk instead? –Janet inquired reaching for the jug.

-That'd be nice! –Jon agreed holding out his empty coffee mug.

Jeffrey did not pay attention to all that. He was deep in his thoughts about how to save these wonderful people from the certainty of financial and moral ruin that is sure to result from their current situation. He could see no immediate solution to that matter. Maybe things will work out for the better, as they most often do.

Bobby stormed down the stairs just then, taking them by surprise. Happy as can be, he shouted a "Good morning" to no one in particular, and grabbed the coffee pot to pour himself a cup of Joe.

The others greeted him similarly, and Jeff gave him a pat on his back.

-We must make some arrangements if we are going to live up here. –Bobby said taking a seat at the table and opening the dialog in a level tone that contradicted his entrance.

Janet served him food straightaway, looking at the young man in awe. He seemed so serious for his age. Or, was it just the unusual circumstances that made him act this way? She wasn't sure.

-What do you have in mind? –Jon asked him to share his thoughts.

-Well, first of all, we need to check around the house to tally the supplies on hand. The bathrooms are fine. -Bobby began on a lighter note. –Anything in short supply should be replenished pronto. Then, we should inspect the perimeter for the possibility of a breach. –he turned their attention to their personal safety.

-What are you suggesting we do about that? –Jon pressed him for specifics.

Jeffrey watched his son and listened carefully to what he had to say. He could not discount Bobby's experience in the Marines that obviously kept him alive. As the immediate future was rather uncertain, they had to consider all options. Even though Jeffrey did not approve the involvement of guns, they could only hope that it would not come to that, if they did not have any.

-While you guys gather the most essentials, I'll drive over to Nevada and pick up whatever I need to make a basic electronic security system. –Bobby offered his skills to improve their safety.

When the phone rang, they all froze in place. After the fourth ring, the answering machine picked up the call. They heard Henry's voice over the speaker.

-Hey you guys! I'm glad you all made it safely! –he said before Jeff picked up the phone.

-Hello, Henry? –

-Hey Jeff! Good to see you my friend. –Henry replied.

-What do you mean it is "good to see me"? –Jeff asked him wondering as he put Henry on speakerphone for the rest of the gang to hear.

-I forgot to tell you before you left that I have had a decent security system installed in the cabin a few years back. – Henry explained.

-Does it work? –Jeff asked with concern. –'Cause it did not go off when we entered the place. –he completed his thought.

-Oh. But it did. Except it does not blare on site, instead, it signals here, at my place. I know you arrived at 11:45 PM and Bobby arrived at 12:22 AM. It's all on record too. I mean DVD! –he corrected himself with chuckle.

Bobby stepped forward to speak.

-Tell us more about it, 'cause I was about to go out and spend money on components to build one! –

-Well it is not too complicated. Look straight up in front of you. Do you see the crown molding? –Henry asked him.

-Yup. –Bobby replied.

-It is made of knotty pine for a reason and it is not only to match the style of the cabin. Somewhere in the middle, if you look closely, there is a small camera looking right at you. –Henry went on.

-I see it! –Bobby said excitedly. -Sweet! It's right there! –he pointed at a spot on the molding; they all followed the direction of his finger with their gaze. Bobby moved closer to have a better look.

-That thing is no bigger than a cell phone's camera! –he noted with enthusiasm.

Henry watched Bobby point straight into the lens, through the monitor of his security system at home.

-That's right. –he said and continued to explain the rest of the system.

They all sighed with relief having learned that it even included infrared sensors as a back up, which actually worked along side the main system. Now they could monitor their surroundings from the closet where the control panel is installed. Henry instructed them in the simple operation of it as well and then he said good-bye, adding that soon he will see them in person.

While Jeffrey, Janet and Jon checked the house for available supplies, Bobby inspected every single security camera and sensor to make sure they all functioned properly. Henry, of course, followed his every move smiling at how thorough he was. When he was done, Bobby went to the console and played back his own tour, unit to unit.

-Sweet. –he said aloud to himself as he was about to close the cabinet.

-I did not pay eighteen thousand for nothing! –he heard Henry's voice from the ceiling.

Bobby turned around and facing the nearest camera held up both of his thumbs to show his appreciation.

-You are the MAN, Henry D'Guard! –he said to an invisible mic, hidden somewhere.

-So are you, Robert! Take care! –he heard Henry's voice from the closet again before the speaker switched off.

-Well, we are looking good as far as household supplies are concerned. –Janet informed the men.

-So, all we need is food, drinks and more clothes. We have plenty of wood in the shed for the fireplace, but I think some coal or charcoal wouldn't hurt for longer lasting heat. –she concluded the assessment.

-Let's head out! –Jeffrey said eagerly and left the cabin in a hurry.

He pulled out the Yukon from the garage and parked it by the Wrangler.

A small, freestanding building is located behind the garage, one they have not yet entered. To answer Bobby's question about it, Jeff only hinted that it contained the fun stuff.

Bobby and Jon took the Jeep.

They winked at one another in acknowledgment that Janet and Jeff would be by themselves again. Besides, they all agreed that the four of them should not be seen together.

A few minutes later they rolled into town.

In an average small town, as the gas station clerk pointed out to Bobby last night, news travels fast.

But, everyone knows that Tahoe is not an ordinary town. For many decades, people came here to get away from the noise and attention of the world. Only recently did the town begin to open up. However, most people still preferred their seclusion and privacy to community living. That is why many attempts have failed to secure large parcels of land adjacent to one another. Some would by land here and later try to join it with their friend's only to be rejected by town planners. An ordinance that dates back to the early sixties, still prohibits building anything other than a single family dwelling on residential lots, the size of which is not limited in any way. Lots may range in size, but one would only find anything under an acre in areas developed after the eighties. This has been done to protect the natural beauty of the wilderness and the lake shore too.

Henry's property is located in one of the older sections; he bought it in '85 for eighty-five thousand dollars. The house, on the other hand, had cost him nearly four hundred thousand to complete.

It only takes ten scenic minutes to get into town; part of the Lake is visible from his porch and from the road as well. The road passes by a few boat launching ramps and piers providing excellent view to the lake.

Bobby first stopped to get propane for the grill. They picked up a five-gallon bottle that fits under the grill and a large one for the gas furnace. Next, as Jon suggested, they raided the sporting goods store.

They did not aim to be fashionable, although everything they bought cost top dollar in that store. Henry had sleeping bags stashed for a family of four, in one closet. He also kept basic camping gear on hand at all times.

Jeffrey and Janet bought casual clothes like underwear, socks, a few shirts and pants, plus jackets. They have not yet decided whether to bother with formal dressing. Then it was time to stock up on food.

The theme was healthy eating. Nuts, berries, honey, vegetables, fruits and fresh bread made the list. So did eggs, ham, a variety of cold cuts; fresh meat like pork chops, veal, steaks and even lamb. They've bought sliced cheeses for making sandwiches and solid ones to cube for wine-sipping in the evening. Beer and wine, of course!

Even the cashier noted that they must have just arrived, for buying so much at once. She also mentioned that they might miss out on some fun community events the way they stocked up.

Janet promised to check back with her about that, because they like a good party, any time.

The Yukon's rear sunk an inch after they loaded all the groceries. The temperature just rose above sixty-five at noon, so they did not have to worry about spoilage. A local coffee shop was not too far away, so they pulled into its parking lot. The flat-green Wrangler was already there, parked just a few spaces from their SUV.

They went inside. Bobby and Jon wore baseball caps now. Acting like two old buddies who haven't seen each other in years, they chatted about friends, family and sports. Inconspicuously, they kept an eye on their friends, who have just sat down.

Janet tied her hair into a bun that enhanced her perfectly proportioned neck and exposed her face.

Jeff had no time, nor any idea how to alter his image just yet. The waitress took their orders just a couple of minutes and fifteen feet apart, as they sat at the counter.

Since they had spent a small fortune already, they kept the orders small this time.

-Hey, its you! –Bobby heard a loud and somewhat familiar male voice call out to him. The man sat just a few feet away from his father, on his left, at the end of the counter.

-Did you find the Motel all right? —the man asked pointing in the general direction of the Motel.

-Yeah, thanks for the tip. —Bobby said, trying to keep the conversation as short as possible.

Jeffrey and Janet had also recognized the man now and began a personal conversation of their own, leaning closer to one another to exclude the world.

The waitress turned to the gas-station clerk with a simple question.

-Who's your friend, Danny? —nodding her head towards Bobby.

She was in her early to mid twenties and fairly good looking, as Bobby would describe her.

-Don't know his name; he arrived last night and stopped at the station. —Danny replied honestly. Bobby felt the eyes of the local folk's zero in on him, as he just became subject of their attention.

-Hey Danny! My name's Robert. Nice to make your acquaintance. —Bobby thought it better not to lie. Sooner or later, they would find out anyway.

-My roommate works at that Motel. He said no one checked in after midnight. —Danny pressed on with his inquisition, after nodding back at him.

-I've changed my mind. Is that alright? —Bobby's voice and manner changed to indicate his annoyance.

-Don't mind him. He is a good guy, but sometimes forgets his manners. Don't you Danny? —the waitress cut in, halting the clerk's inquiry.

-Yeah, whatever…- Danny's attention returned to his food.

-My name is Stacey —the waitress introduced herself.

Hi! I'm Robert.–Bobby smiled back at her as a way of saying thanks.

Janet went to the restroom, while Jeff quietly nibbled on the apple pie he ordered. The low hum of conversation returned as people picked up where they left off.

Bobby and Jon said good-bye to Stacey and waved at Danny leaving the coffee shop a little later.

Jeff also placed the money on the check and pushed it closer to the waitress. He stood up and moved to intercept Janet by the exit of the coffee shop.

Stacey collected their payment and looked after Bobby. She watched him get in the Jeep and drive off. Danny did not care one way or another. He was too wasted from working the night shift for weeks and heavily drinking with his roommate last night after getting off work.

-You believe that guy? What's his deal anyway? –Jon asked Bobby as they closed the doors of the Jeep.

-Don't know. But I guess we better be more careful around here. –Bobby looked at him.

-Maybe its' nothing, but last night he told me that strangers stick out in a small town. Then he described you guys in great detail because we all bought the local map. –Bobby recalled his exchange with Danny.

-'You think he might be a problem? –Jon's concern increased a notch.

-Can't really say. –Bobby's answer was not very reassuring.

The dark blue Yukon was only three cars behind them until Jeff pulled it into a gas station to fill up. Janet paid the operator inside, with cash. The Yukon had roughly a quarter tank of gas in it when Jeff started pumping. Sixty dollars, however, did not quite fill the tank to capacity. Jeff was very disappointed, as it would take fifteen dollars more to get it full.

He shook his head contemptuously when Janet got back to him.

-Look at this! – he said, -It's not even full! –showing her the gas gauge.

-I know; it is why many people, including me, buy only fifteen to twenty dollars worth, each time. –she offered a solution.

-How is that working for you? –Jeff inquired curiously.

-It may seem a bit inconvenient, but I no longer "invest" my money in a full tank of gas that I may not use for some time. Instead, I only buy what I need for the next few days. –she began to explain.

-So, you invest time instead, to get that little gas? –Jeff probed her logic.

-Well, as you know, many people are perfectly capable of planning their trips ahead of time, so it's no big deal. You get to keep your hard-earned money a little longer too. –she continued her reasoning.

-Not to mention the chance to test an old notion that fooled so many so long. The notion of "supply and demand". Let's say for sake of argument that fifty percent of a million people would begin to use this method to reduce their expenditure. –she became more excited by the minute as she went on.

-Let us also consider that a small number of people already do this without realizing. These folks keep their tanks full all the time by only replacing the gas they used up. You follow? –she asked Jeff, taking the driver seat.

-Yes. I mean no. I am coming with you. –Jeff replied to both meanings of the question, hopping into the passenger seat.

-Now, the immediate effect may not be clear, so let's see. Figure about six hundred thousand people only paying $20 each time for a partial fill, instead of $50-70. The money, going into the pockets of the gas stations and the fuel manufacturer is reduced by nearly two thirds. The station will not have to order fuel so frequently either. –Janet now held Jeffrey's full attention.

-Why? –Jeffrey asked testing her logic again.

-Take an even number of one hundred cars per day. Before high prices, they took twenty gallons each, totaling two thousand gallons. That is six thousand dollars at the cashier. With high prices, only forty cars take a full tank, that is eight hundred gallons, and sixty takes only six point six gallons totaling three ninety six. That is eleven hundred and ninety six gallons, a forty percent reduction in demand per day. –she concluded her calculations.

-What about people driving cross-country or have to commute farther? This theory does not work for them. It's impractical. –Jeff put in his two cents' worth.

-Are you being difficult? –Janet shot back, as this argument always got to her.

In her opinion only those people used it who intended to disprove a logical idea for whatever reason.

-No, but…–Jeff began to say only to be cut off by Janet's heated response.

-Like millions of others, I am a person of limited means. Until yesterday, I had a job that didn't pay much, but I thought by sticking with it I could make a difference one person at a time. Call me sentimental if you will. I can't change the world by myself, but I'm willing to do my part to help make it happen. So don't make me work overtime. –she dumped all that on Jeff in a single breath.

-Janet, all I wanted to say was…but they have no choice. –Jeff finished his sentence just before Janet took a hard right turn onto the road that leads to the cabin. He managed to grab the safety handle.

The engine roared and the tires squealed on the pavement just a bit. Then their sound changed to a swooshing low rumble as they transitioned to the hard-packed gravel driveway. Jon and Bobby, already waiting, turned sharply to look when they heard the sound. The Yukon strewn rocks and dirt wildly as it fishtailed up the hill. On the last thirty feet, the engine went silent and the vehicle gently came to rest a couple feet from the garage door.

A faint yet satisfied smile appeared on Janet's face as she shifted into park. Then the doors popped open and they both jumped out at once.

-Wow! Do you always drive like that when you're pissed? –Jeff demanded, catching Janet in his arms as she came around the SUV.

-Always! –she growled, wiggling in his arms to break free. Jeff would not let her go just yet.

-Let me go! –she continued to fight, lightning bolts flashing from her eyes.

-Don't let that fire burn us. It is why I like you so much! –Jeff whispered into her ear.

Jon put his hand on Bobby's shoulder to keep him from interfering. They could see the mood change as Janet stopped fighting back and looked Jeff straight in the eye.

-What did you say? –she could not help asking him to repeat the words.

-Don't let that…-Jeff began to repeat, but Janet cut him off.

-No, no! The second part? –she held his gaze firmly.

The answer was simple. Jeff felt the passion build within him for the last two days, but he could not find the words to express it until now.

-You are a very attractive woman, a breath of fresh air, even when you breathe fire like a dragon. I find you highly desirable, nevertheless.

I feel alive and happy just holding you in my arms! –he spoke softly, only for her ears.

Janet's resistance noticeably softened following his words. Jeff could feel her posture relax as the tension between them dissipated.

-I mean it. –he added looking into her eyes. Janet returned and held his gaze.

-I feel the same. -she said laying her head on his shoulder, as Jeff's arresting arms eased into an affectionate hug.

The sun continued on its path toward the western horizon, dragging its golden rays behind. They swept ever higher on the tall threes with a heavenly glow, creating a sharp contrast as darkness closely followed. Before they would disappear, they lit up the cirrus clouds in spectacular colors. First, they turned even brighter white, reflecting light like giant snowballs, as the rays were now aimed directly at them. Then, slowly they became bright yellow, deepening to orange and blood-orange accelerating through the remaining colors of the rainbow until fading into black.

With sunlight gone, the temperature took a nosedive they could all feel in their bones. Jon and Robert already went inside allowing Janet and Jeffrey a private moment to proceed as they saw fit.

Their emotions generated warmth that spread throughout their bodies making them impervious to the growing cold. After spending a few minutes alone in each other's arms, they finally dared to kiss.

It felt just right, even though it only lasted a few seconds. They swiftly searched each other's eyes and saw acceptance and encouragement. Their second kiss took far longer and overflowed with desire, as their lips locked together passionately exploring the taste and texture of the other. They sensed the desire grow in one another, but it had to wait.

-Let's go inside. The boys are waiting. –Janet gently slipped out of Jeff's arms.

Inside the cozy cabin, they filled the fridge and pantry with the groceries and then they sorted out and put away the other stuff.

Later, everyone helped to make a simple dinner. Jeff and Bobby prepared and baked potatoes to be mixed with sour cream, butter and chives. They put them on the grill's top rack, while Jon grilled sirloin steaks on the lower one, marinated with his own recipe. Janet washed and cut fresh veggies for dipping as well as to steam. Jon and Bobby were sipping beer despite the weather, while watching over the grill, Jeff snuck back inside, beer in hand, to help Janet wrap the veggies in foil. She also made a dip from canned beans, sour cream, lemon juice and improvised a mild spice mix. The scent of the grill carried faraway in the cool evening air. Aromatic smoke of fire logs, drifting from neighboring chimneys, blended with it to create a strange impression. One belonged to the approaching winter season; the other to a lazy summer night. But, they all went entirely unnoticed since the neighbors were either at restaurants or other events, or simply enjoyed themselves in the safety of their homes after dark.

Jon and Bobby smiled, winked or poked at each other every time they noticed how Jeff and Janet would windup next to each other, regardless of what they were doing. They saw them earlier when they wrapped the veggies for the grill and as Jeff mixed the dip under Janet's close supervision. Then they watched them circle the table and each other as they placed the tableware for four. When Bobby and Jon finally brought in the food from the grill, there they were, elbow to elbow, dicing cheese and uncorking the wine for the leisurely chitchat after dinner.

Dinner went by smoothly and quietly since none of them felt like talking much. Although Janet volunteered to clear the table, the men jumped to help. As they figured, that way they could all sit down in the living room together.

Settled in their seats in a lofty mood, they talked about many things. Personal memories from long ago, family events that were happy or sad and other stories about friends or people they knew, all came up. They made a conscious effort to avoid political topics which is why they kept the TV turned off.

They did not want its background noise of subliminal messages.

Earlier, while grilling the food outside, Jon asked if Bobby would care to go out later to explore the nightlife in town. He liked the idea, so they left the house together around ten PM.

Alone at last, Jeff put his arms around Janet's waist from behind as soon the door closed behind the boys. He burrowed his face into her neck, taking deep breaths to memorize the sent of her skin. She leaned her head against his and held his hands to keep him from taking them away. They stood there for a while soaking up all the pleasure this moment had to offer. Their desire for the other had finally spilled over the self-restraint they obeyed until now. They quickly turned to face one another. After a ferocious kiss, they began to move toward the bedroom, playfully wrestling. Pushing and pulling one another up the stairs, peeling pieces of clothing off the other as they went. They were practically naked by the time they reached the bed. They kissed continually and wildly, only separating to catch their breath. Even in those brief moments of gasping for air, they continued to explore the other's body with their hands. Firm grips turned to gentle caressing by fingertips. Jeff slowly slid his left hand down Janet's right side, feeling every rib on the way, pressing gently into her side, stopping for a split second, then continuing over the ridge of her hipbone, his fingers followed the curve of her buttocks and stopped on her sacrum. Jeff felt goose bumps forming in the wake of his touch. Janet returned the favor by running her fingers down his spine, gently pressing her nails into his skin, making him arc his back. She slipped her hand lightly around his hips to the front. There she playfully encircled his bellybutton, and kept moving down, inch by inch…

As one might dare to imagine, things got out of hand at that point; so to speak.

Completely spent, laying side by side, they fell asleep just after eleven. It was the best kind of sleep one could ask for, serene and healing, devoid of dreams. That kind of healing begins by the soul reaching a state of true peace. That message is gradually carried to every cell of the body and a miracle takes place. The body rejuvenates itself by rebuilding old, worn out cells into new ones.

Bobby and Jon were having a good time in the local club. The music was great; the mood was fantastic.

The crowd swallowed them whole upon entering the joint. The people there seemed to know everybody. They freely engaged in conversation with anyone or invited them for a drink or dance. Thus, the boys were soon separated by strangers, who treated them as old buddies. Jon had not been out for years, which is why he felt a bit out of place. His shyness rapidly evaporated as he too was forced to mingle.

The crowd consisted of a reasonable mix of age groups, for such a place. Cautiously edging through tightly packed bodies, Jon managed to reach the bar.

A woman of mid-thirties tended this section of the bar, quite expertly, as far as Jon could tell. She moved about very efficiently. Jon watched her reach for bottle after bottle without looking; obviously she had memorized the exact location of every brand. After completing her current orders, she replaced each bottle to its original spot. In bars, such as this island-type, liquor bottles are usually set up in repeating groups. The groups are separated by racks of snacks, a coffee maker or a cash register. She was slowly approaching Jon, taking orders and filling them one by one. She checked left and right to note new customers waiting for their turn. After serving three bottles of beer to a man, she came right over to Jon.

-Have you been waiting long? –she asked with a genuine smile.

Jon watched her smiling at others as she served them, but not quite like this. He was flattered.

-Not at all. How're you doing? –Jon returned her smile.

-Busy. What can I get you? –she got to the point.

-Jack, straight up. –Jon specified without further ado.

She turned left about forty-five degrees and reached out behind her to get the fourth bottle from the second row. Her right hand produced a shot glass at the same time. The two objects smoothly met on the counter in front of Jon. She slid the shot glass full of J.D. forward and the bottle landed on the shelf.

-Five seventy-five. –she stated the price with a smile equally warm as the first one.

Jon, being a pragmatic man, pulled eight bucks from his valet and laid it on the counter.

-Thanks. —the bartender retrieved the bills and made change for herself.

A fleeting glance is all they shared after that. She moved on to the next customer and Jon casually observed the rhythmic pulsing of the crowd. Minutes later, three women emerged from the shapeless mass. One of them wedged in next to Jon to place their order. Jon saluted her by raising his J.D. and she replied in kind. Small talk ensued and after brief introductions, she invited Jon to join them. He could barely catch her name even though she stood next to him, the names of her friends got lost in the din.

They exchanged some information about one another, but Jon skillfully eluded all inquiries about where, with whom and how long was he staying. The point of their outing was to enjoy the evening, so they refrained from prying. Jon danced with all three ladies politely as a gentleman, but spent the most time with the lady whose name is Claire.

At the end of the night they said good-bye, but agreed to meet again.

Bobby made a connection a lot faster. He did not even make it to the bar before a group of guys and gals, roughly his age, scooped him up. One of the girls deliberately bumped into him, but the guys in her group did not mind as she was flying solo. The girl was Stacey from the coffee shop.

-Sorry, I didn't see you there! —she said, pretending to be surprised, after bumping into him.
    -Hey Stacey! How are you? —Bobby greeted her, unsuspectingly.

He was relieved by this coincidence because it saved him the trouble of finding a girl to hit on while making sure he was not trespassing. He also found Stacey a fitting partner for the night.

-I'm great. What are you doing here? —she asked.
    -Fishing. —Bobby blurted out carelessly.
    -Without a bait? —Stacey asked curiously with an impish smile, while glancing at his flies.

-I'm not here to get laid. Just want to have some fun. –Bobby clarified his intentions, quickly checking his zipper.

-My bad. –Stacey's smile vanished in an instant.

-Oh no, that was very funny… -Bobby reassured her, finally cracking a smile. –Can I get you a drink? –he offered.

-Sure. –Stacey accepted and followed him to the bar.

The crowd undulated like fluid, so they moved with its waves, turning carefully to avoid its current, lest they might be separated. The music was so loud, it limited all conversations to the essentials mostly. After sharing a few bits of information about one another, while sipping their drinks, Bobby and Stacey danced to a couple of tunes they both liked. Bobby learned that Stacey is a local girl who lives here year around. She works in the coffee shop six days a week. They open at seven in the morning and close at ten pm, but she only works eight-hour shifts. It pays her bills, but she has a hard time saving any money. Bobby told her about himself only that he was in town, visiting friends, and he'll be leaving in a couple of days, back to L.A.

They too said good-bye with a promise to meet again.

The Jeep turned white again as the chill of the night swept over it. The small amount of humidity in the air was just enough to form a thin layer of velvety, sparkling ice on its surface.

Jon and Bobby enjoyed the cool weather, since they rarely got to see their own breath in L.A. Jon ran his hand over the top, stroking the cool crystals with pleasure. Bobby started the engine, and then they quickly closed the doors, waiting for the heater to kick in.

-It's not even winter yet! –Jon commented with a sense of things to come, fogging the windshield wit his breath.

-It will be a lot worse then. -Bobby said redirecting the flow of warm air to the windshield and their feet.

The road was slick here and there, but Bobby handled the Jeep expertly. The trees, shrubs and driveway glistened in the beam of headlights as they approached the house. Bobby turned off the engine and they both jumped out. They slammed the doors shut, and listened to the crackling of the cooling exhaust pipe.

By one AM they were fast asleep.

The night seemed to have gone by in a blink of an eye. Janet was first in the kitchen once again.

She walked by the closed doors of Jon and Bobby quietly when she came downstairs. Janet had no idea when they got home, but she wished they have had some fun.

The morning passed as it did the day before. Jeffrey came down as soon as the smell of coffee reached him by way of the heating ducts. They barely had time greet one another before Bobby and Jon came in, disrupting their privacy. They ate breakfast together, while the boys told them about the club and the women they've met. After breakfast, they cleaned up the kitchen as a team.

They turned on the television to get an idea about their status, but the news did not carry their story any more. Some folks say "new wonders last but three days", then they become common-place.

-Ya see? –Jon asked feeling justified for not being overly concerned. –No one gives a rat's ass about what happens to us.

-That's what worries me. When the media drops a story that fast, they've been ordered to drop it. –Jeff countered with unease.

-We should get the local paper, or the L.A. Times to see if they followed up on the story. –Bobby suggested.

-Today's Saturday; which means my boss is off work. I want to call her from a landline to see what she says. If we can find one in this area. –Janet offered.

-Bobby! You and I are now a hunting party. Not for real, just to round up four Walkie-Talkies, in case we get separated. –Jon suggested as the next step.

-Sounds like a plan! –Bobby concurred. –Let's head into town and see what they've got! –he declared enthusiastically.

-Okay, you guys do that. Janet and I are going to try and find a landline within fifty-mile radius. See you back here before dark. –Jeff stood up, ready for action.

This time Jeffrey drove the big, clumsy SUV. He did not care for such a huge vehicle, but for now, this is what they had. Leaving the driveway, he turned north toward Nevada.

Since he still had a slight hangover, Bobby decided to ride shotgun, giving Jon the opportunity to get a feel for the Jeep. Their first stop was the sporting goods store. The sales person recognized them as they entered.

-Nice clothes for hunting! –he pointed at their attire they bought here just the other day.
-Right! –Jon pointed at him in a friendly gesture, treating the man with one of his fetching smiles.
-Say, do you have any two-way radios with a decent range? –Bobby got to the point right away.
-Well, let's see what we've got. –with a hand signal to follow, the man led them to a display case.
He retrieved the keys from the pocket of his uniform and opened the sliding glass door of the display.
-We have three fairly good ones here with ranges up to two, five and ten miles, respectively. –he started to explain reaching for the first one. To save time, Bobby gave a couple of "must have" parameters to narrow the search. The radios must have a range up to twenty-five miles regardless of terrain and handle most frequencies. The salesman apologized for not having anything close to that. To have a few words in private, he took Bobby and Jon into a blind spot of the security cameras. He had been verbally, yet formally, instructed not to offer any information that was not related to the store. He took a gamble.

-Look, I can see you have a dire need for something I can't provide here. A dear friend of mine, on the west shore of the lake, knows a great deal about radios. He might be able to fix you up with something...- –he spoke quickly and anxiously. His hands slightly shaking, he jotted down his friend's name and address with simple directions on a small note pad. He handed it to Jon, who slipped it into his pocket.
-Tell him Harvey sent you. –
Then, he walked back to the floor to assist other customers.

CHAPTER 3

Jeffrey and Janet entered Carson City, Nevada, just over an hour. Jeff took his time and made the drive as scenic as he could without holding up traffic or drawing attention. There, they have found a large retail store that still had a single working payphone, near its main entrance. A rare find these days, as phone companies have been slowly getting rid of, "phasing-out" as they call it, "unprofitable" phones for at least a decade, maybe longer.

God forbid, you forget to take your cell phone, and have an emergency!

-Wow! That is a rare sight! You don't think about it, but when you need a pay phone, good luck finding one. –Janet observed.

-The number of public phones dropped from over two million to just around two hundred thousand nationwide, the last eight years or so. But now, the disappearance of public phones is a worldwide phenomenon. –Jeff shared the relevant part of a report he recently read.

-To find one that actually accepts coins is even harder. –Janet

-Well, I can explain that too. To eavesdrop on calls made from public phones is illegal and they are more or less anonymous when the caller pays with coins. –Jeff began his theory as they walked toward the phone.

-Due to the alleged "terrorists" out there, authorities want to know who's calling who. "Security" cameras have been installed to monitor people in corporate parking lots, like this one. –he continued.

–Just look up there, –he pointed at a light-pole, -that camera seems to be aimed at the entrance, but believe you me, that phone is well within its field of view. It is there "for your safety" or "to prevent vandalism". –Jeff explained.

-I never thought of it that way. –Janet admitted being one who ignore this obvious invasion of privacy.

-Have you seen the movie Phone Boot?- Jeff asked her, momentarily stopping. - The one with Collin Farrell? - she asked, then quickly added, - No, but I've heard about it.

-Well, you might wish to watch it. It's an interesting film, to say the least, and its story line plays out in and around the last functioning phone boot in New York in 2002. Hence its title. - Jeffrey suggested

They've crossed the driveway separating the parking area from the building and arrived at the phone.

–Look, this one still takes coins. –Janet smiled at Jeff with hope.

-Lucky for us. –he smiled back at her. –Make the call quick, please. –he squeezed her shoulders as she moved in to dial the number.

While Janet was speaking with Katherine King, in L. A., about their situation, both in L. A. and in general, Jeffrey went into the store to ask for a phone book. He looked up a couple of used-car dealers and asked the clerk for directions to them. Both were within a couple miles, just up the main road. He rejoined Janet at the phone and they headed back to the SUV. Janet informed him about the search at his home and that Mrs. King had been questioned by the FBI regarding their whereabouts. Naturally, she had nothing useful to tell them. But, because her boss placed her and Jon on administrative leave, Janet said that she won't be calling her anytime soon.

Janet stopped reciting the call, when Jeffrey pulled into a used-car lot.

-What are we doing here? –she asked.

-Since we are not going anywhere backcountry, I want to get rid of this over-sized gas-guzzler. I'd like to get something more efficient, reliable and perhaps civilized. –Jeffrey answered.

-Ookay. –Janet acknowledged with some concern.

Jeff did not have the faintest idea of what he was looking for, and this dealer had nothing that impressed him. Driving up to the other dealership, however, an elegant Volvo XC90 caught his eye from a distance. He parked the Yukon on the street and, hand in hand, they stepped onto the lot. Janet saw a number of fine vehicles, but she realized that almost all had points that worked against them, especially for their needs. Besides, Jeff took off straight toward that Volvo. Janet followed him curiously.

They checked the mid-size SUV top to bottom; tires, rims, body, windows and lights and found everything in near mint condition. Jeff looked under it to make sure there were no visible leaks on the ground, even though he knew used cars are cleaned up daily.

-Can I help you find anything? –a sales person interrupted their inspection of the vehicle.

-Hello there! –Jeff stood up to face the man.

-My name is Garry. –the salesman introduced himself.

-How nice to meet you! Could we take out this Volvo for a test drive? –Jeff side railed a sales pitch.

-Of course Ya can. –the sales person replied.

-The doors are open, if you'd like to check the interior while I get the keys. -with that Garry went back to the office. Janet and Jeff looked at as much as they could within the two minutes it took the sales person to return.

The Volvo was impeccably clean. It had no stains, no smell of cigarette smoke or pets, and no damage.

Janet knew it was not going to be cheap, because, at just over two years old, this vehicle must still have a few years' worth of factory warranty in effect. And the ridiculously low mileage, is that a mistake?

-Here are the keys, sir. –said Garry, holding them out for Jeff.

-All I need from you is a copy of your driver license before you can take her out. –he looked Jeffrey directly in the eye. Jeff was ready for this possibility. He extended his right hand as if for a handshake.

-Will you take this for an ID? It's got my favorite picture on it! –Jeff smiled at his own joke.

Garry hesitated for a split second, but then reached out to shake Jeff's hand, and whatever was in it.

-I'm going to take her around the block once. Be back in less than five minutes. –Jeff promised.

-I'll be waiting! –the salesman warned, feeling that more than one bill landed in his hand.

-There is a blue GMC Yukon by the curb. The keys are in it. Consider it a part of our deal, as trade-in. –Jeff offered his vehicle in exchange.

-Will do. –Garry replied with a official smile, sensing a quick sale.

The salesman was waiting by the Yukon as he promised. With years of experience, it did not take him long to appraise the vehicle's worth. The two hundred-dollar bills in his pocket where damn near his daily pay, which made him very pleased, for the time being mid-day.

As soon as he saw the Volvo come around the corner he started fidgeting.

The question on Janet's mind was how to avoid putting their name on the paperwork. Jeff told her that, somehow, he is going to persuade the salesman to tweak the documents.

The Volvo actually drove, as it should, like a brand new one. Seventeen thousand miles made absolutely no difference since the day it rolled off the assembly line, in Sweden. It handled absolutely stable on the road, with precise steering and road-feel. Its interior is quiet and comfortable, with heated seats. It comes with all the safety equipment that make Volvos so famous.

It even retained some of that "new-car" smell that makes so many people willingly commit to many years of debt.

-Ah, that "new-car" smell! I love it! –Janet exclaimed with pleasure when they first got in it.

-Me too! It makes you feel proud and happy; despite the financial burden it foretells. –Jeff agreed.

-Look! He is waiting for us on the street. –Janet pointed ahead as they turned corner.

-He must be hard-pressed to sell! –Jeff speculated.

He pulled up behind the Yukon. Garry nodded with a smile, but remained close to the curb.

-How do you like her? –he asked as soon as they were in hearing distance.

-We like her just fine. –Jeff replied coming around the Volvo.

-The Yukon looks neat for being nearly five years old. Low miles, clean in and out, no leaks. –Garry noted a few quick facts about it.

-And it drives like a charm. –Jeff couldn't resist adding.

-No doubt. –Garry agreed, but quickly continued: - Unfortunately, I have a bit of bad news.- he said, instantly causing Jeff and Janet become alert, almost alarmed.

-My boss told me, after you pulled out of our lot, that the XC90 has been spoken for this morning, right after we opened for business, he simply forgot to mark it accordingly. My bad. -Garry informed them about his mistake. Despite the minor setback, Garry was in luck and being a seasoned salesman, he moved to make an equally appealing offer.

-No need for concern, we might just be able to fix you up with a vehicle that too might fit your needs. -he said, hoping his prospective customers were not turned off.

-Well, what is it? - Jeff and Janet asked him almost simultaneously.

-Please follow me. - Garry turned to lead the way.

He was heading toward the opposing corner of the lot, the view of which was obstructed by their office building.

There, he led Jeffrey and Janet to another Volvo SUV, a light slate-gray XC70.

Only a few months older, with almost twice the mileage of the XC90, at 30,000 miles on its ODO meter, looked equally clean on the outside. Right of the bat, they noticed its price tag that was listing this vehicle several thousand less. Now, considering a fact that did not elude either Jeffrey or Janet as they walked through the lot, this Volvo XC70 was shaping up to become their new ride. Most other cars and SUV-s were either too small and powerless, or just as large, yet powerful, as the Yukon they were about trade in. In addition to that, the color of paint-jobs of nearly all other vehicles were objectionable as they would screamingly stand out in any natural backdrop.

After a thorough inspection, inside and out, with Garry's help, and the fairly unnecessary test-drive, for which Garry asked to tag-along, they made up their minds already.

During the test drive, Garry drew an expert comparison between the XC70 and the XC90. He listed all the selling points in order of importance, as he thought they might apply to his buyers' needs. Garry was not only an expert of his chosen profession, but also a pretty good judge of character. He explained to Jeffrey, primarily, all the power and fuel related points, while addressing the comfort and safety features, to satisfy Janet's perceived interests, alternating his attention between them. He pointed out that the XC70 is powered by, practically, the same engine and transmission combination as the XC90, which means they both produce about the same horse-power and torque. The difference in gas-mileage is, unfortunately, negligible, only favoring the XC70 by one mile/gallon, in both city and highway driving. Here, Garry mentioned the fact that the XC70 is significantly lighter, at 1.5 tons, than the XC90 weighing in at over 2.0 tons. This alone, said Garry, should have given the XC70 an even better gas mileage, so one must wonder: "What happened?", as he put it. Combining the lighter weight with the XC70's lower profile, one might reasonably expect it to give 20 miles to a gallon of fuel in city driving, and better than 25 miles on highway. After brief pause, perhaps to allow that to sink in, he went on. The XC70 has tighter turn radius, by a couple of inches, perhaps owing to its slightly shorter wheelbase. The XC70 offers slightly less over-all room, mainly because it's built lower than the XC90. Garry did not feel the need to mention safety features in great detail, because most people are familiar with Volvo's reputation on that point. He only pointed at some of the markings inside the cab, showing the abundance of airbags all Volvos now feature as standard equipment. Finally, as they were already heading toward the dealership, he quickly mentioned one fact that remains out of sight for most car- buyers, unless they take the time to read the entire vehicle information sheet. The fact is, Garry continued his account, that many formerly national automakers around the world have been acquired by China over the years. Both Volvo and GMC ended up on that list. Americans continuing to argue for buying "American", should educate themselves of that reality!

Garry decided to close his assessment with a reassuring thought
-As for this XC70, and even that XC90, I can confidently say that they were both manufactured in Sweden, and imported to America before the Chinese acquired Volvo and began to have any influence on their products.- he said, and opened the door to exit.

Before he did exit the vehicle, he quickly informed Jeffrey and Janet, in case they did not realize that he maybe under an unofficial gag-order regarding certain topics, to keep the political commentary he made to themselves.

-Most certainly!- they assured him of their confidence.

-Sooo, are you ready to make an offer on what I'd consider to be the deal of the day?

-I think we are. –Jeff glanced at Janet and they nodded in agreement.

-Please, follow me. –Garry turned to lead the way to his desk.

They walked along the outer edge of the sidewalk. Janet squeezed Jeffrey's hand noting the odd behavior of the salesman. When they got to a point where the distance between them and the office was the shortest, Garry made a right-angle turn toward the building. He ignored the entrance that was facing the lot. Turning right at the rear corner he opened the emergency exit with a key. He escorted Jeff and Janet into a small room, right by the backdoor.

-Have a seat. –he offered as he closed the door behind them.

-What are you asking for the Volvo? –Jeff inquired, ready to make his offer. Garry stared at him and Janet for a few seconds before responding.

-Mr. Clark, you put a lot of faith in your fellow men by walking around in the world like this. –he said suddenly, pointing at the two of them.

Jeff stood up instantly, hearing his name, and so did Janet, but Garry stop them.

-Please, sit down. I don't wish to sound like some Insurance Agency, or MSM Network outlet, but I want you to know, I'm on your side, for real.- he paused momentarily, only to add with some concern and excitement, - Hell, I'm surprised you made it this far without help! –

-What do you mean? –Jeff asked nervously.

-look, Mr. Clark; I know that you, - he pointed at both of them, - are not criminals by any stretch of the imagination. But my advice is this: Never react when you hear your own names. Might be better off using aliases. –Garry sat down so he would not seem imposing to them.

Nevertheless, Jeffrey's spine stiffened and the hair on his neck stood up hearing his name from a stranger he'd never met before. They slowly lowered themselves into their seats again.

-I recognized you the instant I saw you Mr. Clark. Your face and the faces of your accomplices, were flashed allover the news last week. –Garry continued.

They began to wonder just how many other people might have recognized them along the way.

-So, does this mean the deal is off? –Jeff asked, partly expecting rejection.

-No Sir. It only means that we're going to do it the exotic way. – the word Garry used from the financial sector, used to describe high-risk products that yielded the highest profits, until 2008, surprised them.

-We are all ears! –said Janet anxiously.

-I know that simply saying this is never enough to gain a person's trust, but I am gong to say it anyway. You are a good man, Mr. Clark. I read about your symposiums and a person who dares to speak the truth is a hero in my book. That's what you are. The hero of the people. –Garry began his bonding.

-Understandably, you and Mrs. Carter are anxious to get out of here. Let me assure you, if I wanted to turn you in, you'd be sitting in a patrol car by now. I think, the ransom they offered for each of you is an insult! –he said with a smile. – Only a bum on the street would be inclined to rat you out for that much. –

-I hope you're right! –Jeff expressed his concern.

-But they don't watch television, now do they? –Garry pointed out reassuringly.

Janet could not help, but step in. She had enough of this jolly dialogue; she viewed it as a waste of time.

-Garry! May I call you by your first name? –she asked.

-Please do, Mrs. Carter. Since I haven't told you my last name…- Garry agreed.

-If there is a deal on the horizon, let's get to it. If not, so be it. Either way, we must be on our way! –she pressed him to proceed in a voice that left no doubt about her feelings of the situation.

She squeezed Jeff's arm to induce a nod.

-Let's talk about the deal! –he said firmly.

-All right. –Garry agreed, clearing his throat.

-Here's the deal. The Yukon is worth about 16K, the Volvo's around 26. If you have five thousand in cash, I'll hand you the keys and registration for the Volvo right now. Assuming you have your own insurance. –Garry laid out part of it.

-So, you won't give us the title? –Janet inquired within the brief pause.

- The answer is simple, Mrs. Carter. I presume the Yukon is not officially yours, so, regardless of how you acquired it, you'd want to get rid of it. You'll be receiving the Volvo as a loaner from a "friend". See the young man sitting in the front office? He is my nephew and he will "lend" you "his" Volvo with a note. It is still legal for people to lend what they want to people they trust, isn't it? –Garry explained further.

-Fascinating! –Jeffrey noted.

-Indeed. This way the two vehicles will not be linked by paperwork. The Volvo's fate rests with you. On our end, it will be written off as a total loss. In case you're wondering what the 5K will pay for is my connections at the DMV and the Insurance Company. –Garry finished his explanation of the deal.

-Well, that sounds like a small gold mine for you Mr....Garry! –Janet took a deep breath after digesting that pitch.

-May I remind you Mrs. Carter, that I am a businessman. I hope you don't mind me protecting you in the process. – Garry replied with a slight edge in his voice.

Naturally, they did not mind at all. The deal Garry offered was far more humanitarian and friendly in nature than financial, and they also realized that Garry personally assumes a sizable risk maneuvering this deal to completion.

Jeff stood up now and Janet followed his action instinctively.

-Thank you, Garry. Yours is a fair deal, indeed. No paper trail, no implications. If we get pulled over for any reason, we'll have your nephew's "loaner note" to pacify the cops. –Jeffrey summarized the deal.

Garry also rose from behind his desk and took Jeffrey's extended hand to seal the deal.

-Let me make a couple of phone calls to my people, and then I'd like to invite you for lunch, while we wait for the paperwork to arrive. –Garry offered.

He opened the other door and let them out into the main office.

-Steve! Get some coffee for our valued customers! –he ordered the young fellow, who just got off the phone.

-Sure thing, Garry! –Steve jumped to his feet, ready to execute the task.

-I'll be back in few minutes, have a seat, please. –Garry pointed at a comfy-looking couch. Then he disappeared in his office.

Steve asked Jeff how would they like their coffees made and served them accordingly. A young woman in her early thirties looked busy at the far desk, yet she kept glancing at them every few seconds. Jeffrey and Janet couldn't help notice her curiosity and it made them somewhat uneasy. She got up from her desk and filed some documents in a cabinet marked "payments receivable". Then she turned around and came straight over to them.

-Please excuse my being direct, but are you Mr. Clark? –she asked with such a warm smile that rivaled Janet's best.

-Yes, I am. –Jeff replied with some uncertainty in his voice.

-Mr. Clark from UCLA? –she narrowed her inquiry.

-Yes. -Jeff replied again, now with a bit of curiosity.

-My name is Erin Sanders. Four years ago I took history classes for my sociology major at UCLA. –the young woman introduced herself.

Jeff crinkled his forehead as he attempted to recall that time, but failed to remember her face in any of his classes.

-Nice to meet you, again. –he said finally. –This is quite different from your intended course. What happened? –he asked, referring to her current line of work.

-Originally, I aimed for a government job, but having learned the real applications of such studies, I got disillusioned. My hopes of improving the social fabric on a large scale evaporated quickly when I realized that governments are not in the business of improving people's lives. –

-That is a serious conclusion for a young lady that you are. –

-I;ve learned from the master ... -she replied pointing at Jeffrey approvingly.

-But, I hope, I am not the source of your disappointment. –

-Not at all. You just helped me complete the puzzle. It's not your fault that the true picture is not what people would want to see. And, you are right, Mr. Clark. Everybody should be aware of it. –Erin replied.

The door of Garry's office opened and he came out holding up both thumbs to indicate success.

-We are almost there. The Volvo is now under Steve's name and is insured. Both documents are due to arrive within the hour. –he declared triumphantly.

Knowing his uncle well enough, Steve looked at him funny.

-Steve! Sit down and write a note to Mr. Clark, in which you loan your Volvo SUV to him, a longtime friend, for as long as he needs it. Include all pertinent info and date it retroactively, say about two weeks ago. Then sign it. –Garry instructed him briskly.

Steve began typing rapidly and produced the requested document within a few minutes. Erin returned to her tasks, and Garry took Janet and Jeff out for lunch.

The trip, to Harvey's friend's home, took nearly forty minutes. Bobby called him twenty minutes earlier to announce their arrival, but Frank Stillwater was not there when they arrived. His home, a simple log cabin, was less than half the size of Henry's, where Bobby and Jon were staying. The garage attached to the house by way of the laundry room. The clothes-dryer's exhaust was located under the single window, and it was spewing an immense cloud of moisture.

Jon parked the Jeep so that it would not block the way to the garage. It appeared that Mr. Stillwater was in the habit of pulling in there every time. In fact, it seemed, the front door has not been opened for a number of years. The cabin stood about one hundred yards from the main road, in the middle of a man made clearing atop a small plateau.

They got out of the Jeep and approached the front of the house.

-See that? –Bobby pointed at the cloud of moister rising from the dryer vent.

-Yup. He mustn't be far away. –answered Jon.

They carefully weaved thru the clutter that covered the porch and knocked on the door. Nothing happened. They rattled the door, trying to open it, but no one responded to the racket.

-Didn't he say he was home? –Bobby asked in a disappointed tone.

-He sure did. –

-Then where is he? –

-Beats me. –

-Let's look around. –Bobby suggested.

They headed in opposite directions. Bobby rounded the place towards the garage to the left. He put his face to the window and shielded his eyes with his hands, but he was unable to see anything in the dark. In fact, the glass appeared to be painted black on the inside. He tried to open the side door, but that too was locked.

Light wind rustled the under growth, twirling the leaves in front of the cabin that fell from the single oak tree at its side. Jon followed the porch that wrapped around the cabin's right side, all the way to the back. There, it widened to about twelve feet, affording room for a bench, a coffee table of sort, made from a stump and a slab of stone and a couple of roughly hewn chairs. A six-foot wide French door provided access to the porch here, from what seemed like a living room, but it too was locked. In the middle of the deck, a four feet wide stair, consisting of six steps, led to the backyard. The wilderness began just beyond the grassy yard, roughly thirty yards away. Low shrubs edged the woods, providing a natural fence. Trees grew sparsely and, aside from the shrubs, allowed fair visibility to about a hundred yards out. The terrain gently rose to the right for less than a quarter of a mile where a bald rock formation towered over it, a thousand feet high. The slope continued downward on the left, offering a breathtaking view of a valley bordered by more jagged mountains a few miles away. A tree lined creek cut across the valley, flowing to who-knows-where. A two-lane bridge spanned its canal that Jon recognized, as they have crossed over it on the way here.

Bobby came around the garage and trotted straight up to the deck, next to Jon.

-What do you think… –he began to ask Bobby.

-Magnificent view! –Bobby replied too soon.

-...about the place? —Jon finished his question.

-Oh, that! It is a well chosen location, easily defendable. The mountains offer natural protection here, except from the air. —Bobby summarized his observations, pointing at the high rocks on the right.

-The house sits on raised concrete foundation; it might even have a cellar. —he added.

The low rumble of an engine and tires crushing rocks on the gravel driveway echoed in the tree line. They walked to the front swiftly, not wanting to offend the owner by trespassing. They saw a station wagon approach the house and pulled right up next to their Jeep.

-Hello! —a sturdy, but well proportioned, middle-aged Native American woman greeted them.

-I am Ana, Frank's sister. Have you been waiting long? —she asked as she came up the stairs, searching in her bag.

-Not more than five minutes. I'm Bobby and this is my friend, Jon. Nice to meet you. —Bobby stepped forward extending his right hand in greeting. Ana stopped and raised her own right hand in response. Bobby, realizing his oversight, withdrew his hand and raised it in a similar fashion.

-Frank asked me to greet you here and to apologize for him being late. He had to get a few more things to make what you need. —Ana conveyed his brother's message.

-Would you like something to drink while you wait? —

- No thanks, we're all good. —Jon replied looking at Bobby, who nodded in agreement.

The interior of the house seemed normal, clean and tidy. As Bobby and Jon learned from Ana, she's been taking care of it since Frank's wife passed away, five years ago. According to Ana, Frank cherished his seclusion and has no plans to remarry, although he is a handsome man and physically fit. At the age of sixty, he regularly rides his bike, he hikes and in the winter he enjoys skiing. Several times a week, he works out in the back of his garage. He's never been seen by a doctor for anything other than his flesh wounds during the Vietnam War and he occasionally visits a dentist for cleaning. Ana admitted that, by the new standards of society, Frank has one bad habit. He smokes a pipe every now and then.

They were so captivated by Ana's story of his brother, they never heard him pull into the garage. The dishwasher was also running in the kitchen, because Ana continued her chores while speaking to them and its noise masked the sound of the garage door opening and closing.

The three of them got startled when Frank Stillwater suddenly appeared from the laundry room.

Bobby and Jon jumped to their feet to greet him, but Ana beat them to it. She quickly hugged him and took the box from his hands. Frank turned to greet his guests with his right hand raised, palm forward.

Bobby and Jon followed his example.

-I hope Ana did not bore you to death with her embellished stories about me. –Frank finally spoke with a smile.

-On the contrary! We found it fascinating and the legend is confirmed. –Jon said looking at the six foot tall muscular man in front of him.

-I am Robert and this is my friend Jon. –Bobby introduced themselves for the second time this hour.

-Harvey told us about the two of you serving together. Is that right? –Bobby asked.

-I don't know what Harvey has told you, but my memories may differ somewhat from his. –Frank replied.

-He and I served in the same unit at the beginning of the war. We were sent out on a recon mission into NVA land to gather some Intel. We should have known better, yet we forged ahead rapidly anyway. Harvey took point; I was second behind him. –Frank began the story.

The three of them sat at the table now, in the kitchen. The table was surrounded by four chairs, reminder of a time when Frank had a full family in the house. Ana put on a pot of coffee to brew, when she heard Frank begin to talk about the war. He does not talk about it often, but then he keeps talking for an hour.

- Harvey and I knew that we were moving too fast, but we wanted to complete the mission quickly. We'd seen nothing that would suggest a human habitat, yet we've found a small village hidden in the jungle. –Frank continued as the coffee's aroma filled the air.

Ana came in a minute later, setting the tray on the table with four cups, sugar and cream on the side. Bobby and Jon listened attentively as Frank continued.

-The jungle slowly gave way as we cut through it with machetes. Harvey raised his clenched fist to halt us and we all froze in mid-motion. As the last piece of cut foliage fell to the ground, we saw why he stopped. Fifteen huts spread out in a double semi circle, no more than 200 feet away in a natural clearing. The villagers closest to us started shouting in gook and ran toward the village. We had to act quickly, so we burst out into the open to engage them. That's when the first hand grenade went off behind me. I felt the heat and shock of the explosion. It knocked me to the ground. Everyone ducked for cover as a hail of enemy fire engulfed us. –Frank recalled the event without any emotions. Jon and Bobby sat mesmerized by the unfolding action and Frank's cool demeanor.

-Tracers crisscrossed from six directions, shredding vegetation and kicking up dirt. Finally we returned fire, after what seemed like several minutes, but it could only have been ten or fifteen seconds. My back and right leg started to hurt, but I was able move. We spread out fast but carefully to minimize further casualties. Couple of more grenades landed among us, wounding another man, but its psychological effect was short lived. Within seconds, we lobbed six of our grenades in the general direction of the enemy. The skirmish lasted about three minutes and gunfire became more sporadic with each exchange. A gook attempted to throw a grenade, but he was cut down halfway thru his swing and the grenade fell and exploded just a few feet from him. Another wounded villager let loose from his AK to retaliate, but he could only hit the threes as one of our guys took him out with a short burst. –Frank fell silent.

Ana was surprised that her brother gave the shortest possible version this time.

-That's intense! –Bobby commented on the action excitedly.

-How many casualties did you have? –Jon inquired curiously.

Frank sat there for a moment, recalling the aftermath of his first combat experience.

–We lost three men that day. One died instantly, saving my life. His left lower leg hit me in the back, flat, making a bloody mess of my fatigue. I was very lucky, because his fractured tibia could have skewered me. Even so, it knocked the wind out of me for a few seconds. Nearly a dozen small fragments ripped into my legs and I was bleeding badly. The other two men were killed by small arms fire. Harvey and I were wounded and out of action. Only three of our men remained uninjured. Harvey ordered them to search the village. They reported twenty-two dead and six wounded villagers. –

–Wow! That many? –

–Yeah. The wallop of grenades we threw took out most of them, as they were running for cover. Collateral damage is hard to control in the middle of combat, no matter how well you're trained.

We've been told many times that in this war there is no such a thing as a civilian. –

–Did the remaining villagers surrender? –Jon asked considering the odds.

–To our relief, they did. Harvey and I pondered that, while the three soldiers inspected the village. They confiscated all functional fire arms. We kept a few for souvenir and destroyed the rest. Later, we were told that the village did not exist on our maps and there were no Vietcong soldiers either. The villagers armed themselves to protect their village. –Frank finished the story.

–How long did it take for Med-Evac to pick you up? –Bobby asked, not realizing that Frank would rather move on.

–It took more than ten minutes just to find the damn radio in the jungle. When Harvey gave them the coordinates, their response was "What the hell are you doing out there?" They picked us up fifteen minutes later. –Frank began to sound a little unsettled.

–What did the villagers do in the meantime? –Jon wondered.

–They cared for their wounded, put out fires and collected their children from the woods. –Frank answered impatiently. –Look guys, I'd like to help you, so let's get on with it. Shall we? –and he rose from his seat.

–By all means! –Jon looked at Bobby, hinting to drop the subject.

-Sorry about the inquiry, but I had a similar experience in Iraq. –Bobby apologized.

-I doubt it. –Frank said flatly, but gave Bobby a curious look, regardless.

He gestured them to follow and headed toward another room in the back of the house. Ana continued her chores and cleared the table.

After their children moved out and his wife passed away, Frank converted the second bedroom into a hobby-room. It was filled with radio parts, scattered on shelves and on a table by the window. A fully functional, homemade radio set was humming on a smaller desk.

Frank sat in the chair at this desk and looked at his guests.

-Would you like to hear some news? –his eyes sparkled with mystery and excitement.

-Sure! –came the unanimous answer from Jon and Bobby.

Frank adjusted a couple of knobs, disconnected the headphones and the speakers came to life.

-Listen! –he instructed them and pressed a button marked "listen".

Beep, "…are they going to do? ", beep, "Don't know, but they better stay underground!", beep, "That's for sure. They should seek help from people…, like us!", beep, and after a short pause, beep, "They've found some new friends, they did not even know they had.", beep, "They ought to be careful, because some people might turn them in for a dime." beep, and the radio went silent momentarily.

Jon and Bobby looked at each other awkwardly. Frank glanced at them to see confusion on their faces.

-Listen. –he said in softer tone this time.

The different voices continued an invisible conversation over the ether. They did not mention any names, but after a few minutes, the subject of their talk became clear.

The radio beeped again, "…snitches! They are the lowest form of human life!", beep, "They make me sick! Luckily our hero and his friends are in good hands now!", beep, "What do you mean? You know where they are?" inquired a new voice, resulting in a series of beeps, some of which were caused by Frank, pressing the "scramble" button and then the "seek" button.

For a few seconds nothing happened. While Bobby and Jon looked overly anxious, Frank remained confident in his radio system. After two beeps the previous voices came back.

"Where did that come from?" " Who was that asshole?" "Did they find our channel?" beep, "No, they did not!! Relax, People." Frank said after pressing the "speak" button. "They are lost now and it will take several days before they accidentally pick us up again on a random frequency!", Frank released the button. After a beep one of the previous voices replied, "Thanks chief!"

-What is this? How does it work? –Bobby asked.

-Many people would like to know that, but only few of us do. –Frank replied proudly.

-The point is that now you know why Harvey sent you here. –he added.

Jon did not know what to say, and Bobby was just a little too young to put it all together so fast.

Frank stood up and walked over to the table at the window. Bobby just noticed that four hand-held, two-way radios were waiting.

-These here will be able to do just that! –Frank said pointing at the four skeletons and at the "big" stationary unit. Jon looked at the small sets and could not help asking the question that was also forming in Bobby's head.

-How are you going to fit that, in these? –He nodded toward the table unit that was really no bigger than an average DVD player.

-It is almost done. I was working on these for a while and I just needed to get a few components today. Let me get the parts and I'll put them together in a couple of hours. –Frank put them at ease.

He wasted no time, brought in the supplies and got to work.

Jon and Bobby observed him for a few minutes, but did not want to bother Frank with silly questions. So, they went to see Ana, who was just about done cleaning the house.

She asked if they wanted anything for lunch and they agreed to have sandwiches and soft drinks.

Jon knew that two hundred-fifty dollars for each of those radios was a very reasonable price. Bobby later admitted that he was prepared to pay much more.

"Heck yeah, they are worth every penny!" –the two of them agreed.

They would have to get instructions from Frank on proper communications, so they would not break their rules and compromise their system. One thing was already clear about using this system; no names of people or places were ever mentioned. Jon suspected that it would make sense to use common names for all major objects of importance, like cars, airplanes, mountains, rivers, roads and such.

But, before they would get too carried away with their ideas, they had to consult with Frank.

He worked feverishly for nearly two hours, while Jon and Bobby ate their sandwiches and even took a stroll into the woods behind the house. Ana told them how to find the entrance of the trail and how to follow it out to the lookout point, half a mile away. She even gave them a small walkie-talkie, so Frank could call them back when he was almost finished.

The trail was winding between a variety of obstacles and it crossed a timber-bridge that connected two rims of a twelve feet wide chasm, where the mountain was splitting apart slowly. The floor of the forest was covered with the usual debris; decaying twigs, branches and leaves, and even the occasional skeleton of rodents that inhabit the woods. The eight hundred yards of trail did not offer much in the way of fauna. They only saw a couple chipmunks, a few bugs, a lone snail in the shade of the bridge and a few crows. Past the bridge, the trail's incline steepened and made Jon and Bobby breath heavily from the effort. Even so, they made the trip in twenty minutes. The last fifty yards was naturally the steepest, as it climbed to the top of a large boulder via a stairway made of steps carved into the rock or pieces of timbers attached to it. A lightning rod was erected at the top of the look-out point to protect the unsuspecting visitor from a shocking experience that could be potentially deadly. The view was simply breathtaking, something Bobby and Jon had little left to spare. They visually explored every detail of the countryside in the distance, while their breathing slowly returned to its normal rhythm. The rising warm air at the face of the boulder offered a great opportunity to crows to test and hone their flying skills. Bobby and Jon watched with gaping mouths as they rapidly rose through the air as if they were riding an invisible elevator. The crows were not in any competition, but rather having fun, even though they seemed to race past one another. With wings fully extended and primary feathers spread wide for maximum control, they rose precisely and fast. Pitching slightly forward into the rising air, they swooshed skyward just inches from the surface of the rock. Then, as soon as they passed the summit, flown out and away a few feet, they flipped over, folded their wings and dropped like kamikazes. Precisely controlling their flight with just the tip of their wings and tail feathers, they dove into the abyss to repeat the experience.

If true freedom ever existed in the world, this had to be it!

Bobby and Jon had found it an exhilarating experience just to witness it. While they enjoyed the crow's aerial performance, time flew by as well.

Their radio beeped. -My friends! I'm done with the internal modifications and I'm working on the casings. I should have them fully assembled by the time you get back. Beep. –Frank's voice sounded flat in the open space. Just like freshly fallen snow in winter, vast distances can muffle echoes.

Yet, the sudden noise jolted the new friends out of daydreaming.

Beep. –Okay, we're on the way. Beep. –Jon answered a few seconds after getting an approving nod from Bobby. As they began their decent, they briefly noted how the midday sun accentuated the blue-black luster of the crow's feathers.

Frank was already sitting and waiting on the back porch. The four new radios were resting on the coffee table, neatly arranged, side by side.

-Here they are! –Frank announced with certain and unmistakable pride in his voice.

It was well justified, being a master builder of unique communication devices, little known outside of his circles, a fact that only boosted his pride. He belonged to a tight community, into which only privileged people were accepted.

-They look so ordinary! –Bobby blurted out, unimpressed by the units appearance.

-That's the idea! No one else needs to know what they're capable of! –Frank hinted to keep it a secret. Bobby paid him for the radios and they left promptly.

The four fugitives rejoined at Henry's cabin. It was already dark at 6 PM so they decided to stay in for the rest of the evening. Jon volunteered to explain the proper use of the radios after dinner, which they kept simple. Jeffrey offered to make a recipe he enjoyed in Europe, a spicy, homemade version of hamburger made with pork and beef. Janet prepared the veggies to go with it while Bobby and Jon made the table adding four bottles of beer as well.

-These radios are special. –Jon began his intro with excitement, after they cleared the table.

-We have met a very interesting and reclusive man. He's been building com-systems for decades, a skill he learned in the military. Apparently, he and his buddies developed this network that allows its users to communicate without being limited to just a few, easily scanned frequencies. The units he made for us were partially ready when we got to his place. His longtime friend, Harvey, informed him of what we needed and he finished them within a couple of hours, while we waited. The beauty of the system is that with each press and release of the talk button, all units, equipped with the synchronization circuit, will automatically jump to the same channel. On top of the random channel selection, each unit has its own ID, and coding and decoding to make human-speech sound like radio waves from space. This feature however, was only included in our units! –Jon conveyed all that information seemingly on a single breath.

-Does that mean we can communicate undetected? –Jeff's interest spiked, beyond containment.

-That's right! –Bobby cut in, taking over from Jon for a moment.

-The man's name is Frank. He said, this switch, set to 1, allows us to communicate amongst our selves and flipping it to 2, with their entire network. –Bobby pointed to a switch located next to the power button that was being protected by a hard cover.

-Let me demonstrate! –Jon picked up another radio.

He opened the cover and pressed the power button. A LED light flickered red first then turned green, indicating that the unit is ready. Jon made sure the radio was set to 1, and he pressed "talk". The two-way radio in Bobby's hand came to life with a BEEP. Jon stepped back a few feet to avoid feed-back. Bobby quickly raised the volume on his set and they all heard Jon's voice loud and clear.

-Lo and behold! –he whispered. BEEP. Bobby also explained that "these beauties", as he phrased it, can raise the other three in order, from closest to farthest.

A series of raps came from the front door just then.

They all fell silent as they did not expect anyone.

Bobby had a hunch as to who it might be. He signaled the others to stay put while he answered the door. He peered out the window by the door and saw the silhouette of Fred Gilmore.

-Hey! –Bobby opened the door quickly.

-Hey, hey! –Fred responded, stepping forward into light.

-Come right in! –Bobby reached out to pull his friend in from the cold. They hugged briefly, patting one another on the back several times.

Bobby led him into the living room and, after proper greetings, introduced him to Janet and Jon. Jeffrey had known Fred for many years, yet he was surprised to see him here.

-Henry is also on the way. He left L.A. around three PM, as we agreed, after he gave me directions how to get here. – Fred informed them.

-Did you get all the stuff? –Bobby looked at him inquisitively.

-Oh Yeah! –

-I'll open the garage; pull up to the door and let's unload, 'kay? –Bobby instructed Fred.

-Right. –

The others watched as the two friends swung into action. Within minutes the couch and the coffee table were loaded with guns, ammo and hunting equipment for the winter.

-What the hell is all this? –Jeffrey demanded an answer from his son.

-Gear. –Bobby looked in his father's eyes.

-Just in case. –he added with composure. Fred smiled quietly. He had his reasons.

Henry arrived within the hour. He brought news to his new friends.

Janet, voluntarily acting as maid of the house, produced some food for Fred and Henry, after their long journey.

-What's the word in L.A.? –Jon couldn't wait to hear something positive.

-As you all know, the authorities are searching for you. They are not going to stop until they have you in custody. – Henry began in a realistic tone.

-They are searching high and low, leaving no stone unturned. The good news is that this time the majority of people seem to be on the fugitive's side! That is you! –he pointed around the room covering all four of them.

-Did you guys get in trouble for helping us get away? –Janet wanted to know.

-Not just yet. Ed and I covered our end as well as we could for now. However, they put us on unpaid leave until further notice. We all know what that means. –Henry looked around to see if any of them had any doubt, but they were all nodding to confirm.

-We want a peaceful solution to this whole thing! –Jeff expressed his concern that the situation might get out of hand. Deep down, he trusted his son's instincts of preparation for the worse.

-Of course you do! –Henry concurred.

-We all do. –he conveyed the desire of all with whom he had spoken.

-But, - he said, pausing for a few seconds before continuing,- we all remember past events that happened to people who had peaceful intentions, but the media turned them into raving monsters, when they could no longer keep their story quiet. –

-Who is with us? –asked Jon.

-I've met some interesting people who have connections in influential places. Agent Brown of the ATF promised to keep us updated about the investigation and what might be their next move. Sophie Herd is a friend of his. Katherine King of "Good Sam" has solid connections in the media! –

Henry looked at Janet curiously to see if she knew of this. Her expression revealed that she had no clue.

-That's great! –Jon exclaimed.

-We also found some helpful people around here. –he added holding up one of the radios.

-This is all very exciting, but we can't hide forever. –

They all looked at Jeffrey, as his voice expressed genuine concern.

-That is true. However, we want to play it safe and keep you all out of prison. We also need to make the public aware of who you rally are, on the large scale! –Henry offered some direction.

-Dad! Would you be interested in a public appearance? –Bobby cut in after carefully weighing the consequences. Everyone looked at him with mixed feelings.

-Just how public are you thinking? –Jeff asked him back, considering the possibility.

-Wait a minute! –Henry stopped them in their tracks.

-When I said the public should know who you really are I meant a TV appearance, not wasting time with a few dozen souls. –

-It wouldn't be wasting time! –Bobby snapped at the notion. –I've met some people here who could help organize a sizable group, possibly a couple of hundred people. –

-Some already know who we are, yet we are still safe. –Jon sided with Bobby based on his encounters with the local folks.

-Okay! Okay. –Henry gave in.

-What we need to do is to reinforce the public's positive image of who you are. Up to now, the media repeatedly portrayed you as some kind of criminals. That has to change! I am not against public speaking, as long as you're not getting arrested. –he continued.

-One step at a time! –Jeff seemed to be growing impatient. -Henry! Do what you can to line up a media appearance. You are right! The public is being misled; let's correct it! Bobby! Jon! Get in touch with whomever you can to organise that local event. – Jeff declared his intention.

They felt rejoicing now, knowing exactly which way their lives would flow. They approved of it!

For the next few days, Bobby and Jon engaged in meticulous planning and schmoozing in the Lake Tahoe area. Henry, Ed and Sophie performed the same task in L.A.

They learned that Henry actually had a hangar reserved at the Tahoe airport, and instead of driving, he flew back to L.A. to save time.

In order to stay off the grid, instead of calling, texting or e-mailing each other, they've met from time to time at predetermined locations. Jeff and his friends began to use their two-way radios. After just a few exchanges, they mastered their use. The invisible people's network guided them whenever they needed help. Frank must have alerted his buddies to look out for them.

Surprisingly to some, and contrary to popular belief that news of a miracle may only last for three days, the news of Jeffrey Clark and his controversial speeches abroad was steadily gaining momentum.

After a brief struggle to keep it off the air, the largest news agencies around the globe were now rallying to profit from it on an unprecedented scale.

Since they certainly have the manpower to gather and interpret data any way necessary, intelligence agencies requested their assistance in searching for Jeffrey Clark.

However, the flow of valuable information began to dwindle mysteriously and rather quickly.

The L.A. Times managed to make a very lucrative deal to publish a script of Jeffrey Clark's last speech.

Eugene Herald, who is a close friend, colleague and mentor of Jeffrey Clark, came forth to negotiate that contract. He insisted that the material would not only be printed in the paper, but also made available online.

Eugene Herald and Jeffrey Clark made a legal contract, prior to undertaking the series of seminars, which gave Mr. Herald power of attorney in case of unforeseen consequences.

Jeffrey signed it, thinking in terms of legal matters that might concern his real estate holdings and other tangible personal properties. He signed it in preparation for seizures, so he maybe able to reclaim what rightfully belongs to him and his family.

Mr. Herald used his new authority to establish a bank account with direct deposit, to receive all royalties arising from publishing deals of intellectual properties of Jeffrey Clark.

Jeffrey did not consider this possibility.

He and his friends were unaware of this development.

CHAPTER 3

"It's been three weeks since Jeffrey Clark was abducted from his home. News of alleged criminals died quickly without sufficient follow-up in the past, but his story is still getting bigger. Much conflicting information has been released, some by mistake, some intentionally. Because of it, the public now pays attention to every detail and closely follows the story.

The public's rising interest, in J. C.-s whereabouts and his well-being, warranted careful preparation of every bit of information before it's released. Editors were scrutinizing each and every article written by their reporters to maintain the integrity of their news agencies and to assure a consistent story line. However, reporters became interested in the man, and many of them began investigating, independently.

It was unavoidable that truthful information would soon surface about the real Jeffrey Clark.

Major news agencies aim to control the flow of information, just as governments do, around the globe.

But, as the communication-age would have it, the technology to disseminate vital information is in the hands of the general public. Ever since, powerful people are trying to get a legal handle on the Internet. In short, they seek to acquire legal permission to eavesdrop on the private life of everyone. Not only in cyber space, but wherever people might be.

Some time ago, the media began using a broad term for such widespread spying. That term is profiling. It sounds rather harmless, and so, it hides the magnitude of reckless disregard for every human right. Profiling involves every aspect of human life."

Larry Smith kept winding his thoughts ever tighter about the ramifications of the Clark case. He felt safe in the privacy of his NSA issued Chevy Malibu, as long as he kept his thoughts to himself. He turned north from SR123 toward CIA headquarters in McLean, Virginia.

The complex is located in the Langley subdivision of town, surrounded by a forest. Obviously, the site has been carefully selected for its seclusion. Its buildings cannot easily be seen, from any roads or highways, passing by just a few hundred yards away. It is only a short drive from Washington, D.C. to get here, taking I66 to G.W. Memorial Pkwy to SR123.

Smith carefully maneuvered his vehicle through the maze of concrete barriers protecting the gate.

As an NSA field agent, he did not have the necessary security clearance to park near the main building.

Consequently, the guard sent him to the visitor-lot. From there, a small shuttle takes visitors to their destinations. Their status is indicated by a sticker they must wear on their clothes while on site.

"Just like in Disney land." -He thought, boarding the tram - "Except here, the thrill is of a different kind!" –Smith smiled to himself.

Trying hard not to be impressed, Smith could not escape noting that the complex appeared very much like a gigantic beehive. "Worker-bees arriving to deposit whatever they collected in the field, and leaving to fulfill new orders. In case of bees, however, the existence and prosperity of the colony largely depends on the presence of a Queen. Here, it seems, the entire colony operates on a mere hint of authority. No Queen in sight. But, while bees go about their duties voluntarily and indefinitely for the sustenance provided by the colony in return, humans can only ensure their worker's constant activity by fear of punishment. Sadly, only a few are capable of selfless acts for the greater good. The rest must be terrorized into compliance, due to the unfairness of the system" –Smith entertained himself.

He hopped off the tram at the next stop. After checking in with at the receptionist, he went up to the third floor. A young secretary informed him to wait in the lounge and that he shall be called shortly.

The interior of the lounge was furnished in a puritan fashion, contradicting its name. There was no lounging here; only a few wooden chairs and a small coffee table have been provided for comfort.

Smith sat down facing the door. In less than five minutes, the secretary told him that Section Chief Davidow will see him now. Smith got up, and, as he reached for the door handle, he caught a glimpse of David Price, as he was leaving. "Oh, shit. That's not good!" The thought flashed through his mind faster than a lightening bolt.

The next second he was standing in front of Aaron Davidow, Section Chief of Intelligence, CA.

The heavy door slammed shut behind Larry Smith, revealing the soundproof padding that was expertly installed on it during the cold war. Despite his years in government service, an uneasy feeling gripped his heart. Until now, all his interactions with intelligence gathering personnel took place within his own agency or agencies below his level.

Smith has never been called this high up the intricate hierarchy of intelligence community. "The Clandestine Services" He articulated the phrase in his head.

"Maybe I'll learn something new." -he thought swiftly.

-Agent Smith! Welcome to my office! –Davidow's voice ended his thoughts, as he stood in front of Smith, expecting a response to his attempt for a handshake.

-My pleasure to be here, Sir! –he said taking Davidow's hand with a professional, but somewhat measured smile. He squeezed the CIA chief's hand, matching his authoritarian grip, ounce for ounce.

-Please, have a seat. –Davidow freed his right hand from Smith's grip, flexing his fingers to get the blood flowing again; making sure that Smith noticed his annoyance. He did.

-To what do I owe the pleasure of being summoned to see you, Sir? –Smith asked him without delay.

The way he saw it, the sooner they got down to business, the sooner he will be on his way back to the world he knows best. If the bedpan of inter-departmental fuck-ups is about to be spilled on him, he wanted it to be over as quickly as possible.

-You waste no time, do you, agent Smith? –Davidow admitted being impressed, however slightly.

-I've heard that about you. It is a quality we value highly around here. So, I will extend you the same courtesy. You are here because we have a situation on our hands that needs your deeper involvement.

I am sure you know that Jeffrey Clark's case was supposed to go away quietly without any fallout. In Los Angeles, your agency is responsible for making that happen. David Price has just informed me that you have allowed the situation to spin out of control. –Davidow looked Smith in the eye, searching for answers.

-Is that what David Price told you? –Smith asked the chief defiantly.

Almost a minute of eerie silence followed his question, but Larry Smith sat in his chair steadfastly. He remained calm while Davidow watched his body language with great scrutiny.

-Price laid out all the details, up-to-date, and your failure is the only logical explanation. –Davidow said finally. Smith let out an audible sigh, thinking, "That's a relief. Price wouldn't have sullied my name intentionally".

-Sir. –He addressed Davidow.

-You surely know –he began by using Davidow's expression –how information gets distorted as it's passed from one person to the next. If David Price did not hand you my written report I must question the accuracy of that assessment! – Smith defended his position valiantly.

Davidow took a few seconds to respond, because he knew very well, the assessment did not come from Price. He only delivered the reports on the progress of this case and made no accusations for responsibility.

-You do not have the luxury of questioning anything! –Davidow decided to go on the offensive.

-Historically speaking, the CIA carries out international intelligence gathering and investigative tasks, the FBI is the domestic arm of the apparatus. So, you see, when we get involved in domestic issues it usually means we have to clean- up, after something went awfully wrong. Now, we are not quite there yet, but we're getting really close! – Dawidow asserted.

-What exactly do you intend to clean up in this case, Sir? –Smith maintained his defiant attitude, feeling that somehow he was standing on higher, moral ground.

-This is not a domestic disturbance anymore, Sir. Do you realize just how many people are following the fate of this man around the globe? Because, for once, the news is not about super powers flexing their muscles to intimidate one another, as they've done during the cold war and since, but about the fate of a man who dares to stand up for the rights of all. –Smith spelled it out the way he began to see it lately.

-Who gives a shit about what the people think! –Davidow erupted with utter indifference.

-We are NOT in the people pleasing business. We are in the people controlling business! People would stray from the beaten path aimlessly, if we did not give them a direction. –

-Even if it goes against their desires? –Smith injected his own argument.

-That's right! –came the answer from Davidow's lips instantly.

-Since the dawn of civilization, low-class people had been controlled by those who knew better! –he continued to clarify his idea of human civilization.

-Knew what better? Like, how to enslave others, so they wouldn't have to work? –Smith cut in once again. His own words made him cringe at the realization of what brought the world to this day.

-People in control know the direction, others need to survive. They unify them into a solid work force, giving them the opportunity to make a living. –Davidow reasoned on.

-That's how the wealthy justify their actions to harness the energy of the masses to benefit the few, while sipping cocktails on their Yachts. –Smith reiterated his point.

-Wouldn't you? –Davidow asked, testing his fallibility.

Smith had to pause to make sure that he would give a truthful answer. This confrontation with Davidow, and his own views, awakened his conscience.

-Just because I am employed by the government, I still remember to whom my loyalty really belongs. My answer is a definitive NO. –Uttering the truth, felt like a boulder had been lifted from Smith's soul. He stood up.

-You are a fool, Agent Smith! I suggest you read your employment contract carefully, because you are making a grave mistake! –Davidow warned him.

Smith stood unwavering in his renewed conviction, as he responded.

-Mr. Davidow. I know exactly what my contract says, but I chose to ignore it, until today. Since I can't make it any clearer, let me quote The Declaration of Independence for you!

"We hold these truths to be self-evident, that all men are created equal, that they are endowed by their Creator with certain unalienable Rights, that among these are Life, Liberty and the pursuit of Happiness.… That to secure these rights, Governments are instituted among Men, deriving their just powers from the consent of the governed.… That whenever any Form of Government becomes destructive of these ends, it is the Right of the People to alter or to abolish it, and to institute new Government, laying its foundation on such principles and organizing its powers in such form, as to them shall seem most likely to effect their safety and happiness.…But when a long train of abuses and usurpations, pursuing invariably the same Object evinces a design to reduce them under absolute Despotism, it is their right, it is their duty, to throw off such Government, and to provide new Guards for their future security."

He paused to catch his breath and then added.

-Based on that, I always have and always will serve my country and countrymen.–

-Agent Smith! I have had enough of your civics lessons! –Davidow exclaimed, livid with anger.

-You have a job to do! If you cannot do it, resign! If you can, then stay with the program! –he demanded.

-Your question is not "can I do my job", but rather "can I be trusted" to uphold the status quo. Is it not? Mr. Davidow. – Smith wanted an honest answer.

Aaron Davidow has dealt with plenty of disgruntled employees during his career. But this, he thought, was a classic case of The Enemy of the State.

-Clearly, agent Smith, you have no idea how close you are to loosing everything you ever had. Take one more step in that direction and you'll find yourself removed from the system. –Davidow said calmly.

-You have the nerve to accuse me of not doing my job and threaten my existence from the comfort of your plush office? You are a piece of work Davidow! –Smith took the step.

The meeting came to an abrupt end. Davidow drew his conclusions and so did Larry Smith.

Dismissed, Smith left the office; Davidow reached for the phone as the door closed behind him.

Smith returned to his car and left the compound without fanfare, as he had arrived. The guard waved him on as he approached the north gate. The spring-loaded steel spikes, designed to keep vehicles out, clanged loudly as he passed over them. He accelerated smoothly.

"I lived in California so long, I almost forgot how beautiful winter can be in these parts" he thought as he approached the overpass above G.W. Memorial Pkwy. The road was slippery from the early snow, especially on the overpass, and his instinct told him to slow down. When he gently touched the brake with his right foot, he knew something was wrong. The pedal sunk to the floor without resistance and did not come up again. His eyes on the curve of the road ahead, Smith kept his foot off the gas to bleed some speed. Then he searched for the parking brake with his left foot, but could not find it. "What the hell" flashed through his mind and he looked down to see where it was, but now, was not.

Just then, a vehicle crashed into his from the rear. "Oh God..." were the last words leaving his lips, as he frantically tried to maintain control of his car. The large black SUV stuck to his bumper, like a bumper sticker. Smith heard its engine roar and its tires squeal as it accelerated pushing him straight ahead. He spun the steering wheel right to get out of its way, but nothing happened. With a final surge forward the SUV became quiet, as it detached from his, and swerved to stay on the road. Smith's car jumped the curb, crossed the median and broke trough the aging wooden guardrail. The airbag deployed with a bang, peppering Smith's face with fragments of plastic and filling the car with a cloud of talc. Instinctively, he shut his eyes for a split second. His car found a path through the woods, covered with light undergrowth that offered no resistance. At nearly forty miles per hour, it passed the point of no return, in less than two seconds. About fifty feet from the guardrail, he reached a three hundred feet long bumpy slope toward the Potomac River. As he opened his eyes, the car bounced one last time and plunged into the frigid water, followed by a rain of debris, nearly forty feet below the cliff. Bobbing like a cork, the current swept the wrecked car downstream. Within a hundred yards the river swallowed it whole.

A few minutes after the accident, a Search and Rescue Party arrived at the scene. The car was located quickly, as the right corner of its trunk was sticking up, out of the eddy. A salvage truck from a local yard arrived, just a little too soon. The driver was told that they would contact him when the vehicle was processed, so he drove off with a business card in hand. The car could not be reached due to the cliff the river has carved in millions of years, so we're told. Therefore, a heavy-lifting CH-54 Tarhe helicopter was requested to do the job. This beast is rarely seen in this area and is a rather ugly and unmistakable piece of equipment. The urgency of the operation did not give time for a more subtle solution.

Travelers on all roads, within a couple miles distance, took notice and wondered what had happened. An unwanted visitor also appeared in the sky, heading towards Langley. Someone had tipped off the local TV station about the unusual chopper and they sent out one of their own to investigate. The pilot flew faster after he was told where to go. The news crew caught sight of the Tarhe from afar, hovering above the Potomac.

As soon as they got their cameras ready to shoot some footage, the lead reporter's cell phone rang.

He answered the call. After just a few seconds into his call, he signaled the cameraman to stop shooting. The look on his face left no doubt about what he'd been told by the person on the line.

People on the ground also noticed the news chopper, as it headed towards Langley. They watched, as it slowed to hover, just half a mile from its destination. Close enough to shoot the scene.

But, to everyone's surprise, it swiftly flew off in the direction from which it came.

Engineers estimated the weight of the car, submerged and full of water, around five tons. That's about half the civilian lifting capacity of the Tarhe. The car, emerging from the water, would quickly loose weight as it drains. Divers were already in the water, hooking up the cables to facilitate the lift. When they got out of the way, the Tarhe's Pratt-Whitney turbines roared into action. The pilot adjusted the pitch of the rotor blades to tighten the cables. The hammering sound of the blades, produced by the Doppler Effect, echoed far over the landscape.

The CH-54 Tarhe triumphed once again, as it lifted the car out of the river with ease, creating a spectacular waterfall. To minimize flight time, and consequently, cost and exposure, it flew to a secure area at CIA Headquarters. Even so, people witnessed the short trip and noted, what appeared to be an overcoat fluttering in the wind, hanging from the window of the banged up car.

The evening news will announce that Larry Smith was the only fatality of the tragic accident.

Larry Smith is well trained in state of the art communication technologies. He also knows that most governments were capable of wiretapping phone lines and monitoring radio frequencies even before the end of WWI and they did and continue to do so for their own protection.

New technologies make their job a lot easier.

"Telex, an invention that preceded the telephone, is still being used today primarily as a data transfer device. It is utilized by the armed services, fire departments and banking institutions, all of whom require the highest encryption available."

"General use of telegraph services began with the founding of Western Union around 1861, but wider public use spread rather slowly. A little-known fact that in the mid 1860-s W.U. attempted to create an intercontinental system called the Russian-American Telegraph, linking the USA to Europe by way of Russia. This business venture may have led, however indirectly, to the purchase of the state of Alaska in 1867 for a mere 7.2 million dollars."

"Interesting piece of history" Smith thought while paying with cash for a disposable phone days ago.

"Am I smart, or what?" he thought proudly, holding that phone now, still wrapped in a plastic bag.

Standing on the east bank of the river, he shook the excess water off the bag. He was amazed how quickly they begun searching for him and the car. Looking upstream, he paused momentarily to reflect on why. "Removed from the system." he remembered Davidow's words.

By late October, most trees were bare in this region, so he moved quickly to get out of sight. Shivering from his wet clothes, he needed shelter quickly. The sound of an approaching helicopter made the matter even more urgent, so he ran as fast as he could to a nearby building.

The large structure is part of the Little Falls Pumping Station. It is connected to a pair of smaller structures located on Clara Barton Pkwy, by a bridge spanning a small canal. Smith stayed close to its walls and peered around the corner. The chopper stopped right above him, so low that he could feel the down-wash of the rotor blades. He looked up and saw a news copter, no more than three hundred feet above the ground. Then, Smith noticed a huge chopper, getting ready to lift his car from the river.

"Damn you, Davidow!" Smith cursed at the CIA chief. The news chopper did not hang around very long.

Smith has been in government service long enough to know that it has been ordered to leave.

Before moving on, he checked his surroundings, and spotted a "security camera" on one of the smaller buildings. Since he could not get much wetter, he waded across the canal beneath the bridge to stay out of sight. At the first break in traffic he sprinted across the road and continued uphill through the shrubs. He slowed to walking speed before stepping out of the brush onto Mac Arthur Blvd. Once again, he felt satisfied with his ability to prepare for the unexpected; he Googled the surrounding area in great detail before visiting Davidow's office. He knew that only a couple of hundred yards away, in Bethesda, is the Center of NGA, or National Geospatial-Intelligence Agency. The perimeter of the campus is tightly fenced, guarded and monitored by cameras, 24/7, because NGA is a member of the spy community, specializing in aerial surveillance worldwide.

Here, at the edge of the road, he removed the phone from the plastic bag and he put it back in his pocket. After putting the battery in it, the phone took a moment to initialize, during which time Smith kept an eye on the traffic. He did not know how to continue yet, but he knew he could not stay here for long.

To get a better feel for the situation he had to make a call.

As always, the NSA office in Los Angeles, was bustling with urgency.

Phones ringing, people conversing about all kinds of topics; secretaries typing reports.

Like most of his peers, Dale Finch was working diligently when the phone began ringing on his desk.

-Hello? –he answered in a monotone.

-It's me. –he heard from the other end of the line.

-Hey, Boss! How's it going? –

-Its going downhill, my friend. –Smith said to him.

-I know what you mean, Boss! –Finch could hear disappointment in his superior's voice.

-I won't be back to my office anytime soon. Anybody comes looking for me, you haven't heard from me. –Smith condensed the events.

-I don't think anybody will come looking for ya, Boss. –Dale lowered his voice, as he checked to see if anyone might be listening to him.

-We just received a note from the top that you were killed in an automobile accident. The details are sketchy, as they say, but your body has been identified, awaiting autopsy at the coroner's office. –Finch informed his boss.

-That is more than I dared to imagine. –Smith acknowledged sadly.

-Do you know anyone in the D.C. area you can trust? –he now asked of Finch.

-I need you to send him to investigate my accident at the local TV station as quietly as possible. –Smith continued before Finch could answer.

-They might have a brief footage of the aftermath of my "accident". –Smith finished his request.

-Sure thing, Boss! I know just the person for the job. –Finch replied.

–Call me when you have something! –Smith indicated it was time to break off the call.

–Will do! –Finch acknowledged and placed the handset back on its base.

First he called his contact at the phone company that maintained the lines of his department. He used his authority to have the record of the last call made to his desk erased, after he jotted down and quickly memorized the number from which Smith had called him. Then he disposed of the piece of paper in the shredder.

Dale Finch and a few of his colleagues planned to have lunch together that day. They picked one of the best places to have seafood in town the day before.

Their conversation centered on the mysterious accident that claimed the life of Larry Smith.

The FBI was preparing to make a move against the four fugitives. The agents accidentally stumbled upon a piece of information that gave away their location in Tahoe.

Donald Clamp met his friend, Paul Eas and some of their best men, at the firing range for training.

The range is maintained by the city for law-enforcement personnel. Acquired from a decommissioned quarry, it is located in Duarte, in the crotch of the Foothill freeway and San Gabriel River freeway.

Naturally, the quarry has been converted to best serve the needs of people who use the training facility. It boasts a paved road, an air-conditioned clubhouse with locker rooms and showers, a gym room, and a canteen that serves all kinds of refreshments its patrons may desire.

In essence, it is a miniature private club that is paid for by taxing the general public.

Outside, on the other hand, the picture is somewhat different. Each year, the land is arid for almost nine months, and the terrain is rough.

Part of the area is still reserved as a flood-control basin, developed over many decades to handle runoff from the San Gabriel Wilderness. During the "wet season", lasting about four months, the possibility of flash flooding is inevitable. After having a brief chat and some refreshments with their friends in the clubhouse, Clamp and Eas stepped out into the hundred and ten degrees heat.

The range is considered open-air, but some shade is provided for the shooters by freestanding sheet metal roofs. Even though the roof shields people from the direct rays of brutal California sun, under the tin roof, the temperature feels like an oven.

The two tough men carried their gear to the nearest stand.

-Handguns or rifles first? –Eas asked, as they set down their packs.

-Handguns. –Clamp responded.

-Good choice! –Eas smiled as he patted his buddy on the back.

-Revolver or semi? –

Eas pulled out his 44Mag and said, -Revolvers. – Clamp placed his favorite 357Mag on the bench.

-Trade? –he asked.

-Sure. –

They chose the twenty-five feet distance to start. After loading their guns, they exchanged them.

-Ready? Set! Fire! –and on Clamp's command they let loose with a thunder.

Clamp nearly dropped the 44Mag, since he had not fired one of these heavy rounds in years. The recoil surprised him and he only scored a "9".

Eas knew what to except from the 357Mag and maintained control of the gun, scoring a perfect "10". They glanced at each other mischievously and got ready for the next round.

Boom! The two shots rang out almost simultaneously, rattling the tin roof above their heads.

To Eas's surprise the 357 produced a ridiculously light recoil the second time. Unconsciously compensating for what he thought might feel like the first shot, he scored a "5" at the edge of the lower left quadrant of the target.

Clamp on the other hand, managed to score another "9".

-Not fair! –Paul Eas yelled, so Clamp would hear him even with his ear protection.

Donald Clamp only nodded in response, as he concentrated to overcome the effects of recoil in subsequent shots.

They both hand-loaded their ammo at home, and mixed some uneven loads in the guns for fun. Their knowledge to do that safely comes from many years of practice in re-loading and following manufacturer's instructions. They both know that to alter the amount of gunpowder safely they need to know their guns and ammo precisely. The slightest mistake could be disastrous.

They proceeded to fire off the remaining rounds.

Clamps next shot from the 44 was loaded so weakly that it sounded like a 22LR. The medium weight, two hundred and eighty grain bullet dropped to the ground in front of the target. It looked hilarious as it made a small puff of dust at the point of impact. After bouncing just once it rolled to a quick stop.

It is hard to fire subsequent shots accurately from a 44Mag without enough practice, let alone with such diverse loads. Eas also struggled to control his senses, to hold the gun steady while he pulled the trigger.

He managed to pierce the paper with all six shots, but only four bullets landed in the numbered circles. Clamp's grouping told a different tale. With only five holes in the paper, he too managed to get four bullets into the concentric circles of his target.

Overall, their final score was only two points apart.

Both laughing, they took off their eye and ear protections.

-I hope you know what you're doing, my friend! –Clamp turned to Eas.

-That one load actually scared me, dropping like that! The bullet barely had enough energy to leave the barrel! –

-To be honest, I was worried about that one too! Thought it might be a squib. –Eas admitted, teasing his friend. - But, I counted on your expertise not to fire the next round if the bullet got stuck in the barrel. –

-Let's check the targets. –he said, dumping the empty cartridges into a bin.

-We've got the order to proceed with the arrest of Jeffrey Clark. I am going to need your cooperation. –Clamp turned to his friend changing the topic of conversation, as they normally do at this point.

-What can I do for you, Don? –Paul's face took on a more business like expression.

-We are going to have to handle this personally, jurisdiction aside, you and me. I want you to join me when I go to Tahoe this coming Sunday. –

-No problem here. –Paul Eas responded.

At a leisurely pace, they covered the twenty-five feet distance to their targets in less than ten seconds.

-That is crazy! Would you look at that? –Donald Clamp exclaimed pointing at their targets.

-Wow! That's ridiculous! After all these years of training here, we can't do better than that? –Paul Eas could not believe his eyes.

-Don't feel bad. With these loads, I'm happy to have scored almost as well as you did, on these targets. –Clamp saw the bright side.

They marked and patched the bullet holes, adding up their scores.

Eas had a 10, a 5, a 9 and a 6-point shot, scattered widely in the small black field of the target. Total score, 30.

Clamp's showed a 9, another 9 and two 5s, also widely spread out. Total score, 28.

-How many men do you think we'll need? –Paul asked of his friend as they walked back to the benches.

-Bring five of your most trustworthy men, I'll do the same. Including you and me, that's twelve men strong. –Clamp summarized the men-power needed for the plan.

After shooting their other handguns for a while, they put them away and moved to the rifle range. They spent over three hours here, since the range was considerably longer, at one hundred, two hundred, five hundred yards and the longest range at one mile. The golf cart proved handy reaching the five hundred yard and one-mile targets. They checked the closer ones on foot. Each range was also equipped with electronically controlled steel targets. After the first round of paper targets, which they intended to take back to their offices to brag about, they began shooting the steel targets.

It's quite amusing to hear these targets clang, a split second after they go down, a visual cue of a hit. When they fulfilled their need here, they moved to the shotgun range.

-What about transportation? –Eas continued to extract bits of information about the mission.

-I figure, to be low-key, four of us should take a car and the rest of the men could follow in a full-size van. Sort of an outing…, you know? –Clamp pictured the scene in his head.

-Sounds good to me! –Eas agreed.

-When are we leaving?-

-I was thinking Saturday mid-day, we can fly up to Sacramento. I'll request vehicles from the local law enforcement. We'll spend the night in town and drive to Tahoe next morning. –Clamp informed him.

-So, you have this all figured out already? –Paul wondered aloud.

-Not exactly. –came the answer that did not make Paul Eas feel good at all.

-Hmm. –he glanced at his friend with a hint of doubt.

-What exactly are we getting into? Do you know anything else about them, aside from where they are? –

-Tahoe is a nice, civilized area. People go there to relax and enjoy nature. We shall spend a few days sniffing around before making our move. –Don smiled at Paul to ease his concern.

-We will take no rash actions, unless the situation gets out of hand. –he added.

-Okay, then. –Paul was still not convinced of a solid plan, as he unpacked his two shotguns and all the ammo he intended to spend.

He has had a fair share of uncertain circumstances and so far came out unscathed every time. However, close calls always remind him that a little more forethought might have been needed. He never liked to leave too many things to chance.

Some forty minutes later, all ammo spent, all stress released, the two officers of the law headed back to the clubhouse. They relaxed in the sauna's hundred and fifty degree heat, infused with eucalyptus oil. About twenty minutes later they took a quick cold shower.

They firmly believe in releasing tension and stress this way. As some might say, and they do concur:

"A good day at the shooting range can be almost as satisfying, as mediocre sex".

From the range, they headed back to their offices to check today's progress in law enforcement.

In private, Paul Eas had wondered many times about the phrase "law enforcement". It never sounded quite right to his ears. He reasoned that if laws are fair and protecting the people, then why would they have to be "enforced"? Wouldn't the people respect the law enough to abide by it?

But, he rarely pondered the matter any further in detail.

Before hitting the office, he popped into the Italian diner conveniently located just around the corner. Just before five in the afternoon, he could still have a cup of hearty espresso and still sleep soundly through the night.

The shop's patronage was normal for this hour, at about forty percent capacity. The door slowly closed behind him as he proceeded to the nearest stool at the bar. He put his key ring next to the glass case displaying fresh desserts of the day.

Paul never had a sweet tooth, but today he felt like having something delectable with his coffee.

The server knows him well, since he has been a daily customer here for over five years now. They waved at each other from a distance and the server acknowledged his arrival with an additional nod. Paul knew that he would come over as soon as he finished serving the other guest.

He examined the pastries and decided to try the Tiramisu he heard so mach about.

—Hello Paul! —the server greeted him. —Desiring something sweet today? —he asked with a smile.

—Hey, Julien! —Paul responded. —You guessed it; I'd like to try your famous Tiramisu. —

—Excellent choice! —Julien exclaimed with pleasure, as he too enjoyed this pastry, time after time.

—You are about to indulge your senses with a masterful blend of exceptional flavors enhanced by just enough sweetness to create heavenly perfection. This is a match made in heaven, to pair our Tiramisu with your favorite espresso. I'm afraid you'll be hooked! —Julien warned his friend excitedly.

Paul was flabbergasted by his outburst, as their conversations were usually limited to small talk.

He sensed that Julien, a Frenchman by birth, was in a state of euphoria. As chief of police, he instinctively suspected that Julien might be "hooked" on something himself.

He kept an inquisitive eye on him, as he hurried toward the kitchen.

Moments later the door swung open and Julien returned with a plate. He set it in front of Paul Eas and stepped back slightly.

-Whoa! –Paul exclaimed in shock.

An enormous piece of Tiramisu filled his plate. It was about five by five inch square and about two and half inches tall. Julien stood wringing his hands in anticipation of Paul's pleasure or dislike.

-It's a special treat for you, Chief! –He informed his guest.

Paul carefully sliced into it with his fork and brought a piece to his lips. Julien, after seeing delight on Paul's face, turned to make his espresso. The experience caused Paul to moan with the utmost pleasure. He thought it was unmanly to behave like that in public and looked to see if anyone noticed. No one paid attention to him, except for an attractive woman in her early forties. She was sitting just two seats away and casting an envious look at him and his dessert.

-Being friends with the pastry chef has its perks, I see. –she noted with some annoyance.

-You mean him and me? Nah! –Paul replied, rejecting a mistaken insinuation.

He was under the impression that Julien is at least a swinger, if not full-blown gay.

The woman, being a psychologist and highly astute of these matters, had to set things straight.

-I only meant to note the unusual size of your serving. –

-Oh. Pardon me. –Paul said with a giggle. -You wouldn't mind if I...-he began to say while he slid his plate and keys closer to the woman, ...-sit with you? Would you? - he finished his question as he arrived at the stool next to her. Then, he quickly offered to share his tiramisu, before she could object.

-Would you like half? –he said handing a clean fork to her.

-It's way too much for me anyway. I only eat pastries like this once a year. –

She accepted the fork with thanks. Julien returned with the espresso and quickly sized up the situation. He sat the coffee on the counter next to Paul's plate.

-Would you folks like anything else? –he asked them, but obviously directing the question to Paul.

When Paul looked up, he noted a twinkle in his eye, and a slight wink in the direction of the lady sitting to his right.

-Well yeah! How about a coffee to go with that? –Paul asked her, saving the moment by a hair.

-How kind of you. –she accepted his offer. –My usual coffee mocha, please. –

The waiter hurried off to the coffee machine and Paul realized he had not introduced himself yet.

-Pardon my over site, I am Paul? – he introduced himself finally. and you are?-

-I am Sybille. –

Paul paused for a few moments, wrecking his brain to recall bits of information about unusual names.

-Meaning an "oracle"? –he asked finally.

-Impressive! –Sybille's eyes flashed at him curiously.

Paul felt a weird feeling creeping into his soul. One that was liberating and menacing once.

He found this stranger of the opposite sex indescribably irresistible.

His last meaningful relationship ended quite badly, almost four years ago. During the years that followed, his demanding work caused him to suppress most human needs and emotions, even within his own family, over time. The meager pay, the long hours and extreme stress can take toll on most relationships. People, like Paul Eas, who care deeply about their purpose and are devoted to what they do, are also willing to sacrifice everything to succeed. His wife was not happy about that.

-So, what do you do for a living? –Sybille's voice interrupted his wandering.

-I am in law enforcement. –he said automatically.

Inside, he cringed at those words, as he remembered his thoughts about the subject not long ago. Sybille did not notice any change in his facial expressions, but detected his body language.

-Are you good at what you do? –she asked.

-That depends. –

-Well, do you catch all the criminals you supposed to? –

-Almost. –he said reluctantly.

-What is your profession? –he now asked her.

-I am a criminal psychologist. –she answered.

A momentary silence set in as Julien passed in front of them with obvious spring in his step. They watched him move around as he prepared the next order. They could even hear him humming a melody.

-Does he strike you odd today? –Paul asked Sybille quietly.

-I was thinking the same thing. –she said.

-Julien! Do you have minute? –Paul called him over.

Julien's task was not very urgent, so he came back to them, instead of shouting from afar.

-What gives, man? - Paul asked him straight.

-I've heard some mighty good news. For some time now my friends and I were very upset about the way things are going in this country. –he said excitedly.

Julien knows exactly who his costumers are; he thought, it's just as well that he would tell them first.

-What news is that, Julien? –Sybille asked aroused.

-Have you heard of Jeffrey Clark? –he asked them.

-Yes, he a conspiracy nut of sorts. –Sybille said.

-Something like that! –Julien added mysteriously. Paul just listened.

-He is safe for now, among friends. But, he is planning to give a lecture here in town, some time within the next couple weeks. In the mean time, he was asked to participate in a live radio broadcast and he accepted the invitation. –Julien continued.

-Is he a friend of yours? –Paul asked suddenly.

-No, Paul. He is a friend of the People. –Julien cleared it up succinctly.

-Go on. –Sybille encouraged the young man.

-He is sowing the seeds of change… –he said, but stopped abruptly

They all fell silent momentarily, while carefully considering the consequences of continuing this conversation. The unexpected information spiked Paul's interest in Jeffrey Clark. Until now, he did not consider the individual behind the accusations.

He needed more information.

-How could I learn more about this fellow and his work? –he asked Julien.

Julien's fervor seemed to pipe down. Evidence of possessing knowledge beyond the ordinary still lingered on his face, but his body language showed no more excitement.

Sybille observed him attentively, as he adjusted his demeanor.

"He must feel uncomfortable having revealed something of importance." She thought.

"Look straight in his eyes; you know the reason for his inquiry." Julien told himself before answering.

-Search the Net. – was his curt reply.

-We encourage everyone to seek the truth. Just begin searching and you will discover all you ever wanted to know. –He added somewhat mysteriously.

-Who exactly are "we"? –Paul pressed further.

-If you're looking for names and numbers, Mr. Eas, there are none to give. We are a fluid, ever changing mass, spreading truth and freedom. If you will, "We" is short for "We, the People". We are the commoners and we question who they are to rule over us? –Julien emphasized the word.

Silence set in once again.

Sybille gazed at him, gnawing over what he said, extracting its deeper meaning. It all made sense to her now.

The last piece of Tiramisu began to loose its magnificent flavor in Paul's mouth. He has been told many times, that the American people are so deeply divided that they are incapable of coherent thought or action, in any group large enough to pose a problem. (To whom? He now wondered.)

He now shuddered from the realization that the winds of change have been blowing for a while.

"He is still in denial, but everything he's been thought is wrong and crumbling". Julien thought while observing the changes of Paul's facial expression. Then he wondered, "Could he be saved"?

Sybille slipped one of her business cards to Paul, expecting an abrupt end to this encounter.

-Please, take my card. –she said. –I'd like you to call me some times. – Paul Eas looked at the card and put it in his pocket.

-Thanks, I certainly will. It's been a pleasure meeting you. –he said and after dropping money on the counter he said goodbye to Julien too.

-I've got to go. I'll see you soon. –he said with a forced smile, and left the diner.

Paul Eas went straight to his office. He needed to exercise due diligence in the matter before him. He never liked leaving things to chance.

Julien cleared Paul's dishes off the counter and put the money in the register. Neither he nor Sybille felt like talking now. In spirit, she was already preparing for the meeting she was going to attend this evening. They need her expertise. "We have our own think-tank" she thought and the notion consoled her.

"We must be true to the Declaration of Independence" the words of Brent Taylor echoed in Sybille's head. "It is the only way to protect our rights, as free men".

The muddled sound of human voices, the rattling of dishes and tableware began to sharpen in her ears as she came out of her daydreaming.

She looked up and around her and realized it must be late. Her cup and plate were gone, and new people were sitting all around her. The restaurant began to serve dinner already.

Sybille glanced at her wristwatch and confirmed the time. Six thirty, she had to leave, now.

Paul, as any gentleman would, took care of her check. She grabbed her purse and waved at Julien. His lips read, "See you later" as he waved back.

For some reason his computer did not want to cooperate.

It seemed to take forever booting up, to open or switch pages, even scrolling on a page was sluggish.

The websites he found about Jeffrey Clark shocked him and provoked him at once.

Some praised the man to high heaven in such terms as "the new Messiah", "a true Evangelist for our time", and "the Savior of Man".

-I hope they mean mankind. –he uttered involuntarily.

Yet, others denounced the man by calling him "Satan's advocate", "instigator of unrest", and "traitor", just to mention a few.

Paul Eas found Clark's own website, where he posted a concise version of his lectures. After having read the whole thing, Paul could not disagree with him. Clark cited a multitude of facts, from the point of view of an individual's daily life that he, as Chief of Police, also experienced personally, and therefore could not refute.

The more he searched, the more he began to see a pattern emerge.

The sites that spoke positively about Mr. Clark and his work clearly represented a crowd with a deep resentment for "the way it is". Albeit, each considered different alternatives, they all seemed to agree that continuing the same course will lead to certain doom.

They laid it all out in well-reasoned arguments.

The ones that rejected Clark's theories, for being despicable and blasphemous, all seemed to have a palpable favoritism to the "status quo". They all dismissed impending doom and aimed to reassure the reader that all is well.

Being an instrument of power himself, Paul had to consciously calm his mind. He knew he could not afford to make a mistake. This is not a joke anymore.

The stakes are astronomical.

Paul couldn't stop reading. His eyes felt like smoldering embers in their sockets. Well after midnight, with a great deal of effort, he weaned himself off the computer. Although he parked in his own reserved spot, it took several minutes to locate his car.

He drove straight home, but he did not remember how. Went to bed, but sleep did not come for a while. His mind was desperately trying to reconcile it all. He realized that most of what he read flew in the face of his indoctrination. He felt frighteningly insecure and that forced him to reassess his whole life.

Fully exhausted, he fell asleep around three am. His soul writhed from strong emotions and for the first time ever, he had nightmares. Disturbing images flashed before his mind's eyes, but his mind could not discern anything meaningful. His cold sweat saturated the bedsheets and caused him to shiver. He took a quick hot shower and replaced the sheets then slept peacefully for a few hours.

But the nightmares returned once again just before daybreak.

CHAPTER 4

It was 8 pm on Thursday of the last week in October, when Stacey G. turned on the radio.

After a few minutes of commercials, the announcer came on.

"Good evening folks, I'm William Ornotte and you are listening to TRDN, Lake Tahoe's own and only radio station. For those of you joining us for the first time, I'd like to explain the name of our station.

It's been derived from the name of a human gene, or protein, named Triadin. In layman's terms, the function of this protein is to induce muscle activity. It triggers muscle movement in the human body by releasing controlled amounts of Calcium ions. That is an oversimplified explanation, but it should help.

Similarly at TRDN, we aim to induce rapid brain function in more and more human sculls by distributing organic food for thought.

That is why I welcome Jeffrey Clark in our studio tonight. His name must ring familiar to many of you from National TV, since his story became the leading news of every broadcast over the last few weeks. Mr. Clark intends to set the record straight and brings vital information. Please Mr. Clark, enlighten us."

Around the same time Sophie Herd and Karl Brown were having burgers, with curly fries and soft drink. They were sitting in Brown's official vehicle in a parking lot, listening to the same station. One of Sophie's friend told them about tonight's broadcast.

"Good evening folks! My name is Jeffrey Clark."

Close to a million people heard his greeting simultaneously in California, Arizona, New Mexico, Oregon and as far as Denver, Colorado.

"I am honored to have the chance to speak to a broader audience today.
It is a very humbling experience.
You may have heard that I died in a 'tragic accident' recently. Later, they reported that I was still alive, but missing. In a way that is true, but please allow me tell you the real version.
My colleague and mentor helped me to arrange an international tour of seminars, where I spoke about human relations. It became a huge success, as I have found myself swamped by e-mails from folks far and wide, who wanted to hear my opinion on countless topics. After returning from abroad, I attempted to answer some of them, but, disguised federal agents kidnapped me from my home. They took me to a secret facility, hidden from public scrutiny, where they interrogate so-called homegrown terrorists.
Until three weeks ago, I was a history professor at UCLA, yet they locked me up as a criminal. Good people, who believe in freedom and free speech, helped me to escape from that facility.
I am not a criminal and do not accept any such charges against me. Criticism is not a crime; it simply points out the difference between the desires of the public and the aspirations of their government.
A government that suppresses criticism of its actions and refuses to correct them is bound to suppress a lot more.
In my seminars, I talked about the undeniable historical fact that humans have always exploited one another, in some fashion, at times with tragic consequences.
It began some time around the Stone Age, and is still happening today!
Those who aim to control the fate of others, do so to secure an easier life for themselves.
Humanity acquired a great deal of knowledge compiled over many centuries that enables us to produce food and shelter with ease. But

even these basic commodities now cost well beyond the earning ability of not only the individual, but whole families.

This can only mean one thing. Some people out there do their dirty work to keep the rest of us down! The following facts are not intended to make a case for slave-keeping. Quite the contrary.

When humans kept human slaves, the master understood that he had an obligation to take care of his slave's basic needs. He had to feed them, cloth them, educate them in accordance with their duties. He even had to provide basic health care.

It was considered an investment in the labor-force that made his and his family's life comfortable.

Allow me now to draw a comparison to owning domesticated animals, even as pets. Even today, people all over the world rely on the strength of animals to work their land, and haul goods to earn a living. How long would they last, if they did not feed their animals, if they did not provide shelter for them, or failed to call either an experienced fellow farmer, or a veterinary, if that was an option, when their animal got sick, or had trouble giving birth to their off-spring? Not long, I can you tell you that. So, naturally, most sane people fed them, housed them in barns, and did all they could to keep them from getting sick, and dying. The same is true of our pets.

We keep them, for sure, but we feed them, we give them shelter and even love, to keep them in good health, in return for the entertainment and love they give to us.

Do not dare to twist my words around and accuse me of likening human-slaves to animals! For if you would, you'd missed the entire point of my comparison.

Some people will argue that this is not entirely so. Granted, we all known that people exist who are rotten to core, including their soul, or whatever may be left of it. We all know that they do evil things not only to animals, but also to humans.

As slave-masters, these people built alarming reputations. Yet, regardless of the small number of these sadistic slave- owners, emphasizing the suffering they caused can easily overshadow any record to the contrary."

Stacey squeezed Bobby's hand tightly and looked in his eyes, but he said nothing. His father was on the roll and this time he wanted to listen. He raised his free hand, pointing to his.

Jeffrey Clark continued on the air.

"We know that slavery dates back to the very beginning of human history. As depressing as that sounds, what I personally find even more disturbing is the fact that it still exists today!

Technological advancements produced a large number of different "master vs. slave" scenarios. Slaves were bought and sold throughout the centuries. It was big business! Open slavery existed and competed with paid-labor until about the end of the Civil war in the USA. As business competition grew ever fiercer, employers realized their advantage over slave-keepers. A Slave-Master must deny freedom of movement to his slaves to have a steady workforce, while an employer can maintain his pool of employees by the mere illusion of freedom. He does not care if laborers come and go, because the need, to pay for food and shelter, would ultimately bring them back.

Employers realized another advantage that comes from the free movement of laborers. It gave them the edge of bargaining a lower wage, compared to the costs of keeping slaves.

Most likely, prominent business leaders, bankers and politicians attempted to convince the Masters of the South of their misconception, prior to the war. But the Masters stubbornly refused to accept the idea. Most likely, bankers secretly promised huge profits to "businessmen", if they managed to trigger a war, since war yields profits. Never mind the suffering and loss of human life and property. All that means nothing when there is profit to be made! Thus, without further ado, father turned against son, brother against brother to decide the fate of our, then, fledgling nation and the fate of its sovereign people. You all know the result. Slavery has been condemned, in its traditional form, as a violation of human rights. Only a few realize that it was quietly replaced by a "more humane" system that maintains the illusion of freedom through choices. Thus, large monopolies developed; manufacturing unnecessary gadgets and an overwhelming surplus of products from which to choose. We have long forgotten what has real value."

Jeffrey stopped for air. He was glad to have the chance to share his observations without interruption. Questions could be discussed later. He intended to use his time efficiently, to say "What is" and "What isn't".

"An incredible number of people are working very hard to discourage the rest of us from asking why. They want us to accept where we are, and to be grateful for what we have, instead of taking steps to make our lives better."

Jeff said and then paused again to regroup.
His pause seemed so long over the air that people began to wonder if "that was all". Yet, no one moved.
William Ornotte finally broke the silence.

-Well, so far so good! I can't wait to hear the rest. –his voice resonated with excitement. Jeff continued his speech, on cue.
"That was the essence of my lectures. If freedom-loving people decide to come forth, asking questions, I can't help that. What bothers me greatly, is that most people are utterly ignorant of their own status. When someone tells them that they are being led by the nose, they flatly reject the notion. This proves the effectiveness of the PLAN our masters devised and set in motion decades ago. Do you realize what globalization really means? Do you see that globalization is nothing, but the concentration of power? It brings nothing good for the common people, as this power will continue to tighten its grip on our lives. Fear mongering is a tool to sway the public's opinion in their favor."

"The only thing people ever have to fear in this world is a despotic world government! That is what actually awaits us at the end of the globalization process. It will mean the end of national identity. It will mean, and you have seen this depicted in numerous movies, that corporations want to, and will, control our lives, if we let them! They want to ensure that we continue purchasing their useless products in a timely manner. It will mean total mind control, also depicted in some movies, by way of the mysterious nanotechnology. What is that? Is it going to be misused like nuclear reaction? I don't know about you, but I want to trust the water I drink, not to alter my mind. I trust my toaster or blender not to spy on me. I cannot say the same about household robots of the near future, because you may turn off their physical functions, but they might still see and listen. Do you remember Google's announcement about being able to collect anonymous sound bites via a microphone, either built in, or plugged into your computer? Is that really done for marketing purposes? When did we give them permission to do that? Do you think they might be able to collect fragments of images from pixels of your computer screen, and reassemble them into a still image or even a video?

If I can think of that, they certainly can and have already! Ponder that a while.

That is all I wanted to share with you, and if that makes me a criminal in any way, then the work of the devil is nearly complete. Thank you for listening."

-And that was our show for tonight. Thank you so much for your thoughts and concerns, Mr. Clark. I am William Ornotte, signing off from TRDN radio, Lake Tahoe. Good night. –

All radios tuned to the station's frequency lost signal in that instant. A soft static noise followed. Most listeners let out a deep sigh. They have been holding their breaths for some time.

The gravity of the information began to churn in their mind; then they gasped with a force that rivaled the first breath of a healthy newborn.

And what happens after a newborn draws that first breath? I cries out loudly, to let the world know of his or her displeasure of having been expelled from the safety of their mother's womb.

Janet led her man out of the studio, arm in arm, feeling the burden of responsibility. She gave him all the comforting she could by pulling him close to her body. Jeffrey moved with her, like a sleepwalker.

"The skeptics shrug their shoulders with indifference, as always. They do not care one way or another. As passive sufferers of the changes that life throws at them, they are going to wonder what happened.

The concerned, but faint-hearted, always feel powerless to change the way things go. They will be watching the changes, with mixed feelings.

But, those who are keenly interested in the forces shaping their lives, as much as they let it be shaped, will likely take action. Their names fill the pages of history books, identified by historians as people who fought for freedom, revolutionaries and heroes. They make things happen."

Jeffrey Clark reflected on how people may ultimately judge him.

Jon quietly reached out to turn off the radio. Now, he was sure that rescuing Jeffrey Clark was the right thing to do.

He felt a deep admiration for Jeffrey's courage to come forth and inform the public about hidden forces that shape the world, but go unnoticed by most people. Jeffrey Clark helped him see the world with increased clarity.

"We are like blades of grass in a backyard. Softly yielding under the feet that walk all over us; but we always straighten up again. We are cut down to size repeatedly, but never stop growing. Sometimes the mower might encounter a stump, a rock or a forgotten tool, hidden among us, blades of grass. They could break the mower, if they are not removed. They are the equivalent of our human rights, and the gardener cannot afford to miss them."

Jon was proud of that line of thoughts, but he did not share it with anyone, just yet. He remembered a movie he saw years ago in small disjointed parts, its name was The Constant Gardener, or something. He now realized that movie title had sparked his thoughts just now.

It might be worth sharing with Jeffrey.

After all, its story line was rather controversial, if he remembered correctly.

Bobby and Stacey sat motionlessly for a while, holding hands. Stacey could not have been happier and there was no place she would rather be.

-They should be here soon. –Bobby stood and pulled her up with a smile.

It took less than ten minutes to drive home from the radio station. They did not say a word the whole way. Nothing would have sufficed to express their true feelings.

The sound of crumbling gravel under their tires startled an convoy of raccoons, as they turned onto the driveway. The furry critters stayed well out of their way.

The Volvo rolled past a hidden sensor and a row of landscape lights came on to illuminate the road and the vehicle. Jeff and Janet caught a glimpse of a pair of hares, before they vanished in the shrubs. It made them smile all the way to the house.

The electronic warning system, which Bobby devised and installed with Jon, worked like a charm.

A beeping sound alerted them in the house as soon as the Volvo entered the driveway. They came out to meet them on the front porch. The headlights swept over them briefly as Janet pulled up.

Fred stepped out of the way so Bobby could freely greet his father. They talked about him a lot lately and Fred did not miss how Bobby's love of his father seemed to deepen by the minute.

He always loved him, but the quality of his love was now rapidly changing to the highest admiration. Stacey let go of Bobby's hand when she felt his fingers release hers in preparation to welcome his Dad.

-Hey you guys! –Bobby yelled as he hurried down the stairs, overflowing with pride.

-Hey… - Jeff could only manage to say before Bobby squeezed the air out of his lungs, with bear-hug.

-I understand everything you ever told me, Dad. –Bobby said releasing him from his embrace.

-I knew you would, Son. –Jeff replied, filling his lungs again.

-I am sorry for ever doubting your teachings. I see now how ignorant I've been. –Bobby apologized.

-Its okay Robert. –Bobby heard his father say his name that way for the first time. He knew then his father would never call him by that childish nickname, ever again.

Robert and Janet weaved their arms into Jeff's and walked into the house, showered by happy remarks from the others.

The alarm went off Friday morning, at eight AM sharp. Robert and Fred jumped to their feet and were fully dressed in less than a minute. The sound of the alarm filled the house and even though it was not loud, it woke up everyone.

The two young ex-marines grabbed their guns and took up defensive positions facing the front entrance. Robert configured the alarm in such a way to indicate the direction of approaching danger.

Jon arrived right after them and went straight to the door. Before he could look through the peephole, the doorbell rang. Jon heard the sound of firearms chambering a round behind him, as he slowly opened the door.

The fully extended safety-chain stopped the door about two inches from its frame.

-Who is it? –Jon asked curtly, staying clear of the opening.

-Good morning Sir. My name is Ed K. Sea. I am a reporter of the Tahoe Times. –the young fellow introduced himself. Jon peeked outside and saw several others standing by two vehicles far behind him on the driveway. Only he had come to the door.

-Hello there. You know you're trespassing, don't you? –Jon asked him in friendly tone.

-Well, yes Sir. I apologize if my presence upsets you and your friends, but I had no way of calling ahead. –the young reporter stated the obvious.

-I've listened to Mr. Clark's radio broadcast last night and I must say, it left quite an impression. Controversial as it maybe, I believe every word he said. –he said in softer tone.

Jon did not respond. He weighed the pros and cons of the matter. Mean time, the rest of his company filled the kitchen, just out of sight.

-Did you say your name is Edgar Crayzee? –Jon couldn't resist...

-It is Eduard, the letter K, period, and Sea, as in ocean. –the reporter answered as he had done thousands of times before.

-It would be an honor to interview with Mr. Clark. –he added timidly.

-Wait here. –Jon said to him and closed the door.

Robert and Fred moved near the windows, to assess the situation for themselves. Jon had to ask Jeff's feeling about this. He could not make decisions for him; he could only provide support.

After a few minutes of discussion, Jeff agreed to sit down with the reporter.

The smell of coffee quickly filled the house, as Janet worked diligently to meet the high demand. Stacey helped out by making breakfast, adding a variety of mouth watering scents to the mix.

The interview went smoothly and the young reporter was clearly sympathetic to their cause. He wanted to be the first, bringing Jeffrey Clark's true story to his readers in print, which he considered the opportunity of a lifetime. As a reporter of the Times conglomerate, he aimed high. Little did he realize, he was swinging a double-edged sword.

-Lastly, why would you risk your life and the lives of your family, by speaking out so blatantly? –Eduard K. Sea needed a punch line for his story.

-Mr. Sea, I am not a politician. I have answered your questions as clearly and honestly as I could. In that tradition, my goal is to educate people so they may look out for themselves. We can rise above our current state, if we try. There is a lot of common ground in freedom and happiness. WE have conquered the world together and we could share it, without anyone needing to suffer. My hope is that altruism will prevail to help make that happen. I know, I am beginning to sound like a broken record, but that is the essence of it.–Jeff responded.

The reporter finished the interview and thanked Jeffrey Clarke for his time.

As they were packing, the sound of rotor blades filtered through the windows and grew louder with each passing moment. The news crew of the Tahoe Times was surprised by the approaching helicopter, since they did not have any. Jeff looked at the young reporter with a questioning expression.

-I have nothing to do with them. I got up earlier than they did. –Ed K. Sea smiled.

-Besides, all this publicity is going to make you a household name Mr. Clarke. –he patted Jeff on the shoulder appreciatively.

The chopper slowed to hover less than fifty yards from the front door, at an altitude of no more than three hundred feet. The whirlwind of its rotor blades was so strong that fragile twigs and even a few smaller branches crashed to the ground with a sparkly shower of morning frost.

Jon could clearly see a new high-resolution camera, and what seemed like, an ultra sensitive listening device, mounted below its fuselage. He stepped back inside putting his finger in front of his mouth to quiet his companions to a whisper. Robert peered out the window, staying behind a curtain, to see for himself. The chopper looked like an old Police chopper, judging from the way it was equipped. But, it bore the insignia of a TV station from San Francisco on its sides. How they found them, Robert could only speculate.

The possibility of an ambush also seemed very real, so the boys were ready to engage, if it became necessary. Jon took a loud speaker from the closet, another gift from Frank, and handed it to Fred. Its name said it all. "Intimidator", "Max.-150 dBA".

Jon handed him another small item. Fred glanced to see what it was. He saw a couple of earplugs inside a plastic bag, and gladly tore it open. By the time he looked up again, Jon quietly moved around the room, handing everyone a packet. As soon as they all had their earplugs in, Jon signaled Fred the ahead to communicate.

Fred turned on the device and adjusted the volume.

-Are we on? –the reporter from KQED Channel 9 asked his technician eagerly. He could see the house on the screen in front of him in vivid detail, but there was no sound, yet.

The technician nodded and cranked up the volume a bit. The circuitry of the USLD blocked noise of the engine and rotor and was trained right on the house. The only faint noises they could hear were indistinct rustling, and what could be the sound of feet shuffling on a floor.

Then, they heard a door opening slowly. The members of the news crew reflexively adjusted their headsets.

-Are you PBS for real? –Fred asked in his simple way, his voice thundering like the voice of God.

The news crew frantically turned down the volume of their headsets while cussing madly. The reporter noted Fred's crude mannerism and responded in a condescending tone.

-No, man. We are just a mirage, if you know what I mean. –his crew gave him some dirty looks for that. His lack of field-experience is no excuse to behave in such unprofessional manner.

Fred, however, did not care for, nor was he accustomed to, excessive pleasantries.

-A Mirage, huh? You don't look anything like it. I have personally downed two of them in Iraq. So, do not give me that crap! –he snapped back at the news crew.

They could hear his voice clearly despite the engine and rotor noise as if he was sitting next to them.
-What do you want? –Fred asked the obvious question without further ado.

The young reporter apologized for being rude and asked permission to interview Jeffrey Clark. Meanwhile, the crew from the Tahoe Times filed out and got into their vans. Carefully turning around in the driveway, they drove off the property. A few neighbors came out of their homes to investigate the commotion. They scrutinized the chopper and news vans, coming and going, with binoculars and video cameras, just in case the situation turns into a historic event. Some of them still remember the siege of Randy Weaver's cabin at Ruby Ridge in Idaho, and the highly publicized incident in Waco, Texas. They were concerned that the situation might escalate into something of similar nature. Seeing that only media personnel were present, they returned to the safety of their homes.

-Okay. –Fred answered to their request for an interview.
-Set your chopper down next to the water tower on top of the hill. I'll come and get you. –he instructed them.

The sound of the helicopter's engine did not change one bit, only the sound of the rotor did. It changed from an intermittent swooshing to a deeper thumping sound as the pilot adjusted the pitch to produce more lift. The helicopter rose effortlessly over the hilltop where it hovered for a few seconds as the pilot sized up the landing area. He lowered his craft precisely into the opening bordered by the water tank and some trees at the edge of the clearing. Fred pulled up next to them in less then two minutes. Once on the ground, the reporter apologized once again for being rude, after his crew chewed him out, hard. Fred shook his hand and reassured him that no harm was done by his funny remark.

Once the helicopter moved toward the hilltop, Jeffrey and Robert removed their earplugs to discuss the situation. Janet and Stacey also took them out and were finally able to serve breakfast. The excitement was a little too much on an empty stomach. They had a long day ahead of them, because Jeffrey's personal appearance was scheduled for tonight at the town's auditorium. Stacey made arrangements with a friend of hers, who is the son of the owner of the building.

The men agreed, that the more positive publicity they get, the better.

Fred eased off the gas pedal, coasting down the road, as he approached the driveway to the cabin. He saw another vehicle coming from the opposite direction and he had to let it pass before making his turn. But, to his surprise, the DHL delivery van slowed and turned in front of him onto their driveway. Fred followed it up to the house. Inside the house the alarm signaled both vehicles as they passed by the sensors. Robert grabbed his gun and squatted down, ready to fire, as he opened the door to see what was coming. The DHL van pulled up to the steps and Fred parked the Jeep at the garage door. Robert quickly hid the rifle behind the door and stood up to meet the deliveryman. Fred told the news crew to stay put for a moment, so they waited in the Jeep.

The deliveryman carried a small package. It looked roughly the size of a box of checks from a bank. At the door, he asked for Jeffrey Clark, but Robert told him that Jeffrey was not here. The deliveryman said that he was instructed to leave the package at this address, but someone had to sign for it. Robert signed on the electronic device and took the box. In the sender's space, he read the name Eugene H. and his address. The package came as a surprise to Jeffrey, since Eugene did not know where he was staying. Although it did not take a genius to figure that Eugene, being a very resourceful man, must have found Henry. By the time Jeff thought it all through, the DHL van was halfway down the driveway. Only then did Fred allow the news crew to emerge from Jeep.

Jeff signaled Robert to step back inside and close the door, prompting Fred to hold up once again. While they loitered outside, Jeff tore off the excessive wrapping of the box. He found a small note inside that read, "Dear Jeffrey, I am happy to inform you that the publishing deal is working nicely. Here is some spending money, to hold you over. Best Regards. E. H."

Jeff put the note on the table and dumped the contents of the box next to it by turning it upside down. When he lifted the box, they saw a bundle of hundred dollar bills nearly two inches high.

-Wow! —they uttered the word simultaneously.
   -How much is that? —Robert asked his Dad.
   -At least forty grand. —Jeff took an educated guess. After a short pause, he slipped the band off the bundle.
   -My friends, as Eugene says, here is "a little spending money". —and without ceremony, he counted out a thousand dollars to each of them.
   -Jon, put this in the safe for now. —Jeff put the loose bills back in the box and handed it to Jon.
   -We might as well use it, but don't carry too much with you at once. People might think you are criminals, or something. —they giggled lightly at Jeff's allusion.

Jeffrey opened the door and signaled Fred to escort the news crew into the house. Fred reached for the camera and took it from the cameraman, who, at first, did not want to let it go.
   -I'll give it back inside, once we decided where you will set it up. —Fred reassured him.
   Robert pulled a freshly printed document from the printer and put it on the table. They rearranged the room earlier so that the background behind Jeffrey would be as discreet as possible.

Just like with the crew of the Tahoe Times, the computer was also set to record the interview.

After a brief introduction by all the parties involved, Jeffrey informed the young reporter about the rules.

-My turf, my rules. You and I will sit here; you can set up the camera over there. Please read the simple contract on the table and sign it, if you agree. We are going to record the event also, for our protection. –

The reporter picked up the contract and he glanced at Jeffrey and the others several times with increasing admiration as he read it. At the end of the document he nodded, indicating his acknowledgment of the terms and conditions for the interview. He signed it without hesitation. For the first time in his ten-year career, he felt good about doing so. The contract was written in plain English without fine print or clauses.

While the news crew prepared, Jeffrey sat down in the kitchen with his friends to have breakfast. They offered some food to the reporter and his men, but they declined saying they had breakfast already.

The cameraman positioned his equipment to comply with their request. After they were all seated, the interview began.

Half an hour later they wrapped it up as agreed.

-That went really well! –Janet exclaimed with pleasure, once Fred led the PBS crew out to the Jeep.

-I hope you are not getting tired, Mr. Clark! –Stacey expressed concern about the evening's event.

-Don't worry! I'll be fine! –Jeff stood up and hugged her for helping out.

The rest of the day went by as any other. It was just as well, since all this commotion took up the entire morning. Jeff and his friends needed some time to rest and get ready for the evening.

They intended to make it a memorable event.

Robert and Stacey drove into town around three o'clock in the afternoon, to make sure that everything was going well. With five hours remaining until the commencement of the address, they had time to spare.

Janet persuaded Jeff to take a little walk with her, to help clear his head. They went out for a leisurely walk on a trail nearby. The late October air was crisp and clean. Lake Tahoe is famous of its dry weather, even though it receives quite a bit of snow each winter. Even in October, there was a chance of overnight snowing if conditions were right. But today the sky was clear.

As they walked silently, Janet wrapped her arm around Jeffrey's waist and, for the moment, her head rested on his shoulder. Jeffrey watched her beautiful hair flutter in the breeze before landing a deep and appreciative kiss on top of her head.

He reflected on how people find the smallest thing adorable about the person they are in love with, and willingly ignore anything less desirable about them. He smiled. Everything about Janet was adorable.

They looked into each other's eyes with the most sincere and accepting look they could conjure. Jeff pulled her closer and they kissed passionately. Then, having adjusted their stride to one another, they moved in harmony, step for step. The sun was now rapidly descending toward the horizon and the temperature dipped noticeably with each passing hour. It made them turn around so they would make it back before daylight disappeared.

Without their knowledge certain events took place, just a few hundred yards away.

Two men, dressed in fall camouflage, were staking out the cabin and its surroundings. They hiked up the hill from their vehicles which they left by the road. The vantage point that offered a clear view of the cabin and its access roads was selected from satellite imagery. Each man carried binoculars and an insulated canteen, filled with warm drink. Their jacket bulged at the hip and each wore an earpiece and microphone on their collar. Their attention was tightly fixed on Janet and Jeffrey, when a tranquilizer dart hit each man in the thigh. The dose, enough for a horse, took effect in seconds, and both man quietly buckled to the ground. Two other men came out of the woods, and pick them up. They carried the limp bodies to their own vehicles and drove away. In less than ten minutes, a local car-carrier took away the spotter's vehicles. The network takes care of its own.

It was essential to publicize Jeffrey Clark's upcoming lecture to drum up an audience. Stacey's friends spent the last several days advertising the event by word of mouth; and they also posted several signs around town to draw attention to it. With so much effort put into it, in so little time, they were hoping for a full-house.

An hour before the event Robert, Stacey and Jon arrived at the hall and found everything ready as they requested. Jeffrey and Janet arrived some forty minutes before commencement time. They quickly familiarized themselves with the layout of the place, with help from an assistant provided by the management.

Jeffrey asked Jon to make the opening announcement and introduction, which he graciously accepted. Stacey and Robert prepared to great the guests, as they began to arrive. The assistant took his position inside the lobby, from where he would show the guests into the auditorium. The first fifteen people were seated by seven thirty pm. Then, quite surprisingly, the flow of guests slowed to a trickle by seven fifty.

Since no new guest has arrived in the last five minutes, at eight pm, it became obvious that everyone with the slightest interested in Jeffrey Clark's speech was already here. All forty four of them, according Stacey's count. They all ignored the refreshments offered at the concession stand, for two reasons. The event was advertised to be about an hour long, much like a class in school. Also, at this hour of the evening, most people were past dinner time, and the concession did not offer any cocktails.

Aside from that, the people now present were not cocktail drinking types.

The type of people who seasonally enjoy the beauty of Lake Tahoe, especially those who own the more prestigious properties of the area, do not come here to listen to humanitarian speeches.

They come here to get away from them.

Robert and Stacey kindly requested their guests to move forward, near the podium, where Jon and Jeffrey had been waiting. At 8:05 pm, Jon made the opening announcement.

-Dear friends. We thank you for coming out, as it means a lot to us. My newest friend, Jeffrey Clark, will tell you some truly fascinating things tonight. Please, welcome him with open hearts. –

Jon stepped away from the microphone, and walked off stage to take his seat next to Janet, Robert and Stacey, sitting just behind the last row of invited guests.

Jeffrey Clark bowed slightly and began speaking.

-I would like to join my friend Jonathan Doering and great you with his words. –

-My dear friends, we are living in a wonderful time in history. We now have the means to help one another better, than any other time before. This is the age of communication. That is why I believe, it is our duty to inform our fellow men, and women, of all things that bear great importance. –

- What I about to convey to you is priceless. –

Jeffrey spoke for thirty five minutes straight. Within that time, he covered the most important issues facing any individual, or any family today. He spoke in the simplest and most appropriate terms, for the most part. Speaking of family affairs, he stressed the significance of the family unit, and the harmony that must prevail in all of its dealings. It must remain impregnable, for it is under the most merciless siege ever, in human history. He demonstrated his points with real life examples, to which his audience could easily relate. Child Services, Schools, Health Care organizations now act in unison to weaken family, by legally diminishing the decision making power of parents. Jeffrey said, it seems that very soon people may lose the right to decide whether to use health services, or not. Let alone trying to decide the same for their children. There is a major push to establish precedence for forced health care. In some instances it has already been done. Parents can barely decide now how to educate their children. People are fast becoming unfit for parenting, according to authorities. The same authorities fail to exam the economic and social causes that create deadly stresses in every facet of our lives. When we can no longer escape the accumulating stress, and we find that customary methods to relief ourselves of it are denied to us by legal means, the society we live in, is essentially broken.

Jeffrey managed to speak of monetary, employment and even religious issues in this fashion.

The simple minded and good natured people, who took a chance to hear him, gradually became agitated.

Not by his relentless bombardment of their minds, but by realizing that he is speaking the absolute truth. That is always an unsettling thing to face.

Jeffrey could have easily spoken for another thirty minutes, but his audience showed unmistakable signs of needing answers. One after another, they began asking questions, of increasing severity. Jeffrey tried to answer as many of them as he could, but each question became more specific, while becoming bolder.

He had to stop the questioning by suggesting to do their own research. He reminded them that the information age goes hand-in-hand with communication. Acquire the necessary information and then organize house parties. Make them fun and productive, he said, by putting issues up for discussion and let people bring their solutions to them. Then, each of them would be better equipped to counter the onslaught of legalized lawlessness.

All this active debate has actually taken more time than Jeffrey originally intended to spend. In the end, he, Robert and their friends where pleased about the whole evening.

The fact that only forty four people showed up, had no effect on their feeling of success. That means, forty four more people are now doing their bidding.

CHAPTER 4

The trip to San Francisco went very smoothly on Friday. They did not even have stop to use a restroom. This time they took Fred's Jeep, but none of them knew why, since it proved to be a tight fit for five people. About twenty minutes down the road, Robert noticed a couple of ordinary vehicles keeping pace with them. Since they were still on a winding mountain road with no cross-roads, he did not think anything of it. When the vehicles did not attempt to pass them at the first opportunity he still did not think it strange. Later the two cars actually hung back a bit as the road became straighter. It is not unusual for people to travel in the same direction, Robert thought, but there was something about the way these guys stayed with them. By the time they reached Sacramento, he had it to inform his companions about it.

Jon asked Fred to observe them for a while, not realizing that Fred was the first to notice the tail. He had been watching them since.

-They seem to be dressed casually, might be going on a sight-seeing tour. Except there are eight of them. –he conveyed what he observed so far.

-You think they could be FEDs? –Robert asked Fred, who was sitting in a jump seat in the back, facing rearward. He was probably the most uncomfortable, but he did not mind. He'd had worse.

-Can't say for sure. –Fred replied.

Their two-way radios beeped just then, signaling an incoming call.

-Do not try to lose the tail! It is provided by the "network" as long as you need it. —they heard Frank's voice.

-We thought you might be wondering about it. -he added quickly, followed by the automatic double beep as he signed off.

-Thanks a lot! —Jon replied, visibly relieved by the news.

Jeffrey did not want to draw attention to the fact that they were in survival mode and suggested to leave the radios behind with Fred, who volunteered to stay with the Jeep. Jeff, Janet, Robert and Jon went upstairs. Two members of the eight-man team protected the Jeep and Fred. The others surveyed the parking structure and took up strategic positions where they would remain, out of sight.

The receptionist greeted Jeff and his group in a professional, yet friendly manner. She seated them and said that the reporter will see them shortly. Eduard K. Sea soon came out to greet them. He informed them of the process of the televised interview and that they are going to meet the programming director. Jeffrey asked Janet to go with him, so the reporter escorted them to the director's office. He made a generous offer of five hundred thousand dollars for the exclusive right to broadcast it live, not knowing that Jeff would have done it free of charge, for this kind of publicity.

Wanting to be sure that the broadcast would go out live, Jeffrey made the director include that fact in the agreement. It also contained a clause stating that Jeffrey will be given an unedited audio/video copy after the broadcast.

Up and down the west coast, people of all social status tuned in to watch Jeffrey Clark's interview.

Anticipation was high and the feelings of the public were widely mixed about Clark. Some expected to see a white-washed, pre-recorded interview, while others hoped for a live one. Just before noon, people quietly closed the door of their offices to have some privacy. Some gathered around in break rooms equipped with a TV set, others used their computers to visit the website of the station. Many home-bound people also tuned in while doing their household chores.

Exactly at noon the station began to broadcast the special event.

"Good afternoon! My name is Philip Dickson and you are watching a special edition of KQED channel 9. Yesterday evening we announced on prime time news that this segment of our programming will change to bring you Professor Jeffrey Clark! In recent weeks he became quite well known by many of you from all sorts of media coverage. Please welcome Jeffrey Clark!"

Philip Dickson pointed to his left and the camera zoomed out until Jeffrey Clark came fully into view. Jeffrey smiled and nodded toward the camera, greeting the viewers by mouthing a silent "Hello" as well.

The news anchor quickly got through the introduction. His conduct was pleasant and courteous. The viewers heard a brief applause and cheering from an audience they could not see, producing the strange feeling of watching a sitcom.

-Professor, you have returned home two months ago from an international tour of lectures. –Dickson began, narrowing the topic.

-During this tour you have visited Australia, Japan, China, Germany, Egypt, and South-Africa. May I ask why have you chosen these six countries? –

-Originally we had more than a dozen countries on our list, but they declined to receive us for various reasons. In the end, we were happy that such culturally diverse mix of countries would give us time and space to hear what we had to say. –Jeffrey answered like a politician.

-So they were not exactly your top choices? –Dickson asked with a hint of cynicism in his voice.

-You are correct, Mr. Dickson, at least regarding Australia, Japan and Germany. –

-What about China, Egypt and South-Africa? –Dickson pried deeper.

-Obviously they perceived the topic to be pure anthropology. What harm could come from that, right? –Jeffrey replied with a mischievous smile.

-Right. –

Dickson allowed himself to briefly deviate from the standard jargon of journalism.

-Mr. Clark. Your tour created quite a stir in most of these countries and was followed by a general uproar across the board. Did you anticipate such reaction? –

-Regretfully, the "stir" was not nearly as noisy as you suggest, Mr. Dickson, and that surprised me. The "uproar" of the governments of these and other countries, whom were not directly involved, however, did not. I mean, when the people of a nation begin to raise their voice to be heard, their government is sure to respond one way or another. –Jeffrey's voice resonated with a distinct edge.

-What exactly did you speak about in your lectures, Mr. Clark? –

This time Dickson's voice also had an unmistakable edge that Jeffrey noted. But more importantly, the question was not leading in any way and, as a result, Jeffrey took the opportunity to open up.

-In recent decades we witnessed a lot of political maneuvering by the governments of the so called leading nations of our planet. All that maneuvering was intended to distract the people from the simple fact that, in reality, those governments are in full cooperation with one another for a common goal; even if, seemingly, they are opposed in certain matters. –

Dickson's stomach tightened in response to what he have just heard, but managed to keep his cool.

-Mr. Clark, that sounds a lot like accusation! –

Jeffrey did not want to get distracted, but he took the opportunity to address the reporter's remark before he had a chance to add anything.

-Thank you for saying that, Mr. Dickson! You see, labeling my observation an "accusation" is a defensive tactic that has been used throughout history to suppress public expression of wrong doing!

So is anger management! If we allow stamping out such emotions as anger, sadness and fear we could not respond properly to being manipulated into something we don't want, robbed of something we do want, or when our existence is threatened in some way. –

Dickson felt the control of his show slipping out of his hands just then. It was a strange feeling, for this had never happened to him before. The man in front of him is as assertive as he had not seen for some time. He had an obligation to himself and to the Network to regain control of his show or he might face a humiliating demotion. So he appealed to Jeffrey's vanity.

-Professor Clark! –

Dickson raised his hand to redirect Jeffrey's attention, who was still smiling into the camera, and make him notice the courtesy of addressing him properly. Jeffrey noticed and looked at him curiously.
-There you are, just like during your lectures, suggesting that people are being manipulated, robbed and or threatened by some unseen entity. This kind of talk is exactly what's gotten you in trouble. Don't you agree that we live in the best democracy in the world? –

-What are you implying, Mr. Dickson, when you say I got myself in trouble with such a talk? If we live in a democracy, as you say, then I should be able to say anything, just like you or the president.
Especially since the Constitution guarantees that natural right to me as well. –

-Professor, you brought a great deal of scrutiny unto yourself by making defamatory statements. Haven't you noticed? –

-What does it mean, when certain people find it obligatory to scrutinize my life, my actions and my words after I have criticized them for being unfair, Mr. Dickson? If they know that they have not done anything wrong or immoral why do they worry about criticism? –

-It is their prerogative to respond that way when they are being portrayed negatively, Professor Clark. And for the record, you are the one in the spot light for unjustly blemishing the image of our leaders! –

Before Jeffrey Clark could say anything the engineer responsible for lighting the stage of the studio flipped a couple of switches and Dickson found himself in the cross-beam of two powerful spotlights.

The engineer mumbled "Ah, shit" and flipped another switch, increasing the illumination of Professor Clark as well. A split second earlier the cameraman zoomed in on Dickson trying to enhance his point, but only made things worse.

When he refocused, to include Clark in the view, the camera found him quietly smiling. Dickson shot an angry look at the cameras located in the dark corners of the studio, but the view did not change anymore.

The smile soon disappeared from Clark's face as he prepared to take on Dickson with all his intellect.

-Surely, Mr. Dickson, you are not referring to our Great Leaders, who laid down the foundations of our free nation? –

-No, Mr. Clark, the world has moved on since then. I referred to leaders of today in general, just like you did in your speeches, without saying anything specific. That begs the question: If you believe that someone means to harm the public at large why can't you point out who they are? –

-You may not realize, Mr. Dickson, but your question is quite loaded. I am going to answer it in detail in several steps, if our time allows or we could go to commercials right now and keep the viewers in suspense for a few minutes. –

Jeffrey offered a chance to catch their breath before moving into deeper waters. Dickson took it and announced the break to the viewers with a professional smile, looking straight into the camera.

The commercial break was three minutes long during which time some people watching the show up to now decided to flip to other channels in hope of finding something more entertaining.

Philip Dickson and Jeffrey Clark spent the break arguing about their arrangement. Dickson insisted that Clark should refrain from defaming public figures, but Clark maintained that the public has the right to know what those figures are up to. Dickson then corrected himself saying that he meant public officials to which Clark replied that, regardless of what he calls them, they are accountable to the public who nominated them by voting and therefore questioning their actions is the constitutional duty of every voting American.

That's when they received the signal to return to their seats.

-Good afternoon. You are watching a special program of KQED channel 9, the interview of Professor Jeffrey Clark and I am Philip Dickson. For those who are just joining us, Mr. Clark is a professor of history and anthropology at UCLA. Professor Clark had an accident at his home in Beverly Hills, after he returned from a series of lectures on human history, about two moths ago. He is going to tell us what happened. –

Dickson casually rotated his seat to face Jeffrey Clark while the camera shifted and zoomed to include him in the view.

-Yes indeed, I will. Let me begin by responding to the remarks you made before the break. – Jeffrey Clark smiled at Dickson then turned to face the camera.

-Before the commercial break, Mr. Dickson, you said that "the world has moved on since then" referring to our founding fathers and their vision of freedom. From that vision they created the Constitution for the American people who live on this continent, Mr. Dickson! Representatives of each of the original thirteen states signed it, in approval, because it acknowledged the sovereignty of every individual and every state in which they reside. So, when you say "the world has moved on" from the notion of freedom, you can only mean the small group in power today who so recklessly ignore it. But the rest of the people will always cherish their freedom. –

Dickson leaned back in his seat; bracing himself for what else Jeffrey might be able to squeeze into the three minutes he gave him before they came back on the air.

-Then you asked me why I can't point out the specific people who are doing harm to the masses. – Jeffrey continued, adjusting his emotions and breathing to maintain a calm exterior.

"Democracy is the reason for that Mr. Dickson. It is a clever system in which no one can be held liable for wrong-doing. Decisions are made collectively by groups of politicians, who covertly serve their own interests. The process of legislation is designed to hold up anything good indefinitely, while lesser or more cunning measures could be swindled in place. The language in which the laws are written is also too lengthy and complicated to be clearly understood, leaving them open for interpretation as needed.

In my opinion, and you may quote me on this Mr. Dickson, a law that an average human being cannot easily read and comprehend is nullified by default for being "meaningless". We could also apply this idea to the Bible. I know many will cry blasphemy hearing me say this, but its language leaves it open for interpretation by whatever interest might benefit from it, so it should be rewritten in the plainest language…-

Dickson, though not a religious person, cringed at that statement. A second later he thought bringing something so fiery to his viewers might just help his ratings and Clark might discredit himself for good.

-….of every nation where it currently exist – Jeffrey Clark got carried away a bit, once again. There is so much out there the people need to know that he was now struggling to stay focused. He glanced at Dickson to see if he had any more time left.

-Thirty seconds, Professor. –

Dickson wondered if he could recover from his embarrassment, so he gave Clark a little extra time.

-In my lectures… - Jeffrey began, but changed direction abruptly, -…I had spoken about human relations throughout history, clearly demonstrating how power-figures manipulated the rest of the people into submission for centuries. I had shown that the people shook off the parasites repeatedly when they have had enough. Once again, we are at the cross roads. We either continue feeding the blood-sucking creatures, or we scrape them off for good. –

Dickson did not like the way his interview was going, he had to cut off Jeffrey Clark after twenty five seconds.

-Thank you, Professor Clark! – Technicians muted Clark's microphone on cue.

Dickson noticed a warning-light on his prompter and read the highlighted note quickly. Then he made the following announcement.

-We apologize to our viewers for the inconvenience, but we have to interrupt our program to bring you this important breaking news. Diane! –

With that he handed over the screen to another news anchor. The cameras in his studio cut out and Diane Weinetraube appeared on the screen.

"Good afternoon! My name is Diane Weinetraube and we bring you this breaking news on KQED 9." Her voice came over the ether smoothly, without a shred of emotion.

"Just a few hours ago federal agents stormed a compound in La Cresenta, believed to be the lair of a radical group.

David Price, the chief of DHS in Los Angeles, says full investigation will follow to determine the extent and exact nature of the group's operation. According to initial reports, it is clear that they were planning nothing short of a coup. At this point, federal agents legally seized all tangible and intangible property belonging to the perpetrators. Let's go to the scene, in real time with Dan Farley!"

Jeffrey Clark and Philip Dickson sat in their seats and had no idea what the special report was about. Couple of hours earlier the phone rang in the programming director's office. An official from DHS informed him that if Clark becomes too agitating on live broadcast, he is to cut the interview and replace it with the take down of a suspected terrorist group, as a deterrent. Arrangements had been made for this possibility and DHS agents will be standing by, listening to Clark's interview, and will take action if necessary.

They deemed it necessary and now Dan Farley is on the scene.

"Thank you Diane! Our informants called us about something hot shaping up in this quiet neighborhood in La Cresenta, a little over an hour ago. We arrived here just in time to witness federal agents break down the door of the house behind me. We were told that the suspects inside are armed and dangerous so we had to take cover for a while. It seems everything is going according to proper procedure now. There has been no word on the condition of the suspects, just yet. As you can see, agents are still busy sorting things out."

As Dan Farley pointed in their direction, the camera shifted focus to several agents carrying articles, from the home to a trailer where an officer was cataloging each object. Items like, a laptop and a desktop computer, baseball bats, a bag of golf clubs and an office filing cabinet, among other things. A few seconds later the garage door opened and agents drove a 2000 Mercedes ML55 AMG and a 2002 Acura MDX SUV out to the street.

"They are now removing the perpetrator's vehicles based on applicable seizure and asset forfeiture laws. In fact, the entire home became the property of the government. Any property can be seized legally, if that property has been an accessory in a crime.
    We interviewed several neighbors to find out more about the people who occupied this house until today. They all characterized them as hardworking, law-abiding people. No one believes that they would be involved in any crime. Diane!"

"Thank you Dan! An associate from the Intelligence Community advised us that these kind of seizures have increased tenfold since Professor Jeffrey Clark's lectures became widely known. In his lectures he suggested absurd ideas like: credit equals slavery and that our government has been hijacked by financiers, at least since the end of the Civil War. As a result, people who believe such foolishness got riled up and began voicing their discontent. These angry people are disrupting the lives of the rest of us and our government steps in to shield us from their terrorist activities. I am glad to see that my right to live the way I please is protected. Aren't you Dan?"

Daniel Farley was caught off guard by this question, because a neighbor stopped by to inquire about the nature of the commotion, while he was off screen. Hearing his name being called, he turned back to the camera without skipping a beat.

"Yes, Diane. I am sure you are. But, as you will see in a moment not everyone shares that sentiment. This gentleman stopped by to ask us about what is happening in his peaceful neighborhood, because he had never seen anything like this before. May I have your name sir?"
"Me name's Chuck" The neighbor replied.
"Chuck, would you repeat what you just told me about the people who owned that house?"
"No problem, Mr. Fraley. I am always shocked to see government employees, whom we should be trusting, ransack a decent human being's home. It is especially shocking, when that home belongs to a divorced mother of three, who works extremely hard to maintain their existence. Not to mention the fact that her son, blinded by patriotism, no doubt, joined the marines and was sent to Iraq for who-knows-what. And, by the way, is it any coincidence that he served with the son of Jeffrey Clark, whose interview was on your channel just a minute ago?"

"Thank you, Chuck!"
Farley signaled him to wait.

"You see, Diane, there are still decent people in the world, who are not afraid to step forward and raise their voice when they witness injustice. All too often, we go along with what we're told, because the information comes from a source we suppose to trust. I have personally reported, recently, at least a dozen incidents, where I wasn't convinced about the facts, as they were given to us by the authorities."

Diane Weinetraube showed no emotions during Farley's outburst. "Finally, the man has dug his own grave"- she thought silently.

She could never stand Farley for being an 'insolent bastard', as she so often thought of him for challenging the hierarchy of broadcasting.

She artfully motioned to the mixer to cut Farley out and have someone else on the air as soon as possible. She announced a technical glitch and asked for the viewer's patience until they restored connection.

Farley had no idea that viewers could not hear him anymore, so he continued interviewing Chuck. In less than two minutes, however, a crew-member got Farley's attention, and stopped him.

This crew-member overheard a brief cell phone conversation that took place just about a minute ago, between someone from the studio and Nathan Neumann, who agreed to continue reporting.

Neumann stepped in front of the camera, the sound resumed instantly and Neumann apologized for the glitch. Then, he directed the viewer's attention, back to the crime scene.

Back in the studio, Jeffrey Clark had been told by the programming director that his interview would not resume due to the breaking news. Since he was only able to use half the time agreed upon, he would be entitled to half the fee originally agreed upon. After quickly reading the agreement, Jeffrey accepted the money and they left the studio.

When they arrived on the third floor of the parking structure, Jeff and his friends were confronted by a couple of people, who were angry about his religious remarks. The pair did not seem to pose any physical threat, so they were allowed to approach them.

-Hey, Mr. Clark! –One of them shouted at Jeffrey as they closed in. –Are you not afraid of burning in hell for desecrating the words of God? –

Jeffrey slowed his pace while he considered an appropriate response.

-Are you not afraid to accept them as the words of God, knowing well that they were printed by priests, my friend? – The man and his female companion have now been stopped by bodyguards about five yards from Jeff.

-That's why they are the priests, so they can bring the words of God to the ignorant masses. – The man replied with solid conviction, giving his companion courage to speak her mind as well.

-We would never be friends with a blasphemer like you! -The woman said in a tone of disgust.

Jeffrey found himself facing a brick wall. He knew there was nothing he could say to help these two, but he tried anyway.

-Just so you know, I am not trying to rob you of your God, or trying to befriend you. For all we know, he may indeed exist somewhere, and honestly, I truly hope so!
I'm only trying to warn you about evil people pretending to speak God's words to lead you astray. I merely suggest that, if you must believe in something, besides God, believe in yourselves and one another. Or, believe in universal freedom for mankind and act accordingly. God would surely want that of you. Or else, He will wipe the slate clean, once again. – Jeffrey could not think of anything else to say. He was ready to leave.

-You damned right HE exists! Our pastor warned us about people like you, who will stop at nothing to bring down our faith! I'm warning you, Judgment Day is near and you and your cohorts are first to be purged! –the man exclaimed.

-Oh, brother. –Jeffrey sighed with resignation.
-Good luck to you both! –He said loudly enough for the couple to hear. Then he turned and headed toward the Jeep. "It's not worth saving the stupid, when they stupidly reject their savior." He thought, feeling defeated.

The bodyguards stood firmly, blocking the couple's way, while Jeffrey and his party moved further away.
Then, the elevator opened with a ding and four men, dressed in dark suits, stepped into the parking structure. They quickly assessed the situation and took off after Jeffrey Clark and his friends, on foot.

One of them kept a close eye on the couple and the four men who stood with them as they passed by.

Sensing that something was up, Fred opened the doors of the Jeep and climbed into the back. By the time he settled in his seat all the doors slammed shut and Robert cranked over the engine to start it.

The four men in suits steadily closed on them and they were only thirty feet away when they heard the elevator ding once again. They saw the couple hurriedly step inside and disappear behind the closing door. The four casually dressed men, who were standing with them a moment ago, have also vanished.

The exit route of the parking structure leads directly towards the four suited men. Robert Clark, determined to leave, stepped on the gas and pulled out of the stall with enough force to make the tires screech. The four men drew their guns at once, to meet the approaching car with equal force.

-FBI! Stop the car; now! –the man in charge shouted at them, flipping his badge open under his gun.

Robert had no choice but to stop. He realized those four handguns hold more than fifty rounds and someone is bound to get hit in his vehicle if they open fire. The Jeep came to a halt a mere ten feet from the FBI agents, who continued to move forward slowly. A thundering voice stopped them in their tracks.

-Drop your weapons and step away from that vehicle! –the voice rumbled through the parking structure with menacing force.

"Now that sounds like the words of God!" –Jeff thought with a faint smile.

Frank, who decided to lead the bodyguards on this mission, out of sympathy and commitment to Jeff's cause, turned off his "Intimidator" loudspeaker. He now had the FBI agent's full attention.

Robert greeted him with a nod, as he shifted into neutral, but kept the Jeep's engine idling, just in case the opportunity for a clean getaway would arise.

The four FBI agents stopped, still holding up their guns, alternating between the new threat and the Jeep. Frank and his men stepped closer, tightening the circle around them.

-I said drop your weapons! –Frank repeated the order in his own voice after setting the "Intimidator" on the hood of a car to his left, so he could hold his gun with both hands.

"…and that's gun-control…" –he thought.

The man, who seemed to be in charge of the FBI group, shifted his aim at Frank.

- This IS the FBI! See the badge and YOU drop YOUR weapon! –he asserted his position once again.
 -It looks like a replica to me. I can't read either your name, or the name of your outfit. –Frank replied.
 -Put your glasses on and have a closer look, old man! –the agitated agent taunted Frank, feeling secure in his authority.
 -Nice badge, agent… Piccolo? Is that Italian for small? No! Wait! It must mean a baby flute, you know, a woodwind instrument , but half the size of a real one. –Frank fully exploited his demeaning name.
 -Never mind all that! –he stopped the agent from answering when he saw his face contort with rage.

"That touched a nerve!" Frank realized looking at the agent who stood about five foot five inches tall.
 -So, you're feds. That means you are way out of your jurisdiction in these parts! –Frank called it as he saw it.

-What? –agent Piccolo barked in disbelief.
 -Do you have any idea of the punishment for threatening an officer with a gun? You're going to jail for a long time, buddy, just for having pointed that gun at me. So drop it! –Piccolo was not about to budge.

-Okay. –Frank said to ease the tension momentarily, as he began to lower his gun.

But, he stopped when the gun pointed at Piccolo's lower abdomen. An area less lethal when hit, but a larger target, than his head. Frank also wanted a better overall view of his opponent as he prepared for the worse.

-As I said before, you only have authority in the District of Columbia. I'm placing you under citizen's arrest. –He added firmly.

Agent Piccolo also lowered his gun a bit, partly for the reasons Frank did, and partly in disbelief. Never, in his fifteen- year career, has he encountered anyone so recklessly defiant. He had faced common criminals before, high-strung on barbiturates or opioids, who would not yield for a while, but this was different. This man's defiance is rooted in conviction; he could feel it.

-Look! I don't know what you're talking about, but I assure you, you have been grossly misinformed! –agent Piccolo attempted to defuse the situation desperately.

He knew, the longer they kept arguing back and forth, the more likely a bloody ending will result.

To his surprise, Frank slowly removed his left hand from the gun and lowered it by his side with his right.

-My friend! Believe me; you don't have a clue who you're working for! As one human being to another, let's not get carried away by our differences. I want to go home to my family just as much as you do. –Frank attempted appealed to Piccolo's private side.

-All we want is a clear path for our friends, and if you grant that, we could all leave here unharmed. The ball's in your court. –Frank simply stated, keeping his gun lowered at his side.

Agent Piccolo had a tough decision to make.

Anthony Piccolo has been recently appointed to be the leader of this special investigation unit, the sole purpose of which is to seek out and apprehend homegrown terrorists, deemed so by their headquarters.

The investigation part has been done already in all cases, as he and his men soon found out. That left them only the physical capture of the person in question. In their sixth months of flawless operation and having successfully brought in twenty-two alleged criminals, they were overconfident to the point of blindness. Piccolo also had reason to boast about fourteen years of field work without a single injury to himself or his men, despite many shootouts during his career.

He wanted to capture Clark as a crown-jewel of his accomplishments, but not at the expense of the life of his men. To show his desire of a peaceful outcome, he lowered his gun also.

Robert took this as a good sign. Since he could hardly wait to get out of there, he shifted the transmission into "D". The engine's increased power, running the air-conditioning, surged through the gearbox. Robert's right foot was on the brake pedal to keep the Jeep from moving. The excessive slack of the drive-train resulted in a loud metallic clang that ripped the delicate fabric of momentary silence.

Startled by the unexpected noise, the rookie in Piccolo's group accidentally squeezed off a round as he flinched. The sound of his shot triggered an exchange of gunfire that lasted about four seconds.

Within that short time, the man hit by the rookie fell to the ground with a broken rib and punctured lung. In turn, the rookie was hit twice in the chest and once in the head, killing him instantly. The other two agents, responding in self- defense, wounded two of Frank's men. They too were neutralized by the fire of the bodyguards. Frank and Piccolo were frozen in shock for a split second, and then both dove for cover.

People, walking on the street below, thought that kids must be playing with firecrackers up there, as they heard a series of loud pops from the building.

When the shooting stopped, those not hurt in the exchange carefully peered from behind their cover to assess the damages. Frank came out first, closely followed by Piccolo, both of them swearing to high heaven.

-What the fuck, People! Did you just hire this asshole off the street? –Frank bellowed in rage.

-Jesus-fucking-Christ! Look at this shit! –Piccolo swore in his thick Brooklyn dialect, venting his fury.

-I thought we had a way out of this! GOD! –He holstered his gun, concealing it under his jacket.

They began to survey the scene and their men as the rush of Adrenalin waned in their bloodstream. After the heat wave that caused them to perspire heavily, a chill and goose bumps took over in its wake as reality set in.

-What now? –Frank asked wanting to know Piccolo's solution for this mess.

-Turn yourselves in! –Piccolo snapped back.

-We can't do that and you know it! Come up with something more workable for all of us! –Frank urged him to make sense.

-I can take care of my own men; you must control your end of the story. –he added pointing at the two wounded agents.

For now Piccolo seemed unwilling to produce an acceptable scenario. He figured this incident could easily cost him his entire career and could even land him in jail, if he does not play his cards right.

After the initial shock of the gunfight passed, four passengers got out of the Jeep and tended to the wounded men using their first-aid kit. Janet and Jon took charge of the work with skillful help from Robert and Fred. They made Jeffrey stay in the Jeep.

Piccolo retrieved two two-liter bottles of Coke from the trunk of his car and set them down by the scene. Accept for Jeffrey, no one wondered why. As soon as the wounded men were bandaged he intended to douse the bloodstains in Coke to wash them off the pavement.

Meanwhile, some of the bodyguards moved out to control access to this level of the parking structure. Due to the light traffic they only had to turn away a couple of vehicles and a handful of people, who wanted to get off the elevator on this level.

When the injured men were finally helped into automobiles, Piccolo and the bodyguard sent to watch him, came back to speak with Frank.

-Look! I wanted to avoid the bloodshed, so I feel responsible for the rookie's mistake. –Piccolo began.

-This has been his first live run and he was very nervous. You outnumbering us just freaked him out. We all know that I should be calling for back-up, right now, to have you all arrested, but you won't wait for that. –Piccolo continued reasoning, while desperately struggling with his conscience.

He wanted to serve his country's best interest, which, in this case and according to his indoctrination, would mean arresting these people; especially since they proved to be accomplices of Jeffrey Clark.

But, at the same time, a hint of private self that remained hiding deep within his soul argued against it. He just realized that the personal well-being of his men and that of civilians, his actions may affect, has always been his top priority, superseding even the mission's goals. Simply, while following an arrest order, he wasn't supposed to consider personal, political or moral angles of any side.

As a low level operative, he could not deny that the shooting took place, he could not get rid of the rookie's dead body and his wounded men needed medical care very soon. Pressed by time, he only has power to change the circumstances.

-We never made contact with you. Getting off the elevator, we walked into a gang dispute that turned against us instantly. After all, this Los Angeles, is it not? - he asked a hypothetical question. -You, –Piccolo addressed Robert and his company, – turn your Jeep around and leave quietly, but in a hurry. –he pointed them in the opposite direction from which they came.

Frank, a sharp leader himself, gave silent orders to his men at this point. They ran off to execute them, as Piccolo continued weaving his story.

-A deadly shooting occurs, obviously. We are hit badly, but not before we also hit some of them. They pick up their wounded and get away in their cars... —as Piccolo uttered the last words they heard two cars approaching rapidly.

Frank's men boosted them to be used as 'getaway cars'.

-I'll stay behind to tend to my guys and call for help. —Piccolo said to Frank with an approving nod.

Robert started the Jeep and backed it into the stall in which he parked earlier. Then he rapidly pulled out the other way, taking his father and his friends away from the scene. Frank and his men also headed to their vehicles, but not before knocking down the security cameras that covered the area near the elevator and the exit route. The stolen vehicles then sped off, driven by two of Frank's men. Tires screeching around every corner as they went, they burst into the street, forcing pedestrians to run for their lives. Sparks flew as their bumpers and undercarriage plowed into the asphalt. Piccolo, now by himself, picked up a bottle of cola and doused the bloodstains of Frank's men to cover their tracks.

Then he reached for his radio and called in the unfortunate event. The Police and the Paramedics arrived within minutes, during which time Piccolo briefed his remaining men about "what just happened". Because they were not only his subordinates, but also his close personal friends, they understood everything.

CHAPTER 5

Since the unfortunate shooting on early Friday afternoon, Frank and other key members of the people's network have met several times. They concurred that the incident was unavoidable and fully justified, given their task of protecting their principal, as they now titled Jeffrey Clark.

They also realized the urgent need to step up an active recruiting system. It is a sad fact, but people had become unreliable, and these days, can't be trusted even for the most noble causes.

Thus, screening them thoroughly is vital.

All of their new acquaintances made the initial list of 'people to contact', but they knew only a small number of them might suffice. In the meantime, they will use the resources at hand.

Robert, Jon and Fred joined them for the obvious reasons. Each man have some unmatched expertise that they are willing to teach to others. In return, they were instructed on the unwritten, but highly revered, code of ethics and rules of conduct to observe and adhere to within the people's network.

On Friday night they received news from Henry that the arrangements for a TV appearance in L.A are now set.

Eugene Herald managed to have Jeffrey Clarke squeezed into a TV network's schedule, despite the ongoing Presidential Election coverage.

Henry mentioned an interesting yet little known fact about the four-year term of Presidency and the recurring Election Cycle. From the very beginning of the nation, Presidential Elections are always held in a leap-year, such is 2012. Some might wonder why the Founding Fathers had set it up that way.

They decided to lay low and recoup until the proposed date, on Wednesday, the 31st of October. Robert noted that it is on Halloween night, perhaps to make it easier to miss, while families are busy entertaining their children. No matter, it is still much needed national exposure.

They limited their lives to the most basic activities, such as eating healthy foods, exercising, grooming, reading and just passing time by observing nature and her simple rules at work.

Janet took Jeffrey out on short walks in the woods, but never farther than a third of a mile from the cabin. By now they knew all the paths that crisscrossed the landscape, leading from one spectacular site to another, so they could keep their minds in neutral and cruise on autopilot.

After the walks, the warmth of the fireplace eased the late-October chill in their bones, and the crackling of the firewood soothed their mind while they meditated to the rhythm of the rocking chair.

Saturday went by in this fashion and it seemed like a good way to go for the next few days as well.

The direction of the future was now very clear in Jeffrey's mind. There was no turning back, and the certainty of the thought gave him the resolve needed to press on. He solemnly planned his speech and manner of delivery for next Wednesday.

It did not take long before this idyllic lifestyle was interrupted again.

Saturday night, a member of the network reported to Frank that, while working his night shift at the local airport, an unannounced private jet touched down precisely at 23:32 pm. Twelve passengers got off the plane, all wearing suits. After renting three vehicles for the next week, they drove off quickly.

Frank alerted his spotters around town to stay sharp, looking out for these vehicles. Within ten minutes, they reported back that the vehicles were seen pulling in to three different motels in town, all around the Police Station. The strangers promptly entered their rooms, at each motel, and stayed out of sight.

Only then did Frank inform Robert of the disturbance. They deemed the affair harmless enough, but to be safe, they decided to keep these strangers under surveillance until they leave town.

In addition to the state of the art security system, they posted guards around the cabin, to monitor movement beyond its boundary. Frank Stillwater insisted on it.

Clamp and Eas settled in for the night with their men, each in their own motel rooms.

For security reasons they used their direct-connect phones for communication. They formed three four-man groups and Clamp and Eas each lead his own. The most experienced man led the third group. Using conference-call among the leaders, they could easily coordinate their actions. The other members of each group received orders to perform their duties by verbal command.

At midnight, the phone rang at the Police station. The sergeant on duty acknowledged the arrival of the southern constituents. He proceeded to inform the local Police chief of the same, according to his instructions for the night. The Police chief auto-dialed the numbers of the ten commanders tasked with backing the southern constituent's actions. One hundred men in all were thus put on alert in minutes.

Throughout the night more vehicles trickled into town and gathered at near Police station.

Eight cars and six full-size vans were needed to mobilize and transport one hundred men. They responded to ten-codes, sent down the chain of command. The codes 10-25, 10-20 followed by the abbreviation L.T.P.S., code 10-36, at 0500 told them to show up at the Police station by 5 am, latest.

When the last few men arrived at 4:54am the chief was standing at the entrance, urging them inside.

-Good morning Sir! –a young officer greeted him enthusiastically.

-Say Chief, whose idea was to use ten-codes to call this rally? The text message was great, but man, those ten-codes are ancient history. Thought they've been dropped years ago! –he added before the chief could respond to his greeting.

-Son! Just get your ass inside! –were the most polite words the chief could say at this hour.

The briefing room was bursting at the seams, not quite large enough for so many men.

Clamp and Eas were standing by a make-shift display showing the surroundings of Henry D'Guard's cabin in the hills. The chief of the local police joined them and Clamp addressed the men.

-Good morning gentlemen! –he began in his usual confident voice.

The men glanced at one another, because what they were about to do was not a bit gentleman-like.

-I'll keep this short, since you all have been briefed earlier on your tasks. However, the sensitivity of the situation requires me to remind you that we are to execute our duty as quietly and stealthily as possible. You all know this area better than any of us from L.A., so we rely on your knowledge. This satellite image shows the complex we are to raid this morning. Take a closer look at it and let me know if there is anything you think might become a problem. –with that he turned his attention to the crowd to see if they had anything to add.

They seemed comfortable enough with the plan that only a low hum of general agreement resulted.

-Does anyone have any concerns at all? –Clamp pressed, as time pressed him to get the mission started. Finally the young officer, who got himself noticed by the police chief for his remark, raised his hand.

-Okay! –Clamp took notice of him as well. –What's your observation, officer? –

-Well, Sir. –the young man stood up. –The plan seems fine, but they have the higher ground and thick woods surround the cabin. That makes our advance rather difficult and, judging from the large clearing around the main structure, we'll be out in the open for the last fifty feet of our approach. —the young officer pointed out.

This time the previously indistinct and low hum of discussion grew a bit louder and more defined. Clamp caught bits of phrases like 'his right', 'we need smoke', 'we need helicopters' and alike, so he had to respond quickly.

-Excellent point. —he exclaimed over the noise. —But, as I have been informed, many of you have military experience in addition to law-enforcement training. That makes this operation just another field training. Does it not? —he grew impatient seeing doubt linger in their eyes.
  -What is your name, officer? —he turned to the young man, who raised that doubt.
  -Jim Kent, Sir. —
  -Well, Officer Kent, I am sure you can, if you stick to the plan! —Clamp encouraged him and the others.
  -What's your specialty, Officer Kent? —he asked next.
  -I am an Expert Marksman, Sir! —Jim Kent declared confidently.
  -Fabulous! With the chief's permission, -Clamp turned to the chief to get his approval, -you shall be under my direct command. —Clamp finished his request as the police chief agreed.
  -Give this man a headset so I can communicate with him in the field. —was Clamp's next and final request before he dismissed them.
  -Lets get to work! —he said and walked out of the briefing room.

On their way out, each man received a topographic map of the area surrounding the cabin.
  They rolled out at ten minutes passed five on Sunday, giving them barely an hour to get into position before sunrise.

Jeffrey Clark and his company were peacefully asleep, knowing that a small army of people were looking out for them. The security system of the cabin was also working like a dream.

They had nothing to fear.

Robert turned over and gently put his arm around Stacey to cuddle, when the numbers on the alarm-clock changed to 5:50 A.M., and then it went black. So did the built-in clock on the oven and the cable-box, along with the night-lights that dimly illuminated essential parts of the cabin. Robert opened his eyes as his brain registered the sound of the back- up generator coming on.

For a few seconds he was in pitch-black darkness and momentarily confused. He propped himself up in bed and listened to identify the noise. The night-lights flickered to life then and, as his eyes pierced into the darkness, made him squint. He now clearly heard the low and distant hum of the generator and realized that the main power must be off. He slipped out of bed and went to the window. Not a single glimmer of light was visible anywhere, except for a gray hue rising on the horizon to the East.

He rushed out to the hallway and bumped into Fred, who was also awakened by the generator. He already dressed and grabbed Robert's arm quickly, but gently.

-Hey! Something's up. Put your clothes on. –he whispered to Robert.

-'kay. – Robert whispered and hurried back to his room. Fred headed downstairs as Jon came out of his room.

-Frank just called. He says: Boogie men are lurking in the woods. –He whispered to Fred.

-Get more details on that. –was Fred's condensed response as he passed by Jon towards the stairs.

Jon headed back to his room to get the radio. From that moment he would not be caught without it. He found Robert and Jeffrey in the hallway, discussing the situation. They greeted one another with a swift hand gesture and each man noted the other's readiness for whatever ever might happen.

Janet and Stacey also began to stir in bed as they noticed their men missing. By now, everyone had their radios turned on and attached to their belt.

Jon fixed his earpiece and called out to get more details.

The four guards, posted around the cabin by the network, remained invisible. They dressed in insulated camouflage clothing, as the weather called for warm clothes this time of year. They also counted on the bad guys to have infrared sensing goggles. Heat-sensing technology is so advanced that devices can pick up even the slightest difference in temperature, which is why the guards wore wet suits with a full face mask under their clothes to reduce their heat signature. Of course, their individual alertness and cunning also helped them to remain unseen. The bionic-ear also came in handy.

These men, being devoted outdoors-men, invested big money in this kind of equipment to enhance their field experience.

They all heard Jon's call and responded one by one.

-South, 40 yards from base. 30 men are closing slowly, 100 yards out. Widely spread. – reported the first one.

-West, 50 yards from base. 25 men about 90 yards out. Loosely closing. –advised the second.

-North, 60 yards out. 30 men closing at 90 yards. Loose formation. –the third one tried to keep it shorter.

-East, 70 yards out, 27 approaching quickly, almost on top of me. –the fourth man could not make it any shorter.

-Thanks. –Jon acknowledged and got off the air, but kept his radio on.

-That's nearly full circle. –Fred visualized the enemy units.

-Yup. –Robert looked at his father. –At least the terrain is on our side. –he added with a smile.

Paul Eas watched his friend, Donald Clamp conduct the operation like the expert he had become over the years. He requested satellite imagery and video feed of the cabin and its surrounding area, all of which rapidly downloaded to his laptop. When the download completed he opened the stills, each in its own window and started the live-video in another.

He enlarged each still image to full screen and examined them.

-How old are these? –Paul asked curiously.

-No more than two minutes. –Clamp said and zoomed in on a ridge. It seemed like a good spot to observe the cabin from the South, given its elevation and sparse vegetation. He decided to send Jim Kent there, who reported difficulty seeing the cabin from his current location.

-Jim! I got a new spot for you. –

-Let me have it, Sir. –Jim Kent responded.

-Go east-north-east two clicks, find the trail and head north half a click. That should get you there. –

-I'm on it. –

Clamp adjusted the video feed and watched Jim as he changed direction, advancing to his new location. Clamp and Eas were sitting in one of the vans, the engine of which was idling to keep them warm. The image on the computer was coming from an infrared camera, showing all warm objects in its view. They could see rabbits scurry out of the way of the figure they perceived to be Kent.

It was still dark.

Clamp zoomed out a bit to see more of the surrounding area. Twenty five yards ahead on the right of Kent's path they spotted what appeared to be a pair of deer.

-Hey Jim. Look out for deer in the dark; twenty three yards ahead on your right. –Clamp warned him.

-Thanks, but you missed the skunks back there. –Kent responded, confirming his identity in the video.

-We thought they were rabbits, either way they were not big enough to harm you. –Clamp explained.

-Gee, thanks. –Kent whispered as he approached the spot where he figured those deer might be.

-Okay. This has been most entertaining, but I should be out there with my men. –Paul Eas got bored just watching electronic surveillance images.

-Right. You know the plan, Godspeed. –Clamp released him and adjusted the video to see the progress of Paul's men.

-Wait! –he yelled quickly, stopping Paul halfway through he door.

-What's up? – Paul turned back

-Look over here! –Clamp pointed at the video.

Paul's men were slowly advancing, just like the rest, cautiously probing the area ahead. But, not far from them, Clamp spotted another solitary deer. He zoomed out more to widen his view. He could see half of their men moving toward the cabin. But, he also noticed other creatures out there like rabbits, squirrels, chipmunks, a lone fox and more deer.

The behavior of the presumed deer seemed a bit odd to Clamp.

-What do you make of this? –he asked his friend.

-...and for God's sake, shut the door, I am freezing. –he added, with fake annoyance.

Paul shut the sliding door and sat by Clamp. He felt his cell-phone vibrate with urgency as he sat down.

Jeffrey and his friends clearly heard on their radios:

-Wait for them! Let them get closer! –Frank's voice came over the ether.

Robert and Fred were looking at the monitor of the security system. It was still pretty dark out there, but dawn was breaking fast. It already provided enough light for the cameras to produce a decent image.

-Wow! Look at them! –Fred exclaimed seeing just how many people were coming for them.

-Yeah, but look at them too! –Robert rotated the camera to show key positions he was made aware of by Frank. Over fifty people maneuvered out there to counter the approaching force of a hundred.

Not impossible odds.

-This could get ugly, I'm afraid. –Jon expressed his concern of a possible bloodshed.

-It could, but remember, they are the ones turning it ugly! –Robert pointed at their enemies.

The four guards placed for the night began to retreat, carefully rushing from cover to cover. The morning light rapidly intensified and they could not maintain their positions any longer. They made their last report before the advancing enemy units could get within hearing distance. Now they had to move fast to get out of their way. As instructed, they headed back to the cabin, making a mad dash through the clearing to reach it.

At this point, all parties began losing their stealth and cover. For the Feds, that meant losing the element of surprise.

For the network, it meant losing control of the situation, if they were in control of any of it.

Paul instinctively reached for his cell-phone. The text message came from Sybille.

She wrote: "I had a bad dream. Today is NOT your day! Be careful! I want to see you again!" Clamp noticed the change of expression on his face as he read the message.

-What is it? –he asked.

-Nothing. –Paul responded flatly as he folded his phone before slipping it into his jacket's pocket.

-See how they move, cover to cover? Those aren't deer, they're human! –Paul noticed the odd behavior on the satellite imagery.

-Shit! –Clamp exclaimed realizing his oversight. Switched on his radio and broke radio silence.

-Ambush! –he called to his units.

One hundred men froze instantly hearing that word. They frantically peered into the receding darkness to find the threat. The only human-like figures they could see now was far ahead and retreating.

They radioed for clarification. Clamp laid out the situation for them as best as he could, interpreting the images and video available to him. Then he searched for Jim Kent.

In the mean time, the guards made it to the cabin, helped by the momentary delay of the advancing foe. They took their pre-assigned positions.

Clamp found Kent just when he reached those deer-like creatures. They pounced on him from behind cover and, after a brief struggle, he was completely subdued. The two creatures, now acting very much like humans, carried him away in the direction of a small parking lot that serves a nearby look-out point. Clamp quickly checked to see if his units were up there and ready, but they were missing.

Paul Eas stared at the screen in awe.

-I've got to go! –He said to Clamp once again and pulled open the sliding door. He wanted to be with his men.

His feet never touched the ground, as a powerful gloved hand shoved him back inside the van.

As the door slid shut, a small hissing canister bounced on the floor after him and rolled out of sight under the seats. The rays of the rising sun grazed the tips of the pine trees, making them look like gigantic glowing match sticks. A pair of real deer passing through, curiously looked at the strange creatures crawling around in their woods, then swiftly vanished in the wilderness.

The home-made 2cc canister depressurized, filling the van with its contents in about five seconds. Clamp and Eas began gagging and tearing within two seconds of its introduction in their space and were now convulsing. The men standing outside their vehicle, holding all the doors shut, observed their thrashing. They were not going to let them pass out completely, so ten seconds after the canister landed inside, they opened the doors and pulled out the two government agents swiftly. Now, in near full daylight, Clamp and Eas looked a horrid mess, their eyes, noses and mouths running uncontrollably.

The leader of the dispatch pulled a couple rags from his pocket.

-Here. Clean yourselves up. –he said handing the rags to the suffering men.

-Wait! Wash your faces first! –said another masked civilian, who brought a couple of jugs of water. They watched patiently as the humiliated government employees washed and wiped off their faces.

The police sharpshooters, whose job was to cover the cabin from afar, were taken out one by one. Some of them were simply tackled by well placed sentries of the network, then gagged and zip-tied. Others had to be tranquilized as they passed sentries in a distance, attempting to reach their destinations. They were all brought to a makeshift camp, by hunters of the network, who captured them. The hunters found it amusing to apply the ancient term hunter-gatherer to themselves, with a new meaning.

The network's code requires the conduct of all members to be as non-violent as possible. Increasing degrees of violence is permitted only in the face of imminent and life threatening danger, commensurate to the level of danger present. This is why each member is armed to match the opposition's capability. So far the level of aggression only escalated to physically subduing their opponents, which is as humane a solution as it can get, under the circumstances. But they know that dealing with the Feds almost always results in the use of lethal force, especially if the Feds perceive the situation threatening to their very existence.

This explains why the Feds are here in the first place, armed to the teeth and ready to use lethal force. Somehow they must be under the impression that their existence is at stake.

The main body of the force commissioned by the Feds closed within sixty yards of the cabin, despite Clamp's warning of an ambush. Here, they still had plenty cover, and they could position themselves to have a clear shot of every opening of the cabin. There was no ambush they could see, except for the fifteen meters of clearing around the cabin, they'd have to cross if they get the order to attack.

They've found it strange on this freezing cold morning that all windows were fully open, as they could see no reflection. Curtains and blinds were covering every opening, however, but they did not seem to move with the breeze.

Each team's leader knew what they had to do, but they waited for an order that seed to be delayed.

After a while they called for it, but no one answered. At least not right of way. A minute or so later an unfamiliar voice responded and identified himself as Captain Frank Stillwater, Marine, retired.

The chief of LTPD took it upon himself to communicate with him.

-I don't know who you are or what you think you're doing, but I want you to know this. You are in deep trouble already for interfering with this operation and I suggest that you return command immediately to Donald Clamp, the director of the FBI. Do that and your sentence will be light. Do it not and we'll make certain you'll rot in jail for the remainder of your natural life. –he said, clearly upset by the unexpected outcome.

-Listen, bureaucrat, I am a Native American Indian, in case my name did not make it clear. As such, I prefer to live in peace and harmony with nature and my fellow humans. Are you a fellow human? –Frank asked looking to make a connection.

-Whatever. Go back to your nature and fellow humans; I have a job to do. –the chief turned off his radio. Frank Stillwater switched over to the network's band.

-Damn! I think he is going to move! –he let everyone know of the impending attack.

-Well then, we didn't get up so early for nothing! –One of his Vietnam buddies replied with a chuckle.

The four sentries, who retreated to the cabin a little while ago, knew the drill. They quickly loaded a smoke grenade onto their rifles and lobbed them into the woods. The grenades landed halfway between the invaders and themselves. Smoke began to build and spread rapidly. They repeated the process in a hurry and, under cover of the thickening smoke, entered the cabin as instructed. The fugitives inside greeted them with quick hugs and handshakes of appreciation. But they had one more task to complete before they could settle in. Once again they loaded their rifles with grenades and lobbed those close to the tree line. These grenades did not pop on impact as they were fitted with a time delay.

The chief of LTPD, as he now found himself in charge of the mission, ordered the men to move forward.

Those with military experience noted the color of cover smoke and advised him that it is safe to enter. No one reached for their gas masks as they moved through the thick smoke, nearly loosing sight of one another, despite being only a few feet apart.

Still enveloped in smoke, they reached the edge of the woods.

-What dummies! They provided smoke to cover our move.–the police chief ridiculed their opponents.

-Not so fast, chief! Remember, this could still be an ambush! –an older undercover officer warned him.

-We have our own smoke do we not? Load it! –the chief ordered.

-Let loose! –he ordered next.

The barrage of smoke grenades, fired from amid a cloud of smoke, flew aimlessly and hit the cabin walls on all sides. Some fell short of the building, landing just right to provide the best cover. Most of them rolled right up to the walls, some actually bounced back a little. A couple of grenades found the windows. One of these sprung back from the tightly secured blind, but the other slipped inside.

Before it could fill the room with smoke, Stacey came to the rescue with a plastic shopping bag. She scooped it up into the bag and tossed it outside the door then she quickly shut and locked it.

The smoke built fast outside and some of it filtered back into the cabin, but not nearly enough to hamper the occupant's vision within. However, they lost sight of the invaders and thus braced for their charge.

The smoke began to disperse in the woods, allowing the invaders a fleeting glimpse of the cabin before it vanished again in the smoke they just lobbed at it.

In all that commotion they did not hear the sound of the half-pound sized teargas grenades as they began to release their content.

-Lets mo... –the chief managed to say before a coughing fit came over him. His eyes started running and he and his men were hunched over, gasping for air. The entire group was in disarray within seconds. They evacuated the area like madmen, away from the cabin, stumbling over the landscape and one another.

The defenders could clearly hear the coughing, gagging and cursing of the invaders through the thick smoke. The morning breeze began to lift the smoke-cover, and they witnessed their hasty retreat.

The sight invoked a feeling of victory, which caused the defenders to break out in laughter. But, sensing that it might be a short lived victory, they braced for the worse.

Donald Clamp and Paul Eas were taken to one of four rallying points set by the leaders of the network's team. During the last hour or so, as soon as Frank and his handful of leaders sized up the situation, they made calls to thirty or so additional members to come help out if they can. Seventeen showed up and now manned these points. The enemy combatants they brought here were lying about, gagged and bound with zip-ties.

Donald Clamp, once regaining his vision, sized up the situation for himself. He and his friend, Paul Eas, were bound together, back to back, lying on their sides, freshly deposited among the others.

He recognized some of his own and Paul's men gathered here in similar fashion. As he looked about, more people were brought in, still coughing and tearing profusely. For the most part, he was responsible for these men, so he demanded to speak with the leader of his captors'.

-Hey! –he yelled out to the nearest masked person he could see.
-Who is your leader? I want to talk to him! –

The man addressed came over casually.
-Who are you? –a raspy voice asked Clamp from behind the mask.
-I'm Donald Clamp, Director of FBI, from Los Angeles. Where is your leader? –Clamp identified himself.
-He is busy. –came the indisputable answer.
-Hey! Stop talking to that man! Blindfold and gag both o' them! –shouted another masked man, who overheard them talking.

Thus, the guy had no choice, but to gag and blindfold the two of them.
-This is fucking embarrassing, you know that? –Paul managed to say despite being muffled, but his distorted voice conveyed his anger clearly.

-Shut up! –the man who gagged him knelt down and shoved Paul's head into the fallen leaves briskly to enhance his point. Then got up and returned to his post.

Paul's cell phone vibrated in his pocket again. Good thing he set it on silent mode, otherwise he would have lost his phone just then. The feeble buzzing of the phone was muted by the thick cover of fallen leaves beneath his body, as he lay on his side.

The brief massage, that he would only read several days from now, expressed Sybille's concern for him. "Where are you? I hope you're safe! S."

Almost two thirds of the retreating men, who could barely see where they were going, were picked off by members of the network waiting for them in the woods. Quickly bound and gagged, they were deposited in any one of four collection sites. The remaining thirty five or so men, now separated from the rest, also gathered in small groups, but they did so on their own. They were told, no matter what happens, the mission had to be carried out. That meant that they had no choice, but to storm the building. Unfortunately for everyone involved, that is just what they were going to do.

Way early for a Sunday morning, the residents of the area were awakened by the unusual racket. One after another, they rose to hear orders being shouted, thumping and swooshing noises followed by bursts, all of which echoed far and wide over the hilly terrain.

They witnessed huge clouds of smoke as it engulfed the D'Guard residence. Then, they saw dozens of men dressed in battle fatigues approach the cabin, ready to invade it, but pull back haphazardly.

Most neighbors had no idea what was happening, but clearly a siege was under way.

They made forty nearly simultaneous calls to the local 911 system, causing a temporary overload. The defenders inside Henry D'Guard's cabin were ready.

Accompanied by four ex-military men, they were now eight-men strong.

Even Jeffrey Clark had a rifle, since he realized the seriousness of the situation. If all these people willingly put their lives on the line for him, he must join them in defense of his own life.

Deep down he still hoped for a nonviolent solution, but historical evidence is to the contrary.

By giving his speeches, he only intended to open a dialogue for change. A change, that could save his country and government, from going down a dangerous path, that was all he wanted. God only knows, the government might be too far down that path. There is no salvaging it in its current form. Perhaps, not at all, by peaceful means. Looking back at the events of just the last twenty years, the direction in which the government has taken this country is disturbing, to say the least. Not just domestically, but globally as well. We move farther away from the possibility of peace and freedom each day, as we force secret agendas onto foreign peoples. But who is behind all these events? Whose agenda are we pushing around the globe, and why? That is as murky as the swamps of Louisiana.

"Here they come…", Jeffrey thought, "…to capture me, and my friends, for speaking the truth." Next, a quote attributed to George Orwell flashed through his mind:

"During times of universal deceit, telling the truth becomes a revolutionary act." "Isn't that the God damned truth?" -Jeffrey understood the message of the novel 1984.

A young and impressionable officer, with high hopes of rapid advancement in the police department, took command of the remaining police force. To him, taking this cabin seemed like a training exercise.

Suppressing the occupants by live fire from all sides, sending a relatively small unit to break down doors and enter their hideout. Then, it is just a matter of minutes to handcuff every one inside.

He gave the order to commence firing.

The first bullet, fired from police weapons, came in through the kitchen window and struck Stacey in the shoulder. Janet saw her collapse and rushed downstairs to help her. She too was hit in the leg as she jumped off the stairs. The balusters of the railing splintered under a hail of bullets behind her.

Robert and Jeffrey cried out in anger, seeing their ladies go down.

-You bastards! –Robert shouted to overcome the incredible noise of bullets riddling the cabin. Everyone dropped down and stayed behind cover while deadly fragments of building materials flew about. Razor sharp bits of glass and china filled the air. Chunks of wood flew in all directions, torn off the frames of doors and windows. Having opened the windows in advance helped somewhat to minimize the amount glass debris flying around, but it still proved to be the most dangerous kind.

Robert, Fred and the four ex-military men of network were ready to repel the imminent attach.

They knew that an assault team would burst through the door any minute, if they did not stop them in their tracks. As most of the police fire concentrated on the ground floor, Robert agreed to the four men to get a bird's-eye view of the situation from upstairs. They took their positions upstairs and spotted the assault team moving toward the cabin. The leader of the ex-military group shouted the direction and strength of the enemy force to Robert and his friends below. As soon as the enemy gets in full view they will open fire.

The police used lethal force first and wounded two innocent bystanders already, so their response with lethal force was now holy and justified.

It's been nearly two minutes since the police began firing at the house. Meanwhile Jeffrey and Jon provided first-aid to the women. They pulled them to safety in the hallway between the stairs and the living room. They stopped the bleeding with field bandages, and gave them some morphine. The women's moans and cries could be heard even upstairs before the morphine eased their suffering.

The incoming fire slowed and stopped just before the assault team reached the edge of the woods. This time they wore gas masks and peppered the house near the point of entry with teargas. They waited a few seconds then charged into the clearing.

Six guns opened fire in the house, simultaneously. They kept firing until all, but one, assailant fell to the ground. He made it to the door, not realizing he was alone. Support fire erupted from the woods to cover him, this time engulfing the upper floor. The lone officer busted the door open eagerly and entered the cabin. The instance his foot touched the floor inside, a golf club struck his right forearm before he could release the doorknob from his left hand. The shank of the club bent slightly from the impact and his arm slumped as both the radius and ulna snapped in the middle. The force of the blow sent his gun flying, out of his lifeless hand. The momentum carried the officer forward, but clearly he was not welcome. Another club whooshed through the air and struck his left shin just as he put his full weight on it. The tremendous force of the club shattered the tibia and fibula with a loud crack and they buckled. He fell and slid a few feet, coming to rest by the coffee-table of the living room. He screamed at the top his lungs, but his screaming, muffled by his gas-mask, quickly faded to a whimper. Jeffrey snatched up his gun from the floor and Jon was about to shut him up by stuffing a dish cloth in his mouth, but he did not have to. The officer shook as the trauma overwhelmed his senses, on the way to pass out. He weakly mumbled a few words after Jonathan pulled of his mask.

-What have you done to me? –

To which Jon responded with the question, -What were you going to do to us? –then gave him a shot of morphine as well.

All ten members of the assault team were down with non-lethal wounds. The defender's aimed mostly at their arms and legs. Still, some of their injuries may result in permanent damage, but they knew the risks they took when they joined this task-force.

The twenty or so law enforcers in the woods came under fire as well. That fire came from afar. The network's snipers put half of them out of commission, also by shooting at their extremities. The remainder scattered in the woods, only to be captured shortly by the patrols of the network.

Sirens of emergency medical vehicles echoed in the distance as they made their way to the scene. A few police cars also attempted to reach the cabin, but were stopped and disarmed a long distance away. The whirring of news helicopters, mixed with the noise below, drove all creatures of the woods into hiding.

By seven AM the neighborhood was overrun by medical and news personnel, in addition to the disarmed policemen, whom were relegated to traffic control duty.

They were forbidden to communicate with news reporters and each officer was accompanied by a member of the network to ensure that they wouldn't try.

The only activity permitted was the recovery of all the injured people from both sides of the conflict. At the time the first ambulance arrived and was sent to the cabin, about ninety percent of the wounded had already received first aid treatment from the Net-folks. The EMT-s only had to carry them out of the woods.

Janet and Stacey were on the way to the nearest hospital, accompanied by Jeffrey, Robert, Fred and Jon. The four ex-military guys stayed behind to secure the cabin.

Reporters were on the ground trying to make a story out of the big mess. The first images went on the air uncensored. They showed Janet and Stacey being loaded into an ambulance, innocent victims of a gunfight initiated by government agents, and taken away in the company of their loved ones, followed by two civilian vehicles.

Surprisingly, noted one reporter, police officers seem to be in close cooperation with civilians, instead of their usually tight control of the scene.

CHAPTER 5

Sybille worried about Paul, even though she barely knew him. She detected a decent person behind his forced, official demeanor, she considered worth rescuing. Since the day she met him in the diner, she felt a deep conflict brewing in his heart. Like someone torn between good and evil.

Her expertise is the detection of malevolence, which is why so many famous people relied on her services. Politicians, bankers, investors, judges and attorneys, upstart and seasoned business people alike seek her advice. Although they represent the highest paying segment of her business, she prefers to serve the masses. Her peers think she is nuts and avoid her company.

Now, on her way to another meeting hosted by Brent Taylor and organized by his activists, she checked her phone once again. Still, Paul did not respond.

"Damn. I knew something was wrong." She thought flipping the phone shut.

Passing a store front, she glanced at a flat screen TV inside. The 5 O'clock news was on. She paused to watch it. A stakeout of sort turned into a wild shootout in Lake Tahoe.

"Federal agents, in cooperation with local police, raided the hide out of alleged terrorist, Jeffrey Clark. Authorities believed the terrorists were outnumbered ten to one, yet they defeated a company of over one hundred agents with ease. As you will see from the video recorded earlier, they had help. The fire fight ended with twenty casualties, but no fatalities"- the announcer's lips moved while Sybille read the captioning.

Sybille watched as the camera panned over the landscape showing some people involved in the clash. She recognized Paul, sitting on the ground among a group of men. They were guarded by armed civilians. Although uniformed officers were present, clearly the civilians had control of the scene.

What the hell happened here? She wondered.

The footage was cut short by a civilian guard, who put his hand over the lens. His voice could be heard briefly, ordering the cameraman to stop recording. The announcer came back on.

"As you can see our news crew has been removed from the scene by members of a group identified as the People's Network. We will continue covering this developing story as soon as the authorities restore order at the scene." The broadcast turned to commercials and Sybille walked on.

Well, well. That was weird! Sybille considered what she had just heard.

The scene was under the control of a civilian militia. The People's Network. Who are they? Five minutes later she arrived at the meeting. Two men stood guard in the hallway.

She smiled as she approached them. "Hello boys!"

"Hello Sybille! Good to see you!" Karl G. Brown welcomed her.

"Welcome! The meeting is about to begin. –Henry D'Guard opened the door for her.

She turned inside and proceeded to the front row, as she was expected to contribute to the discourse. Brent Taylor welcomed and introduced her briefly to those who may not know her.

Then he proceeded to finish up his opening speech.

"…as I was saying, most people watch or read the news, having been conditioned to only see and hear what the media wants them to. Consequently, they form opinions based on suggestive information. People are so shockingly complacent and trusting that now the government can do whatever they damn well please!"

He allowed his emotions come through, as he always does when a point must be made.

Taylor concluded his speech quickly and invited Sybille to join him on the podium. She walked to the microphone briskly and adjusted it to her height. Seeing familiar faces in attendance time after time, like Julien, Sophie and Ed Forsythe, means they have a steady base.

A warm feeling of hope welled up inside her as she addressed her audience of seventy or so people. "Ladies and gentlemen. It gives me a strong reassuring feeling seeing you all here tonight.

You certainly posses the same desire that Mr. Brent, Professor Clark and I have in our hearts. We all wish to create and live in that better world for which our forefathers laid the foundation in the Declaration of Independence, the Bill of Rights and our Constitution. The determination in your eyes tells me that we are making history." Sybille aimed to resurrect their slumbering patriotism.

The intensity of the applause proved that she was on the right track.

"As a psychic, I tend to have visions of that world."

"But first, I'd like to ask, have any of you heard the news about the raid on Professor Clark's hideout?"

As she suspected only a few raised their hand. The majority had no idea.

"There; you see? Most of you are still unaware that a raid had in fact taken place in an attempt to capture Jeffrey Clark. I have just seen the TV report of the raid and its aftermath. From that report the existence of a civilian force came to my attention. They were able to protect Jeffrey Clark!" she paused to let that sink in.

People whispered to one another in incredulity. Their whispers grew loud enough to force Sybille to raise her voice. "Listen to you!" they heard her shout.

They fell silent and listened.

"You are completely unaware of your power! Just now, each of you had only whispered, but your whispers combined were louder than my amplified voice!"

"Imagine what would happen if you raised your voices together, with a purpose."

"Visualize now the 545 elected officials who dictate our lives! They can only be heard by three hundred million of us through the loudspeaker of authority that we gave them. It is that same authority we now fear, having forgotten its source!"

Sybille felt the power of oratory for the first time as the crowd responded. "The source is US!"

"Yes…" she whispered into the mike, when the roar subsided. "…and we will exercise our authority!"

Brent Taylor has been a big fan of her for some time, but her ability to appeal to people's senses greatly surprised him. He clapped so hard, in sync with the rest, his hands hurt.

Sybille waved indicating that she had more to say.

"I saw a voluntary, civilian militia in that report, not unlike the one our forefathers intended to cultivate to call upon in time of need. This militia managed to capture and disarm cops and feds alike with minimal casualties. They now hold them in makeshift camps, bound by zip ties. They relegated uniformed cops to traffic control duty, under their close supervision. Ultimately, they even removed the media from the scene." Sybille conveyed what she saw in the report. "Who are they?" someone asked the obvious question.

"They call themselves the People's Network" she answered. "We should get in touch with them!" suggested another person. "And that is what we shall do!" Sybille promised.

"Right here, right now! Please, call in Mr. D'Guard from the lobby." she signaled to no one in particular near the entrance.

A young man in his mid-twenties was awakened from his slumber by a woman in her late thirties who held a small boy in her arms. She pushed past the comatose youngster toward the hallway. A moment later she returned with Henry D'Guard.

"Henry, would you please, come up here! I'd like to introduce you formally to our friends." Sybille called to him eagerly.

Henry walked toward Sybille, tall and self-confident as always.

He had just received word of the outcome of the siege at his cabin in Lake Tahoe. Sybille put her hand over the mike and spoke a few words with him when he stepped next to her. The brief exchange ended with Henry's consent to introduce him. The audience could read his lips saying yes as he faced them. She removed her hand from the mike. "Ladies and gentleman! I'd like to introduce to you Mr. Henry D'Guard!" she began.

Henry bowed his head slightly accepting the sporadic applause.

"He is one of the few brave people who rescued Jeffrey Clark from the talons of the authorities and he is the man who provided him with shelter for the last month or so." she continued, when Ed Forsythe jumped to his feet leading the next round of thundering applause, shouting "Go Henry, go".

Sybille stepped away from the microphone.

"Thank you! Thank you!" Henry shouted waving his hand in appreciation of the warm welcome, thus signaling his intention to speak.

The applause halted as quickly as it started.

"My friends!" Henry addressed them for the first time.

"I am not the man who deserves this kind of ovation. I have simply done what many of you would have done in the same situation! The man who really deserves our cheers and support is Jeffrey Clark!"

He was cut off momentarily by cheers from the audience.

"To most people he is only known as a "terrorist", or an "anarchist", as the media consistently labels those who dare to question status quo."

Henry paused briefly to allow them to reflect on that.

"He is just a humble history professor, who cares about humanity! He is not a leader of anything. His only intention is to help us see clearly what is happening and why! So let us not put the burden of leadership on his shoulders. Instead, we should work together to change the course of human history in the direction WE want it to go!"

Henry stepped back slightly from the mike as applause exploded across the audience. Sybille moved closer taking hold of the microphone.

It took a few seconds until the applause subsided.

"As you see," she said "Mr. D'Guard is a very modest man and he has a point! The government is already hounding Jeffrey Clark for being outspoken. Let us not cause anymore trouble for him! Instead we should help spread his message! We should let our elected officials know that we want them to act as true statesmen, once again!"

A brief, but enthusiastic outburst of cheers followed her words.

"I believe Mr. D'Guard maybe able to contact the People's Network."

She turned to face him as she said "We ask you to tell them that many people sympathize with their actions and wish to join forces in shaping our country to our liking!"

Henry D'Guard accepted it graciously.

After that, the meeting quickly turned into a brainstorming session of what they want to accomplish and in what order. They knew it will not be easy, but they knew it had to be done, not only for the American people, but for the people of the entire planet. They all wanted America to remain the leader of the free world. They want to show to the rest of the world, what is written in the Constitution created for the people of America, in the Declaration of Independence and the Bill of Rights. They must explain it all, in full detail, as the concepts presented in those documents may seem "alien" to most people today.

The world must know that the combined message of those documents is universal and eternal.

It applies to every human equally and it does NOT give power to any group of people to rule over another!

The current practice of "Democracy"will end swiftly, along with the 51% dictating policy to 49%. Democracy is a code word for socialism and ultimately communism.

America was founded to be a Republic, and the people will return it to that form of governing. Not to be confused with a People's Republic, which is just another code word for communism. See China, for example.

At the end of the meeting, they all felt elated and a bit overwhelmed by the scope of the task.

Later that evening Henry D'Guard called Jeffrey and his friends. They were pleasantly surprised about the growing number of groups, now acting in accord, nation wide. Jeffrey was grateful for the people's decision not to expect him to be their leader, but pledged his support for the new direction of their movement. Returning to a Republic form of Governance is the Right direction, as far he is concerned.

He also informed Henry that Janet and Stacey will make a quick and full recovery, as they are in good care. The captured feds will remain in custody of the Network for now.

In turn, Henry conveyed the joy shared by all of "their friends" that Jeffrey and his companions remain safe and free. He then suggested that, due to the raid, it would be wise to do the TV interview in L. A., ASAP, instead of waiting for the scheduled date. He'll be in touch with Jeffrey as soon as he has set a new date and time.

The Network-people used the fed's vehicles to transport their detainees to a local hotel. As it is often the case among people, a friend of a friend pulled some strings, ever so slightly, and they were given permission to use the ballroom of the hotel. The ballroom has its own rest rooms and all of its windows had functional shutters.

Cots and lockers were provided by various sources and by the time the convoy arrived at the rear entrance, the place looked like an emergency shelter set up by FEMA. The hotel's manager agreed to provide food right from their own kitchen.

All agents and officers were disarmed at the time of their capture. No one was allowed to keep anything that could be used to communicate with the outside world.

The people of the Network proved highly skilled at logistics operations. They cataloged all personal items removed from their detainees. The injured were taken to a number of health care facilities around town, under close supervision of the Network.

This being their first large scale and open public action, they had to make sure it was done as cleanly as possible. They even video taped crucial instances to support their non-violent intent.

By eight AM that Sunday morning the entire law enforcement network of the west coast was buzzing like an over-turned beehive. Nearly all of their resources were now committed to "handling" their predicament. They could not reach any of the agents who were physically involved in the raid.

Satellite imagery showed the location calm and activities seemed well organized. Groups of people were loaded into vehicles then driven off in all directions. They observed check-points being set up on all routes in and out of town. Cell phone communication in the area dropped to zero, as service providers reported all their towers disabled at this time.

They have sent out repair crews, but all reported being turned away by a civilian militia.

Some form of negotiation was now inevitable, so they waited for the rebels to make their demands.

Four hours later it became clear that no demands would be made. During one of many meetings aimed at formulating a plan to respond to the developments at Lake Tahoe, a young and brighter than average officer pointed out the fact that the People's Network are the defendants in this case.

As such, it would make no sense for them to make demands, except for one: to be left alone.

Lake Tahoe and its residents seemed to have settled back into their normal routines by one pm.

The news crews have all returned from the scene and they were promptly and properly debriefed. Their accounts of what is happening in Lake Tahoe all point to one conclusion.

The enemy combatants are peaceful. They will not initiate any armed conflict, but they will use force in self-defense.

The People's Network peacefully took control of the local Cable TV and Internet Service Provider and the Telephone Company as well. The only phone lines they left operational were landlines. The video footage of the raid, captured by the security cameras around the cabin, has been slightly edited to show only the action sequences and was uploaded to the Internet. The local radio station did not have to be occupied by the Network because it is operated by local independent journalists.

They actually offered to broadcast an announcement concerning the wide spread cell phone outages.

The announcement informed the public about the existence of the Network and that it had temporarily shut down all cell-towers serving the Lake Tahoe area. For more information about this action people should request their copy of a written pamphlet by calling 1 800 638-9675, or 1 800 NET-WORK, from a landline.

Of course, people are not entirely helpless and they realized that VOIP communication over the Internet was still available. So friends and relatives now sat in front of their PCs and Laptops using webcams and microphones.

Cell phone companies noticed the gaping hole in their service area around Lake Tahoe. But there wasn't much they could do, as repair personnel sent to restore service were intercepted on all roads leading to town.

The leaders of law enforcement organizations are also competent people, the general public would certainly hope so, and they were ready to make their next move.

High resolution images of Lake Tahoe flickered on hundreds of computer screens and monitors, up and down the west coast, linked to spy satellites, in FBI, CIA, ATF, and DHS offices.

They watched as the Sun gradually disappeared behind the horizon, slowly leaving the west coast in darkness. At the same time they saw the lights of Lake Tahoe come on, illuminating its area as an island in the wilderness. The night temperature was expected to sink well below freezing at that elevation.

"Okay people, shut them down!" David Price gave the command at 6:30 pm.

A subordinate sitting in front of a computer typed in the grid-code for Lake Tahoe, precisely defining the area he wanted to affect. Then he pressed the "enter" key.

David Price stood by him, watching a monitor that showed Lake Tahoe all lit up one second, and disappear in darkness the next. Even he thought that the image was quite profound, for the screen now showed a large black spot, nearly a hundred miles in diameter, where Lake Tahoe shimmered just seconds ago. The town plunged into the darkness of the wilderness surrounding it.

-I guess we'll see how they fare by morning. –Price said patting the man on the shoulder, who executed his command.

Residents of Lake Tahoe found themselves without electricity for the first time in a long time. But, as people living in relative isolation from the world tend to be, most of them were prepared.

In the least, they had flash lights and candles; at the most, they were equipped with back-up generators. First, of course, they attempted to restore the main source of electricity, but soon realized the cause was not local. At times of need, sooner or later people begin to communicate and negotiate for commodities with one another. For now, food was not a concern, since most homes had reserves and the cold weather provided all the refrigeration they needed. What they really missed was electric light.

Arrangements were made to exchange power for fuel and one generator after another rumbled to life. So much for tranquility, people agreed, as their generators' steady hum echoed far over the hills.

And so, to the amazement of law enforcers, after only about an hour of blackout, Lake Tahoe reappeared in the middle of their screens, getting brighter with each light coming on.

Thanks to the Internet, the news of the attempt at capturing, arresting and possibly even killing Jeffrey Clark, on the spot, had traveled all over the world. Even though the number of people paying attention to what is happening in the world at any one time is ridiculously small, it only took a week.

How was that possible? It's simple.

One only needs to apply the principle theory of most "network-marketing" schemes to this event.

It goes like this: If only one person paid attention at a time, and that person passes on the news to just two people, who in turn pass it on to two others, and so on, an exponential growth curve is formed. Based on the "doubling-effect" of the theory, if the news could reach only half the population of planet Earth in just six days, doubling on the seventh would mean that not a single person would be left out.

Jeffrey Clark had given his last Television interview on Thursday, the 1st of November, following the raid. It was successfully arranged by his new friend Henry D'Guard and his old friend Eugene Herald.

Not as soon as they had hoped, but still ahead of the Presidential Election by a few days.

Professor Clark skillfully dodged any questions that could potentially incriminate him in any way.

He made it abundantly clear that his lectures have always been purely historical in nature. His only aim had been to analyze human relations. Statements he made were taken out of context and deliberately misinterpreted by certain officials, which is why he was "kidnapped", as he now understands it. Further he expressed that he was drugged for two whole days while "they" tried to "convince" him that he suffered from seizures as a result of the Kawasaki's disease which he survived in his childhood.

His rescuers told him that what may have happened to him if they left him in the custody of the authorities is anyone's guess. The FBI, the ATF and local police interpreted his escape as proof of being "guilty as charged", even though he was never formally charged with anything. They seized all his properties, as if he was an "enemy of the state".

Yes, his attorney did file a lawsuit to recover his property, but it could take years.

Disturbing news of similar cases now circulate on the Net from independent news sources. They report a dramatic increase of search and seizures carried out against American people on mere hunches or simply because they dare to criticize recently enacted laws. The last time he checked, criticizing laws that circumvent and/or undermine the founding documents of this country is not a crime. Jeffrey asserted his belief that the government is accountable to the people under the Constitution, especially when the president was elected on the promise of transparency. Except transparency only seem to apply to the general public, who are now under constant surveillance. So much for the right to privacy.

Jeffrey flatly rejected any responsibility for other people's thoughts and actions.

How they interpret his words and what conclusions they draw from them is their business entirely.

Jeffrey summarized the essence of his lectures by saying that human history has always been a struggle between people with God-given-rights and people with Gold-given-rights. In other words, it is the struggle of people who cherish their freedom against those who want to take it away.

The people want to know who, and why, would want to take away their freedom.

The people can handle the truth, but the governments might have a hard time explaining why they are deliberately trampling the rights of their people.

At this point the reporter thanked Jeffrey Clark for sharing his views and time, ending the interview.

His clever move did little to hide what had already come to light since Jeffrey Clark returned from his tour of enlightenment. Hundreds of thousands of independent truth-seekers have been working very hard for decades, across the globe, to expose what must be exposed. The public's reaction to Professor Clark's lectures encouraged them to intensify their efforts. Many government's and international corporation's dirty laundry is now fluttering in plain sight on the Net, and the mood is ripe.

Countless and nameless angry groups are on the move, and they move in unison.

Acting on their own initiative, they band together, inspired by the belief that a better world does exist. People, fed up with lies and schemes, now demand accountability never seen before.

The world is rapidly changing in the wake of "full disclosure" that is well under way.

Throughout the year TV stations reported news of rebellion against the establishment in many countries. Over the last decade the leaders of at least half a dozen countries were removed by instigated clashes, but the true reason remains unclear. Most of these leaders were portrayed as dictators and monsters who have committed heinous crimes against their peoples.

Despite the commitment of mainstream media to spew propaganda, alternative news-sources insist that ulterior motives are behind all this.

Instead of taking news at face value, one must take a more in-depth look at things. While looking, one must remember to "follow the money" as it is the surest method of uncovering the truth.

After the interview Jeffrey and Henry headed straight to Burbank Airport, where Henry's jet was waiting. Jeffrey wanted to be by Janet's side, although she and Stacey were protected by his son and Fred.

Eugene Herald assured him about his financial situation by explaining the full extent of the deals he had made on Jeffrey's behalf. Publishing rights and other investments were now producing profits in excess of fifty thousand dollars each month.

The people of the Network in the Lake Tahoe area had it all figured out. For quite some time they were planning a new, local, economic structure that would be impervious to the effects of the outside world.

Local business people were invited to friendly gatherings where they discussed new possibilities.

When Jeffrey and Henry got off the plane at Lake Tahoe airport a small delegate of the Network greeted them. As a courtesy, they informed Jeffrey Clark of the rapidly improving condition of Janet and Stacey.

Then they invited the two of them to a local meeting of the minds, as they called it.

The meeting took all of two hours and many details were laid on the table. A localized monetary system was proposed, along with involving farmers and ranchers of nearby areas, even though it meant covering a fairly large geographic area. Lake Tahoe isn't exactly farmland, as they all know. The few farmers and ranchers that were present pledged to help in recruiting additional people who might be interested joining the network. As long as people are involved in it equally, producing and transporting goods to exchange could be handled internally within their locale. One major point of the meeting was to settle the dispute of what they would use for a medium of exchange and from what would they derive its value. Jeffrey pointed out that even the current FIAT Money System has been working rather flawlessly, because people accepted the value of its units to be just what they saw printed on the face of each bill and coin. Regardless of the fact that, since the 1970's, the American dollar had nothing backing its value, whatsoever. He then suggested that hourly human labor might be a good universal basis for a new currency. Further details would have to discussed, naturally, but it could lead to the equalization of monetary values between all nations. After all, we are all humans. Therefore, human labor should have the same value in all nations. The people attending the meeting agreed to ponder that concept, and promised to evaluate it, in comparison to other proposals.

After the meeting, Jeffrey and Henry felt renewed hope that people can indeed change the world for the better. They exchanged some ideas on the way to the cabin, but they had more burning issues at hand.

Robert called to inform them that Janet and Stacey were about to be released from the hospital, as they pulled up to the cabin. Robert and Fred arrived withing the hour bringing their ladies home.

By now, the signs of the raid have been cleaned up, the broken window is re-glazed. The four men assigned to the cabin had done a fabulous job.

After expressing his gratitude, Jeffrey insisted to pay them generously.

Then, he reached for his radio to call Frank. They talked for a couple minutes, during which time Frank pledged his continued support and protection to Jeffrey Clark and his family. Jeffrey promised to continue educating the public relentlessly about matters of vital importance. He also told Frank that the thought of hiring a body-guard had crossed his mind recently, but now his entire family may be in need of protection.

"Consider it done." - Frank replied, and assured him that he will personally hand pick the body-guards.

Jeffrey Clarke knew that he was now in a position to help people not only by his lectures, but he could also provide financial help, if need be. He discussed that with Frank for a while, and in turn for the protection they offered him and his family, he offered to finance the expansion of their facilities and acquisition of new and necessary equipment, to which Frank replied with sincere thanks on behalf of the Network.

They said goodbye and promised to keep in touch. They meant it.

The captured agents and policemen were systematically processed by the Network over the next few days. They identified each by genealogy, going back as far as was possible. They informed them that their personal identity is going to be made public information, including but not limited to, DOB, all known addresses, level of education, former and current employment records, and so on, as long as they intend to work for any of the uniformed services, or Alphabet Agencies. The captive federal agents and police officers were then given an affidavit to sign. It clearly stated that they were treated with the utmost consideration throughout their detention to which they attest, and they willingly forfeit any right to pursue any legal or lawful retribution. After some hesitation they all signed their own copy of the affidavit, in front of a Notary Public who authenticated the document. They received a final check for good health, along with all their personal articles, including their firearms, less ammunition, and the agents and officers were free to go, at last.

Several days later, the American people have learned that the sitting President has been re-Elected.

www.ingramcontent.com/pod-product-compliance
Lightning Source LLC
LaVergne TN
LVHW041909070526
838199LV00051BA/2548